I0713009

Defeated Dogs

Quentin S Crisp

Defeated Dogs
Paperback
Publication Date: 04 July 2013

Copyright Quentin S Crisp

Cover Art copyright David Rix
Introduction copyright Brendan Connell

Credits
Quentin's haircut: Jazz Topalusic
Quentin's trousers: Dominika Kieruzel
Quentin's shirt: Emily

ISBN: 978-1-908125-20-0

www.eibonvalepress.co.uk

dedicate this book to dogs of all breeds, to analogue recordings, to those who are the living disproof of theory, to those between one thing and another, to long dead gods and to ghosts unbelieved in, to the sentimental, the unreconstructed, the voiceless insane, those who choose damnation, those who have only themselves to blame, those who bring the average down, those who never write history, those whose way of life is drawing to an end, to sticklers, grammarians and gatekeepers, to the pretentious, to the purple stripe, the garment's brilliant hem, to those who are fascinated and not yet liberated, to the woo, to the hookworm, the mosquito, the ichneumon wasp, and all those not needed, to those dying in inconsolable terror, to my unspeakable nemesis, to little me and little you, to the judged and the judge and the noose of time above them, to pride, the greatest or the most trivial of all sins, and to the dying art of confession.

"Inside of a dog it's too dark to read."
~ Groucho Marx

Contents:

INTRODUCTION

"The masses are prone to perspicacity in minor facts, but to stupidity in the major ones."

This is what Ko Hung said.

Never, since history began, have more people been able to *speak* English. Never, since the language began, have fewer people been able to write it well.

Who can find joy in its depths, appreciate its magnificence—its abundance?

The Earth is engulfed in a deluge of words—words clumsily skewered together like expired meat on a kebab, charred by the fires of inanity and seasoned by the clumsy hands of technology.

"Verbiage-fakers: you gulp down all that is on the plates, before wise men can dine or even get a bite."

Hermias said this; and that some are grateful for the rush of this never-ending sewer, in which bawdy romances whirl about the precincts of gauche volumes intended for the pre-pubescent members of our society, we can have little doubt. But we also know that, ultimately, beauty attracts. Bandinelli is forgotten; Michelangelo forever remembered.

Mr. Crisp was born in North Devon in 1972. His parents were vegetarians and ran what might well have been the first vegetarian guesthouse in England. Crisp has, for the most part, avoided meat to this very day, giving "strength to his body so that it might contain his soul," as Eunapius says.

The first word he spoke was 'brontosaurus'. While he was still at a tender age, his family spent a period in Israel, and young Crisp returned with a cage full of smuggled preying mantises. Being naturally inclined to humour, in Secondary School he secretly put woodlice in his hair and then shook them out on his desk, causing a crisis, as the teachers thought they were giant headlice. The following year he hitchhiked to High Wycombe in drag in order to attend a concert of the German heavy metal band Accept. One of the band's roadies, a middle-aged transsexual who went by the name of Robin Roma, was able to get the young Crisp backstage. The two afterwards corresponded with great frequency and at Roma's suggestion Crisp had his first foray into 'publishing' by producing a photocopied magazine of mermaid pornography, the discovery of which earned him two weeks suspension from school.

This same Roma later became a Buddhist monk in Thailand, and it was through him, in fact, that I first discovered Crisp's work, him giving me a soiled copy of *The Nightmare Exhibition*.

"Where you see bodies, I see forces tending towards each other by a creative impulse."

So said Balzac.

One of Crisp's GCSEs was Television Studies. As he could only find one other boy to work with, he convinced this latter to film him putting on a wedding gown and marrying himself, the footage then being used for a video for the song 'Woman' by the Anti-Nowhere League.

Ikku Jippensha said, "travelling means cleansing the life of care".

Studying for a bachelor's degree in Japanese from the University of Durham, he went to Maebashi, Japan, where he spent ten months at Gunma University. He boarded with a barber and received complimentary haircuts; went back to England, and then back to Japan again, to Kyoto, having received a Monbukagakusho Scholarship, through Kyoto University, in order to study the works of Higuchi Ichiyo.

There is a rather amusing anecdote about his return to England after this second stay. It would seem that one of the first people he met upon his repatriation was Mark Samuels, the noted writer of strange stories. This latter found Crisp's speech patterns so distorted from his continuous study of classical Japanese that communication was almost impossible. The incident was the inspiration for the Franklyn Crisk character in his story 'Glyphotech'.

Crisp is known for his vital prose, his legendary green woolen scarf, his love of tea, his fear of certain kinds of fruit, and his suspicion of all things *digital*.

"My lowly self has sat quietly out of sight, for I was not fitted to the times, and my work has been out of tune with the day. Whatever I said ran counter to popular belief; every step I took was against the direction of the masses."

So said Ko Hung.

For many years his work has been followed by a rather elite group of readers and its quality has placed him amongst a unique group of writers, not as part of any particular school, but rather as one of those *who should be read.*

"Great desire to begin another story; didn't yield to it. It is all pointless."

So said Franz Kafka.

To earn a living, Crisp has done various things, such as testing software for mobile phones, freelance writing, and teaching English at a nursery school in Taiwan. At one point he was employed in London as a 'Green Champion' which entailed him going to low income housing blocks and informing the tenants on various ways they might be greener, such as getting them to recycle, ride their bicycles to work, put bricks in their toilets, etc. And throughout all this, he has, fortunately, continued to write, despite not being petted by the soft hands of the large publishing houses.

He has written numerous short stories, several novels (a number of which are, as of this writing, still unpublished) and lyrics for the band Kodagain.

"Why talk about insects when the whole world is before you?"

This is what Shih Nai-An said.

To call Crisp's stories simple would be to malign them; to say that they are complex would be to slander, for the highest art is that which, in its directness, its naturalness, says what it has to say without pretence.

The stories are not marked by imaginative paroxysms in which vapid thoughts are tethered together with the tails of absurd beasts, and neither are they studded with knowledge flaunted. There is in them much of the sort of realism used by Patricia Highsmith—much of the same sort of introspection. In Crisp's case, however, the introspection has a much quieter tone—and the strokes of his brush, so to speak, are more often broken, giving the stories a heightened sense of mystery. The world is not always *exactly* what it seems.

Gold and vermillion rarely enter into his palette which consists primarily of white, indigo, grey-green, and yellow—the colours used to paint trees, flowers, mountains and people—but even then, the ink is not wasted and is treated as if it were more valuable than money.

One might call these stories restrained, but the word naturally calls to mind tension, and in them the reins are let loose and quiet observance given its chance to roam.

Lu Ch'ai said, "Neither complexity in itself, nor simplicity is enough."

In other words, great distances are pointed towards with a simple gesture. Simple things are made beautiful with direct presentation. The composer sees the common with eyes uncommon and finds the sublime in the poverty of his surroundings.

"To be a man, that is to say a participant of the infinite, one must abjure all fraternal conformities and wish oneself special, unique, absolute."

These words Remy de Gourmont wrote.

With powerful simplicity Crisp evades banality. Detail is perfect, but gives way to sweeping gestures. Eccentricity, the most precious thing in good writing, is achieved without violating natural order.

> So many people have stood in my way,
> But I am not afraid.
> I brush my teeth each day
> With new, improved yuugen.

These are words written by Crisp for the Kodagain song 'The Iowa Writers Workshop Lacks Yuugen'.

Author's Note

The phrase 'defeated dogs' is an English translation of part of a Japanese idiom, '*makeinu no tooboe*', or 'the distant howling of a defeated dog'. Although perhaps 'distant barking' would be a more accurate translation. If I understand the idiom correctly the subtext is this: two dogs have had a fight, and the defeated party has slunk off to a distance, where, rather than admit he has been roundly drubbed, he begins to bark as if he is the winner, or, at least, as if he is offering a sincere challenge to his rival along the lines of, "If you weren't a coward you'd come and fight."

The stories selected here, although some of them are quite recent in composition at the time of my writing this, represent a kind of backlog for me that I hope is a retrospective—something I can move away from. I was there when they were written, of course, and, except in one or two instances, I don't actually feel very removed from them now. I imagine that to the reader they might sound like distant howling… or barking.

THE FAIRY KILLER

Faye was wrapped up in the blanket of her thought. Everything had become as warm and vague as the colours behind closed eyelids.

She sat cross-legged upon the floor, hugging her mohair stomach and gazing at the tree that she had decorated with such delicate attention to detail. She had placed each star and each glass ball as if placing the notes on a cylinder in a wind-up music box. Now the tree played the silent tune of her whimsy. The fairy lights with their sweet, delicate colours, were each one like the heart's innermost knowledge of peace. The same thing might have been found represented in an old, incense-musty – but still delicately coloured – painting in a conventional, religious form, such as a lotus blossom. The fairy lights threw strange, magnified shadows on the wall, and powder-puff splashes, and strokes of colour and reflections of tinsel as taut as springs.

Faye had invested such time in decorating the tree, it was only natural, now that she sat down to appreciate the results, that she should be repaid by a kind of bonus time that was no time at all.

Something not quite thought and not entirely feeling was taking shape. This invisible magical something may have been inside her, but it wore whatever was before her eyes and expressed itself through that. And so the Christmas tree was a perfect diagram of her daydream.

The branches were clouds and the lights stars. The clouds were sleep and the stars waking. The sleep was life and the waking between-life. The life was the body and between-life was the heart.

The twinkle of lights, where she had placed the pegs on the cylinder of the music box, were a lullaby. She was half in the sleepy world of life and half the magical waking of between-life, listening to the lullaby that told it all.

The ceiling light had been dimmed. In the semi-gloom, Faye's face looked as if it were illuminated by candles, and flames seemed to glisten in her eyes. She was a honey blonde, slightly chubby. When she walked she let her weight fall heavily on one foot then the other so that she swayed like a bell. On the bridge of her nose was a bony lump. There was a honey-blond line around her lips, as if they had been cut out with scissors and glued onto the collage of her face. This year she had blown out the flames of eleven candles on her birthday cake.

Now warm silence purred like a fire. Familiarity itself was a kind of magic – like the familiarity of the mirror-eyes sewn into the purple macramé cushions on the settee, or of the mud-streaked Wellingtons that crumpled the bottom of the heavy white curtains in front of the French windows. Her woollen jersey hugged her tightly, creating the tactile equivalent of an after-image around her body. But as well as this, the warm magic of familiarity, there was a cold magic, too. It waited unseen beyond the heavy curtains and the French windows. It whispered through cracks and crept across the carpet, caressing her now and then, so that she shivered. Out there in the night, separated by a flying-dream distance of cold air, a shivering as big as the rain-wet sky itself, was the single magic that made it possible for all other things in the world to be magic.

In that room, with no one there to see, Faye's lips began to move. No words came out. In front of her on the floor was a tiny xylophone, each metal note a different colour. She picked up the beater as if it were a painting brush and the xylophone were a palette that she could dabble in. She would choose the notes by their colours and paint a little tune, the kind that might come from a wind chime brushed by those cold fingers of air. She had already dissolved so far into synaesthesia, with all things losing themselves in metaphor, that a single object became a circular paper-chain of metaphors, and it was no longer possible to tell which link in the chain was the first. Perhaps she could play this synaesthesia on the xylophone. She played a few halting notes. Yes, the silent tune had become audible. The notes of the music box winding down. She recognised it, and half-sang, half-murmured along with it.

"Twinkle, twinkle, little star. How I wonder what…"

She let the song trail off and looked at the tree again.

"I have those lights in my life. I have those lights in my life now."

At that moment, someone walked into the room through the open door.

"It's dark in here, isn't it? What are you burbling about?"

The ceiling light winced suddenly into brightness. The hand that turned the dimmer switch stopped just before it reached maximum power, as if measuring a discrete yet firm compromise in the instant of a single twist.

It was Faye's mother, Joan. Faye twisted her torso round and looked over her left shoulder, making a display of her contortionism and pretending she was about to lose her balance.

"Nothing," she said, blinking.

"More of your saucy nonsense, I'll be bound," said her mother, stringing together phrases clearly meant to be heard in inverted commas. "Anyway, just thought I'd let you know that we're expecting dinner within the hour, so if you wanted to go out on one of your gallivants you'd better wrap up warm and do it now."

"Yes," said Faye, still blinking and teetering. The two of them looked at each other in silence for a while.

"What?" said her mother.

Faye affected to lift up her arms with great difficulty and stretched them towards her mother.

"Hug!" she said.

Her mother walked over as if about to pull her sleeves up and do some gardening. She arrived at the spot where Faye was frozen in her comic contortion.

"Come on, then," she said, and Faye stood up and put her arms around her, clinging tightly.

Joan was wearing a black, short-sleeved top. Even through her jersey, Faye was aware of the touch of her mother's flesh. Her arms had become slightly flabby with the onset of middle age. There was a toad-like coldness and softness to this flab, which only seemed to Faye to emphasise the warmth beneath. The very cold of those arms was like a goodnight kiss. She could smell it. All this was wordlessly dear to Faye.

After an interval of tightly squeezed silence, her face still pressed sideways against her mother's chest, so that her jaw could hardly move and her words came out all adenoidal, she spoke.

"Mum, isn't it strange that I exist? Do you think it means something good?"

"You are a funny one, Faye Brion."

"But I'm the last, aren't I?"

"The last what?"

"The last Faye Brion. There'll never be another me, will there? I'm very lucky, aren't I? But sometimes I get scared 'cause I'm too lucky. It makes my tummy wobble."

They continued to hold each other tightly for some time. Eventually her mother loosened her grip and Faye slipped from her arms in silky relax with a hiss of fabric.

"That reminds me," said her mother, though quite how it reminded her was not clear, "I've had a phone call from your Uncle Jamie and he's coming for Christmas, so we're giving him your room while he's here –"

"Oh, Muuuuuuum!"

"Yes, I know, darling, but it's either you sleep in your sister's room, or you share your room with Uncle Jamie, and I don't think you'd want that."

"Blech!" Faye stuck her tongue out in disgust. "But Mum, why does he have to come? I hate him soooooo much."

"Faye! He is my brother, you know."

"Why do you have to have such a horrible brother?"

"Well, we don't choose our relations, do we? Anyway, you should give him a chance."

"This is Uncle Jamie," said Faye; she puffed up her cheeks and cast her eyes upwards, looking about the room in a bored, conceited fashion. "I hate the way he just sits there with his arms crossed and his legs open like he knows everything and he's king of the world."

"Well, like it or not, he's coming, so you'll just have to make the best of it, my dear."

Jamie Blight, thirty-six years old, was a graduate of Cambridge, where he had read philosophy and distinguished himself with a first class degree. As a post-graduate his PhD had been concerned with the philosophical definition of truth. Upon completing his studies he had taken a position as a lecturer at the same university. Three years of this, however, had been enough for him, and he had left to put his talents to better, and more profitable, use as a management consultant. Over the years, his crusade to rectify the muddled thinking of those around him had led him to publish a number of books. So far he had produced three volumes – *Thinking Straight, Offences Against Logic* and *Thoughts You Should Not Think*.

Jamie was still a bachelor and, having few commitments in his social life, when he found himself at a loose end it was not unusual for him to pay a visit to the Brion household. Jamie clearly considered such occasions a chance to put his feet up more than anything, since, apart from taking the opportunity to speechify on the views he had already expounded in his books, and to root out fallacies in the thinking processes of his kin, he showed little interest in communication. Most of the time he would bury his nose in a newspaper while he munched on a slice of toast, or tap away on a laptop computer.

Right from the start he had made a bad impression on the two girls. Faye, in particular, had taken a dislike to him. This was in part an instinctive, even a physical dislike. But it was also partly due, perhaps, to the fact that Faye was the elder of the two sisters, and Jamie therefore felt more able to talk to her 'as an adult'. It seemed that his intent was not malicious. He was simply unable to tolerate expressions of thought that did not conform with his own views of logic. Faye, for her part, was unable to tolerate the constant demand to justify her thoughts and feelings using Jamie's logic, or any logic at all. If anyone had wished to create a vicious circle of antagonism, they could have done no better than observe how the two personalities dovetailed to achieve this. On occasion Faye had been reduced to tears by her uncle's attempts to clarify her thinking. There was the time, for instance, when he had asked her about her vegetarianism. "But how do you know the animal feels pain?" he had asked. "How do you know I don't know?" had been her reply. When he had logically overturned all her arguments and asked her why she still thought eating meat was wrong, she had said, "I just do." This simply was not good enough for Jamie, and his insistence that she give a well-reasoned answer had, on this occasion too, been the cause of bitter tears.

Joan had been obliged to talk to Jamie more than once about his bullying search for truth, but he had been quite incapable of understanding what he had done wrong. How could a simple insistence on logical conversation, logically be upsetting to anyone? Exasperated, Joan had given up trying to appeal to sympathy, and instead had used explanations designed to flatter his logical mind.

"She gets upset because she's *not* logical, Jamie. You can't expect her to keep up with you at her age."

Still, if Jamie was tolerated within the Brion household, it was because the members of that household did not take him altogether seriously. Mr and Mrs Brion were naturally concerned if there was another altercation between Jamie and Faye, and their sympathy was with her rather than him, but when Faye's tears had dried or her temper died down, they would joke with her and tease her, and she would usually end up laughing.

Once Joan had actually made the effort to read one of her brother's books. If it had not been written by her brother there's no doubt she would have given up after the first chapter, since the author showed no consideration for his passengers in the vehicle of thought he had created. However, she persevered, as much as anything curious to investigate the cogs and wheels of her brother's brain, and for two or three weeks she was to be seen sitting about the house with her reading glasses, concentrating intently on the book in her hand.

"What are you reading?" asked Faye one day, unused to this look of concentration in her mother.

"It's Uncle Jamie's book," she replied. "It's called *Thinking Straight*."

"Is it called *Thinking Straight and Narrow*? Is it, Mum? Is it called *Thinking Straight and Narrow, Like an Arrow that Killed the Sparrow*? Is it, Mum?"

"You're full of saucy nonsense, girl," her mother replied, with the warm irony of post-modern mothers up and down the country.

"Yes, I am," said Faye, "I am the source of all nonsense."

Perhaps because the house had been in the family from before the steep rise in property prices at the end of the twentieth century, the Brion household had that natural feeling of home about it that had once been so important in England, and, at the same time, so taken for granted. Although the house itself did not have so many rooms, all the rooms were spacious and well furnished. The ceilings were high and the walls hung with paintings and tapestries. This, in combination with the large garden, made the place seem almost like a manor house. Indeed, there was even a folly in the garden, albeit on a small scale. This was a dove-white summerhouse with Doric columns and a statue of Aphrodite at its side. It was really only big enough for four or so people to sit in. The Brions referred to it as "the temple".

Faye had spent a great deal of her childhood in this garden, where her daydreams were given free rein to frolic, and her parents had been only too happy that they had not needed to prise her away from the television. It was perhaps not to be wondered at that Faye had grown into such an abnormally imaginative child. Summer after summer, winter after winter, she had pretended that this was the garden from her favourite book – E. Nesbit's *The Enchanted Castle* – and lost herself in rapture at what enchantment had made visible only to her.

Faye's habit of playing alone in the garden, had, over the years, become as robust and immovable as a great oak tree. Because, in this solitary play, Faye often appeared to be performing a curious kind of dance, like someone riding an invisible palfrey through a mimed allegory of adventure, her mother had come to call this play "gallivanting". Faye showed no sign of stopping this childish behaviour as she grew older, and her mother, recognising some sturdy life-force in it with which it were best not to tamper, did little to discourage this gallivanting, even on wet and wintry days.

It seemed there was still a little time for gallivanting before dinner on the day Faye decorated the Christmas tree, so she put on her quilted coat and pulled on her Wellingtons in a hurry, eager to make her cheeks red in the cold outside.

She exited the house via the kitchen door, stepping from the warm yellow zone of stove, kettle and wooden table into a world as damp and silvery as a snail's trail. She shivered a little, as if feeling cold water from a puddle on her shoulder blades. Her hood was constricted in a circle round her face. Her hair spilled out of it into the winter air. For a while she simply stood and looked at the garden.

The rain that had fallen earlier that day had stopped, but the entire visible world seemed waterlogged. The rain still held dominion, it had simply ceased its invasion from the clouds and colonised the Earth, going about its soggy business more quietly in drips and trickles. Even the air seemed permeated with a fine silver haze. The paving stones beneath Faye's feet glistened. Something in this universal dampness, in the sound, sight and smell of rainwater slowly losing the hard edge of its coldness and slackening into puddles and mud, quietened Faye's heart, so that she could not move, let alone gallivant. This, too, was a kind of wonder.

The house was one of a number of detached houses that lined a dirt track leading away from the main road. In the summer, the trees that stood in an avenue along this track would form a broken canopy above, and screen the gardens and houses from the view of passers-by. Now, as Faye looked down the garden to her left, those trees were charcoal skeletons, here and there the blue light of a street lamp making wet limbs gleam and allowing a partial view of the track, its centre a raised bank of gravel on either side of which were runnels of muddy water.

To the right, the garden rose in grassy undulations, inset here and there with flowerbeds, rockeries and solitary trees, to the wall at its summit.

There had been no snow so far this year. Winter had a watery slackness to it in place of frost. Still, there was something in the air that said "December". Faye could feel it on her cheek. And just as some unspecified light made halos on the paving stones, so there was a halo in the newly washed air, a magical tension distilled from the slackness. And Faye, her chest a little tight, breathed in this air, and when she breathed out again, after all, there was enough of witchy winter in that air for its magic to become visible as white mist.

She stepped from the paving stones onto the lawn and began to squelch across it in the direction of the temple. Somehow she just didn't feel like gallivanting in the usual way. She wanted to sit in the temple for a while, and just be quiet. But as she trudged across the sneeze-wet grass, a secret grin of excitement crept up on her. She wanted to go to the other place. She didn't have much time, and she might be late for dinner, but she wanted to go. Yes, she would go! She didn't care. She laughed and started to run, a little awkward in her Wellingtons. She passed the temple and reached the back wall of the garden. She paused for a moment to rest, watching the puffs of breath from her mouth on the air. Here were the trickling, mossy bricks she knew so well. Everything was vivid with the pins-and-needles of intimacy. The curling wet leaves on the ground were breathing misty with her. She followed the wall to the corner. This was where bits of timber and miscellaneous burnables were kept to build bonfires with, and also where, for as long as Faye remembered, a pile of stones that looked as though they were left over from the building of some other wall had been abandoned. These stones formed a broken staircase to the top of the brick wall, on the other side of which stood a great sycamore tree. In this staircase, now half-covered with leaves, Faye could hear the wild, thorny voice of the field beyond, and the ruddy-cheeked wind that roamed over it.

She clambered haltingly over the stones, one hand against the wall, the sound of her movements strange with no one but her to hear. Then she was astride the wall. The ground of the field beyond was nearer than that of the garden. She swung her other leg over so both Wellies were dangling above the tussocky edge of the field, and then she launched herself with her palms, her ankles almost buckling when she landed.

Without pausing, she started to run. It was not just because there was little time; her excitement would no longer permit her to walk. The wide benighted field seemed made for nothing but running. There, at the edge of the field, was a clump of sapphire darkness that said deep, deep, deep in the chest is an unexplored continent, and this is the shape of its nameless coast, surrounded by stars. And this darkness, which seemed a part of the sky, was where Faye, with thudding heart, was running.

She drew closer, close as the blue-white surf of the evening air, and slowed, breathless. Now she shivered as if something had got inside her coat, her sister putting an icy cold hand on her back for a joke. But the shivering was in her chest, and it was not entirely that of the cold. It was the shivering of magic. The cold was part of the magic, of course. It shivered her insides and the outside world all up together, the familiar of the flesh mixing with the wild of the rain and stars like colours running in a watercolour painting. A shine of cold on the side of her chest like the rubber of her Wellies. A woollen smile in the crook of her finger. A swirling cup of hot melody in her hair. Outside the stars shiver, and inside the body twinkles. My heart is a torch, she thought, an electric torch beam in the how-exciting dark.

Yes, the flickering wings of yes a light amidst the trees. The lights that say, it's true, my heart, among the trees, where the sheltered ground is soft and the air still.

Faye came to where the field became a slope, and the dark copse seemed to spill over the edge of the world, and she leapt over the edge and ran staggeringly across the slope into the trees, and the lights said yes it's true still true as it always ever was and will be and they rained down upon her in a flickering spiral of wings like sycamore seeds.

Greg, hunched in his long army surplus coat, swung the dog chain in one hand and called to his border collie, Trips. He stopped and saw her galloping figure emerge out of the gloom. Waiting, he let his gaze wander over the lonely fields. For some reason his attention was drawn to the copse of trees at the top of the hill opposite. Dead shadows. The branches had been bled of all colour by the night. It looked like some lunar grotto flanked by petrified growths of gargantuan moss. Then there came a sound. For an instant he thought it was an owl. But no, how curious! In the crisp emptiness of the night he could hear the sound of a little girl singing. He could distinguish no words. For that matter, he was not sure there was a tune. There was only the silence of night and this girl's single voice. He half-wondered if there might be something wrong. Perhaps he should go and investigate. And what would he do when he found only a little girl singing? He looked around again. There was no one else here. Why should he go and investigate? Besides, there was something odd about the voice, and he would rather just forget it. He shivered. Trips was now by his side, looking up at him expectantly. Uneasily, vaguely hoping that he never heard anything about that voice thereafter, he walked on.

It was two days before Christmas and Uncle Jamie had arrived yesterday. Despite his bored and waspish manner, he also had something of the glow about him, as any guest must do in this season, of one who had come in from the cold. His body seemed to sneer lazily across the cushions of the settee while he read his usual newspaper, an expression of disapproval on his face, as if he had been asked to correct all the mistakes.

Usually the family would eat dinner in the kitchen, but since they had a guest they had decided to be more formal – and less cramped – and use the sitting room as a dining room. Faye's sister, Tegan, was upstairs and her parents were busy in the kitchen. Feeling a little put out of her usual routine, Faye had volunteered to lay the table. She was now setting the last of the plates upon the tablemats. All that remained was to bring in the food when it was ready.

A little unsure what to do next, she glanced across at her silent uncle, whose presence she could not help being irritated by. He wore an expensive, charcoal grey suit and a white shirt with no tie. Faye had a sneaking admiration for the suit. Even if her uncle had no manners, he at least made some concession to the illogical common sense prevalent between people by being well dressed. That said, he was well dressed in a way she did not care for. This regard for his own appearance was further displayed in his bald pate, which he had shaved when his hair had begun to recede noticeably. Uncle Jamie was not fat exactly, but he was somehow red and puffy. The word 'waspish' conjured images of a thin person, but in Uncle Jamie's case, the poison of his own waspishness seemed to have swollen his flesh. His physique expressed a mixture of the discipline that had brought him his current lifestyle, and the material comforts of the lifestyle itself. The self-satisfaction in the outer layer of flab covered a balancing musculature of extreme *dis*-satisfaction with everyone else.

Jamie must have noticed that his niece was examining him, because he folded his paper and looked up at her. Perhaps mirroring her boredom and loose-end-ish-ness, he discarded the paper on the cushion next to him and made a strange, deliberate attempt at conversation.

"Very helpful of you. Your mother tells me you also decorated the tree."

Faye lowered her eyes and nodded.

"But I like decorating the tree," she said.

"And you don't like laying the table?"

She laughed. He was really just asking questions for the sake of it.

"Not particularly," she said.

"Well, what's the difference?"

This must be one of his philosophical questions. Why else would someone ask the difference between decorating a Christmas tree and laying a table?

"Decorating the tree is… I don't know. You can do what you like. Laying the table is just something you do 'cause you have to eat."

"Interesting."

Faye laughed again.

"Do you know the best thing about our tree?" asked Faye, forgetting herself.

"No, what is it?"

"We've got a fairy on top. Most people these days have angels. I hate angels. They're rubbish. Fairies are much better. It's an heirloom, you know."

"I know," said Jamie. "I remember it."

He paused.

"And why are fairies better than angels?"

Faye sighed.

"Well, never mind," she mumbled.

"Pardon?"

Suddenly she looked up at him.

She actually pitied him with his endless strings of silly questions. He was like someone bent over with his nose to the ground, following a trail with a magnifying glass, not realising that if he only stood up and looked around he would be able to see what he was looking for. At that moment Uncle Jamie did not frighten or irritate Faye. She understood that while he crouched, she held her head up high. He had no power over her.

"Well," she said, confident of bewildering him completely, "if you actually saw one you'd know why, and you wouldn't have to ask."

She felt as if she were dancing lightly around him on fairy wings, sprinkling beautiful magic dust into his eyes. She was free, and he could not catch her.

He was silent. Somewhere in that silence there was a change; her triumph became unease. She felt her wings might fail her. Then he opened his mouth.

"But you see, I don't believe in fairies."

Faye gasped as if suddenly pierced by a cold blade.

"Don't say that," she managed in a half-whisper.

As if he found this performance distasteful, Jamie said in an even tone, "What? 'I don't believe in fairies'?"

Faye's face went pale and she trembled.

"You mustn't say it."

"Why can't I say – "

Since her first gasp it had looked almost as if Faye were paralysed. In fact, all strength had drained from her at her uncle's words. She felt like a useless jelly, unable to do anything but tremble. But when her uncle had begun to speak again, as if from nowhere a flame leapt up in her. She picked up one of the plates from the table and flung it at him. He ducked, raising his arm to shield himself. In her fury, Faye's aim had been wild, and the plate smashed against the wall.

She was half horrified at what she had done, but the flame continued to climb higher inside her. She stood, breathing heavily through flared nostrils, as if they were a bellows feeding the furnace within. Her mouth was set in a bow of scorn. Her uncle looked up as he drew his arm away, his face serious. He was not amused by this hysteria, and would not back down to it. His expression was one of contemptuous warning, like someone who has agreed to a fight.

Faye wanted to spit, or scratch his cheeks till they bled. Instead she just stood there, feeling the flames rising within her and staring into his eyes. She hoped that even a ground-snuffling, half-blind creature like him would understand the hatred in her stare.

At this point Joan marched into the room.

"What's all this racket?"

She must have meant the plate. Faye's heart thudded, but she kept perfectly still.

"I'm talking to you, young lady," bellowed Joan.

With her eyes still fixed on her uncle's, Faye spoke.

"I don't want him in the house. Make him go away."

"Now, just what is going on here?"

Faye turned to her mother.

"He said he doesn't believe in…" She stopped, unable to finish her sentence, and pointed to the fairy on top of the tree.

"And?" said her mother.

"Mum! You know that every time someone says that… every time someone says that a fairy dies."

Joan turned to her brother.

"For God's sake, Jamie, try not to wind her up. Have a bit of consideration, won't you?"

Seeing the pieces of plate on the carpet, she bent down to gather them up.

"I'm sick of it. I really am. I'll have to put muzzles on you both… Another plate gone. We'll have to buy a new service soon."

Jamie, in the meantime, had found his voice.

"I really don't see that I've done anything wrong. What kind of world is it where you can't express a rational view like…" He paused and looked at Faye. A smile flickered on his lips, "Like I don't believe in fairies, I don't believe in fairies, I don't believe – "

Faye shrieked and lunged, her nails bared, ready to claw out his eyes. Her uncle did his best to fend her off, and Joan, too, discarding the shards of broken crockery, leapt in to try and separate the two.

"Pack it in, the pair of you. I ought to bang your heads together."

She finally managed to drag off the assailant, who by this time was sobbing uncontrollably, but not before Jamie had sustained an injury. Three claw marks showed scarlet on his left cheek and there were weals on his throat.

"Go to your room now, Faye Brion. I'll deal with you later."

The irony of the post-modern mother had vanished from her voice.

"And you," she turned to her brother once Faye had left the room, "Don't you dare – don't you *dare* – complain about that mark on your face after you deliberately goaded her like that. I mean it, Jamie, I will not have this fighting in my house."

Faye lay on her stomach with her face in her pillow. She was beginning to feel hot and stale, like someone who had been binging on sleep. However, whenever she thought of moving she realised there was nowhere she could go, and she felt wretched again. She couldn't even get under her duvet and curl up properly, because her uncle had slept in the bed the night before, and she could smell him on the sheets. She had even had to turn the pillow over to put her face on it. This was worse than being ill. She wished that her uncle would hurry up and go away so that she could wash the sheets and have her room back.

She couldn't go downstairs. Her mother had told her not to come down until she was ready to make a full apology. And she wasn't ready. It was true she had been sent to her room, but she felt all the pride of someone who had gone off in a sulk and was waiting for everyone else to notice and come after her. That they would not do. So she was stuck. Perhaps if she could cry again she'd feel a little better, but for the moment her tears had dried. When her mother had come to her room she had cried and bawled and used up a great many tissues. Despite her anger, her mother had been unable to refrain from giving her a hug, whereupon she had cried all the more.

"What's the matter, love?" her mother had asked as she rubbed her back.

"You… You don't understand," said Faye, her throat clogged with tears, "He's *killed* them. He's a murderer."

Unsure how to answer this, and being well aware how ill-advised she would be to try and reassure Faye by explaining that since fairies did not exist they could not be killed, Joan had simply kept a worried silence and continued to rub her daughter's back.

But if Faye could not go downstairs – and this tormented her more – she was also unable to go out into the night and visit that other place.

She needed to go there now more than she ever had before, but she was afraid. There would be tears and pain, much worse than any she had felt so far, but more than that, there was the fact that it was partly her fault. Why had she been so stupid as to talk like that to him? She had been… over-confident. Yes! Like so many human beings that she hated. Like Uncle Jamie himself. That's what had led to disaster. And her arrogance had brought on his arrogance. He had sprayed out his opinions in his usual way, and released the deadly pollution of his arrogance like CFCs into the atmosphere. But no, the damage was not a side effect of his arrogance. It was true that he had said those words because he really didn't believe in fairies. And in his stupid, piggish way he thought he was being funny and clever. But, even if he did believe in fairies he would say he didn't, just in order to kill them. She was convinced of it. He did it deliberately, as if what he sprayed was pesticide.

She sighed and lifted her face from the pillow. Inside her chest a tearful ache persisted. As well as sadness there was hatred in that ache. She could call Uncle Jamie a pig – for some reason her hatred created a block and she couldn't express it beyond that single word – but he himself would never know or care just how horrible he was.

Despite the ache in her chest, it seemed to Faye that everything was quiet now. She looked out of the window. From here she could see the front of the garden, all webbed with silver. This was the kind of silky quiet that seemed to say, there is nothing left to do, you have to face the terrible sadness that is waiting for you.

Almost directly below the window was the roof of the portico, and twisting tightly around the pillars supporting that roof were thick vines of wisteria. Faye had climbed down those vines before, a long time ago.

It was time for her to make a move and meet that vast, silky quiet. She slid the bolt from under the hook on the meeting rail of the lower window frame and pulled down the upper frame to let the night air into her bedroom.

Faye tramped alone across the darkened empty field, her resignation a kind of heroism. She was pale and listless, as with a terrible emptiness. So terrible was the emptiness that it might have been a cold kind of glory, like the cold that seeps into an open wound. Before she had drawn very near to the copse of trees at the field's edge, she felt herself suddenly in the presence of a monolithic sadness. She stopped in a kind of reverence, and an effusion of tears pricked the world wetly into stars. These tears were her mortal offering to that immortal monolith. They were a token, but a spontaneous one.

Faye knew all about fairies. She knew the stories, and she knew what in the stories was true, and what false. The stories often spoke of a mist that travellers pass through in order to enter the realm of fairy. There was such a mist, but it was not so much one you saw as one you felt. Last time she passed through it, the mist had been a kind of shivering. This time it was tears.

From somewhere in her tears a light leaked out, spreading like dye. It was a single light among the branches of the trees, wild yet familiar, waiting. She ran through the blur of her tears to meet it.

Once she was beneath the branches she felt that warmth of softness she knew so well. She stopped and wiped her eyes. There, in the crook where a branch met the trunk of a tree, was Juniper. Faye's first emotion when her tears cleared and Juniper came into focus was relief. This was the first fairy Faye had ever met, years ago, at a time from which all other memories were vague or lost. Juniper alone remained vivid and unchanged from that time. The light that came from Juniper's body was to Faye a tie closer than blood. Juniper's body shone in such a way because, though solid, it was not made of flesh. It was more real than flesh. It was precisely that greatest of all realities that humans deny by being realistic. It was real because it was devoid of the human impurity of realism that finally makes it impossible to feel anything at all. And it was strange and eerie because it was so beautiful. This creature, so clearly quick with life, and to the human eye so clearly other, was neither male nor female, only beautiful. It was naked, or seemed to be, but calyces of light grew naturally to gird its slender hips, half-hiding a gossamer flowery growth beneath.

Juniper raised her head slowly from the branch where he had been resting her cheek, and turned his green eyes upon Faye, her gender seeming to change as he did so, like the image on a schoolgirl's ruler that is transformed by movement. He said nothing; instead his silence spoke. The green of her eyes were a starburst as cool as the point where reeds meet water in a pond. Where usually a tumbling company of fairies would be here to meet Faye, now there was only one, as on the day they first met, a solemn reminder of the meeting that was her first link with and invitation to the world of fairy. Beyond Juniper there was only gloom. The light of the other fairies was nowhere to be seen.

Tears crabbed their way once more down Faye's cheeks. Juniper inclined her head to one side, quizzically. There came a voice like wind in the water reeds.

"What have you done, Faye Brion?"

"I'm sorry. I'm sorry. It was my fault. I tried to beat him. I tried to show him I'm better. But I'm not. I'm a stupid idiot, and you must hate me."

The creature tumbled in nonsensical movements from the branch. He did not move like a human being, or any other animal. The whole principle of her movement was different, as was the stuff from which he was composed. Faye, long ago, had let fall from her childish tongue a word she thought described these tiny, exquisite movements, at once so fluid and so jerky; 'dropsical', she had called them, not knowing the word might mean something else in the dictionary.

And so Juniper moved all dropsically across the leaf-strewn soil to where Faye stood. Juniper had no real size. When she moved this was especially apparent. He was tiny, yes, but only in that she could fit anywhere and was also preternaturally delicate. But this attribute of 'being tiny' also meant that his body, or parts of her body, were liable to appear suddenly close-up, twitching huge and fine as eyelashes, as if magnified by a powerful and limpid lens. More than that, this disruption of scale had a knock-on effect, making the relative sizes of everything else infinitely variable. By the time the fairy thing had reached the place where Faye stood, he seemed perhaps two or three feet tall. But since Faye was the only yardstick for such measurements, and since she could no longer be sure of her own height amidst the enormously looming bark of tree trunks and the strange fertile paving known as soil, such measurements had no meaning, after all.

Juniper's hand touched Faye's elbow and light seemed to flush through her body. The fingers had landed there only for an instant, like a butterfly, before flitting away again, but in their untameable, uncatchable butterfly way, they had made Faye feel more special than one of her mother's longest, tightest squeezes.

"And so you were afraid to come to us, poor Faye, and poor, poor Juniper had to wait so long for you. But what you have done is only what we have done through you, dear Faye, our last and most precious human sister. We've stayed away from the human world, but then we chose to try again with you. What happened with your uncle was inevitable."

"But something terrible has happened, hasn't it? Something truly… solemn."

"Yes, Faye. We share it. I will show you. Do you know what it is that 'solemn' comes from?"

"No, what is it?"

"It's time, Faye – the human trap. It's the striking of a clock, you see. Sometimes it strikes, and everything cracks and changes. Do you understand?"

Faye nodded.

"This is difficult for you, Faye, so difficult. Come with me, I'll show you."

And Juniper rustled away through the trees, the flickering iridescence of her wings beckoning Faye to follow. In the world Faye had left behind, separated from this by a wall of invisible mist, the seasons came one at a time, as did day and night, and now it was a winter evening. In this world, day and night and the various seasons were wonderfully mixed, just as shadows and sunlight are mixed in leafy dapples by the canopy of a forest. The copse of trees that Faye had approached from outside had been near leafless, but the trees she walked among now were so thick with leaves it was impossible to glimpse a world beyond them. Winter was present amidst these trees as a damp darkness of hue, a silvery web of frost here and there, and as pools of air as beautiful as pure, cold water. Even now Faye could not suppress her excitement in this world, and when she passed through these pools, it showed in the filigree of her breath chased into the otherwise invisible silver of the liquid air. But there was spring here, too, in hazy carpets of bluebells, and summer where a yellow-green light occasionally broke through the leaves, too dazzling to allow the eyes to see out where it came in, and autumn in fallen horse chestnuts and rich soil smells. And all of it, all of it so limpid as to be alien. Futurism, alienage, surrealism – they were contained in the very crystallinity of colour and of the air that communicated colour without touching it. Despite his luminosity, Juniper seemed always on the point of disappearing, as if by camouflage, in this world of eerie freshness.

A nowhere darkness, invisible as the air itself, made the freshness of certain sections of the wood particularly intense. Juniper was leading Faye to one of these sections now. Here the positions of the trees seemed to attain a certain regularity, like standing stones, and crowded round in concentric circles filtering the view of what lay beyond. Faye was only aware that the intensity of darkness here threw the presence of certain living lights into relief, but she could not see much more than that between the stern, straight trunks of the trees. She thought for some reason of Juniper's description of 'solemn' as the striking of a clock, and about the cracks that might appear with that striking. But she had no time to dwell on this, for Juniper was already squeezing through the screen of trees, and Faye did not wish to enter the fairy-litten clearing too far behind him. And so she stumbled into the moss-deep bower all unprepared for the scene that met her eyes, or rather, the air that fell upon her heart.

Of course, this was not the first time she had burst in upon a secret fairy place, but what struck her now was not the usual tottering wonder of the fairy revel. It was a wonder altogether darker and more terrible.

Usually, when she passed through the mist bordering Fairyland, Faye would be greeted by a kind of spring rain, the drops of which were fairies. As if rain fell upon a pond, these drops did not simply fall, but splashed about in directionless chaos. And Faye would feel herself a tiny part of the teeming pond life, the size of a pond-skater, and just as the fairy droplets were magnified about her, so that in their microcosmic way they were gigantic, so in their splashing acceleration of the miniature they achieved slow motion; drops of water magnify the water fleas inside them; in slow motion the mercurial acrobatics of each droplet can be seen, each beat of each wing.

But this time there were no such dancing splashes of fairies. This time there was stillness. The fairy folk were scattered around the clearing, each an example of the weird semi-camouflage that Juniper, too, possessed. It was a camouflage of strangeness, a trick played on the mind. The fairies did not so much blend into the background as make the background strange, so that it was hard to tell which was background and which was fairy. The whole scene became a painting by Arcimboldo, in which figures seemed to emerge from twig, leaf and berry, before merging back again. Some of the fairies were thin and prickly, like little thorn bushes. Some were knobbly and fungoid. Others, like Juniper, tended towards the floral, spirals in their bodies budding and flowering. Others still had spent their lives at a masquerade whose jumbled costumes once belonged to crawling things or flying things.

The reverse camouflage of the fairies caught the eye, as did the glow of their bodies. But that glow was not now gooseflesh fresh; it was intimate as candles. Because, usually, when the fairies were gathered in a group, the tumbling and gambolling never stopped, it had seemed to Faye that it never could stop. To see the fairies now, simply crouched or huddled, perfectly motionless except for a flicker of wings here and there, suggested to Faye something against nature.

But all this was peripheral – in the branches of trees and amidst the living fractals of ferns. In the centre of the embowered space there was indeed movement. It was this that the other fairies watched so intently. But it was not the movement of revelry. It was slower movement, more purposeful, the kind of broken, rhythm-less movement to be seen in those with work to do. Perhaps this movement was infected by the objects that the silently toiling fairies handled, though they seemed at pains to keep a distance from the objects, which they moved with the aid of twiggy stretchers. The objects were embodiments of a devastating contradiction; they were fairy corpses. To Faye, a fairy was the very opposite of death. She knew what had brought this about, but even so, as she watched in horror, she could not help asking silently, "How is this possible?"

There were now four of the corpses laid upon the ground. It was little wonder that the other fairies did not want to touch them. The very air around them seemed different. Where their living fellows glowed with reality, their bodies springy and warm as flesh, without the decay-prone element of matter itself, the corpses no longer glowed, but instead were ravaged by the bleak light of filthy realism. They had been transformed into mere matter, and putrefaction had quickly set in. They looked like the pitiful, white-bellied, tooth-baring corpses of shrews that Faye sometimes saw amidst the leaf litter on the woodland floor back in the human world. There was something else in the scene before her that Faye had never seen before in Fairyland – flies were buzzing around the corpses. Indeed, the maggoty smell of death had become sharp and insidious on the air.

What were these strange objects that once had been fairies? It was not enough to say they were corpses. Although they were not ugly as such, they were harder to look at than the most hideous examples of the fate of human flesh, either living or dead. Their beauty had faded only a little, but there was something vastly sinister in this slight change. It was the mixture of the real and the unreal – whichever one took to be which – that made these objects not ugly, but somehow unclean, unholy.

Faye remembered that she had come from the unreal world of the realistic. To see what its touch had wrought here disturbed the foundations of her being. Such damage might cause the universe to buckle. How had she ever come to this place without causing such damage before? Who was she?

Juniper, flitting at her side, spoke:

"Do not stare at them, sweet Faye. Your precious mind is troubled now. Your defences are low. We do not want to lose you. Diseases spread in troubled minds, dear child. Take my hand."

Faye felt a sweet presence in her left palm, like a melting snowflake.

"It's easy, Faye, easy as my hand. Don't let it cloud your mind."

Just then there was a bustle from the foliage beyond the bower and two more fairies arrived with another object on a litter between them.

Faye's expression displayed a puzzled concern, then her eyes widened in recognition. She let out a shriek that, if by chance it were heard in the human world, would have surely been recognised as a sign that the world of fairy was close by. As soon as the weird note had passed her lips, she rushed forward. But the stillness of the fairies surrounding the bower was deceptive, for now a dozen or more of them were on her in a single flickering of wings, holding her back by dint of some strength that inhered in the glow of their limbs.

"Cloudberry!"

Tears burst from Faye afresh as she called the name of the latest fairy to be numbered among the corpses.

Cloudberry had been a lissom thing, crowned with white petals instead of hair. The friendship she had given had been magnified for Faye a thousand times by the fact that it was – should have been – undying; Cloudberry's spirit had come to hover in Faye's heart like a sweet fog. But now that fatal dawn of realism had crept over Cloudberry. The fog was evaporating. What had been beautiful when it lived, in death looked only freakish.

Faye's voice was jagged as she called the name of the vanished fog, feeling a harsh burning in the emptiness it left behind. A friend closer to her than daydream itself, the playful genius of that most useless and most precious thing, the heart, had, by the malicious-fingered interference of some useful, worthless other, ceased to be. The worthless thing was malicious *because* it was worthless. It must destroy anything of value. That much was clear. But how and why had it been granted such power?

"Four," Faye was bawling, "He said it four times. I heard him. I counted it over and over in my head. Four. He never finished the next sentence. I swear it! I scratched his face before he could. The pig! The stinking pig! Not Cloudberry! Cloudberry can't be dead. It's not right."

Juniper's calm voice was audible above the pain in Faye's heart. It soothed her in its dew-like clarity, but she did not want to be soothed. For if she were soothed she would accept what the calm voice was saying, and the moment she accepted, the thing would become true.

"Faye, dear and sweetest Faye, listen to me. Poor Cloudberry was not the only unlucky one. Even one death would be too many. But there is no mistake. And Cloudberry is not the last. There are seventeen killed by the words from your uncle's lips."

"Seventeen? But…"

"When you went to your room, when no one else could hear, he put his hand to his cheek and said the words again, slowly, thirteen times."

"Horrible! Horrible!"

With these words she unwittingly accepted that which she had hoped to deny forever, and a sickness took up occupation in her heart. Her pure tears ceased to flow. Instead she watched as the remainder of the corpses were brought out one by one from that place where they had been laid temporarily to stop the spread of the infection within them. If her heart was sick, her mind was in fever, and there was nothing for her to do but to let the light and the movement and the voices of the fairies be a hand upon her brow, not healing, perhaps, but simply stroking and being present through the brimming pain that made her as passive as doom.

Presently, all seventeen bodies were arranged, like the radiating petals of a wilting flower, upon the earth that is the last home of so many living things. Somehow it did not seem that the earth, or any other place in the universe, could ever be the home of these bodies. What was to be done with them? They required special treatment – not so much funeral as dangerous waste disposal – in accordance with the fact that they now belonged neither to the fairy nor the human world.

The fairies who had been engaged in carrying and arranging the remains of their fellows now drew back and formed a circle. They appeared wan, and there was a weariness in their manner, as if they had fallen under the wilting spell of the corpse-petalled flower at their centre. They linked their delicate fingers together as if threading the severed heads of daisies in a chain, and then they began to dance.

Faye had seen this kind of dance before. She knew that, when it was over, mushrooms would sprout where the fairy feet had trod, and a fairy ring would be formed. The movements of this dance were, as usual, 'all dropsical', but now all that was jerky in the dropsical equation was removed, and there remained only the sadness of a drooping fluidity.

Round and round went the circle of linked hands, round and round that fluid sadness in the midst of Faye's fever, the quiet dance seeming to speak to her in the eerie-meaningful language of dream, of cycles grander and vaster than nature itself – at their zenith higher and at their nadir lower – and revolving now upon the grim axis of a pile of plague carrion. These were not cycles of time, and in Faye's mind as she watched, time came unravelled, its coils twisting unevenly on top of each other, like images multiplied and overlapping in the vision of a drunk.

She heard Juniper's voice at her side. That slow dance, that cold dance had seemed to leap as close as the hallucinatory flames of her own fever. Hearing that voice, suddenly the dance seemed inaudibly remote, like the surface of a distant star seen through a telescope. It seemed to Faye now that she could never see the end of such a dance. There was no end, unless it was some catastrophic meeting of the invincible elements of plague and flame. Even to Faye, such sights were forbidden.

"This way," said Juniper, and flickered off into the trees at the side of the bower.

Faye followed Juniper's glow like a heartbeat, a voice inside her head, her own breath keeping her warm. They moved through leaves and lucid darkness, as if they did not move at all, but all things moved around them.

"… we don't have the power for that," continued the ignis fatuus voice, without which Faye would have been utterly lost. "Forever! Oh, when there's a piece of forever in it, precious Faye – do you understand? Our magic doesn't work against forever. We're only little things with little tricks. But for you we will put our tricks together. Only, sweet Faye, it's a hurting time. It's difficult. Even for us. But I have to ask you – do you want to be our friend forever? It hurts me to ask. We should have known the time would come. It's difficult with humans – "

"Juniper! Don't talk to me like that, please. Why do you have to remind me I'm human? I know. And I'm sorry for what I've done. Believe me. I'd understand if you didn't want me to come here anymore. Only, please let me come again. Please let us be friends forever. I knew that I should never talk to people about fairies. They're too stupid and ugly ever to understand. But please let's be friends and not talk about me being human… If that's okay."

"Of course, sweet Faye. We love you, too. We don't want to hurt you. But saying, 'Let's be friends' is not enough. We have to do something. The dance will stop the poison for now. But it won't make it go away. You have to help us. You know human and fairy. You can pass through the mist. You can take the poison away. It's the only way we can be friends now. I'll show you."

"Yes, of course, Juniper. I'll do whatever you want. I'll do anything. I'm so glad we're friends. Nothing else matters. But I don't think I'll ever understand why you chose me. I'm nothing special."

"Not in the human world. Nothing is special in the human world. But we know who can play with us. We had to have you, Faye. You know how to twinkle. That's why…"

The appearance of the forest around them was changing. The bark of the trees seemed to be knotted with disease and the leaves looked pale and lifeless. There was in everything the suggestion that the forest was becoming a swamp. A forest is not trees, undergrowth, birdsong. All these things are simply the colours in forest's palette. A swamp is not mud, gas, creepers. These are merely the brushstrokes of swamp. Here one spirit, one style, was giving way to another. The same subject matter, depicted with the same materials, was distorted into something utterly different. Here the body of the forest had become malignant and tumorous.

The trees thinned out, their deformity increasing and their leaves becoming sparser as they did so. It was as if, for an instant, everything had been liquefied by a flash of heat ten million times hotter than the sun, only to solidify when the instant had passed, into shapes that were somehow not right. The *substance* of everything, also, had been affected by the shock, so that nothing had quite returned to a state of fixity. Names no longer seemed applicable here – the branches were not branches, the roots were not roots, even the soil was not soil, since all these things had melted closer to an undifferentiated waxiness.

Faye and Juniper came to the last of the tree-objects, beyond which, for some distance, was a swamp where everything had deliquesced into utter shapelessness, like a mixing of different-coloured paints until they formed only swirls and spikes of nasty blacks, greys and browns. Beyond the patch of swamp could be seen, through a dismal haze, more of the ruined trees.

Juniper stopped here, hovering in mid-air under the warped appendages of a howl of frozen matter.

"You mustn't go further. The line between you and it will disappear. This is where it happened. We call it a 'twisting'."

Faye was about to ask why it was called a 'twisting'. It was true that where a semblance of shape remained in anything, that shape did seem awry, as if the principle behind form itself had been perverted, but she was not sure that this was the explanation. There was also the way she felt when she looked at it – twisted inside, as if she saw the future here. This was not anything that could be purified by cycles of life and death. It was something removed from nature. Neither life nor death could save it. It was matter transmuted into seemingly indestructible nightmare, and nothing could reverse the process. It was not devastation, from which something might grow afresh. It was worse than that. It spoke of eternal continuation in a state of sludge. As Faye surveyed this most ultimate of all stagnations, however, she noticed something. The area where all trees, undergrowth and soil had melted away into quicksand seemed to dip towards the centre. Moreover, amidst the distorted residue of the shapes that once were, could be traced a slow and sombre pattern, like a wave swelling beneath the viscid black of an oil slick. It was a spiral. As soon as this pattern became clear, Faye was convinced that she was looking at the kind of pit that is formed in the sand of an hourglass as it trickles away. Where was the swamp trickling away to? Was it a kind of nowhere? The sludge could never be destroyed, she was sure. Did that mean that everything was turning inside out and into a universe of sludge? The implications of the scene seemed to swing spiral arms in such wide arcs that they swept out quite beyond questions of whether the human soul could endure this or not. The human soul would simply be trapped alive in the sticky pitch bog.

"How can we stop it?"

Her question seemed to see-saw on the balancing point of the moment between wild despair and equally wild hope.

"Usually we go away to the farthest parts of Never, where no bridge of mist from the human world has ever been built. We're safe there. But if you want to be friends with us we must keep the link. When the last of the bridges goes, then we set the world adrift and bye-bye misty forever. But we have a little plan. Shall I tell you?"

Faye nodded once. Juniper smiled the strangest smile that Faye had ever seen, and pointed to the ground. There, next to the agony of serpents that had been roots, were other objects sprouting in shapes expressing poison as some trees express the otherwise invisible passage of the wind. These objects, the only things that seemed still to grow here, though they grew in the spirit of the twisting, were mushrooms.

When Faye eventually came down from her bedroom, after first climbing back up into it, there was a very professional looking Melolin dressing applied to her uncle's left cheek, held in place by surgical tape. It was white, like a bandage, not the flesh-tone of the usual sticking plaster, and covered most of the area between ear and nose. Faye's father was a doctor and her mother a nurse, so this sight was no great surprise to her. Probably her mother had tried to propitiate her brother a little by treating the scratches as a serious wound.

Tegan had gone to bed, but her parents were still at the table in the sitting room with her uncle. She apologised to him in front of them. Faye's manner seemed to suggest she had thought things over and come to a genuine change of heart. Her apology was given with good grace and no signs of reluctance. Her uncle looked silently into her eyes as she spoke. His expression was unreadable. He seemed to accept her apology, perhaps with a suggestion in his patience that this was only what was due to him. Only the white flag of injury on his cheek gave a hint of bitterness to his silence.

When Faye had finished her apology, he gave his. In fact, his apology was given with markedly less grace than hers. It was very clear that he was not accustomed to apologies, and was embarrassed, reciting the words briefly and without feeling as if they were an unpleasant formality whose meaning he did not understand.

Faye sat down at the table with a prim motion that resembled a curtsey. Suddenly she was a mime of modesty, as if she were putting into practice recent lessons in deportment. Her mother glanced at her sidelong, seeming to detect more saucy nonsense effervescing just beneath the surface display of nervous control. There was something charming about this mixture of demure lowered eyes and unspoken riddle; the riddle itself, challenging anyone to guess what was truly in her heart, radiated in deliberate waves of mystification from every ivory-nervous movement of piano-player fingers, from the very upward curve of her eyelashes.

Her mother got up from the table, breathing in through her nose and watching Faye out of the corners of her eyes, her lips twitching and her head wobbling almost imperceptibly as if to say, "I know what your game is." She disappeared into the kitchen and returned with a plate of cold dinner, which she set before Faye.

"Well, young lady, you must be hungry," she said, and returned to her seat.

Faye began to pick unenthusiastically at the quiche. She seemed thoughtful for a while. Finally, still looking at her food, she spoke.

"I've learnt another reason why it's good to be vegetarian."

Although she did not raise her head it was somehow apparent that she was addressing her uncle.

"Oh?" he said, after a moment.

"Yes, do you remember I couldn't give a proper reason that time?"

Jamie seemed wary, and only murmured. Faye continued.

"Meat uses up too much of the world's resources. It takes much, much more water and food to feed the animals to make a meal for humans, when humans could be using that water and food for their own meals."

"Well, that's true. Viewed simply in those terms, it's an inefficient way of feeding ourselves. But other factors must be taken into consideration, such as the economic infrastructure – "

"But what about the world's resources? There are too many people."

"Too many to continue forever in our current lifestyle if nothing changes. But it will change. Science will develop, *is* developing new technologies that will enable us to cope with whatever environmental changes we have to face. For instance, in terms of food, we will soon be able to genetically engineer chickens without wasteful body parts such as legs and heads, and so increase the efficiency of food production –"

"That's horrible!" Faye interrupted again.

Her mother looked as if she were ready to intervene. Even her father, leaning back in his chair, showed a certain attentiveness in his expression that was more than a casual interest in the conversation.

"Why is it horrible?" asked Jamie, simply and calmly.

"It just is. Really. Don't you think that's at all horrible?"

Jamie simply smiled, almost sadly, as if to say he was constrained to silence in order to keep the peace, but that the truth was so obvious he need not speak it anyway.

"Why do the animals have to suffer just because humans are greedy?"

This time, the sad smile of knowing melting into his voice, Jamie responded.

"Let me explain it to you. Do you know about DDT and penguins?"

Faye shook her head.

"Not long ago a number of environmentalists kicked up a fuss because they claimed that DDT in food production was harming penguins.

They seemed to consider this a problem. There was a fundamental fallacy underlying their reasoning. DDT is harming penguins, therefore we must stop production of DDT. But, you see, this doesn't follow at all.

"People are the only thing that is of any importance. And do you know why? Because people are the only things capable of defining what is important. Penguins have no idea of what is important and what isn't. Whether they exist or don't exist makes not the blindest bit of difference. Or, if they are important, it's because human beings find it amusing to look at them in zoos and make wildlife documentaries about them. There is absolutely no criterion whatsoever for establishing anything as being important outside a human frame of reference. Therefore, since penguins are not a matter of life and death for us, we must simply weigh the value of the amusement with which they provide us against the financial and other costs of ceasing to produce DDT. That is the only way to proceed without confusion. And if penguins become extinct, so what? They will not be missed any more than the dodo."

Was it the white badge of injury that gave Jamie license to speak like this – that badge flaunted as both weapon and shield – or did he simply have no idea of the power of his words? Faye's parents looked ready to restrain uncle and niece at any moment, but Jamie's speech had taken on a quiet momentum of its own and there seemed no logical point at which to stop it. Jamie's confidence that he could say what he pleased seemed to cast a spell. It seemed no one could touch him while he spoke. So he sailed to his conclusion without meeting any resistance. When he finished there was silence. In one attempt, without pausing, he had composed something perfect.

"I suppose you're right," said Faye at last, and speared another piece of quiche with her fork.

Relief emanated audibly from her parents.

"Of course," said Jamie. "It's a very simple matter."

With the sudden easing of tension, the conversation moved on to other things. Faye's father, Gregory, asked Jamie about the square-faced quartz watch that flashed out from beneath the sleeve of his suit jacket when he jerked his arm. It was a Versace Landmark, and very expensive. Jamie held out his arm and Gregory admired the baroque horologe. The face was black, inset with a number of dials. Despite a suggestion of the ornate in the design, there was something sleek and cold about its angularity, as if it were an automatic handgun. Gregory remarked with interest the silver Medusa's head at the twelve o'clock position. The two men began to talk about accuracy in time-keeping, the piezo-electric field generated by quartz crystals, the higher rate of vibration used to divide time in atomic clocks, and so on. Gregory wondered aloud, almost wistfully, if the impossibility of making a time piece that was one hundred per cent accurate meant that time was nothing more than a convenient fiction.

"It must always be accurate to the thousandth of a second, or the millionth of a second, or... However much you reduce the margin of error, that margin exists. It's a gap, not a point. And any gap is big enough for the whole concept of time to escape down. A bit like... sand in an hourglass..."

Faye kept quiet during this conversation. At length she finished her dinner and her mother, as if she had been waiting for this, picked up her empty plate to take it to the kitchen.

"I'll give you a hand," said Gregory.

"Don't be silly," said Joan.

But when Joan left the room, Gregory was following her. Soon voices could be heard from the kitchen. They left behind a silence. The two remaining in the sitting room were aware that the blurry voices, removed by distance, probably concerned them. Faye looked at her uncle and smiled, as if she found this fact amusing. Her uncle gave her a blank look.

"Can I have a look?" said Faye, her tone of voice that of a young girl talking to some favourite of the adult world who spoils her.

"Pardon?"

"Can I have a look at your watch?"

"Oh yes. Of course."

Jamie extended his arm so that the watch emerged again from beneath his sleeve. Faye leaned over the table intently, the swish of movement somehow transforming her into a warm concentration of respiration.

She stared at the watch, flicking her fringe and moving her head from side to side. Then, without saying anything, she extended both her hands, almost in the manner of a child trying to catch a lizard. She put one hand on the veiny back of her uncle's hand, and the other on the flesh of his forearm below the wrist, so that the watch was framed between them. Her uncle did nothing. He gave off an aura of awkwardness, but remained entirely passive, as if the lizard Faye had caught were playing dead. She pulled his arm a little closer and stared at the watch for some time, moving her head slowly and minutely from side to side. Her lizard uncle continued, patiently, to play dead.

"That's funny," said Faye all of a sudden, and quickly removed her hands, "It's stopped."

"It can't have."

Her uncle withdrew his arm as if suddenly realising that he had been tricked and had left it there too long. He checked the dial, his face lined with irritation.

"What did you do?" he said.

"What do you mean? I didn't even touch it."

Jamie continued to scrutinize his watch in perplexity. Faye stood, stretched and yawned.

"Oh well, I suppose it's time for bed." She spoke the words against the ball of her fist, watching her uncle out of the corner of her eye.

It was Christmas Eve, and the house was full of a kind of lazy excitement. Most of that excitement, it seemed, was contained in Faye. From late morning, as if to prove that yesterday's apology was heartfelt, she began to question her uncle earnestly about correct thinking. She announced after lunch that she intended to do some cooking and banished everyone from the kitchen so that they could not spy on her while she mixed her special, secret recipe. Her parents, used to such caprice, humoured her. By mid-afternoon the lazy excitement seemed to have become so distinct that it was manifest as a warm, sweet, baking smell.

Faye opened the kitchen door to let the smell waft through to the other rooms. While she was waiting for her confections to cook, she bounced into the sitting room, where Jamie was reading a science journal, plumped herself down on the piano stool, and began to play a restless medley of Erik Satie and The Beatles. She would break off one tune halfway through to start another, only to return to it again without finishing the other, as if she could not make up her mind what to play. Finally she settled on 'Strawberry Fields Forever', and played this through three times before getting up suddenly to run to the kitchen.

She called her mother down from upstairs to help her with the finishing touches. Then she appeared, smiling and breathless, leaning against the door jamb of the sitting room.

"Uncle Jamie, I've got something for you."

He looked up questioningly from his magazine.

"Come on. In the kitchen," she said, and disappeared in a twirl of tresses.

In the kitchen, on the sideboard, was the result of Faye's whimsical labour. Lined up in rows on a metal baking grid, like a small harvest bounty, was a golden brown hoard of cakes in pleated paper cups.

There was a moment of sugary silence, such as some declare signifies 'an angel passing overhead'. In that whisper of a moment, Jamie saw the cakes spilling over their paper cups as purely abstract objects. Some strange, yeasty reaction had caused them to effervesce into existence out of nothingness. And now they were frozen in time, like impossibly congealed soap bubbles disguised with dyes.

Faye's eyes sparkled, and her lips quivered.

"Fairy cakes!" she announced in denouement. "Go on, try one."

"Go on, Jamie," said Joan from her position by the draining board, "She's made some especially for you. They should be just about edible."

Jamie stepped forward and reached out his hand to take one of the cakes.

"No, not that one," said Faye, laying her fingers on his wrist. "These ones here are for you. I made them separately, because of your nut allergy. See, they've got your name on them."

Jamie picked up a cake from the indicated batch. Sure enough, on the top, in icing, had been written, "For Uncle Jamie."

Faye watched intently as Jamie slowly peeled off the paper cup. He seemed to be examining the object, like an entomologist who has discovered a new species of beetle. Faye's eyes were wide as he ceased his examination and bit the foam of cake crumb in half. He chewed for a while and then seemed to swallow prematurely.

"Interesting flavour," he said, still searching out debris in his mouth with his tongue.

"It's my secret recipe," said Faye quietly, not taking her eyes off him. "Do you like it?"

Jamie frowned and didn't answer, but finished the cake nonetheless.

"Have another one," said Faye. "There're plenty more."

He seemed unable to hide his reluctance. Whether the first one had tasted unpleasant or he simply found the idea of cakes made by the hands of a child distasteful, was hard to tell. Whatever the reason might have been, he acted out of keeping with his usual forthright nature and consumed a second cake. He chewed slowly, as if the experience taking place in his mouth were impossible to assimilate at normal speed, as if his taste buds required a longer time to analyse the data they received, and, as if after such analysis, they were still unable to identify the experience under previous categories of good, bad, indifferent and all their various sub-categories. A thoughtfulness spread over his features, seemingly in waves generated by the working of his jaw; perhaps it was this thoughtfulness that allowed him to speak so thoughtlessly.

"Peculiar. They don't taste real."

Joan, too, was nibbling on one of the cakes. She laughed at her brother's remark.

"I'm sure he just means they're extra diaphanous, dear."

Faye's only response to this remark was a twitch at the right side of her mouth.

"Now you've eaten my special cakes I can show you to my secret, special place."

"Oh, you are honoured, Jamie. She's never shown anyone else."

Jamie looked at his sister.

"Special place?"

"Don't ask me. She doesn't deign to explain these things to the rest of us."

Faye was tugging on Jamie's sleeve. Her excitement was unmistakeable. There was something she desperately wanted to share with her uncle. Perhaps she thought that if she laid herself open, and if he really understood her, then he would change, that, in a sense, she would win by surrendering.

*

The clouds that marbled the sky were like the webbed craters of the moon. Indeed, there was something stony about them. Their presence was like the hard, cold touch of granite when one presses one's head against it in weariness, and sighs. They were calm and yet troubled, like the lofty brow of a lunatic. From their underbellies they seemed to spread a glowing soot of darkness across the land. Beneath their vast, smudged canopy, two ill-matched figures traversed the Brion family's lawn like some lop-sided pantomime beast. The tall half of this beast strode forward silently, eyes fixed ahead, but seeming to see nothing; the shorter half had an irregular gait, sometimes skipping, sometimes running, sometimes just walking fast. This short half also chattered and glanced about, often looking up to the taller half for reaction and finding little.

They came to the corner of the garden, where the stone detritus formed a ruined staircase, as if the stone itself were a sort of lumpy creeper clinging to the brick wall. Here they stopped for a moment. Two white clouds of breath made empty speech bubbles on the air.

"Is this it?" asked Jamie.

"No. We have to climb over the wall."

"Over the wall?"

"Yes. It's not far. I do it all the time."

So saying, Faye started up the leaf-slippery stone pile, pausing at the top to look back. Her uncle was following her. She turned her face once more to the cold open space of the field before her. No one in the whole world could see the expression on her face now. There was only the icy air surrounding her pale skin, and all that she could see from this high place. Once they had both dropped into the field below, her uncle would not turn back. She was sure of it. The two of them were alone, and she was leading the way. Surely nothing would stop the magic now. It was *her* mind thinking, *her* heart willing and *her* hands guiding, and destiny was this icy air, allowing it all to happen, allowing it because she had dared. The spark of her daring had ignited this magic. Yet, she supposed, there were still unknowns in the wind. If the magic were to spread its flames across this field and into the trees, she must hope that the wind blew with the flames and not against them. Sometimes, because of unknowns in the wind, fires seem to burn themselves out. She would time the spread of the fire with her strides, hoping all the while that it did not die away. As if not knowing and not caring where she would land, she jumped from the wall. Moments later there was a heavier thud that told of her uncle also striking the sod after the brief tumult of freefall.

Without saying a word, Faye started forward, the hobbles of grass awkward under her squirming ankles. There were nervous hooks in her chest that connected her with the castled branches of the distant copse of trees. The hooks belonged *there, now*, and could not tolerate this anomalous distance in time and space. And yet, Faye could not run. Instead her walking pace threatened to break into a trot, as on the imaginary palfrey of her gallivanting.

Her uncle caught up with her.

Since that drop from the wall he had begun to feel peculiar, as if the tumult of the fall were with him still, making ground and sky unsteady. He had, in fact, become more than usually aware of the unsteadiness of his own body, of his unprotected head shaking like a badly handled camera in mid-air, of the sea-sick, ship-like motion of all things.

This strange mood, which only seemed to grow on him as he tried to shake it off, was in equal parts physical and mental. At first it seemed it had come upon him suddenly, but then he grew unsure, and thought he could trace it back to before he climbed over the wall.

These reflections were interrupted by the high, chattering voice of the small human presence in front of him. Acknowledging that presence as human in his mind suddenly made it seem unutterably alien. Still, he was glad of the distraction of that trilling voice.

"We're going to those trees," it said breathlessly.

"Do you like trees?" it continued. "There aren't many left now, are there?"

He could not find his voice. Somehow he actually seemed to have misplaced the link between his brain and his tongue.

"Do you know that, by the time I was born, all the air of the whole world was already polluted? That means I'll never know what a normal winter or summer was like. Never ever. That's because of people like you inventing cars and stuff, isn't it, Uncle Jamie?"

His tongue moved sluggishly.

"I didn't invent the car." He wanted to say more, but could not.

"No, that's right, isn't it? You're not clever enough to invent anything, are you? You just say, 'This is incorrect thinking, that is incorrect thinking', don't you?"

He did not answer.

"Anyway," continued Faye, "that's why I like the trees. They make me feel like I can remember how things should be, how the world was without cars and pollution."

She looked back over her shoulder at him and laughed. He did not understand how her laughter was related to her words. The laughter was a language of its own that he did not speak. Faye's upturned face was whiter than river foam in the smoky blue gloom of the evening. Was it the twist of her smile and the angle of her face? Whatever it was, her face seemed to have become distorted, like a rubber mask. Perhaps it was the simple enigma of being human that had previously made her seem alien. Now the impression was even stronger. She looked like a little witch, or a goblin. But just as Jamie had been unable to decide whether the taste of that cake were pleasant or unpleasant, now he could not decide whether this face were repulsively grotesque, or bewitchingly beautiful.

It was because she was a child, he decided. For some reason, out here in the night, alone with Faye, he had been granted a revelation of the inherent strangeness of children. This was Faye, age eleven, almost twelve. But while something called Faye would continue to exist, this particular Faye, in its own way perfect and fully formed, would vanish utterly. It would be discarded along with outgrown clothes. But where those clothes might still have a physical existence, this Faye would be a non-existence, an absence, the very nothingness from which those clothes fell away, the invisible doll that was all that could now protrude from those sleeves, from that polo-neck, from the bottoms of those jeans, from the tops of those socks.

At this revelation, Jamie's heart gave a double-thud. Was this strangeness what was meant by love? The thought was distasteful to him. It was a curious and temporary trick of the mind. He pushed it away, but found a sick taste permeating his body in the emptiness it left behind. Then another thought occurred to him. Is this what his sister felt towards her child? But how was it possible to live with such a giddy, sticky, disturbing emotion? It was a kind of madness. Indeed, from the sick, twisted taste it left behind in his body, he felt sure that it *was* madness.

Faye had turned to face the front again. The back of her head, covered by blonde hair, gave him an impression of intense heat. Though they lacked expression, the backs of people's heads were capable of projecting a sense of intimacy similar to that associated with faces – this thought flitted across his mind as he continued to stare at Faye's bobbing head in fascination.

What was he doing out here? This was one of those nights that he had heard of somewhere when one's life suddenly seems to begin and everything is changed forever. Once again, he did not understand the meaning of his own thoughts; he even found something frightening in them. But they were only thoughts, he decided, terrifying as they were, and he let them swing wild into the vast night. He realised that he half-believed Faye would show him something that actually fulfilled the promise of the queasy feelings fluctuating through him. This something was undeniably the object of hope as well as fear. The scratches on his cheek, where her fingernails had torn his skin, began to itch and throb strangely. He looked up from the pilose fingerprint of her scalp to the mad, mad twinkling sky that tilted above.

The copse was close now. They started down the slope at the edge of the field and cut across to the dusky sanctuary of the trees.

Once within the embracing circle of the branches, where the air was somehow different, as if they were, indeed, inside, they both stopped. In the sudden blood-tide of silence, Jamie had the impression they were not alone. But when he turned his head, the movements he had sensed escaped from his field of vision. No doubt this was some deception perpetrated by the moon.

"We're almost there," said Faye, the small flare of her voice suddenly illuminating the huge darkness.

She walked over to him and slipped her hand in his. The hair prickled on the nape of his neck.

"You have to close your eyes. It's not far. I'll make sure you don't bump into anything."

The request seemed so preposterous that Jamie could not begin to argue with it. He closed his eyes, as instructed by his inscrutable guide, and the white foam of silence around the rocky cliff of his head was transformed into a furious symphony of colour. The peculiar tension in his body – tight as violin strings – since he had come out into the night with Faye, probably meant that this orchestra had been raging in him all along, just waiting for him to close his eyes and hear.

Now there was only the hot, dry hand that led him, the pulsing music of intertwining and off-branching colours, and the great unsteadiness of the unseen world he trod. Once or twice he came close to falling over, but each time, a breath sweet as blackcurrant had come close and the thud of a second hand had come with it, making sure he kept his feet. These thuds stirred up a sugary agitation within him that congealed into cramps here and there, and elsewhere turned into a thrilling current of such fibrillating high speed that it seemed constant and static. One such current seemed to flow between his hand and that which led him.

Suddenly the hand was gone, replaced by cold air.

"You can open your eyes."

Jamie's heart was now beating at such a rate he was afraid that it might fail him. His breath was snagged at various points of inhalation and exhalation. Full of foreboding, he opened his eyes. He blinked a number of times. For some reason, as soon as he saw Faye standing before him, he knew something had gone horribly wrong. Somewhere something had got twisted up, and now it could never be untwisted. A fire – a disastrous fire – had been started, and the terrible smile on Faye's face told Jamie that she was the heart of the blaze.

He looked around himself to survey the licking flames of catastrophe. These flames came in a form very similar to the orchestra of colour inside his head. Although it was night, and the sun had gone, Jamie saw that Faye and the surrounding trees seemed to breathe and burn with colour, and the colour spread with a smoke-smell through the darkness. But it was not only the colour that was wrong; there was also a kind of unearthly luxuriance here. The trees were shaggy with leaves, as at the height of summer, and leaves, branches, creepers, earth – even Faye's menthol-smooth cheek – all seemed to be melting and dripping with their own luxuriance. Shadows thrown by no visible light shifted like centipedes of time-lapse decay. And in the melting and shifting, and in the vivid breathing colours could be glimpsed shapes of unknown creatures, as if their camouflage had become momentarily ineffective while they changed positions.

The acrid smoke of colour must have got into his lungs, because he felt sudden shooting pains, which earthed themselves on his previous areas of sugary cramp. He looked back towards the figure of Faye, who already seemed cut off from him by a curtain of heat haze. Her expression was that of cold satisfaction. In that coolness he sensed something like a lost reality.

He tried to trace its exact outlines with his eyes. Only that coolness could save him now.

"Faye," he said, "what have you done? What did you put in those cakes?"

She smiled briefly and pointed to his feet. He looked down to see a ring of grotesque mushrooms surrounding him. They seemed to emanate waves of distortion.

"The fairies told me their secret recipe," she said.

The matter-of-fact tone of her voice cut deeply into him. She was utterly beyond his reach, and had told him so firmly, though her words themselves contained no such meaning. Hearing her speak those words was like falling off a cliff.

He tried to move forward, perhaps to grasp at that coolness with his hands in the hope he could drag himself out of this, but the heat haze defeated him.

"Why?"

"I had to make you know how horrible you are, and how much I truly hate you. Do you understand now?"

"Faye, this is important. Have you ever eaten these mushrooms? Do you know what they do?"

"The fairies told me – you're going to a place you can never come back from, Uncle Jamie." She paused as if her very hatred made her breathless. "If you're an example of important human beings, then I think I'd much rather live in a world of unimportant penguins. You won't be missed any more than the dodo."

Now he understood. Deception was trying to destroy him. Deception could not bear for the truth to exist anywhere, since the existence of truth was inimical to it. This was what he had fought against all his life, and now he was meeting the grave and desperate core of that struggle, in the form of a dangerous little girl. Of course, this was the deception of innocence, the deception of the heart – how fitting that word should in itself be a deception, referring to nothing more, in reality, than a muscle that pumped blood. As savagely as he had felt his severance from Faye moments before, now he felt his hatred for her, long suppressed, igniting within him.

As if sensing this, she spat. He had never seen her spit before. There was something obscene in it.

"Do you understand now?" she said.

This half-invisible fire was long since out of control. He knew this. He was only afraid of losing the truth in it somewhere. The truth… Where, before, he had lost the link between brain and tongue, now he seemed to have lost the link between brain and thought. They were isolated parts of a burning building.

"Yes," he managed to say, staring her in the eyes. With that hiss of a word the flames leapt higher within him, both scorching and icy, composed of the naked meeting of her hatred with his. The flames filled her eyes as she stared back at him; she knew the 'yes' that seemed to seal his doom was a kind of defiance, and that the anguished flames of their meeting like this would never die inside her.

The curtain of heat haze between them rose higher until it surrounded him in a vortex like a distorted fairground mirror. What he saw in this mirror was himself melted down into mercury and smeared across a two-dimensional plane devoid of gravity. He thought he could make out an insane Bacchanal of dancing figures beyond the quivering reflection, and Faye was not the least wild among them.

One of these shadowy figures suddenly grew larger in a panic of insect wings and burst through the protean surface of the mirror in a flickering splash, as if erupting from the pulverised body of Jamie's own reflection.

Hovering before him, like a daddy-long-legs made of pearl, was what Jamie knew to be the ultimate source of his poisoning. It was a fairy – a creature of such sickening beauty that it surely came from some plane of existence beyond his imagination. At the sight of this impossible thing his soul was filled with loathing. This was not the swooning beauty that relied somewhere upon an admixture of death. Such beauty, though it did not interest him, was at least human and familiar. This was a beauty that was quick and exquisite and trembled with constant movement. It was the beauty of unopposed life, and for that reason it was deadly.

"Do you know how fairies are born?" asked the creature suddenly.

"No."

Without becoming explicitly aware of it, Jamie was beginning to feel that he had already died, and that this was the inevitable interrogation that awaited his lingering consciousness.

"The sunlight creeps across the moss in the early morning, when no one is looking, and it reaches a place where a mushroom sprouts from the soil. Around the mushroom is scattered dew that will soon evaporate into mist. But before it does, the sun touches it and throws up a tiny rainbow. The rainbow arcs over the mushroom, and, in that instant, a fairy appears. There are other ways, of course, but it's the same in the end. From a precious moment, seen by no one, an eternity. Because fairies are like diamonds – they should live forever. And what should live forever, you have destroyed, seventeen times."

"How? With my words?"

Jamie paused, and smiled.

"That's right," he said, "Because I don't believe in fairies. I don't believe in fairies."

However, the fairy remained before him, lace-wings flickering, its face tightened with inhuman scorn.

"Your words have lost their power. You use them because you believe they will kill us."

"But fairies don't exist. There's no proof. No evidence."

"And you? Do you exist? Why don't you try and prove your existence?"

"Of course I exist."

"Prove it."

"Well, it's obvious… because… I think, therefore I am!"

"Those are not even your words. You try to prove your existence with the words of another. You already know that you don't exist. Is that not the final truth you have been searching for?"

Sure enough, as he heard these words, it seemed that he did know it. He knew it in his bones, or rather, in his absence of bones. The words 'I think therefore I am' were like a hook, and attached to that hook was a repugnant, wriggling worm. Something had believed itself to be an identity composed of hook and worm. But now that same something saw the hook, and knew it was not the hook; it saw the worm, and knew it was not the worm. Moreover, the worm was dying on the hook. And the something disappeared like a face composed of fruit or fish disappears as the perspective shifts.

Jamie looked down and saw that his feet, his ankles, his legs, were twisting and distorting, turning into a tarry, swampy substance, and collapsing beneath him. His head was thrown back. The fairy was disappearing out of the mirror vortex in the same flickering insect panic with which it had arrived. Vision broke up like clouds. Those heartbreaking clouds, were they heaven? Something warm and fragrant rained down upon a face that was not there.

The front door clicked closed as if sealing the air-tight silence of the house. The silence suggested waiting, and anger. Faye simply stood blinking in the warm airlock of the hallway, noticing afterimages of the wall and banisters, somehow whispering to her of the terrible and perpetual anti-climax that was reality. She swayed, uncertain how to move forward.

There was mud on her face and clothes, and leaves in her tangled hair. Suddenly the silence thumped with footsteps. Her mother appeared at the bottom of the stairs and slowed to a halt. The anger in the house had stewed up a kind of slow motion that froze everything the instant before it stung, making it hover unbearably, before letting it strike at normal speed.

"Where the hell have you been?"

Faye did not answer, but only gazed about vacantly.

"Where's Uncle Jamie?"

A smile or a twitch flickered at the corner of Faye's mouth and she looked at the floor.

"Who's Uncle Jamie?"

"None of your nonsense, now." Joan's voice almost cracked in fury. "Where is he?"

Faye opened her mouth.

"I... I don't believe in Uncle Jamie."

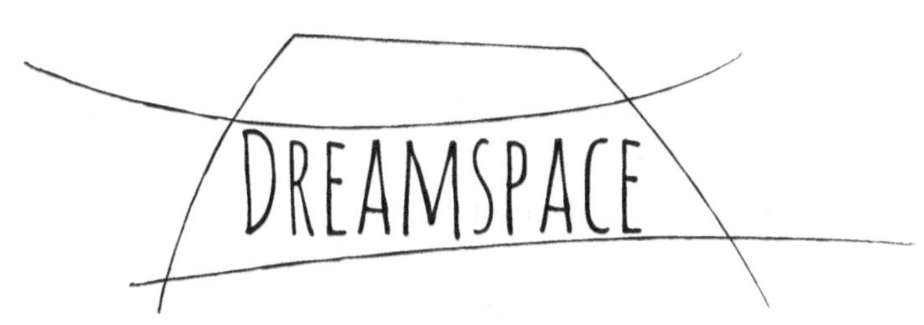

DREAMSPACE

Lester's eyes rested on the fencepost, tufted with splinters, like repetitions of the grass at its base. Clara tugged at his fingers. Brought back to the present, he looked down at her and flashed a smile. She met him with a look of limpid concentration; her tiny brow knitted, but her eyes as unclouded as the newest thing on Earth.

"Daddy, I want to go in."

"Not long now. We've just got to wait for the other people to come out."

She leant her shoulder against his thigh, as if she were lackadaisically storming a portcullis with a battering ram. Lester enjoyed the warmth of the soft battle wordlessly. A veteran of such campaigns, he scouted around with hawk-like leisure in the midst of the fray. Clouds had been passing over all afternoon, occasionally obscuring the sun. The day was bright, but windy. If they had been at sea, the conditions might have been described as choppy. From here, there was quite a view of hills and fields, beyond that in which the fair was being held, so that the fairground seemed almost lonely, isolated. The patchwork of the landscape was not merely that of the hedge-lined pastures; the shadows of clouds also made a shifting piebald.

Not far from where they were standing, strategically and also picturesquely removed, was an unusual group of people to whom the eyes of those queuing sometimes silently returned without emphasis, as cows may gaze at passing traffic. Most unusual of these – in fact, unique – was a figure with shaven pate and a strange shawl or cloak thrown over his shoulders. He looked like he might be a fairground impresario, of a strange sort, or perhaps even a kind of priest. The others in the group pointed bulky cameras at him, and a long microphone covered in yeti fur.

After a pause, a man in a khaki coat who had been bending, straightened and said, "Okay, let's try that again. Remember we've probably only got about one or two minutes air time with this, so we need something simple. We can let the camera roll. As long as there's something in there we can edit and use, it's okay."

The shaven-pated man nodded soberly. He looked both suited and unsuited to this.

"Who is that man, Daddy?"

"I told you. That's Morgan Dinos. He made Dreamspace, where we're going to go in now."

"In now?"

"In a minute."

"But who is that man?"

Lester seemed stuck for an answer, as if he had exhausted all means of explanation. "I don't know," he said. "He's Morgan Dinos."

The conversation seemed likely to limp in this meandering way until it was their turn to enter what Lester had just called "Dreamspace" – a word Clara had accepted far more easily than she did the identity of Morgan Dinos. Perhaps this was peculiar, since it was Dreamspace that Morgan Dinos was attempting to explain to the camera now, trying and failing to find words of sufficient simplicity to satisfy the director of the camera crew. Even at a purely sensual level, Dreamspace was an anomaly. It was an attraction, yes – a curiosity. If one wanted to be more specific, one could say that it was a 'bouncy castle'. But one would have to qualify this as "a kind of bouncy castle", before going on to elaborate. It was a large, multi-coloured, inflatable structure, bearing a passable resemblance to a castle, or a pavilion, but also with something about it of the squashed, rounded shape of a flying saucer. This indeterminate nature of the exterior, and something indescribable in the details of the design, was strange and disturbing enough, but the real enigma of Dreamspace was what lay inside. Nothing, apparently – nothing but sound, shape and colour – and yet hundreds, and over a number of days, thousands of people had lined up in order to know that enigma for themselves. If this had been a queue at a cinema or theatre, those coming out might have been able to spoil the surprise for those going in by telling how the whole thing ended, and so on. There was no danger of spoiling the surprise here, since those who emerged seemed unable to communicate the kernel of the enigma even if they tried. Occasionally someone in the line of those waiting would hail one of those who had had their turn, perhaps being acquainted in some way, or perhaps having grown jovial on the general atmosphere of novelty, and ask what it was like. The responses were various, but all had one thing in common.

"Interesting," says one man, scratching his head as if searching for words.

"Amazing," says a young woman, with wide eyes.

"Well," says an older man as if about to divulge some little known titbit of great profundity, "you'll see for yourself."

Some even tried to be specific. A young man who looked like a student had been stopped by the camera crew earlier and asked to describe the experience.

"It's good," he said. "Very clever. There are different colours and sounds, and everything changes depending on where you stand, and... It's good. It's like walking in an optical illusion."

Even such attempts as these somehow left it clear that there was something unique about Dreamspace that could not be understood by analogy.

Now Lester watched as the camera crew began filming again. The wind played with the collar of Morgan's cloak in a dreary sort of way. He looked, Lester reflected, a little like a superhero, or super-villain. It was hard to tell which, because clear distinctions of that kind belonged to Hollywood. Removed from an environment of gloss and Technicolor, all super-persons must look something like this. The dour weather – somehow not the weather for smiling, despite intermittent brightness – and Morgan's British accent, meant that his caped figure simply appeared out of place, seeming to fribble at reality in a camp, ambiguous, vaguely troubling way.

Lester had missed some of Morgan's explanation.

"...came by the idea by accident, really."

"You didn't spend a long time designing and developing Dreamspace then?"

"I did. But that was after the basic idea had just happened in front of me. Accident is very important to art, actually. Part of learning to be an artist is learning to let accidents happen. I was working on an art installation with Chris Bolam, to do with the effects of light, and we were planning some kind of spectacular finale to the exhibition, and someone said, 'Why don't you just blow the whole thing up?' It was a kind of joke about deconstructionism, but it ended up being a very constructive comment. I hope, though, that what Dreamspace will do is to take apart our normal ways of seeing and experiencing the world, and let something else, unknown, enter in…"

Morgan continued in a similar vein, seeming to trip over himself in his attempts to fold in as many references and ideas as he could to leaven his explanation, while at the same time trying to accommodate himself knowingly to the medium of television. It seemed he was able to discard his self-indulgence like a cape, however, when he wished, revealing something of the populist ingenuity that had, through him, shaped an idea that had drawn thousands of people, from as diverse social backgrounds as could be imagined, in this country and others, during the course of the past few months.

"Dreamspace is all about you," he said. "It's nothing to do with Morgan Dinos. That's just an accident. It's a new piece of art each time someone steps inside, because what it does is simply make a space where your dreams can come to life, in the middle of the day. And the best bit is you can take your dreams home with you for free. Better than a goldfish in a leaking bag of water. I think."

At this point, Lester noticed that the queue had started to move again and a space had opened up in front of him.

"Come on, then," he said, and led Clara through the gate in the wooden fence that surrounded the enclosure in which Dreamspace buoyantly loomed like a cross between a circus tent and a clown's balloon.

Lester wondered, as they approached the curved and swollen edifice, whether they would be stopped again before they got inside. At the entrance, two attendants were counting people through. Lester was mildly surprised to find that he and Clara were just at the tail end of those who were ushered in this time. The dark green smell of crushed grass came with milky sweetness to his nostrils, and a strange sense of freedom rose and expanded in him as the two of them crossed the threshold into a shady place of filtered light, from which straight lines had been banished along with any shades of black, white, grey or brown. Lester felt soothed by coolness and at the same time tingled with the unearthly lightness. The inflated ribs of which the space was made gave a little beneath the feet, but were surprisingly hard with the air inside them. The tingling seemed to radiate from these ribs as a soft fizz of coloured light.

"Is this Dreamspace, Daddy?" asked Clara.

"That's right. We're in Dreamspace."

He hoped it would not be a disappointment to her. There was someone else with whom he wished he could share this experience, for his own sake, and for Clara's, but that seemed now impossible, whatever the urgings of his heart, which pleaded always for things to start again at the beginning. However, if what Morgan Dinos said was true, and dreams came alive in Dreamspace, then whatever dreams came alive for Clara would also be alive for him. Perhaps it was ridiculous to expect too much from a fairground attraction, but it seemed that you had to make dreams come true at every chance you got. The fact those chances were meagre only seemed more reason to do so. At the very least, Dreamspace was not everyday life, and that alone gave it an advantage as far as dreams were concerned. Lester, knowing that there was nothing in particular inside Dreamspace, worried that it might be too intellectual or abstract for Clara. Then again, thinking back to his own childhood, he remembered how things that might have been unremarkable to an adult had seemed quite magical to him, forming a core of nostalgic consolation at the centre of his existence. Perhaps, when Clara looked back on this day in years to come, whatever she might think of it now, she would find that it had been transmuted in such a way, and so he would always be with her, alive in that part of her that was dream.

From the entrance of Dreamspace they could go either left or right along a short, chubby passageway that formed a kind of antechamber, screening their view of the real interior of the place, and thereby heightening a sense of wonder and anticipation.

"Which way?" asked Lester.

"That way," said Clara, pointing to the right. "No. That way! That way!"

And so they went left.

They emerged, after a few paces, into a cavern of multilateral symmetry, in which brightly coloured stalactites met brightly coloured stalagmites, creating a hive of hourglass columns that stretched away with the bewildering appearance of a room multiplied to infinity by mirrors. It was an eerie effect. The ellipses created by the columns, in fact, had the appearance of countless mirrors that reflected only each other, and then only in the sense that they contained each other. Human figures disappeared, confusingly, into these mirrors, or stepped limpidly from them, like satyrs appearing and disappearing in a flute-haunted grove.

As he trod forward on the springy ground, Clara's hand still in his own, perhaps to prevent her from floating away, Lester felt his scepticism dissolving. There seemed to be a natural sense of awe about the place, as if it were some kind of quivering, jelly cathedral. The solemn antiquity of a stone cathedral was replaced by a garish otherworldliness, but the effect on Lester was not dissimilar. The atmosphere of each commanded the kind of respect that made you look slowly around and up without even thinking about it. Another difference between a traditional cathedral and this, apart from the colour and texture, however, was the obvious fact that this was intended as a kind of playground. Since there was nothing to see in the sense that you might see things at a gallery, or in a zoo, it seemed best for Lester to let Clara run around as some of the other children were doing. And since this was not really a bouncy castle, running was more appropriate than jumping on the spot. The shrieks and squeals of the children somehow failed to dispel the solemnity of the multi-coloured twilight here, but echoed strangely, Dreamspace acoustics seeming to have their own particular strangeness, different from, but bringing to mind the acoustics of a public swimming baths. And with this echoing, and with the tented shade of filtered light, there was also a distinctive tent-like smell, almost rubbery.

Another thing that might have prevented the unearthly atmosphere being shattered was the music. 'Ambient' was the word for it, Lester supposed; there was no tune, but mainly wafting veils of sound, at once drifting and watchful, as if some alien emotion, full of anticipation, had been made audible on the air. The sounds must have been electronically generated, but Lester found himself now unable to take electronic sounds for granted. Where had they come from actually? What were they made of? Certain reverberating whorls might almost have been whale-song, but the music here shaped sounds that, although they sometimes suggested life forms, seemed to come from a world where the only life forms were mineral, or of a variety of other, unknown orders of being outside the animal and vegetable. For a moment, Lester was almost angry reflecting on this. It seemed as if this were not the kind of music that children should hear. But seeing how the children were enjoying themselves, he supposed this was, after all, a priggish adult attitude, wishing to protect children from the strangeness that was perhaps even their natural element.

This thought occurred to him and suddenly the interior of the tent took on the aspect of a forest. It was a gloomy, leafless, colourful forest, which made up for its lack of branching trees with the subtle luxuriance of its sounds. Though these sounds were not birdsong and animal cry, yet they were something like them – the equivalent of those sounds in the forests of the world from which children come.

Lester laughed quietly to himself and shook his head at the strangeness of the thoughts that had crept up on him.

Clara frolicked with a lamb-like bobbing motion between two of the coloured stalagmites.

"Don't go too far," said Lester. "I don't want you getting lost."

The idea of getting lost inside an inflatable fairground attraction seemed unlikely, but he wanted to keep her within sight, anyway. He followed after her.

As soon as he stepped between the stalagmites he found himself in a kind of elliptical avenue, which renewed in him the cathedral-like sense of awe. It was ridiculous for an inflatable castle to be awe-inspiring, but it was, somehow. Morgan Dinos must have known what he was doing. There must be particular combinations of line, colour and sound that awoke a very ancient, serious feeling in humans, he supposed. Maybe if he were an architect he would know how it was done.

Clara was some distance ahead of him along the avenue. One or two people crossed their path, as if they were lost in a separate maze that somehow intersected this.

"Don't go too far away," he said again. "Make sure you can always see me. You might get lost otherwise."

"Okay."

He looked back the way they had come. He could still see where they had stepped through into this avenue, but there was something about the way the place looked that disturbed him. He felt as if the stalagmites and stalactites that made this hive of pillars could somehow shift and obscure the way back, like sand burying tracks in a desert. This really was a weird place! He was not sure it was much fun, exactly, but it was weird. Rather than architecture, it now seemed to Lester that Morgan Dinos must have made use of the secrets of hypnotism in some way. He looked like a hypnotist. Perhaps there was some element of practical joke in all this, just as there usually was in the acts of stage hypnotists. Otherwise, it was just weird; pointless and weird, without any focus.

"Daddy, I want to see what's there!"

Clara was pointing to what seemed to be the end of the avenue, where swirling lights were visible, moving in time to the music in a way that invited with mystery, as if something was taking place.

"Come on, then," said Lester.

When they got there they found that there was a kind of chamber, like a cave, where the music was different – a kind of churning, wheezing rhythmic skirl – and lights had somehow been made to dance across the surfaces without casting the shadows of the people inside. There were bubbles, too, coming up from what looked like the pipes of a pipe organ, and filling the air with an iridescent blizzard. A few children were dancing and hopping about, not really in time with the music, while a larger number of adults looked on. Lester felt suddenly dizzy. He stopped to steady himself and let Clara run to join the other children.

After a while she ran back to him, colliding with his legs and grabbing hold of them. He gave a jolt at the impact and looked up just in time to see a woman on the other side of the chamber looking at him. She smiled, and he smiled back. It was because of Clara that the woman felt easy smiling at him, he knew. And the smile he returned was of a bland, public kind he had never known before having a child. The woman's own child, also a girl, ran back to her, and she whisked her up before smiling at Lester again. A ridiculous fantasy now played out in Lester's head. It was silly, of course, but it was private and ephemeral, and he did not feel especially ashamed of it. Their two daughters would play together, and they would start talking to each other, and they would find things in common, including singledom, and exchange contact details. Was it really so ridiculous? Wasn't that how it worked for people like Lester, and perhaps for people like this woman, too? The idea was attractive, but seemed too airy and frivolous to pursue when he and the woman were both weighted with responsibilities and life specifics.

Clara ran off again to chase more bubbles, stopping now and then to clap her hands on one of the fragile spheres. Lester looked about at the faces, laughing, smiling, or in unreadable repose. The garish colours made the strangers here seem almost alien. Lester's dizziness still had not left him, and now he noticed a clutching, constriction sensation. Something was very wrong, but he did not know what. He felt a nasty sense of oppression. The faces appeared to be leering now. Or... Were the others here aware that something was wrong? Lester had never felt quite like this. It was as if he were having a nightmare while still awake. He found that he was gasping for breath. Then a kind of understanding came to his rescue. He was having a panic attack. Madeleine used to get these all the time. So this is what they felt like! At least he was familiar with how to cope with this situation. He had to get out of this place. Snatching up a surprised Clara in his arms, he strode from the chamber into an avenue beyond like that by which they had come.

"Daddy. Daddy. I want to go back in."

"Wait," said Lester. "Daddy doesn't feel well. Let's have a rest."

He crouched down and held Clara against his thigh. He remembered that Madeleine would sometimes breathe into a bag when she had her attacks. Something to do with oxygen. He was carrying a polythene bag of things they had bought today but he did not want to empty it, or sort through it for a smaller bag, so he hung his head and tried to breathe slowly and deeply. Surely there were attendants in this place? If someone came he would ask.

"Are you okay, Daddy?"

"I told you, I'm not feeling… well… darling. Why… don't you… tell me… a story?"

"What story?"

"Any story. Your favourite."

"Well, there was a little duck girl, and she lived in the woods. And the house was very tiny, and square. Like a tent. And every day she would fry her eggs for breakfast. And then she'd go for a walk. And in the tree was Rarius, and she stopped under the tree and said, 'Please don't eat me, Rarius', but Rarius said, 'I am going to gobble you all up, because you are a bad duck girl!' And the duck girl said, 'but I've never done anything wrong. Please don't eat me up.' But Rarius said, 'Yes, I'm going to eat you all up, yummy in my tummy.' And the duck girl said, 'But I don't want you to eat me up. What can I do?' And Rarius said, 'well, I'm going to eat you anyway, with my great big mouth, and my teeth which are thiiiis big.' And the duck girl started to cry…"

The story continued in this way without seeming to make much progress. Lester felt unable to concentrate on it, though he tried. And yet, the story kept intruding on him with a growing insistency. He realised that, for some reason, it was only making things worse.

"Okay," he said. "That's enough."

Clara stopped. The silence felt strange.

"That's… a good story," he said. "Tell me the rest later."

"Why can't I tell you now?"

"I can't… concentrate… Sorry."

There was a silence while he continued to struggle with his breathing. He realised that his extremities were tingling and turning numb. He had to do something.

"That nice lady in there," he said.

"What nice lady, Daddy?"

"The one…. with the… blue and grey… jumper… Tell her to come… Go on…"

Clara slipped away, seemingly only too happy to perform this task.

Lester, alone, felt entirely abandoned to the strangeness of his panic, and his bodily sensations. It was extraordinary, as if he could feel the whole world in his body, and yet he was also entirely numb. He closed his eyes, but still saw the colours and shapes of Dreamspace, more distorted and abstract than ever. It seemed to him that the entire universe was some kind of weird trampoline and that, through him at this moment, it was experiencing one of its dizziest bounces.

"Hello."

How wonderful. It was the voice of a stranger, an adult.

"Mummy, what's wrong with the man?"

"Sssh, darling. Excuse me, are you all right?"

Lester had managed to nod. Even without looking, he knew that the woman was crouching over him, and in her voice he heard the fringe of her hair hanging over the concerned features of her face. He knew the exact tightness and elasticity of her jeans where her buttocks touched her ankle, forming the mouth of a long, narrow, perfect inlet to the bend behind her knees.

"It's a panic attack," he gasped out, and suddenly even wondered if he were not exaggerating. His breathing seemed easier now.

"Is there anything I can do?"

"I don't know. I think… It will pass. Do you mind…?"

"Mind? Waiting? Anything else?"

"Just waiting. Just waiting is fine."

"Okay. It's Okay. I'm here."

She was a good person.

Lester found his body now becoming the stage for a strange battle. Part of him must have known that an opportunity like this was unlikely to present itself twice in a single lifetime. A kind of urge for dramatic expression was rippling through his body. He thought of Madeleine and the disdain she had shown for him in the later stages of their relationship. Now even the most pathetic aspects of his psyche and experience could bubble to the surface and be accepted as a kind of medical phenomenon that was, nonetheless, emotional. Some opposing urge that might have been called 'discretion', or 'modesty', fought against this expression, but such conflict only served to make Lester's shuddering, his twitches, and so on, more convincing and more likely too induce sympathy in the onlooker. He heaved a sudden intake of breath that had about it the rattling wetness of a sob. Now, he realised, almost with disbelief, a hand was stroking his hair. It was hard to let go sufficiently truly to appreciate the situation. Soon another hand joined in with a stroking, patting motion, this one tiny.

"Gently. Gently," came the voice of the woman.

And then there was a third hand, also tiny.

"Aaah," came a little girl's voice.

"Are you making him better?"

"Yes."

"Thank you," Lester managed to say in what sounded to him a congested, snivelling voice.

"Are you feeling better?" asked the woman.

"Yes. Thank you. I think I'll be better soon."

Perhaps to her credit, although maybe it was a simple matter of tact, the woman did not immediately withdraw her soothing hand. The other two hands, however, disappeared from his sensations except as a tapping, fluttering memory.

Lester truly did feel incapacitated by what had happened, and was not confident that he could try to stand up without falling over. His fists had become quite knotted, so that for a while they had frozen fast with a spastic look about them. Now that tight numbness was just beginning to thaw.

The woman continued to talk to him with a calm that was almost professional and which contained that inimitable compassion that was the reason so many people, male or female, would always prefer a woman as a counsellor or confidante when it came to the most personal secrets. The two girls chattered a little, too, and at intervals one tiny hand or another joined the adult hand. The woman also spoke to Clara, asking her name, introducing herself as Judy, and introducing her daughter as Briony. When Judy turned her attention once more to Lester, he heard Clara repeating something to do with the story she had just been telling.

Finally, he lifted up his head, rubbed his eyes, and let out a deep breath.

"I think I'm okay now," he said. "Thank you for helping me. I don't know what I would have done otherwise."

"That's all right. Do you know what brought it on?"

She had asked this before and he had shaken his head.

"I'm not sure," he said thoughtfully. "I think it might have been something to do with that room. Only, there was something else, too. A kind of…"

"Yes?"

"Oh, I don't know. Nothing, I suppose. Where's Clara?"

Perhaps his voice betrayed more panic than was necessary or appropriate, but Judy seemed to understand the tenor of his concern and fall in with it. She stood immediately, and called.

"Clara? Clara?"

Lester struggled to his feet and looked about in dismay. He added his voice to Judy's.

Seemingly from some distance away, but not answering, there could be heard the fey chatter of Clara's voice. Lester and Judy exchanged a glance and started in that direction, Judy carrying Briony on her hip.

The maze-like quality of Dreamspace seemed to threaten frustration, and this must have formed part of the anxiety that Judy and Lester now seemed to share, but perhaps there was also something else, something in the tone of Clara's faint, incoherent gabble. Actually, they found her quite soon. Relieved, Lester wondered whether he had been exaggerating the malevolence of this place to himself.

Clara was in what might have been called a glade, or possibly a grove – one of the weird, colourful groves of Dreamspace whose foliage was alien sound. Here, she was running from the bole of one branchless tree to another, staring at each in such rapt fascination she seemed not to be aware they had arrived, and apparently answering the ambient chatter festooned in mistletoe bunches from the non-existent boughs with chatter of her own, in which it was hard to distinguish particular words.

"Clara."

Her father's voice was not enough to break her excited trance. Lester had to call her name three times before her communication with the unseen things of this place could be interrupted. After the third time however, when his voice became louder and sharper, she stopped suddenly and looked back at him with an expression almost of irritation, which he in turn found peculiarly hurtful. This expression was soon replaced on Clara's face, however, by something like simple confusion.

"Don't run off like that, darling."

"But it called me, Daddy."

"What do you mean? What called you?"

"Rarius."

"Rarius?"

The name had an unpleasant association.

"Rarius I was telling you about."

He remembered.

"In the story. I see."

Then he realised that he did not see at all.

Judy had put Briony down and she, too, was becoming absorbed in the peculiar sounds of this glade.

"I wonder what this is all about," said Judy.

From her tone, Lester had guessed she was talking to him and not Briony.

"Yes, it's very odd," he said distractedly, still thinking about what Clara had said and watching her turn once more to the edge of the small space to answer some goosey honking and clicking noise. "It makes me think of those games. I forget what they were called. The lights flashed and they played a tune, and you had to copy them, or answer, or something."

"I know the ones you mean. We never had one, but I remember."

The truth was, Lester wanted to leave at the first opportunity. He felt there was something badly… misjudged about this place. But he was like a teacher to whom the pupils had stopped listening, and he did not want to do anything strange or sudden in front of Judy, or, if he came to that, leave her without acquiring her contact details.

Clara was now talking back to the garish emptiness – if 'talking' was the right word – in a kind of clicking and honking gibberish that was rapidly destroying Lester's patience.

"It's funny how kids seem to understand these things quicker than adults," said Judy.

There was something uncertain in her words, as if she had not yet allowed herself the kind of advanced doubts, nameless as they were, that Lester now entertained, but she was preparing, at least, to leave the public highway of unquestioning affirmation.

"Who are you talking to?" Judy asked Clara.

Clara turned around and looked at both Judy and Lester.

"It's Rarius," she said.

Of course, Lester loved Clara for her creativity and imagination. He was, after all, a modern father. But there were times when he noticed a kind of stubborn consistency in her make-believe that disturbed him. Children were not endlessly cute, and it distressed him to encounter things in his daughter that, in their strangeness, were not endearing to him, but hinted of a largeness and wildness beyond his comprehension, a realm into which he was not invited, could not follow, and perhaps did not even wish to follow. At times like these his authority wilted and he was lost.

"Who's Rarius?" Judy was asking Lester now.

"I don't know."

"It's Rarius and Acky," said Clara.

"Acky," muttered Lester to himself. "Is Acky the duck girl?" he asked, remembering Clara's story.

"No," said Clara, and looked up at him with those intense, cloudless eyes. "I'm the duck girl," she said. "I'm the duck girl, Daddy."

Lester stared at her as if dumbstruck.

He looked up. There were some peculiar droning, whistling noises somewhere in the background. They seemed to be coming from somewhere outside Dreamscape. And they were rising.

"Judy," he said. "I'm sorry, I think we should leave."

"You're leaving?"

He nodded and met her interrogative gaze with a wordless frankness. He did not know how to translate it into words, and he hoped that she would understand without them. Judy nodded in her turn and looked to Briony, as if to gauge whether she were ready to leave also.

The distant, whistling drone continued to rise. Clara was looking around in something resembling awe.

"It's going to be a visit," said Clara.

"What?" Lester could not keep the anger and alarm from his voice.

"Rarius said. It's going to be a special visit soon. Rarius said. It's a big surprise. Like a birthday. He said it's coming soon, in a minute. And there'll be him and Acky and their big beaks all full of teeth, and lots of bouncing flowers, and I mustn't be scared…"

Lester realised that the ominous tingling of his panic attack was creeping back into the edges of his sensations.

"It's starting again," he gasped.

"It's Rarius," said Clara. "Daddy, I'm going to be the duck girl again. It's Rarius."

Once again it seemed to Lester that his panic had somehow broken down the barriers between his body and the rest of the universe, so that his sensations seemed to extend to the entire world of which he was aware. This time, however, there was a terrible and incredible difference. Something must have anchored the world last time, but this time there was no anchor. His panic was not his own, after all, but that of everything. Judy, too, was looking around with real fright as if their environment had become suddenly and mysteriously hostile.

Everything was filled with an unspeakable nausea that seemed to make the very teeth in his skull revolting to him.

"It's moving," Judy murmured under her breath, and she turned and snatched at Briony just as the world shuddered and pitched. This sly combination of shapes, colours and sounds had finally done its work and, just as certain tones may shatter glass, so this combination had melted all that was solid in reality. There was a sudden whoosh and all the shapes and colours became distorted. Dreamscape was full of screams. Lester himself fell to the floor, or would have thought so, except that there no longer was any such thing as floor. They were in space, spiralling into a mangled kaleidoscope that seemed about to suffocate them. They were catapulted upwards, and yet they were falling, and there was nothing to hold on to. Lester called for Clara. He heard her voice, but could not see her. Everything was melting.

*

The screams inside the great dirigible ghost-train that was Dreamspace were echoed by screams from those outside in the field. How it had happened perhaps not even an expert could explain, but something stealthy in the day's troubling winds had crept under Dreamspace and suddenly, almost as if deliberately, had ripped it, with all of nature's hidden strength, from its moorings, so that at first one wing of the inflatable structure, and then almost the entire thing, had flipped into the air like a balloon-framed house in a tornado.

From amongst the drab huddle of dark-clothed onlookers, too astonished and appalled to do anything more than stare open-mouthed, Morgan Dinos had rushed forward, his caped figure looking now horribly appropriate, and had grasped one of the guy-ropes in an attempt to restrain the incredible flight of this multi-coloured castle. A handful of others rushed to follow his example, but the lightness with which the mere air had lifted Dreamspace was deceptive, and they may as well have tried to restrain an ocean-liner in its launch. The ropes were torn viciously from their hands, and they were lucky not to have been lifted skyward themselves.

No one had seen such a thing before and no one knew what would happen. Would Dreamspace float away like a hot-air balloon? The fears of those watching were as giddy and uncertain as the air, and it seemed that there was something bottomlessly airy in the fate of Dreamspace; without a bottom to their fears, no one knew if they were soon to suffer the solid impact of death. They were helpless and unable to prepare themselves.

The impossible thing, however, came to an end, and when the laws of the possible reasserted themselves, just after Dreamspace had rolled like tumbleweed for the distance of half a field, it was, for some, fatal.

Lester stood palely and watched as Clara was lifted onto a stretcher. A whole fleet of ambulances had been needed, and no one really seemed to understand why. It was meaningless. A gust of air from nowhere had brought carnage and a taste of strangeness that could never be explained or eradicated. For Lester, this fatality had not reinstated the much-needed line between possible and impossible as it had for some. Clara showed no outward physical marks that she was anything other than asleep and dreaming, those eyelids soft as violets closed now over the clear, cloudless eyes – no sign, that is, apart from nothingness itself, in the absence of breath and heartbeat. And though Lester was going with her, into the terrible back of the ambulance – which, like a church, was the closest that humans could come to an authority that comprehended, formalised and thus protected from death – still she was going away from him, and would be going away from him for ever. To his gasping horror, he found he could not cry. It was as if he had been rendered physiologically incapable, as if his tears had been cut out like the tongue of a mute. This was like no death of which he had ever heard. Clara had been snatched away by a dream, by an airy fist in a jester's motley glove. Somehow – perhaps here he would comprehend impossibility once more – he would have to tell her mother.

He turned to Judy and Briony, weirdly reassuring in their unhurt condition, and made a jerky, broken-off goodbye, before turning back to follow the stretcher that was being lifted and taken away.

Garish colours, swelling and distorting, collapsing and suffocating, had kept Lester awake for the better part of a week. Talking to Madeleine had been the hell he had known it must be. His red eyes gritty, he sat in his armchair, in a flat without the heating on. Tomorrow, too, he would take off work. He might as well, he realised; it was a Friday.

Often now he thought about those two panic attacks. He had not suffered another since that day, but he had been left with a curious physical sensation like some process unfinished inside him. It felt as if a bubble that was both emptiness and pain had arisen from deep within, only to become lodged somewhere in his chest or throat. He kept opening his mouth in a goldfish-like motion between gasp and yawn, as if to disgorge this bubble. But it did not move or burst. It was stuck. This sensation had another aspect. As well as feeling he could not release something that was inside him, he felt unable to take in something that was outside. He had never known such a feeling before, and he could not account for it. When he checked he seemed to be breathing normally, and there was no sign of further hyperventilation, and yet, however deep the breath he took, it felt as if he had not breathed in sufficiently, or even not at all, so that he had become conscious in his breathing, and tried to swallow air as he would food or water. He did not know if he would ever recover.

There was something in him now, something rat-like and unclean, and he wondered if, in fact, it had really always been there. And yet, there was no doubt that he had to live his life, that if his rat-like uncleanness was to be mitigated at all, it was *only* by living his life.

Next to the telephone, on top of the wicker table, was a scrap of paper torn from a notebook, and on it was written the name 'Judy Wicklow' and a telephone number.

The question was – one of a few very significant, one might easily say 'burning', questions to occupy him this week – did Judy really need this? Did anyone need this?

Judy had given him her number after the thing had happened for which he still could find no words. He had thought so when she stroked his head, and he had been right – she was a good person.

Sighing, he stood and walked over to the telephone, as if there were nothing else in the world that could be done except either sit in the armchair or walk over to the telephone. He reached out his hand and lifted the receiver. He lowered his eyes as if asking forgiveness. He began to dial the number.

After my father had his stroke, he became even more attractive to women.

Downstairs, cross-legged in front of the stove, I worked on my translation of Nagai Kafu's *Dwarf Bamboo*. I had returned to the author's Preface, which, being written in classical Japanese, was especially difficult to render in English. From upstairs there came the sound of voices and laughter. I sighed and paused in my work, then read over what I had just written. Kafu was explaining the work's strange title with reference to a conversation between himself and the gardener:

> Bamboo is held an elegant plant, but amongst its varieties, *okamezasa* (dwarf bamboo) is one by humans much trodden, and much pissed upon, growing in profusion always at the edges of fields and the sides of footpaths, like weeds. Ah, the perplexity of the poor gardener, instructed by this bloody-minded old man – fancying himself refined in having such tastes – to plant that weed in his garden! Behold in this the very heart of my pitiful work. And examining the life-story of this novel's hero, too, such a title could surely not be thought of as strained.

I wondered if I would ever finish this useless task of translation. I pictured death overtaking me in some absurd and meaningless way while the manuscript was still incomplete. There it would lie, on my desk, or in a drawer, pages covered with my childish but crotchety handwriting, never to be read by another soul.

The window, beyond which lay blackness, was an unseeing eye, its condensation a glaucoma of indifference protecting it from the world, leaving it only with unguessable thoughts. I got to my feet, unlocked the back door, next to the window, and went out into the night. The atmosphere was damp with something between rain and mist. It was as if the whole cycle of precipitation were visible, with the clouds becoming rain, which refined itself to mist, which coalesced again into clouds. In this night of never-ending mist and rain, the cottage and my life were a single, worm-eaten mushroom, forgotten in some rotten nook.

I looked out at the other cottages, lightless and silent, and at the trees and hedges lining fields that rose into hills. Above them all, screened by the clouds, shone the silver disc of the moon.

The clouds, spreading over the entire night sky, were bunched together in what the Chinese call 'fish scales'. It seemed to me, had they been absent, I would have clearly seen the harvest moon as a tarnished orb with a single glowing ring around it. However, the clouds caught the glow of the moon and transformed it. What I saw above me in the vast and lonely night was a great, silver gong of concentric circles, broken into scales. The mist between the clouds was the endless reverberation of that gong. Strangely enraptured, I listened and seemed to hear. It was a tintinnabulation slowed down to the roar and wash of ocean. That tintinnabulation seemed to form a word, a word that I understood, and did not understand, a word I had never heard before.

Tzimtzum. Tzimtzum.

I stood there, by the back door, and listened for some while to that silver sound, aware that the ear that heard was the tattered ear of a worm-eaten mushroom.

In the morning I was preparing my breakfast when my father went out the back door carrying a bucket. In a minute he had returned. He closed the door behind him and looked over to where I stood by the breadboard. He stopped then, and began to speak, not so much – it seemed to me – because he thought I required explanation as because there was something he wanted to tell someone, and I was there. As he spoke, I noticed that he had not yet put his teeth in, so that his upper lip was collapsed, changing the whole impression of his face, and reminding me, as it always did, of my own descent towards death.

"I worked on a dream I had recently," he said. "It was a powerful dream. Since then I've been taking my urine out and putting it on the garden. It's what our family have done from generation to generation – this is what the dream told me. But these days it's been forgotten. The way we live now, it's like something's been taken away from us. I feel…"

Here he paused to wipe a tear from his eye and regain his voice, which was choking with emotion.

"…I feel that we've lost our connection with the land. They took it away from us, the same way they stole the church from the people. They stole it from us. We don't have our church any more.

"So… I want to give back to the soil that has grown me. I've taken life into my body, and now I pass it out with something added. It's rich in nutrients – good for the soil."

I nodded thoughtfully and my father continued up the stairs with his empty bucket.

I took my bowl of breakfast to my room and ate it sitting on my bed. Space is a luxury of which there has been little in my life. Confronted by my room's usual disarray, I wondered just where I could start in order to make sure the day would represent progress towards something. However, I had long since lost sight of anything to progress towards. For me there was only a miscellany of odd projects (such as the translation of *Dwarf Bamboo*) that meant nothing to anyone. These projects had become a physical maze of books, written notes and so on, taking up the floor of my room. This literal maze was also a conceptual model of an abstract maze.

Somehow I had strayed into the woods. I knew they were only little woods, and comically grotesque, without the majesty of the vast, dark forests to be found elsewhere in the world, but for some time the feeling had been growing on me that, indeed, I would never leave these woods as long as I lived. I would never come to their border. I would never see full daylight. I would never know the expansiveness of a traveller who apprehends his destination in the distance and feels he is getting somewhere. So then, how to occupy myself for yet another day in these same, dwarfed woods? Since I could not think of anything that would make a difference to my long-term situation in the slightest, I decided to go out into the garden, split a few logs with an axe, and confront the dilemma again when I had finished.

*

Outside, as I remembered, was the space in which my life was secretly rich – the space that was not mine, except in as much as it was also time. I had had time in my life to take walks – the same walks day after day – and to feed the pony by the end of the old, dried-up canal track. To put it another way, poverty had been my luxury, and it had been as meaningless and useless as any other luxury.

As I had intended, I split some logs, but soon found my purpose deserting me. It occurred to me that I really spent very little time enjoying the garden, and that it was there most of all as a place simply to linger wordlessly. If I was lucky, my luck consisted in the fact I was able to do this.

I put down the axe and the mallet and I trod the stone steps that descended to the bottom of the garden. It was really a very small garden, so that 'explore' seems the wrong word to use, and yet, in as much as I had never really looked at what had always been there for me to look at, I truly was an explorer.

I was naturally drawn to the slender and leafless tree in the corner of the garden, where the angle of the wall was also the angle of one quiet road meeting another. I did not even wonder what kind of tree it was, though now I come to write about it, and cannot name that tree, I do wonder. At the time the question in my mind was whether the tree were dead or alive.

Because it was leafless, I supposed it might be dead. Its branches were gently aflutter with decorations, turning it into one large wind-chime. Shells hung from its twigs on strings, and lucky silver charms of the kind people once put in Christmas puddings and still use, perhaps, for charm bracelets, and here dangled a small thurible and there a St. Christopher, so that the ornaments were numerous enough – and therefore close enough to each other – that they set up a clinking, skeletal murmur with each breeze.

I was reminded of the Christmas tree my father had once found for us to use in that other, better world of my childhood. In fact, it had not been a tree at all, but a bare and twiggy branch that he must have scavenged from the beach or a walk in the hills. As such, its advantages over a normal

Christmas tree were at least twofold: It obviated the necessity of killing a tree for the sake of ritual, and it had cost no money. There was also the advantage that it seemed a creative and original choice for a Christmas tree. That had been decorated with fairy-lights, glass baubles and so on. I wondered, then, if the tree now before me, in the garden, were not the same thing – a mere decorated branch made to look like a tree. If it were, that would explain its lack of living green. And yet, despite the grey bareness of the twigs here, something in the calm smoothness of the bark suggested life and the supple growth that curves from the mystery of sap.

Looking down to the soil in order to inspect the roots – to see, that is, whether the tree had any – I noticed the earth seemed to be damper here than elsewhere, and there was a slight trace of bubbles, as if from dish-water. I guessed that it was this tree in particular that had benefited from the golden liquid nutrients recently bestowed upon the garden. This was evidence – perhaps even proof – that there were roots here to absorb those nutrients. This leafless tree, I decided, was, after all, alive.

I don't know why this thought made me so meditative, but under its influence I sat down upon a nearby rock that had been placed between flowers, my back to the empty road, closed my eyes, rested my chin in my palm, and felt the breezes of the day on my tired face. They seemed to invite me to slip forever into a cool sleep of sadness. Their caresses made me nod towards the heaviness of dropping off. All the while I heard the tintinnabulation of the tree's hanging ornaments, as if the wind were playing a harp made of silver and bone. Clacking glissandos and zigzag cat's paws of miniature glockenspiel made me think of the last foaming tassels of little waves among pebbles and shells on a beach, as if the sea were a robe fringed with tiny silver bells.

Tzimtzum. Tzimtzum.

So caressed and teased in an empty dream of wind and sound, I sat, or floated, or I simply was, or, then again, a shifting shadow of thought, was *not*. When at length I unclosed my eyes, the immediate appearance there of a sunlit world (and my body resting within it) so vast and yet as light in its suddenness as the perching of a butterfly upon a flower, was a dazzling surprise to me, and I blinked at it to tame its reality to my eyes.

It was only after I had managed to stop blinking that I understood this new reality as well as seeing it. I was not where I had been. I sat in the relative cool between walls the colour of dust and honey. The limited purview revealed by the gap where they ended in parallel was of a town square – a kind of plaza – stone-paved, which it seemed the sun had kept clean and pleasant from some time without a date, a munificent and unpaid caretaker. The air that was the main occupying element of this area had about it, to one who had lived with such things, some indefinable sad freshening of ocean. I knew that we were close to the coast. There were voices in the square, not large against that fresh but idle air – smallish and isolated within it, comfortable in a wakeful emptiness, and clear as wall-carvings. The language spoken was not English and the gentle sharpness of everything was such that I quickly realised the strange specifics of this world; I was in Italy.

It has always seemed to me a kind of cosmic paradox that in a universe so vast a beam of light would take countless human lifetimes to traverse it, concepts such as 'Italy' not only survive, but are to some deeply familiar, like some eternal, secret knowledge that is no secret at all, a dream that for a few becomes everything and is taken for granted. There I was, then, in the dream called Italy, remembering its familiar secret. At that moment, the secret seemed redolent of the tinkle of bells. I heard them, jingling in rhythm with the footsteps of someone in the square, and I could not help being drawn out from between those two walls by a rare curiosity, of the kind that people perhaps only know when they awake in the midst of a dream to find it rich with meaning and mystery.

I looked about me and saw the eternal ordinary of time and place, a moment of daily life that assumed – but did not reveal – a whole history of preceding moments. It was the usual freshness of here and now, in which the inhabitants, of course, notice nothing strange, but to me it was full of wonder. The square was surrounded by cafés and hotels, between which there ascended or descended steps and narrow, sloping streets. I did not see the source of the jingling, and forgot it quickly when my eyes fell upon two figures seated at a table outside a café to my left. I saw in them, or rather, I recognised with my entire body, another cosmic mystery, akin to the mystery of Italy. This was the mystery of 'likeness', or heredity. I knew the two people there, though they were younger than I had ever known them to be. They were my paternal grandmother and grandfather. I steadied myself with one hand against the wall as I made some surprisingly lucid, but to me titanic calculations. These calculations seemed assisted by something in my environment, by the very stones surrounding me. I was setting foot here for the first time – *how* was a mystery – but I knew where I was. Nan and Grampa used to come here each year, if they could, on a cruise ship. It was the ancestral home that Grampa's father had left behind. Perhaps the cruise ship was even now in the bay.

I would have said that I did not know what to do. In fact, it did not occur to me that I had to do anything. I was seized by a vital fascination. I watched and listened as if at any moment I would be given information touching upon all the questions at the very foundation of my existence.

Tantalizingly, the information did not come. I remained captivated. My grandmother, Elsie, had, I thought, a beautiful and very tragic face. Everything about it was heart-shaped, like the faces of forgotten film actresses. And yet it was a profoundly ordinary face – the face of someone who would never truly be known, who was hardly known to herself. By contrast, my grandfather, Frank, was alert and outwardly open, while retaining a sense of nervous circumspection, almost as if he were trying to appease the tragedy in my grandmother whilst keeping secrets from it.

"Your leg still hurting?" asked Frank.

Elsie's fur-trimmed coat had slipped off the back of her chair, and she was bending to one side to retrieve it.

Frank watched her with such attentive eye-movements it was as if he knew he was being watched in turn and was making asides about his wife with the quickest of flickers.

"I told you it was just a minute ago," she said, before returning to an upright position.

"Should have left the coat in the room, really."

I wondered if I should approach them. They were my grandparents and yet they were not my grandparents. There was a tenderness in what I witnessed that made my tendons quiver. The routine of it all was as namelessly known to me as a woman's thigh in shadow beneath a table, and the cool, homely soil-scent of that shadow. Then it came to me that I felt this aching tenderness because I had not yet been born. Perhaps it was impossible for them to see me, not knowing me as I knew them. Perhaps it was not impossible, but would merely be cataclysmic.

I hesitated, my very soul in that hesitation.

As if it had started up to fill the gap made by my hanging back, there came again that jingling sound. Turning instinctively, I found its source. A woman in a long black dress was crossing the piazza. She wore also the black hood and veil of a widow, though there was something outlandish in her attire that made me wonder what her provenance might be. She strode with such striking sense of purpose it was as if I saw a ship with the wind full in its black sails cutting keenly through the crawling glassy waves of the sea. I noticed her brown hands, shocking where they emerged from her sleeves. It seemed to me they were the colour of new-baked bread, yeasty with the pride and passion of all that rises directly from its own nature, without instruction and heedless of censure.

I could not see the bells that must have made the jingling, but I guessed they were perhaps the kind that dangle from a chain around the ankle, as their silver shiver came in time with the woman's steps.

After only a second or two, it was clear that her undeviating course would take her to Frank and Elsie's table. It seemed to me then that I must have hesitated because I was waiting for this stark arrival. The woman stopped perhaps six feet from where they sat, and stood silent, as if confident that her presence was enough to command attention. Her confidence was wholly justified.

"Hello. Who's this?" said Elsie in a quiet and doubtful voice.

Frank turned around quickly, as if his constant alertness had found a small outlet in motion and made him react too keenly.

"What does she want?" asked Elsie.

As I watched, I could not help remarking the contrast between the standing figure, so charged with moment in her attitude, and the seated couple. The latter had seemed to me fine and glamorous in this different age that was their element, but their glamour was plebeian and domesticated. This other creature perhaps had no glamour at all, in the latter-day, degraded sense of the word, but her presence was a veiled lightning. I have said she was outlandish – more in demeanour actually than in attire – but perhaps I would do better to say she was unearthly. And yet, to say so would suggest she was ethereal. She was not. Rather, it was as if the sun-beaten rocks and earth of the region had become woman and walked.

Frank's astonishment was almost that of someone who has been caught out, or someone who is suddenly in the company of two people who do not know each other but know him in very different ways. It seemed a while before he remembered himself sufficiently to try and regain his composure. When he did, however, all the circumspection behind his alertness took over, came forward and asserted itself in a new posture of iron rigidity.

The woman beckoned with one hand.

"*Venga! Venga!*"

Frank shook his head wordlessly.

When she repeated her invitation, he shook his head again and said "No" in English, with icy decision. The woman started to talk then, rapidly, in Italian.

"What's she saying, Frank?" asked Elsie.

"You tell me, Else. Your Italian's better than mine."

The woman continued her glossolalia.

"I don't understand what you're saying," said Frank. "I don't understand. I don't speak Italian."

With a gesture of exasperation, the woman gave up and walked on, looking back once, then twice, before disappearing up one of the steep roads from the piazza.

"What was that all about?"

"Don't ask me."

Witness to this scene, I had thrilled with a kind of paralysis. The yes or no of the outcome – of my grandfather's response – I felt certain was of profound and urgent importance. His entire life – somehow I knew it – would have been different had he said yes, and he had tried his best to master himself, to dispense with all fuss, and to eliminate all signs of weakness, as, there and then, he made the decision he thought necessary.

Where, moments before, I had been paralysed with the grave decision that I witnessed, now I was torn that it had been made. Part of me stayed with my grandparents and part of me went with the disappearing figure in black. At first it seemed the part that stayed was the greater part, but then I realised my eyes were only following the woman, and searching the place she had disappeared, and that the greater part of me was with her, or longed to be. And then thought ceased and my legs moved beneath me, carrying me in haste past the table where were located two lives of many without which my life would not be. I left them to shrink once more into the sad unknown of all that is hidden from me.

With a billowing relief that was close to wonder, I turned the corner the woman had turned before me and saw that, after all, she had not vanished, though she was some way ahead. I was too intent on keeping her in sight to care very much whether I was observed in my turn. I pumped my legs hard against the gradient. I think I even wished to be seen. The woman did, indeed, look back at one point, and must have noticed me ascending in her footsteps with hunched determination. However, with some distance still between us and the veil that obscured her face, it was impossible to tell what her reaction was. It might have been complete indifference, and when she turned once more forward and continued without any quickening of pace, I was struck – and stung – by the impression that it *was* indifference, or some lofty knowing akin to indifference that was equally as humiliating to me.

My sense of humiliation acted as a spur, and since my pursuit was not in any way discouraged by the woman, my determination to follow and find – perhaps – what my grandfather had disowned was only strengthened. We passed out of the town, and, looking back, I saw how the streets and houses crowded down to the rich blue enamel of the Mediterranean waters, the rooftops reminiscent of some civilisation of coral and sea anemones exposed by the tide. The buildings, it seemed, had grown up together and were all apiece. There was little or no sign of the new replacing the old. The town itself was a kind of living rock formation, unchanging in its antiquity, staggering in its vertiginous yawn. Fearing I would lose ground, however, I turned again and hurried after the untiring figure ahead of me.

We began to climb, the interval between us varying little, into a mountainous terrain of scrub and rocks and quiet dust. The sun was fierce and serene, and glowered upon the rocks and earth in such a way that my eyes cooled themselves with an inkiness like that which belongs to thunder clouds. I was sweating profusely, and wondered how the woman could move with such steady composure swathed in her black clothing. There were stone steps for us to ascend, ancient and seemingly hewn from the very rock of the mountain. They were as narrow and precarious as the vertebrae of some behemoth of the world before humans. The landscape itself was the petrified remains of this stupendous monster. The very way in which the steps were worn spoke to me of a span of time far greater than that usually encompassed within my mental horizons, as if something had been exposed that was usually covered. The darkness and strange texture of the stone were the darkness and texture of the antediluvian. The steps ran into each other like the guttering of some incredible candle, used to illuminate the reading of a book known only to the gods. The wax had absorbed the dust of the pre-human study before hardening once more into something both soapy and igneous. At times I stopped, exhausted, and looked out at the flashing convexity of the sea, a shield on which the fiery blow of the sun was falling continuously with a silent, delirious pounding, or down at the shrinking, archaic fantasy of the town, which now appeared the maritime equivalent of that house of sweets into which Hansel and Gretel had been lured. I grew dizzy on such occasions, and the stairway seemed to sway as if it were some endless rope bridge. My vertigo was almost that of someone scaling a mountain-high ladder, but this vertigo only seemed to push me up from below, and so I continued to follow the nameless woman. For her part, she looked back from time to time. I began to feel that she was leading me.

When the sun had worked me upon the anvil of the steps so that I felt myself quite boneless and malleable and white-hot with lack of will, I saw that the woman had reached a plateau and no longer ascended, but walked along a horizontal plane. There were perhaps fifty steps left to me before I, too, gained the plateau. They were harder than the uncounted hundreds of steps I had so far climbed put together. Almost on my hands and knees, I staggered onto the level shoulder of dust. To pretend that I had not been following the woman would have been absurd, but I was too enfeebled to care about such things in any case. I sat down in the dust and wiped the sweat from my face with both hands. I almost felt that, in doing so, I made myself a *tabula rasa*.

It occurred to me that the blank I experienced was not *my* blank exactly. The town was still visible below. Surely we were not far from it. I was sure, however, that we had come to a different time – a different *kind* of time – to that which prevailed in the piazza. I had an inkling of what time had pitched its pavilion there. It was from a period before my birth and after the births of my grandparents. This seemed a reasonable – though no longer an impregnable – assumption. The time whose invisible banners streamed in the air of this plateau was a preceding time. My grandparents' time was contingent upon this as I was contingent upon them. And yet, this time also seemed to comprehend their time in the way that the plateau commanded a view of the lilliputian town. My grandparents were encamped in the pavilion of the present – of *their* present. This plateau, somehow, surrounded them. Had my grandfather known that to step outside that small locality would be so soon to step into something deep and vast and other?

"*Venga! Venga!*"

I heard the voice of the woman for the first time since the piazza, addressing to me the words that she had first addressed to my grandfather. No longer so sure of myself, trembling in all my limbs after the sustained effort of the climb, and half chilled where the wind caught my sweat, I stood and walked in wary obedience towards her.

The plateau widened in her direction. She was standing amongst piles of stone that still bore some semblance of a symmetry imposed by human mind and human hands. There were low bushes there, too, and skeletal trees.

Drawing close, I saw that the woman was standing at the side of a well, next to the ruins of some gaunt and ancient building, and had drawn a bucket up from the well's liquid heart, to hold it perched upon the rim of the encircling wall.

"Drink," she said.

If it had not been for this instruction, my awe in her presence might have baffled me. Receiving that instruction, I knew what to do with my awe. In awe I drank and splashed my face, and poured sweet, crystalline chill upon my head. The water hardly seemed wet. It was the blood of the rocks, a liquid quintessence of the cold, pure darkness that formed strata of the sediment of shadow deep, deep underground.

When I had finished, sprinkled with jewels of water, and as if knowing anew my own depths with the depths of my refreshment, I turned and saw that the woman had tossed her veil and hood into the dust at her feet, which were bare. Her hair was dark and long, and her face was the same yeasty colour as her hands. She looked neither old nor especially young, but so alive and so without disguise that I could not be unmoved. It came to me that we are taught to apologise for all that is alive in us, taught that it is obscene. Unadulterated life, though it may have the most graceful of manners, is not polite. Life itself is the true enemy of the censor. Now I beheld the uncensored face, as beautiful and ready as that of any hawk.

Obscurely ashamed because I had no face to meet this face that was its equal in nakedness, I averted my eyes, casting them again upon the discarded veil.

"Who were you mourning?" I asked.

"The mourning is over," she said. "Be happy. Be free."

I smiled half a smile.

"Perhaps I shall," I said. Then I looked her in the eye again, suddenly, my head cocked a little to the side, almost as if to shield my eyes from the scorching brightness of the sun, in this way hoping to cover my guile, and I said, "You speak English."

"We speak the same language now, yes," she said. "All once spoke the same language, before the tower was built and fell. Are you glad to be here?"

"Yes, I am glad."

"Do you want to know why you are glad, and why we can speak together like this?"

"Yes. Tell me."

I felt a strange confidence growing in me, like that of a hunter who knows his arrows will strike home and fell the hart that is his quarry.

"There is another spring here. Its well is not this well of stone. Its well is in your heart and mine. We're close to it now."

I looked about me.

"I can't see it."

"Yes you can. You can see its outer parts, at least."

Then she strode across the dust as if she were walking upon water, and laid her hand upon a broken and teetering column of masonry.

"Here," she said.

She turned and looked at me, and her smile was that of someone who had known me before, a smile that seems to say there is no happiness and no glory like the happiness and glory of return. And yet her smile was wistful, too, and conveyed a patient wisdom. She was waiting to see how much I understood.

"This is the Chapel of the Forgotten Tears of Christ," she said.

Her voice was not the sanctimonious voice of a teacher or official guide. She spoke as if referring to a member of her own family, and yet the respect evident in her voice was magnified greatly in its power for being the supple respect of living flesh and blood.

Her eyes flashed and met mine.

"As you can see, the Chapel is ruined. Show me your ring."

"My ring?"

"On the forefinger of your left hand. Who gave it to you?"

She had come forward now and held my hand in both of hers. The skin of her palms was hot and dry. It seemed suddenly as if I had not been touched by a human being for hundreds of years. I remembered with the contact of her flesh something for which there were no words except as phantom clues such as 'community' and 'passion', something I had missed without knowing ever since my mind had taken form around my name.

"My father," I said.

"Where did he get it from?"

"I don't know. From Italy."

"And here," she said, "I have one like it."

She showed me a band of braided silver on the forefinger of her left hand.

"When the tide goes out," she said, "in your land, it goes so far out that on the beaches sometimes it seems like the sea was never there at all. But you walk in the sand, and you smell the sea, and you hear it. You know the sea was there, and that if it did not go out, you would not be able to walk like this, with the crabs and the sea-snails, on its muddy bed. Isn't that true?"

"Yes, it is."

"Do you know what that's called?"

"I don't know."

"There's a word for it – a very old word. But never mind that. It's time for the tide to come in again. You have come to restore our church. Your heart should be glad."

"I am glad," I said again. "Very glad."

I heard then a gentle clinking, a stir of tintinnabulation. The woman stood still with my hand clasped between her palms. The sound was not from her.

"There's something only you can do," she said, and with one hand keeping its grip on mine while the other escaped, she led me through a breach in the shattered walls of the long-forsaken chapel. Roofless, the place had the feeling of some courtyard in a desert haven. It could have been a garden, if it were not for the fact that nothing grew here. Nothing, that is, except for a single tree, slender in its trunk and its branching limbs, which sprouted leafless in one corner. From its twigs there hung rosaries, silver crucifixes, shells and other ornaments. Occasionally a breath from nowhere made them ripple with sound and motion, as if they were eternally borrowing life from the high mountain air, clacking bones forever dead, continually resurrected.

The floor of the chapel had also been ruined so that it was now mostly dirt, with traces of broken masonry and mosaic. Of what remained of that floor, and all the floor had once supported, there were shapes and objects telling plainer than language that there had been human burials here. As if the leafless tree were its headstone, one of these graves was set in the same corner of the chapel, now little more than a rectangular mound of slightly raised earth, surrounded by a fragmented frame of stone. Against the wall next to this nameless grave were set a number of tools that might have been left behind by whatever unknown hand had first dug the grave. Seeing this I had that feeling, once again, that had taken hold of me in the piazza, of being in the presence – on the threshold – of a decision whose implications towered to the sky. Mixed with this, and complicated by it, was the mysterious confidence that had begun to percolate through me a little time previously. Something in this mixture of feelings – something I could not yet comprehend – prompted me to let go of the woman's hand, whose touch was so charged and so comforting, and to look about the rest of the chapel's interior.

In the corner opposite the grave and the tree I saw what at first seemed to be a funeral bier. I approached and examined it. There seemed little sign of age in the surface of this slab, and it almost shone in the peculiar atmosphere of that plateau, as if freshly hewn. On and about it were a number of artefacts that shared the troublingly pristine quality of the bier. There was – incongruous in a chapel – a mirror in a frame of bronze, a candelabrum, a censer, a stoup, a thin dagger in the shape of a cross, and a number of other items.

"This is a strange place," I said, when I felt her hand upon my shoulder.

"All places are strange," she said, "when the tide is out. Would you like to come to the end of strangeness?"

"Wouldn't that be strange, too?"

I turned around and she drew back.

"I cannot tell you anything," she said. "Things are as you see. If you wish to restore the church, it is never too soon. I suppose you haven't heard of the loneliness of God."

"How can God be lonely?"

"How can God not be lonely? Look into your heart."

I nodded.

"I understand. I'm sorry. What do I have to do?"

"You must dig."

And so I dug, with the tools that someone had leant against the broken wall. The moment my hoe struck the dry earth, I realised that I had been impatient for this, that this was the hard and wordless work I had procrastinated to avoid, increasingly suffering the strain of my own procrastination.

The woman sat upon the bier and watched, dangling her legs, while I felt myself dissolve in sweat as I broke and turned and shifted that sweet and hallowed dust. I knew that the woman could not help me in this task. I did not want her to. For once it seemed that I would accomplish something real and complete quite by myself. No one else would be able to take credit for my work – not even God.

At times I wiped my brow and rested, leaning on the shaft of the hoe or the spade that I was wielding. When I did, I was unable to refrain from glancing behind me at the woman. She watched without boredom, seeming never to look away. I would turn back to my work, each time, with an image of her in my mind, and each image grew into the next. It seemed to me that she was the future – a future of such mystery and possibility as the high mountain breezes that cooled me where I dripped in perspiration. I did not know her name, and did not ask, but it was abundantly clear to me that she was You, the nameless You of whom I had heard in one love song after another. I had often thought, fleetingly, in my life before, that I had met this You, and I had always been miserably mistaken. After a number of such mistakes, it had come to seem to me that this very common and vulgar thing, the love song, was something other than it appeared. It was not a lie, after all, but it was not true in the way that young and foolish people supposed. It had an esoteric truth, which I had sensed before and which now, in the presence of the woman, I was coming to understand with some precision.

I do not know how long my excavations had continued before I uncovered something in the earthen wall of the grave, set in an alcove of fragmented stone like that forming the outline of the grave itself. Shining within the alcove, as pristine, beneath a layer of dust, as the items surrounding the bier, was what appeared to be a silver chalice.

I stopped and regarded it for some time, and the woman descended from the bier and came over.

"We're almost there," she said.

This buried alcove seemed peculiar to me, like something still living though it is embedded in rock. I gazed at it a while longer with puzzled wonder before continuing.

The woman was right, as I had known she would be. It seemed only a few moments later that the spade I was now using struck something quite different to the covering soil.

"That's it," said the woman from above me, and she climbed down into the grave with signs of excitement and delight radiating from her every movement and expression.

"You'll have to climb out," she said. "There'll be no room otherwise."

Again, I did as I had been instructed, and from the edge of the open grave looked down while the woman swept the dirt aside with her hands to reveal the timbers of a coffin. Not long since she had been wearing the veil of mourning. Everything in her attitude and motion now expressed some curious ecstasy I had never seen before that was in some way the very reverse of grief.

The lid of the coffin must have been divided in two. When she had sufficiently cleared off the dry soil, the woman lifted open the upper half of the coffin while she continued to straddle the lower. I am not sure now what I had expected to see, only that I had expected something. What I saw was a shock to me, but it immediately eliminated all other possibilities from my mind and became the inevitable. It was myself I saw, arms folded across my chest, eyes closed, with skin and hair soft and lustrous, without decay, as if preserved by whatever had kept certain other things in that chapel immune to the depredations of time. The chest seemed still, without the rise and fall of breath, but the face was radiant, serene, and an impossible smile tingled over the closed lips, so that I thought all sense of something sweet and potential in the dust I had removed had derived from this buried object. It was a thing that so magically defined life that even in death it did not die.

Then the woman smothered that face with kisses as passionate as the agonies of grief, and tears passed from her cheek to his, soaking them both. It was as if she had forgotten there was someone else here to observe her actions. I drew back from the edge of the grave, not wishing to watch any more. Turning my back to the hole, I rested my eyes again upon the bier and walked over to it. I exhaled with a wild resentment, and kicked a stone. The confidence that had been growing in me had not gone. It continued to grow. But it had become twisted now, and bifurcated. I thought of how my grandfather had said no to this woman, of the immovable obstinacy of that refusal, and I nodded grimly. Ideas piled up swiftly in my head, and feelings in my heart.

The woman called my name. When I did not respond she called again. Eventually I walked back to the edge of the grave.

"Why didn't you answer?" she asked.

"I didn't know who you were talking to," I said.

She looked at me strangely.

"We have to get you out of this coffin," she said.

"Isn't that a desecration?"

"It's a desecration made by love and life. Do you think there is any desecration here? You can see how close we are. All desecrations will be redeemed. Look! Your life is here in front of you."

"Is it my life?"

"What else can it be?"

I shrugged.

She sighed.

"You can't leave this undone," she said. "Beneath this coffin, there's more. There's the spring whose well is in your heart and mine, which has kept you alive even in death. Once we get you out of the coffin, we can begin."

"What's that?"

I pointed to the chalice.

"It's another well," she said. "Life flows from it forever. But if we dig deeper—"

"Yes, I understand. What was that word?"

"What word?"

"A very old word."

"Yes. *Tzimtzum.*"

"Yes. *Tzimtzum.* Do you want me to come down there again?"

"No. Wait a moment."

She got to her feet and began to climb from the hole. I helped her up.

"There's something I have to explain to you," she said. "Maybe you already know part of it, or have guessed, but you need to understand it all. I don't think you quite—"

Before she could finish, I drew out the misericorde that I had sheathed in my belt, behind my back.

She looked at me in silence.

"Speak," I said.

I needed to see her face as she saw the dagger in the hand of the one she had just been kissing. I needed to hear her voice and feel her trembling heart as she saw the scorn on the face that she had so lately baptised with her tears.

"What are you doing?"

Her dismay was as undisguised as had been her passion. It was unbearable, but now, my heart breaking, the only answer I could give was to plunge the blade into her soft belly.

She looked down, open-mouthed. In her blood was all her tenderness and pride – a personal and sacred treasure that none should know who she had not initiated in the mystery herself. Now I was pillaging that treasure, and pillaging only to waste and dishonour it. As her deepest warmth coagulated around my fist, I saw the horror on her face and knew that the worst of it lay in the fact that it was *I* who pillaged. There was no hate, no anger in her face or in her voice, only the horror of violated trust, the horror of someone who does not understand.

"No," she said, and I had never heard a single word so poignant. And then, "You don't know what you've done."

In her words there were disbelief and something like pity, unless it was simply that the disbelief was pitiful.

My anger was quickened. My heart was sick with resentment and despair. I drew out the blade, and, as if it were myself I wished to punish, myself I wished to slay, I plunged it again and again into that place where her noble, precious heart still quivered.

All too soon she lay upon the ground, robbed of life.

I fell, and wept on her motionless legs.

*

Still my crime was not complete. I had become a jackal, a hyena. I cut a length from her black dress, and onto this I placed those objects I could take away – the candelabrum, the censer, the mirror and especially the chalice – before folding the fabric and knotting it into a sack. I had been right – as I discovered – about the bells attached to her ankle. There was a shimmering silver circle of them. These, too, went into the sack.

I rolled the body into the grave and shovelled some earth into the gaping hole, but soon threw down the spade.

Whatever natural feelings I had once possessed, I had disfigured them all. My emotions were beheaded things, voiceless, lumbering monsters that could finish nothing.

I took the sack like one accepting a curse and I left the chapel behind me, a fleeing shadow. I could not return to the town. I had to climb the steps again, higher, till they took me across these mountains and on my way to places where I was a stranger, setting foot for the first time.

As I ascended almost to the highest point of that stone stairway, my loot clanking on my back, I was seized and pierced by a wild sense of hope and joy. *She is not dead*, I told myself. She cannot be. I have only done what I must to ensure our sweetest reunion at the very end of time.

I heard then a shriek like that of a seabird, and, reeling in confusion, almost tumbled back down the deadly emptiness of air and mountainside.

I stopped then to steady myself with my free hand on the rock before me.

She is not dead! It was such a spinning and giddy ecstasy of hope – as if something flashing in the air above had dazzled me – as I had never known before. I drew the dagger from my belt again. The blade was still red with her blood. There was no hope. How could there be? I had never hoped like this before that crime of irreparable despair. This must be the natural madness in the soul of the murderer – a bright rebellion of hope and faith. I looked at the cross of the misericorde. Here was the proof of her death, here the blinding flash of hope and here the curse with which that hope was now forever made riddle and mystery.

*

I began a strange journey. By the blood-stained blade I carried, I knew it was a quest, although I did not know at first what kind of quest it was. After all, how could I bear to know, when it was a quest of the unthinkable, and when it had started from the terrible end of hope? What further end could there be after the end with which the quest had begun?

I was successful in selling one or two of the items from my sack at the first village to which I came. My communication, I noticed, was somehow charmed. I spoke the language of the villagers without the need to think. Since this blessing seemed uncanny to me, and since the horror of my crime was still not far behind me, I took the money I had made, hurriedly bought provisions, and moved on.

I stopped among some scrub and dark-boughed trees on a slope of vivid saffron earth, and cut a loaf with my only knife. It had not occurred to me to buy a different blade, but now I saw that everything I ate would be as if cut for me with the blade of murder. The crumbs I forced into my mouth tasted of the disbelief in her last words and the desolation of her final silence. I had turned the entire world that supported me into a broken, poisoned Eucharist of sickness and hate.

In that place, alone, my body and soul dumb to speak of the deformed urges, ecstasies and shudders that now moved them, rather than speak or pray, I took that knife and with it cut, determined, an inch or so below the toes of my left foot, until that foot was blunt and bleeding, pollarded. My entire life, I thought, would soon be lost with the dizzying spurts of blood.

As I watched, however, the red fountain slowed and stopped. There was half a foot, a section of bone and meat open to the air, but it had become self-contained, this wounded bodily extremity seemingly latching on to some anomaly of belief or perception in my heart to guide its physiology. I flung the chopped-off toes away for the birds to find.

Cutting myself a staff, I limped on my way. In the hours that followed, I witnessed a grotesque miracle. The pale skin of my truncated foot began to grow over the wound that tickled with flies. It moved like oil slowly filling the bottom of a pan into which it is poured. Observing it now and then on my journey was like watching some exotic, half-hideous flower that blooms and closes before your eyes according to sinister sensitivities known only to the world of plants.

Such healing was more than luck, and I felt the miracle's obscure menace. My wound had been sealed over with soft, round, ivory flesh, like a large, stubby ball of thumb. It was as if I had been born with this deformity. At least I was growing into a creature more suited to my journey. I looked, now, like a life-long beggar and vagrant. I did not always need to sell what I had acquired or stolen. I could beg for alms.

The gift of languages – wherever I went I could speak the native tongue – and the gift of healing, were, it seemed to me, part of my curse, and there have been plenty of people, in all times and places, who understand what is sinister in luck and ominous in blessing. I thought of what she, behind that gory, unthinkable barrier of time and deed, had said, was there still saying, that the chalice was another well from which flows life. I took it out, often, from the sack, to examine it, and saw how it shone, and felt some chord in me played by fingers of its light. I knew very well what this object was. There were some who believed that there was no object more precious on Earth. And it was this object that formed the basis of my quest. For some the quest would have been to find it. I had already found it. My quest, therefore, was to dispose of it, but I knew I must do so appropriately. To choose how I passed it on – how I rid myself of this article – that was all that was left to me. And my strength to do so came to me only from the memory of my grandfather shaking his head and saying no.

Without such a quest to occupy my thoughts, there was nothing for me but to be haunted by the one whose dying had made me a murderer, and who yet lived on, atrociously, in the glamour that opened to me the locked gates of all language, in the unnatural healing of my mutilated foot, and in the shining of that chalice. Afraid that, in her death and its many wonders, she would somehow return to me, one night as I sheltered in a disused granary in Austria, I took out the knife again and did something that was greater agony than anything my body had previously known. I cut the nose from my face. Blood poured into my mouth from the ruin above it, so that I spluttered and choked, almost drowning in my own spilt life.

The influence of the chalice saved me on this occasion, too. The blood swiftly ceased to flow, and a delicate, moon-coloured membrane crept over the new orifice at the centre of my face. My neck now terminated in a living skull, a death's head. My fear of seeing her again was quelled a little. I had a face that was adequate to meet hers. Hope trembled again beneath what remained of my fear. I had made myself a scarecrow to earn the secret powers of the soul, and in earning them came to symbolise them physically. The crooked, half-foot, skull-faced beggar – behold the power in my form! I had shaped myself into a creature worthy of my crime, and worthy, therefore, of my unholy possession of the stolen chalice. Still, I felt myself fugitive as I clasped that chalice in my pale claw.

So I wandered, begging and buying and selling. I was a beast of ill-omen. But just as some see the curse in the blessing, so some thought they saw the blessing in my curse and hoped to gain a little of that blessing by contact and commerce with me, drinking from a poison spring as if it might cure them. I sold almost all I had first taken from the chapel, except for the dagger and chalice. The silver bells from her ankle I sold before too long. It had been partly their jingling that tormented me with the sense of a reappearance forever imminent, but never now – a soon-not-yet, soon-not-yet that made each step I took a tinkling of heralds of the Day of Judgement. It was the silver voice of love, recalling me always to the innocence of new life, but before which I could only stand as one in chains, to be sentenced and condemned. I sold these bells to a hare-lipped and sentimental whore in Salzburg. I told her that each time the bells rang a heart would beat with love for her and that one more link in a silver chain would be forged around that heart, and one more silver coin would pass from those hands to hers. But in my own heart I told myself that for each time the bells rang she would conceive a sorrow that would cause a hundred tears.

Even after I sold those bells, I was followed by a familiar tintinnabulation. As the sun accompanies the steps of a traveller during the day, and the moon at night, so it accompanied mine, moving through the world, as it seemed, by virtue of my movement, and disappearing for long stretches into the obscurity of silence only to be revealed once more, as if by parting clouds, in the bells of a street performer, the splashing of a stream beneath a water-wheel, the jangling of a passing carriage, the clinking of bunched keys on a ring. At one time I stood, transfixed, listening to the chime of nearby church bells. In English, of course, a child knows that the song of a church bell is "ding-dong, ding-dong". It is a round and melodious sound, often jubilant, sometimes dolorous. However, in my stolen sack of unlucky charms and trinkets, I carried something that opened my ears to other languages. That melodious "ding-dong" became cracked and fuzzy in my hearing. There was, instead, a sound that fizzed and hissed with a constant inner sparking. *Tzimtzum. Tzimtzum.*

I looked, and the steeple of the church appeared to me then crooked, like a shadow thrown upon jagged rock, and the face of the clock was glowing like a forge. From the glow there emerged, as if from the haze of immense heat, a shimmering pattern of concentric circles. The circles began to warp and blur and spin into a spiral. All the while there came that buzzing chime, of bells speaking some other language than that I once believed native to them. *Tzimtzum. Tzimtzum.* I had been hearing it, of course, for a while now, but before it had been something like a silent sound, a suggested sound, the echo in my mind of a sound in my ears. Now the sound in my ears was growing closer and closer to the echo in my mind. The two were converging. I saw the very vibrations upon the air of the loud clanging of those bells, the waves of concentric circles that made all the town seem to shift in an undersea way, the houses, roads and shops becoming crooked, watery shadows.

Tzimtzum. Tzimtzum.

Hardly able to keep my balance, I limped away on my staff in fright. Behind me that crackling chime of *tzimtzum-tzimtzum* sounded like laughter issuing from the dry, scaly, lizard-like lips of a very old man. I even seemed to see his tapered tongue wriggling skittishly like a lizard's tail.

As my purpose became clearer to me, so also did the need to disguise the chalice that I carried. Above all, this meant finding some way to dim that object's lustre. It was a spangled capturing of light whose effect was something like that of a strong white beam thrown upon a cinema screen, except that the screen, in this case, was what most would call reality. Reality seemed pale and worn-through in its presence. Even a person who had never heard the name by which this object was best known would nonetheless recognise something more than mundane in that luminosity. The layer of dust that had covered the chalice when I first saw it had not been enough to dull this light. The needed disguise would not be easily achieved.

My travels became a search for any means by which the chalice might be tarnished, dented and begrimed. When walking lonely dirt tracks, I let it drag behind me on a string. I threw it into the flames of burning houses, not caring for the burns I suffered in retrieving it. I made it sticky with the blood of slaughtered pigs, and mired it in the slops of abattoirs. I baptised it with the vomit and bile of dying men. I dipped it in the ink used to print scandal-sheets and spattered it with the wax of purloined funeral candles. Slowly, the layers of ash, dye and unspeakable filth began to take hold and accumulate in a glorious, heterogeneous crust that appeared to me more precious in its vile nacre than the silvery shine it obscured.

I came to Bohemia, and it happened that, as I was beginning to be satisfied with the baroque crust on the chalice, I entered Prague. Limping across Charles Bridge on feet that seemed to bleed their ache into the stones they trod, I looked at the dark avenue of statues that stood witness to my progress – St. John of Nepomuk, the Pieta, St. Francis Seraphic and St. Anna – looming icily as black ocean spray frozen in time, and I knew that what I thought of as my quest must be accomplished here. The air had about it that tender sobriety of twilight that seems to distil all things into a vision at once infinitely pellucid and infinitely evanescent. This solemn twilight emanated from the very stones of the city. Prague, it seemed to me, in all the world must be the very capital of twilight. On the other side of the cold and melancholy Vltava, the triangles, domes, trapezoids, ovals, arches and spires made such a grand miscellany of shape against the empyrean of clouds that I remembered the town of the jagged church steeple whose bells had spoken an alien language that echoed over the wavering undersea streets.

There was something kaleidoscopic about Prague, with its castle, its Synagogue and its astrological clock – at which one day I stared until I was afraid to stare any more – that gave me the impression of things converging. Things converged here like the pattern of coloured beads in a kaleidoscope converges with its multiplied reflections before being swallowed up in them; they converged as the sound of '*tzimtzum*' in my mind and in my ear had converged that time, and continued to converge on other occasions since. As if spiralling from one holy site to another in pilgrimage, I entered those establishments of drinking and entertainment that are known as places to be avoided. Although I saw strange things at each of them, the strangeness was exoteric, to be understood at a glance. The people of this world are required to present themselves in a certain way in public and feel, therefore, that they have crossed the forbidden border into true living if, in a dark but crowded place that is both public and hidden, they engage in activities diametrically opposed to what is otherwise publicly known and seen of them. Most of the strangeness did not extend further than this. However, when I sold a trinket here and there and asked where else I might sell, one name recurred as something proposed for consideration, and then dismissed. My sense of convergence became a crackling of lightning when I heard that name.

Establishments of ill repute in some sense look out upon the reputable daylight world as if they are merely a dark corner one backs into. But some who back into that corner cease to look out upon the world they have left. They turn and face the corner itself until, by some mystery of the converging of kaleidoscope patterns, and the shifting and self-swallowing of those patterns, the corner opens up and shows a space beyond. The windows of this new realm no longer look out upon any reputable place where daylight comes. They look out on an endless, resounding darkness where something like ragged tapestries seem to flutter, and occasionally a whining, a moaning or a chanting can be heard, followed by cold wafts of obscene incense and a timpani of charnel things.

The name of the place was Indra's Web.

At first, none would give me directions there, claiming ignorance. However, the information finally came to my ears. At one tavern I was asked to leave by the landlord. He did not want me peddling my wares on his premises, or perhaps he simply did not like the look of me. I asked where else I might expect to sell my wares so that I might eat and live. He looked at me with unflinching hostility.

"Indra's Web is the place for you," he said, as if he were telling me to go directly to Hell.

"How do I get there?"

He hesitated (perhaps he had not anticipated that I would take him seriously), and then he smiled in sly derision and gave very exact and complicated directions.

106

The night is always on its way to becoming dawn, so that to speak of the depths of the night can be deceptive. And yet, if the night is only a brief interlude, it is also true that it is the natural time of dreams, and sometimes these dreams seem to leak and infect even the waking aspect of the night. When I stood outside Indra's Web, I sensed that the night had been contaminated in just such a way and that I had come to a curious hinterland in which place had escaped the usual governance of time. It was obviously a foul and dangerous part of the city. Steps led down behind a building amongst unsleeping tenements. At the bottom of the steps was a windowless door, scratched, stained and battered, and above this door was a sign painted in a careless script, dubiously proclaiming, "Indra's Web". On other signs, now obscured by soot, pigeon's droppings and diverse unknown filth, were older names, many of them now illegible. Still other names were scribbled heavily in chalk on the bricks around the doorway. It was as if the place were essentially nameless, and was known by a name that was only an echoing, ever-changing Chinese-whisper. Perhaps, I thought, in the same way that there was no real name, there was also no true owner.

I hobbled down the steps, trying to become the shadow I cast – a thing that in its weakness was nonetheless invulnerable and could mingle anywhere with impunity. I knocked on the door with my staff. It opened an inch or two, and from the darkness within a voice hissed, "Who sent you?"

The landlord had been well-informed. I gave the name he had given me – that of Meyer – and passed inside.

"That way," the voice hissed again, and a grimy finger pointed along a short passage. Then the owner of that finger was gone into some hole of darkness within the darkness.

This, I knew, as I saw the shadows upon the interior wall, was the centre of the spiral of my pilgrimage. For the first time, upon entering such a place, I was afraid. I felt that my disfigured face and my crippled foot were mere disguises that might be seen through at any moment. There were sounds here – a kind of bedlam of laughing and singing, along with the intermittent wheezing of an accordion – but they did not mingle in that warm ambience called a hubbub. Instead, each voice seemed to shape itself with slow, narcotic clarity within the element of a nightmare silence, as beetles and other small creatures underwater are enveloped in silver film. I could hear with great closeness and lucidity the scrape of my one-and-a-half feet upon the gritty floor.

The short entrance passage ended and I came out into an open space, dimly lit with lanterns and candles, where wooden pillars, stone pillars, raised floor areas, dank, low, half-walls of stone and tattered folding screens formed a minimal sense of partition. It seemed little more than a cellar – a truly cheerless place – though a large one. Huge barrels loomed out of the darkness to the far left, and next to them was a tiny counter, behind which stood a man with more the look of a watchman about him than a landlord, as if he had goods or information only for certain people who he would know by a word, an introduction or shared knowledge. There were jars and bottles on makeshift shelves behind him, containing liquids of all colours and, clouded by murkiness, vague pickled objects. On the counter was a large demijohn half-full of some yellow potion.

The air was webbed with a sweet but oddly sickening smoke, which made me shudder as if my flesh had turned chill from the inside. I glanced briefly at a group of men around a table in a corner, partly partitioned by a low wall. One of them was smoking some kind of shisha. His beard was stark and stiff with grease and his flesh was pale as with fever. More than in any of the places I had previously visited, I knew that I should not let my eyes linger on the habitués, and so I looked away. I had seen enough of the others at the table, however, to know that I was far from being the strangest creature here.

The name of the place, even if it were only the latest name in a series, was appropriate to the point of inevitability. Any place where drinks are sold and imbibed is a mixture, in atmosphere, of the public and private, but I had never known such an eerie mix of those two qualities of atmosphere as this. It was as if the web of smoke were an actual web, by which the nervous systems of all the bar's inhabitants were extended quiveringly onto the unwholesome air – extended and linked together. And any agitation in one quarter of that tense, nervous web was immediately communicated in spidery vibrations to every other quarter. I did not feel threatened – as in the other squalid holes I had entered – because of the explicit violence of a fist-fight or a stabbing (which here might have eased the tension), but because of the sense that I had interrupted something, with my presence, that I did not understand. A fly, I imagine, does not understand what it is that tangles its legs and wings when it is caught in the silver strands of a web, but it knows, when it feels that web tremor, that something unspeakable has found it and is approaching.

I did not wish to buy a drink here, though I guessed the name 'Meyer' might help me to do so, as it had helped me at the door. I looked away from the various half-lit groups of figures and towards a stone arch, beyond which was a suggestion that the vaulted ceiling continued. The smoke of years and decades – perhaps longer – seemed to have accumulated on the air and the layers so formed became increasingly visible towards this arch as endless rings of furrowed waves.

The dread that overcame me as I gazed through that arch into the unknown turned to chill fatalism. The fatalism, in its turn, grew into a sense of grim defiance and perversity. I moved then to an unoccupied table nearby, whose surface caught more of the scant light than the others, and on this, with a deliberate emphasis of gesture that brought also a clanking emphasis of sound, I set down the sack that had been my burden for so long. Without a word I loosened the knot and spread out its corners on the table. Then I began to arrange the items it had contained in two neat rows. All that remained of my loot from the chapel was the misericorde, still sheathed in my belt, and the chalice, which now stood in one of the two rows mentioned, between worthless gewgaws I had picked up on my way – a mandrake root on one side and a Jew's harp on the other.

As I set about this task I knew, by means of that nervous, vibratory web of smoke, that various pairs of eyes were turning to me. I had gone through a similar performance before in this city. It was a ritual by which I amplified within my heart my contempt for all the people of this world, laying out before their eyes all manner of gimcrack, and with it the chalice, which was worth more than this orb called Earth that is their home. Encrusted now as it was with layers of filth, this was no longer a vessel that people would care to drink from or wish to use as ornament. Those who passed the chalice over in favour of some cheap pendant or bogus relic did not realise that they were, in relation to life, no more than the dirt that caked this chalice and obscured its true radiance.

"All items for sale," I said, without looking up from the table.

Somehow my ritual seemed to take on a different meaning here.

One or two ragged characters approached to examine my wares. Purchases were made. Even here, however, it seemed that the chalice went unrecognised. I began to wonder whether I had even needed to disguise it. Disappointment was spreading from my tongue like the taste of bitterness when I became aware that I was being observed closely by a figure seated at a table somewhat to my right set against the frame of an empty, unmanned counter. The figure would not have stood out in most crowds, I decided, but he stood out here. He wore a dark suit which matched in its impression of gravity his equally dark hair and moustache and the paleness of his face and hands. His head gave the impression of strength rather than subtlety, his skull being of a square shape and his face seeming concave, dented towards the eyes and the top of the nose. This concavity gave his eyes a quiet but remarkable intensity. When he moved, it was not with grace, but with abrupt energy, his movements seeming always to stop before they had reached a natural conclusion, as if the very nature of this man were a form of self-control that had stunted him and which yet brewed within him a tremendous power.

This man had a companion, and that companion was more peculiar. It was human – it must have been – although something made me question this assumption. It had the appearance of being a very old man, and perhaps the age of this creature had caused it to wither and shrink, because it was tiny upon its seat, like a child. Size and age vary within human beings, and I do not believe that the simple extremes of senescence and smallness here mixed were enough to account for the aura of utter repulsiveness that this creature possessed. I began to wonder, as I glanced at it now and then, whether it were perhaps possible that this was a hybrid of human and something else. Could one of the parents have been an ape of some description? This idea did not convince me and I began to think instead of some of the more hidden and less celebrated adventures of science. Whatever had made this creature – and what was the god of which such a thing could be the image? – it was distinguished not only by its physiognomy but also the clothes it wore. They appeared wrong, somehow, in this setting, and reminded me of the sense of timelessness that had impressed me before I had entered, and of other very peculiar thoughts and feelings I had experienced when gazing through the stone arch.

The creature's atrophied legs were bare and it wore what at first appeared to be a loincloth, which I soon realised was a flannel nappy. Covering its torso was a white nightgown, stained and torn, and too small even for this runty frame. These clothes looked as if they might have been stolen from an orphan, and the moment this idea occurred to me, a nasty suspicion took root in my heart. Augmenting the impression of something simian about this being was the collar and leash, like that I had observed used to tether the monkeys of organ grinders. The other end of the leash was in the black-suited man's left hand.

As I watched, this foetid homunculus produced a tankard from beneath the table and passed it across to the man with the moustache, its manner that of skin-crawling tenderness. Its mouth twitched and wriggled into an infantile grin as if in a combination of scatological amusement and sly, bestial pride. The pallid man received the tankard and peered into it approvingly. Then he quaffed, his Adam's apple bobbing. His expression when he set the tankard once more on the surface of the table was that of a connoisseur savouring and ruminating. He took another quaff or two and then, with strangely deliberate vindictiveness, splashed the rest of the liquid in his companion's face. The creature flinched and cringed sickeningly and the man gave a short laugh.

"A taste of your own medicine," he muttered, meaningfully.

Not satisfied with this, he threw the tankard itself, which bounced off the creature's skewbald and mangy skull. It flinched again, more pathetically than before.

The man looked over in my direction, then back to his leashed companion.

"Get up! Get up!" he said, and, standing himself, walked towards me.

There was still a punter at my makeshift stall, but, half turning his head and seeing the other two approach, he hastened away. I noticed again the abrupt, bullish movements of the man with the moustache. Nothing about him seemed to flow, and yet there was a kind of precision or discipline to his manner. Even that may not be an accurate description. I had the sense that what appeared unnatural and arrhythmic to others was to him, in fact, very natural. Nonetheless, there was something of contradiction here. His outward form was stiff and inflexible, but inside he was different. It was as if he were a living version of the tankard he had just hurled at the homunculus – a solid, strong vessel containing some unknown liquid.

The creature on the leash, yanked along with unnecessary vigour, when not stumbling, crept forward in a stooped and fawning manner, all knock-kneed and pigeon-toed.

Standing before my display, the man glared at me. His eyes moved up and down, assured in their appraisal. When I first saw him, I had found his face undistinguished – the kind of face it is hard to picture when it is not present, since the features do not seem to add up to any very individual impression. The entire head seemed unformed, a kind of rough prototype. And yet, that confident, sardonic glare and those sour, contemptuous lips brought to the face a burning quality that told me that this was no run-of-the-mill human being now examining me with the same commanding detachment as that with which he examined my wares.

He picked up the items one by one, seemingly amused with what he found. His creature turned its moist eyes on me.

"Shall I sing for you?" it said.

I stared back in fascinated horror.

"Shall I sing for you?" It repeated the question, apparently puzzled at my silence.

"It seems these choice objects are not going for a song," said the moustache, with a sidelong, downward glance at the creature.

As this was happening, I heard a rapping at the door by which I had entered this place. The door must have been opened and the newcomer was admitted. There came a rasping voice – the same voice that had hissed at me only a little while previously.

"…an acquaintance of yours. Said you'd sent him."

I could not catch all that was spoken.

"Oh yes? Where is he?"

"Inside. He has no nose."

"How unusual."

"Do you know him?"

"Perhaps."

"Said Meyer had sent him."

"But who is Meyer?"

"What do you mean?"

"Never mind."

Then there emerged from the dark passageway into the ambient gloom of the smoky cavern, a thin figure in a buttoned-up jacket and a peaked cap. His eyes seemed to glow with the reflections of candle flames as he looked in my direction. Immediately he had seen me and my strange customers, he retreated to the tiny counter where the sentinel of the demijohn held vigil. Here he acquired a shot glass of something greenish and then turned to watch the unfolding transaction.

Finally, the moustache picked up the chalice, his hand extending leisurely, but his grip on it sudden. He nodded to himself and frowned, then held it up the better to catch the light. Even in that dim cellar, beneath stalactite scabs and rinds of unclean matter, there was a silver gleam that turned encrustations of the foulest colour pearly.

"What do you want for this?" he asked.

"That one's not for sale."

"Then why is it on display?"

"A mistake."

"I don't think so."

"It's an heirloom."

"Maybe so, but not yours."

"Yes. It's been in my family for a long time. That dirt is our history."

"I can believe that the dirt is yours, but I'm not buying that. Dirt is dirt cheap and in plentiful supply, and I have already more than I need."

"It's a sacred trust – we must protect the chalice, and pass it on to our children."

"But you won't be having any children, will you? I have a child here, though, on this lead. I think I'd like to pass this on to him."

"Why do you want to buy it?"

"Why don't you want to sell it?"

"I've told you."

"This is not your heirloom. How did you come by it?"

He searched my face as if to find the answer there, but I said nothing.

"You cannot have acquired it by any proper, moral means."

It seemed to me then that this person might even be some kind of policeman – he had the manner.

Then he smiled.

"But, quite frankly, I'm not a very moral person. I won't inquire into how you got this thing. I do know you've been looking for a buyer, however. I've heard of your presence here in Prague. I've even seen you. And now here you are. And here I am. So, what do you want for it?"

I grew afraid. I knew that I had, indeed, come to the end of my quest. All that was left to me of free will was to name my price.

"Beat me," said the creature on the leash. "Please beat me!"

And with its right paw it pulled down the nightgown from its left shoulder and showed where the flesh was bruised and scarred, and where a loathsome spider danced within the filmy cell of a pustulent cyst.

Immediately, the moustache dealt a strong, backhanded blow to the creature with his left fist. The creature sprawled easily upon the floor and then got to its feet again, its long, yellowish tongue licking the blood from its upper lip and probing its nostrils.

"Get to your seat," said the moustache.

The creature obeyed, and its master looked to me with eyebrows raised as if in extension of his previous question.

"I don't know why you want to buy it," I said. "It's worthless, like all this junk. It would make me laugh if you paid even ten hellers for it."

"Yes," he said nodding, "that would make me laugh, too."

He threw the coins on the table and looked me in the eye as if we understood each other.

"I've met people like you before," he said, shaking his head in contempt and disbelief. "Well, Villiers here needs a new piss-pot, anyway."

And he took the chalice and turned away. I heard a chuckling, as if that sound emanated from his black-suited back. He passed the chalice into the paws of the creature, who took it greedily, the expression on its face at once crafty and moonstruck.

"Villiers," said the man, "our desires are no longer to be denied. Let us depart."

I watched as Villiers hopped from his chair and allowed his master to lead him through the rippling smoke to the stone archway and beyond. For a while their steps sounded. Then they became muffled, and soon I could discern nothing audible from that direction, except, finally, a creak that might have been a door, then, briefly, voices, then nothing. The smoke billowed back from the arch, rolling on a draught of chill air.

I had the peculiar thought, as I watched the turbulence of that smoke, that I had understood something of the nature of corruption. It is a word that conjures up images of languid curves, of a beauty that, in being seductive, has become wicked and poisonous. The man who had just been here, however, and had left a billow of smoke in his wake, despite the rigid angularity of his spirit and his form, was undoubtedly the very soul of corruption. Its whisper lingered in the air with his departure.

I swept the last, leftover goods from the table. There should have been no surprise in the fact that all remaining to me now was worthless – empty and worthless. Such had been the predictable end of my quest from its inception.

I staggered from that den of wanton sinners, fools, lunatics and aspiring demons the way I had come. A despair had descended upon me now that was the equal and counterpart of that maniac hope that had torn me like a veil on the mountainside after her murder.

"My darling, mother, sister, child!"

I repeated this mantra of grief as I climbed the stairs again to the eternally indifferent street, warmly uncaring in its blanket of night and the mere fact of its existence.

I wept as I hobbled away from that place. In dwarfing my grief, the world itself was dwarfed. In failing to notice me, it proved its own insignificance to my soul. All that was left, therefore, was my homeless grief, and that was all I cared for.

After I had turned one or two corners, I heard footsteps. They were merely part of the world that I had forsaken and I gave them no thought until I found that I was no longer walking alone. The man in the peaked cap was now beside me. I glanced at him as I limped miserably along, but said nothing.

"Where are you going?" he asked.

I had been walking without any destination in mind, since the world, anyway, had ceased to exist except as a dungeon cell of memory and mechanical fortune.

"To the river," I said. "I want to see the river."

"Then we're going in the wrong direction," he said. "It's this way."

I made a sidelong study of the man's features while he looked ahead, navigating our route. His face was, in some ways, even closer to a skull than mine. His cheeks bore hollows that were almost scars, and there seemed little in the way of flesh between skin and bone. Blood, however, he did have. I saw it mark out his life in pulses on his temple. His eyes were stark with the same hot life, as if he drew all his sustenance through them rather than through his mouth.

"I believe I know what you just did," he said.

"What did I do?"

"You sold what has no price."

"Is it your business?"

"Perhaps. After all, I'm the one who sent you, am I not?"

"You are Meyer."

"That's right."

"Who was the other one? The one who… bought it?"

Meyer sighed as if unsure how to tell what he had to.

"No one knows for sure. He's a kind of spy, so they say. I've been watching him a little, but I feel sure it's dangerous to watch him too closely. He doesn't belong here, and he comes and goes in mysterious ways. No one knows what his purposes are, but it seems sure that of all the people who have passed through Indra's Web, looking for… all the things that people look for there, he is one who is certain to become someone. If he himself is not known by the world soon, then his deeds will be, or their consequences. His name, if names have any meaning, is Somerset-Maugham."

"What is that creature that was with him?"

"Perhaps that's even harder to say. I had a strange conversation with it once, when it was there in Indra's Web on its own. I tried to find out its relation to Somerset-Maugham. It answered readily, as if it were a kind of innocent, incapable of lying. It said it was his child. This seemed improbable, so I questioned it again, and it replied, almost like a pupil reciting a lesson, that the child is father to the man and that the man – Somerset-Maugham – was in the same way father to *it*, the child-creature."

"In the same way? It's his future."

"Perhaps."

"Is that possible?"

"Who can say what's possible?"

Night was beginning to recede from the sky. The faint tints of coming light seemed to me an intimation of vast and weary sadness.

"What have I done?" I said in terrible lamentation. "It's too late. It's too late."

We came at last to some steps leading to the ceaseless dark waters of the Vltava, and there we stood.

"It's too late," I said again. "What can be done?"

We talked for a while as the solemn dawn approached.

Meyer did not seem hopeful about the possibility of reclaiming the chalice from Somerset-Maugham.

"Let us say, then, that, here on the banks of the Vltava, we are standing in a different world than that which saw the sun rise yesterday, and that, hereafter, the rays of the sun will always be colder, and dreams will cease to be the language of the gods, but will become only the gibbering of the nervous system, like the rattling of a skeleton, let us say we have set foot in a new world; even so, we must explore it, and make what lives we can within it. We even may seem to remember a world that the devil, triumphant, has erased from time – remember things from outside of time, things that never were. To remember such things…"

But something strange was happening to me, and sometimes I could not understand the words he was speaking.

The dawn was not far off now, but a mist was thickening along the river. It seemed to me as I watched the water lapping close to my feet, one whole and one maimed, that I was not a human being at all, but had merely imagined myself to be. I was instead, a kind of piecemeal doll, something like a chest of drawers, with a drawer where my heart was, perhaps, and a mirror for a head, a clock for a stomach, one leg stolen from a chair, and another made from a bellows, a hand of clay and an upper arm of alabaster, a bookcase for my left shoulder and a birdcage for my right. I was inanimate, but had been animated by some covering of dream-flesh. That flesh now seemed to be drying up and shrinking away, so that I cracked and felt myself about to crumble.

From somewhere further along the wide, sombre flow of the Vltava there came a sound as melancholy as the cry of geese. I suppose it was the clanging of a bell on some river barge. It was as meaningless to me as the voice of the man still at my side.

Then, for a moment, I thought I understood that clanging, that funeral peal of piercing hope.

Tzimtzum. Tzimtzum.

Momentarily, the words of the man beside me, too, made sense.

"…again, still, remember I'm the one who sent you. As such I say, fate will not forget. Fate will not forget."

Then there was only clanging and mist and the sound and movement of water, growing darker.

*

When I opened my eyes, still sitting upon the stone in the garden, the scene was illuminated to me by an inner sense of strangeness. I thought of dusty Gethsemane, which I had visited as a boy, and where I had sat and watched the crawling of ants in sunlight and in shade. Then I thought of the Japanese fairy tale, 'The Dream of Akinosuke' as retold by Lafcadio Hearn. Akinosuke had fallen asleep beneath the cedar in his garden and dreamt that goblin courtiers had come to take him to the kingdom of Tokoyo, where he had wed the king's daughter and been sent to rule with her over the island of Raishu. Together they had reigned for twenty-three years, until the princess had died. When he awoke he told his friends of the dream and they advised him there was an ants' nest beneath the roots of the tree. Digging it up, they had found the topography of Tokoyo in miniature, and even the grave of the dead princess – a female ant – marked by a tiny stone.

A dream of twenty-three years…

I looked towards the leafless tree in the corner of the garden. Of course, I wondered what I would find if I dug up the soil at its roots, but I did not do more than wonder.

All that day I scratched my head and scribbled notes about dreams and fairy tales, trying to reconcile them with what appeared to be their attractive opposite – a doctrine I had found encapsulated in the two words '*amor fati*'. I came to no conclusions.

"Nonetheless, something has to change," I said, as I laid down my pen that evening.

I slept and I dreamt a vivid but relatively ordinary dream. In the dream I was going to visit a friend from university. I arrived at a sandy, mist-enshrouded beach as the gloom of evening was descending. There were rows of beach huts full of rowdy, drunken strangers. I found an old, red telephone box and made a call to my friend, but there was no answer. So I set out to find his house without guidance. When I found it, he was not there. I was let in, and waited in the front room, but he did not arrive. The girl who had let me in – one of his housemates – eventually got up to go to bed. As she did so, she said, "You can't stay here tonight." She was angry, and I realised I was not welcome. I tried to telephone my friend again, but to no avail. Finally, I assured the housemate that I just needed to collect my things together and would not be there in the morning. I'll sleep in the street, I thought to myself. She was not entirely satisfied with this arrangement, but at last agreed and went to bed. Eventually I was ready and about to step through the front door when the door of a downstairs room opened and another girl – another housemate – appeared. She asked me where I was going and I explained. "Why don't you sleep in my room?" she suggested. I appreciated her offer, but declined. I had promised the first girl I would not be there in the morning. Quite resigned to my fate, I turned to step out into the cold.

It was, indeed, cold, when I awoke the next day. I made myself a breakfast of porridge. I had switched to porridge recently, tired of the fact that the manufacturers of other breakfast cereals gave me no choice whatsoever on the question of sugar. If I wanted to eat their cereals I had to conform to what was apparently the taste of the general public – the disgusting, vulgar taste for sugar, sugar and more sugar. Gazing at my porridge in the saucepan, I thought of how I loathed human beings. As the porridge bubbled and swelled, however, I fell into a bleary-eyed daydream. I remembered the fairy tale 'Sweet Porridge', in which there was a magic pot that would not stop producing porridge. I felt I could understand where the inspiration had come from. Porridge was, indeed, a magical and monstrous food, appearing to well up from nowhere before your very eyes. As child, the thought of a world drowned in porridge by the magic porridge pot had quite distressed me.

I sat on the stiff settee in the front room, gazing at the unlit fire as I ate. My father descended the stairs behind me, bucket in hand – as I saw in the mirror above the fire – and went out through the back door. Before very long, he returned. He placed the bucket halfway up the stairs and then sat in the chair by the fire.

"Did I tell you I've got swine flu?" he said.

"Er… No."

"I have. I can feel it invading my lungs and draining my energy. What have you been working on?"

I exhaled, sighingly.

"Nothing, really."

"No special projects?"

"A few projects. Nothing special. I just don't feel motivated."

"Isn't there something you're interested in, some kind of inspiration?"

"I suppose there is. I'm just not sure anyone else is. I'm tired of horror, anyway, tired of 'the Scene'. You know, I read something the other day, someone was describing someone's writing as 'deliciously bleak'. How can you be 'deliciously bleak'? It suggests to me that the person who used that phrase doesn't actually take the bleakness seriously, and yet he wants more… like Oliver Twist. Because it's so delicious. Maybe the Oliver Twist simile doesn't work. Anyway, he wants others to produce this bleakness so he can consume it. He very clearly doesn't take it seriously – although he probably thinks he does – but he wants the author to go on taking it seriously and living a bleak life so that he can produce more of this authentic, secret-recipe bleakness. It's pathetic."

"It doesn't matter what they want. What do you want?"

"I don't know."

I continued eating my porridge for a while, and then spoke again.

"I mean, why don't they read some philosophy, or something? Take a look at the long history of human thought and spiritual endeavour that modern science flatly dismisses as not worth thinking about."

I nudged a heap of books with my toe to indicate my meaning and they collapsed onto the rug. It came to me that I had two whole feet, and I thought again of the strangeness of my own twenty-three-year dream.

Returning to my room, I was unsettled and could not concentrate on anything, so, after I had dressed, I decided to go for a walk.

Passing the tree at the corner of the garden, I thought to myself, *Nothing will change if I don't dig up what's buried there*. But what if I dug and found nothing? What then? After all, the crime had been committed in a foreign land, before I was even born. For that reason, it seemed to me, I could never escape its influence. For that reason, however much I dug, I would always find nothing.

In any case, I thought, what I need right now is a spade. As I walked, I was overcome by a feeling of almost infinite gravity – that everything might depend upon the blade of a single spade and what I did with it. What would the future be if I did not dig? What would it be if I did? How could I know which future was which, and which future did I want, anyway?

I turned down the narrow canal path. The canal itself was long since dried up and filled in, but a narrow path still ran along its route. I passed the Japanese knotweed and went through the newly erected kissing gate. In this area was a patch of ground that had often absorbed my attention. Next to the path, where once the canal had been, was something that appeared to be a separate world of its own, a kind of grove, almost like an unfinished or abandoned ornamental garden. Some juniper bushes (one grey and dying), some stringy grass, a scattering of small rocks and a clump of bamboo added to this impression. Branches overhung this world-in-miniature, and a slope of trees and ferns rose up from it on the other side from the path. Here, depending on the season and the weather, was a shallow pond. It filled and drained away very swiftly. Sometimes I would be staring at the reflections of skeletal branches in water, and sometimes I would be staring at an expanse of dried mud carpeted with dead leaves. In the early summer I had walked by when there had been water, and I had noticed the congeries of black-eyed jelly-blobs from which frogs were soon to spawn. On later days, I had dipped my hands in the water and scooped up wriggling sweet handfuls of gelatinous life. Then I spent some time away from the area. When I returned, it was passing from high summer to late. The pond had almost entirely dried up. I looked for tadpoles or frogs, but found none. The patch of bamboo made me think of Kafu, and I wondered if I could write a short, meditative piece in the Kafu style, under the title 'Tadpoles', but I never did. And I never had, since the hatching of the tadpoles and the subsequent drying up of the pond, seen any frogs in the area that might have survived from that time. What had become of them all?

I stopped now and pondered this question again. The pond had reappeared and once more disappeared, and was now a patch of leaf-strewn mud sufficiently dry to walk upon. What futures had proceeded from this now empty beginning? Maybe the majority of the tadpoles had died before reaching adulthood, picked off by blackbirds and grass snakes, turning upon each other cannibalistically and becoming stranded when the pond shrank away. Probably some did survive to become frogs, however. And these, perhaps, were mangled by malevolent grimalkins, eviscerated by cars, crushed by those who wondered why their front door was not closing tightly, picked off by herons, now, instead of blackbirds. How many lived to die of old age?

Love and happiness are portrayed in popular culture as very commonplace things – things that we have by default and only lose temporarily. The truth is rather more like that of the survival of frogs to old age. Surely, very few, if any, make it to that end. Such a truth becomes more naturally acceptable if, instead of saying "love and happiness", we say "*eudaimonia*". The word has such a ring to it, such a mythical ring – a ring like "the Holy Grail" or "the once and future king".

Looking at the parched mud, my sense of time became confused. It had been waterlogged and drained, waterlogged and drained so often that it seemed to me the events related to this patch of ground could be run in any order at all with much the same result.

The creases and furrows in the mud became, before my eyes, mountains and ravines. A wind blew suddenly. I closed my eyes and heard, from someone's back garden on the other side of the path, the tinkling of a wind-chime. There was only that sweet gust of air and the scattering of notes.

Tzimtzum. Tzimtzum.

Hanging from its wooden frame within a stone alcove, again and again the battered gong was beaten, until its vibrations became cacophony. Finally, the cords that held the gong came loose, and the gong fell noisily to the ground where it rolled a little way before collapsing like a spinning top when it loses momentum. Carved into the stone of the alcove, and now revealed by the fall of the gong, were the following words:

> *Thams cad mnyam rdzogs sgyu ma'i rang bzhin la*
> *Bzang ngan blang dor med pas dgod re bro*

> Since everything is but an illusion,
> Perfect in being what it is,
> Having nothing to do with good and bad,
> Acceptance or rejection,
> One may well burst out laughing.

> Longchen Rabjampa

The wizened hand that held the beater, its scaly fingers terminating in long, twisted fingernails, drew back, and then cast the beater aside. An old man, the hand's owner, sat in an alcove opposite that of the gong, his body twitching with spasms of laughter as if to demonstrate the truth of the inscription. He must have been crouching in his filthy niche for some time, because a number of spiders had woven their webs over his body. Now he stirred and tore the webs, and the spiders scattered over him in the primordial panic of their kind, for whom the world is nothing but a battle between different mouths and different stomachs.

The old man descended from his perch to the narrow lane of stone, his limbs as thin and delicate as those of some dying bird. The hair on his head was long, but hung in patches, like Spanish moss. Instead of a nose there was only a fungoid orifice from which dribbled green and yellow mucus. Beneath this hole, his shrivelled mouth was an almost toothless vortex of wrinkles. His shrunken frame was covered in tatters, as if he wore the ripped and scorched scraps of battle pennants scavenged from the scene of a massacre. He began to hop and lurch down the sloping lane, between the walls of rock, his gait made eccentric by the fact that one of his feet had no toes, instead ending halfway in a leprous ball of flesh. Companionable rats joined him as he went, rubbing against his ankles and threatening to trip him over. Some tinkled, apparently with silver bells that dangled from their scrawny necks. He continued to laugh, apparently delighted by their attention.

The lane debouched onto more level ground, made uneven, however, by piles of stone and by even larger heaps of carrion. Most of these were dry bones now, some remaining connected as skeletons, some separated from the atomies of which they were once integral parts. The old man paused here to sniff deeply so that the mucus wriggled like a burrowing centipede in the cave of flesh that was his nose. Once again he was delighted, the sights and smells that met him seeming to fill him with a joy that bordered upon hilarity. He danced now, and tumbled, grotesquely nimble, towards a tree that stood in the bare earth a little distance beyond the last of the charnel cairns.

Coming to the tree, he ceased his cackling, stood for some moments as if in wonder or puzzlement, and began to pace around it. The tree was slender and leafless, growing only a little taller than the man himself. From its branches there hung bones, no doubt pilfered from the near and very plentiful supply. When the wind stirred, they made a clacking sound.

In the dirt at the base of the tree had been etched the furrows of a spiral, its centre being the point at which the roots met the earth.

As if it had nothing to do with him, a tear slid down the old man's filthy cheek. Then he began to relieve himself, making sure that his cloudy urine fell into the furrows, as if to deepen and reinforce them. He stepped, crab-like, to the side, attempting to follow the spiral in an unbroken line to the centre. He laughed again now. Surely he could only have been thinking of the two bodies buried somewhere beneath those roots, one on top of the other – the female and the male.

His jet of urine faltered and died away.

He regarded the branches of the tree once more, with an expression between curiosity and reverence. It was certain, anyway, that the tree was alive, leafless and hung with bones though it was. From the end of one drooping branch there depended a fruit, slightly larger than the man's hand. Its skin was waxy, the colour ranging from yellow, through orange and brown, to red – all the colours of autumn leaves, with the freshness of spring, the colours of earth and also of fire. The shape of the fruit was that of a tetracuspid star, its six astroid rays pointing in the six directions. It was a fruit unlike any that had ever been seen before.

A single life consists mainly, it seems, of obscure little nooks, like the dark crags of a rocky coastline, receiving quiet sunlight and pouring rain with no one to witness or care. Taken together, such crags might add up to the map of a country. But the complex, fissured line of this map cannot truly be said to go anywhere, and certainly cannot be translated into language. The country might be given a name; some may even know the coastline well enough to think of that name when they see it. Who, however, can look at such a map for very long without the country disintegrating once more into the nameless crags of a line that, however it twists, can serve as a frame of reference only for absurdity and nowhereness?

Once in my life, many years ago, I visited Sado-ga-shima. It was my useless recollection of this episode that brought to my mind the image of the craggy coastline, both literally and as metaphor, and I can think of few better examples in my life of the kind of obscure biographical nook to which I refer than my visit to that lonely crag of an island.

I knew a little about Sado-ga-shima before I ever went there. The name is often shortened to Sado, which, even to the ears of the English-speaker, I think, conveys something of the character of the place, sounding, as it does, like a conflation of 'sad' and 'shadow'. In fact, the two characters with which 'Sado' is written are a rather archaic ideogram for 'help' and the more familiar ideogram for 'cross'. 'Ga' serves a function somewhat like 'of', and 'shima' is 'island'. Thus, altogether, the name might be translated as 'The Island of Assisted Crossing'. Of course, 'assisted' here is what I am tempted to think a rather Japanese euphemism, since Sado was once an island of exile.

The first recorded banishment, of the poet Hozumi no Asomioyu, took place in the year 722. His offence was to speak ill of the Emperor. The last recorded banishment was in 1700. For nearly a thousand years, it seems, Sado was an island oubliette. It was considered the ends of the Earth

– a place of no return. It was the very entrance-hall of death. Here, the exiled were as far away from life as they could be without actually crossing over that silent, stony threshold of which there is no other side. Here, sat upon that cold doorstep, there was only bodily existence, and the wait for bodily existence to end. That, I believe, was the intention – a punishment that was a blade's width away from a death penalty, as if the condemned were taken to the guillotine, but, because the blade had been lost, were obliged to sit at its foot and die of old age.

I wonder if Hozumi no Asomioyu wrote any poetry after he was exiled. I don't believe that I have read any of his poetry at all. I have, however, read more than one poem about island exile dating roughly from the era in which he lived. Here's one from Sangi Takamura:

> *Wata no hara*
> *Yaso shima kakete*
> *Kogi idenu to*
> *Hito ni tsugeyo*
> *Ama no tsuribune.*

> The plain of the sea
> And the scattered isles before me,
> As the oars creak and groan.
> O, fishermen, let her who waits
> On land for me know of my fate.

There is, I am afraid, some poetic license in my translation – the creaking of oars, for instance – that must be excused; I believe poetry is better translated in spirit than word for word. With or without such license, the poem conveys a desolate, briny loneliness. The scattered islands are like the world disintegrating on the edge of nothingness. The island in this case – to which Sangi Takamura was banished – was Okishima, but the principle is quite the same as that of Sado. I have the impression, reading this poem, that these words were the last the world heard of this unfortunate poet before he disappeared into a solemn white haze from which nothing can be retrieved.

The poetry of that age is full of the same loneliness, offering an eerie view of nature quite different to the idyllic view sometimes found in Western art and literature:

Awajishima
Kayou chidori no
Naku koe ni
Ikuyo nezamenu
Suma no sekimori.

How many nights
Has he awoken to
The cries of plover
Crossing from Awaji island,
The guard at Suma Pass?

Once again, we are at the very edge of the world, whose boundary is marked by the gateway of the pass. Beyond the pass is the infinite and hazy loneliness of wild nature, with its sounds of wave and cries of wheeling seabird. The human world is dwarfed by this cold loneliness. Even in the very capital of the human world, in Kyoto, for instance, you can feel the icy hiss of this loneliness on your skin, and in the echo of your heartbeat. The farther you go from this insignificantly tiny human centre, however, the more that loneliness seeps into your bones.

Geographically speaking, Sado is '*Nihonkaigawa*', that is, rather than being located on the Pacific side of Japan, it is on the side of The Sea of Japan. Interestingly, the effect of such a location seems to be that the island is even more desolate and ends-of-the-Earth. I suppose it's impossible to be objective about such a thing, but I am not simply promoting my personal view on the matter. Before I ever went, or dreamed of going to Sado, I remember having a conversation with a Japanese friend about the '*Nihonkaigawa*' of Japan. He asked if I had ever been to that side, and I had to admit it still lay outside my knowledge. The Pacific side, he told me, was entirely different. It was a prosperous area, as represented by the fact that the *shinkansen* ('new trunk line' or 'bullet train') stretched along the Pacific Coast, notably from Tokyo to Kyoto. The *Nihonkaigawa*, he explained, was not so prosperous. It was hard to put into words, or say precisely why, but the *Nihonkaigawa* was somehow '*kurai*', or 'dark'. It had, he suggested, something of the uncanny atmosphere of the old Japan, and, he added with a sardonic smile, when foreigners had stayed a very long time in Japan, many of them ended up crossing over to the Sea of Japan side, and settling there.

None of what I have just set down, however, formed any of my motivation for visiting Sado, or even occupied the foreground of my consciousness when the decision to visit was made. I had been studying in Japan on an exchange programme, and my brother had come to visit me in the weeks before my return to England. We visited many parts of Japan during that time, often going to those places I recommended. Sado, though, was entirely my brother's idea. That is, he had, in a way that mystified those to whom we mentioned the matter, somehow decided that he wanted to visit one of the many little islands dotted around the coast of the four main islands in the Japanese archipelago, but I cannot remember quite what the process was by which we arrived at Sado as a destination. Probably the reasons were purely practical. Although there was no real financial justification for it – rumour had it that the convenience of a government official was involved – the bullet train did run to the coastal town of Niigata, from where a ferry could be boarded to Sado.

I don't think I ever asked my brother why he wanted to go to an island like Sado, and probably it was not a question that could be answered; it was simply a fact that he wanted to. I have vague memories of sitting in a travel agent's looking through brochures and timetables. I remember enough of the brochures to recall that, not unsurprisingly, they made Sado sound a very attractive tourist resort. I imagined, after perusing them, a kind of idyllic fishing village, as one might find somewhere in the Mediterranean, with soft, coloured lights along the seafront reflected in the waves, and music wafting out onto the warm evening air from the glowing interiors of bars and restaurants in which staff and customers knew each other well and had lost all sense of time. This, I thought, would be the kind of place we discovered on Sado. I am not sure why I would imagine such a thing, since I had never been anywhere in Japan that would lead me to suspect the existence of a hidden Mediterranean paradise there. The brochures did give out, however, that Sado was unlike anywhere else in Japan, and presented the place as cheerfully rustic whilst emphasising the importance of the sea in daily Sado life. Of course, difference is far from being a virtue in Japan, and maybe I also subliminally picked up something wrong about the brochures, as if those who had produced them could not quite make the 'difference' that afflicted Sado sound bland enough.

This faintly disagreeable impression comes back to me now in the form of an image from one of the brochures. That image was of crabs. To be specific – and it is, after all, an important detail – they were spider crabs. There was nothing else in the picture, only a heaving (in my imagination) mass of red, spiky spider crabs. They filled the entire frame, as if this were only a tiny glimpse of a whole universe in which spider crabs by themselves formed a kind of shoreless and bottomless ocean, not moving in the fluid, surging manner of the seas of Earth, but with the creaky, jerking movements of those spindly, segmented limbs, their claws and shells tapping feebly against each other and creating a bony rattle that blurred into a distant roar.

I suppose that the image was meant to convey the idea of marine abundance. This was a dripping cornucopia as held in the hand of Neptune. And thinking about it now, I even have the feeling that this was one of the reasons my brother wanted to visit such an island. Even I was impressed by this and other, similar, images. I imagined us sitting in a kind of bistro amidst great platters on which there teetered mountainous piles of crabs, whose legs we had to crack between our teeth one by one, and from whose shells we had to scoop out the pulpy flesh before licking them clean. I have no idea, however, why such an image would be in any way attractive to me. Surely I must have been secretly daunted? Though quite capable of eating fish, I could by no means describe myself as a seafood gourmand. In fact, the consumption of things native to that eerie other world of the sea had always struck me as a kind of dietary perversion. On the occasions I have ventured to try that perversion for myself, I have generally had to make a concerted effort not to think about what I am eating. Often I might find myself biting into the flesh – if that is what this weird substance is called – of a prawn, only to be overcome by the previously suppressed realisation that this is a crustacean, the kin of woodlice and other such creeping things. In short, recalling the image now, rather than abundance, I find it conveys to me a kind of flesh-crawling disgust such as one might have on parting someone's hair and discovering a scalp seething with head-lice.

In any case, we made our arrangements and bought our tickets. In time we were standing on the deck of the ferry, watching the city of Niigata recede. There was so little of the seaside about it, it was as if the burgeoning grey of urban expansion and industry simply did not have enough space to accommodate it and would soon spill into the sea itself. As if signifying the truth of this impression, the water churned up in the sluggish wake of the ferry had taken on something of the filthy, lifeless grey of the city. Its green was not a sparkling aquamarine, but a murky, detergent colour, and whole fleets of litter – polystyrene cups and coke bottles – rocked in the spreading ripples, and dead rats floated belly up, as if they had found the one environment too toxic for them.

The motion of the boat in the water and the smell of the waves conveyed to me something of the romance of travel and of things maritime, and brought back obscure memories of some halcyon summer before I ever knew that the great ocean-liner matinee was not eternal, and that it was someone else's past that simply lingered in my nostrils, alternately quickening and soothing my heart, and was not my own future – before, in short, the end of the world became a part of daily existence for me. The romance chugged away in the background, like the engine of the ferry, though it was a romance polluted to dullness. After a while, the dullness in the romance became too much and we retired below deck to find some comfortable place in which to spend the crossing.

We had bought cheap tickets, so we had to try and find an empty space in an area devoid of seats, in which families had laid out picnic blankets to mark their territory, the competition being considerable. Nonetheless, we were lucky enough to find a small patch of this lower deck not already taken. We staked our claim and took it in turns to go to the toilet, or to buy food, and so on, enduring the cramp and the tedium as best we could. I remembered, once again, that what seemed picturesque and glamorous to me in theory – crossing the sea by ferry – had predominantly, in my experience, been uncomfortable and almost unbearably wearisome.

At length there was a tannoy announcement that we were approaching the island, and my brother and I went out on the upper deck once more, where the slightly queasy staleness of our journey was blown away by the fresh sea breeze. Even as the dark hump of the island grew on the horizon, time seemed to have slowed almost to a halt. The announcement of our imminent arrival had been made, but our sense of arrival was thwarted as the ferry juddered on and on interminably. Even having reached the vicinity of the island, we had to circle the coast before we came to a port. I do not have a particularly vivid memory of my first sight of Sado. I recall it now simply as a darkness looming out of the mist. There were sheer cliffs rising up to a suggestion of vegetation. Despite the fact that this was a mere speck on the map, I was impressed, as we drew closer and settled into a course parallel to the coast, by the great size of this wave-battered rock. It did not seem to be the kind of island that someone could easily walk across in a day. I felt more inclined to think of it now as a small country. However, I did not receive any impression, as yet, that the place was inhabited.

When the ferry eventually docked, this, too, was a numbingly slow procedure. I remember a mechanical hiss of slow release, and water pouring from the side of the ferry, or the dock, or both. The hydraulics of the docking procedure awoke in me, once more, a sense of glamour, though of a colder glamour than that I had felt at the outset of the journey. This was life – independent, lonely, adult life, such as I had looked forward to as a child. In childhood I had been capable of glamorising anything at all, and there was a particular glamour attached for me to any inexplicable accoutrements of the adult world. For some reason this glamour was best represented by any meeting of machinery and water, such as a dam, or a water-treatment plant I remember visiting on a school trip. I suppose the fact the world contained such complex workings, such instruction-manual detail, creating mystery out of the mundane and obscuring what was closest to our daily lives, fascinated me. Truly, looked at from an equal distance, the life of an engineer in a hydroelectric dam and the life of a comic book hero are both equally magical.

The boat had docked at a concrete wharf, a kind of artificial spar jutting out into the sea from the natural land. When eventually we descended from the boat to the wharf by a set of steps like those by which you descend to the tarmac of an airstrip, I felt as if we had come to a completely barren and isolated man-made environment, like an oil-rig. There was a small building here, which might have been a shop, or some sort of office. I suddenly felt so lost that I wondered how we would ever leave that wharf. Maybe the building was a tiny bar, with no room except for a few bar-front stools, where we would be forced to drink some kind of potato spirit, and eat crabs, while waves lashed the wharf, until the next ferry came to rescue us, if we were still alive.

"What do we do now?" I asked.

My brother did not seem in the least bit fazed. We simply had to find transport to the youth hostel where we had reserved a room. Our first task, therefore, was to locate a telephone.

The strange thing is, I have absolutely no memory of what happened next. I suppose it's not unusual to have these gaping black chasms in one's memory, but the very fact that this is common and the past is an inaccessible ruin terrifies me. I remember that for a while I was close to panic. I presume one of us must have made a telephone call, and, since I was the only one who could speak Japanese, it was probably me. However, I also have a feeling my brother took charge of the situation. Somehow or other we must have found a way – by bus or by taxi – to our lodgings, since the fact is, we did arrive. My next (or almost my next) memory of the island is of us wearily, but with some relief, stepping through the gate of a silent, sun-bathed building that it had cost us some pains to find.

In fact, finding that youth hostel had taken me back to another time. I grew up in the countryside, and I am at home with the rural. It is only in adult life that I have learned that this is not 'normal' – that is, the tenor of our age is determined by urban values and it is almost entirely urban voices that dominate our airwaves. Because of this, the country has become more a part of my identity than it was when I took it for granted. To live all one's life and to die in the city – this is a notion very strange to me, like living in a house and never stepping foot outside. But the country is always waiting, like the gate through which we finally stepped, like an old story – always waiting at life's beginning and end, or heard here and there in snatches, reminding you of where you came from and where you are going. And there the signs are fewer, the silences longer and deeper, and interaction with one's surroundings less filtered by words and machines. We simply had to find our way by walking and looking, and, if we met someone, by asking – by trusting our senses and our judgements. Such a process of looking for your destination in the country is bound to take you into country time.

This, at least, was the notion of countryside to which I was accustomed by what, after all, is a peculiarly merry green world. Nature in England – deciduous and dewy – was already half tame before the English country garden, before kings hunting boar through wooded tapestries, before druids ever treasured mistletoe. The soil gives birth to all things, and a landscape shapes a culture, as climate tempers the heart. I believe this firmly. In England, the soil naturally gave rise to Hobbiton and the Shire. In Japan… Well, that is what I hope to convey.

The silence of the untidy garden, half grown for vegetables, half for flowers, outside the youth hostel, and its rustic anonymity, which had almost caused us to enter the neighbouring gate, were to me refreshing, like something deeply known. But we had already come across evidence that this was not quite the countryside with which we were familiar. The air was a little too humid, and the vegetation tangling either side of the deserted roads we trod, a little too tropical. On our way, at the bottom of a sloping road that climbed eventually to the hostel, we had also found something that interested us. It was a vending machine for soft drinks, of the kind that is ubiquitous in Japan, reportedly even dotting the slope of sacred Mount Fuji. It stood at the corner of a hairpin bend and seemed to be in danger of being reclaimed by encroaching nature, whose green tangles were creeping stealthily around its edges. We were thirsty from our exertions and the vending machine had to us something of the mirage-like attraction of an oasis. However, it seemed we had to endure our parched throats a little longer. The machine was not in working order. This decrepitude was lent a touch of the grotesque by a detail that for some reason caught the imagination of us both. Inside the plastic display casing of the machine was a bright green frog – the kind I believe are known as '*amagaeru*' – somewhat resembling an Amazonian tree-frog. It was dead, and appeared to be stuck to the transparent casing, as if it had run out of oxygen whilst trying to find some point of egress. There was something of enigma about this vacuum-mummified frog; how had it found its way into the sealed machine in the first place?

> *Yaemugura*
> *Shigereru yado no*
> *Sabishiki ni*
> *Hito koso miene*
> *Aki wa kinikeri.*

> To the loneliness
> Of my hut, now thickly vined
> With lushly layered weeds
> No human visitor comes,
> No guest, but only autumn.

> Egyō Hōshi (Heian Period, birth and
> death dates unknown).

> *Yaemugura*
> *Shigereru Sado no*
> *Hanbaiki.*
> *Kowareshi naka ni*
> *Kawazu shinikeri.*

On Sado Island
Overgrown with creeping weeds,
A vending machine.
Nothing works; inside
A small green frog has died.

Quentin S. Crisp (1972 – ?).

The quiet wrong note struck by this discovery was temporarily forgotten when we arrived at our lodgings. The building was a rickety wooden structure of the traditional Japanese kind, with a sliding door that rattled in its groove. The interior, however, was pleasantly clean and cool, and natural light bathed a stone-flagged floor. Immediately inside was a desk that answered for a reception, and this faced a Spartan kind of common room with an old leather three piece suite. A passage led off to a barracks-style bathroom and narrow stairs ascended to the first floor. The place seemed deserted, the silence of that thick, tingling, almost tangible variety often found within old wooden buildings – a silence you seem to feel in your throat as you breathe.

Upon the reception desk was the customary bell for service, at which I tapped experimentally. We decided that if no one came we would simply sit and wait, since we were exhausted. For a while there was no response. I tapped again, a little louder. Eventually a bent old woman shuffled out from the passageway and stopped in astonishment when she saw us, apparently not used to the sight of foreigners. Since we had not reserved our rooms under a Japanese name, I had not expected such a reaction. Still, my previous experiences in Japan had been such that I was not particularly surprised, either. For a while she seemed to panic as she visibly struggled for words in English that might excuse her from the trouble of dealing with us further. I swiftly stepped in and demonstrated, not entirely without apologetic nervousness, my command of Japanese, explaining that we had, in fact, booked rooms over the telephone. The woman did not seem as impressed with my language skills as most of her compatriots, and wasted no breath on the usual flattery. At least, however, she was slightly mollified. She continued her shuffle until she had installed herself behind the reception desk, where she opened a ledger book, licked her finger and turned its pages. She had some difficulty with the unfamiliar name, but we were there, after all, and she seemed satisfied, if rather grudgingly, that we were not lying.

"You're early," she said.

"Early?"

"The rooms won't be ready until five."

"Well, can we put our luggage somewhere until then?"

"You can leave it here. But if you're going out somewhere, you must be back by nine o'clock. One of the house rules is that lights go out at nine. There's no talking allowed after nine, either, as it disturbs the other guests. Also, there's a deposit to pay. You can pay the rest when you leave. How long do you want to stay?"

I said that we wanted to stay two nights, since that was the reservation we had originally made, anyway. We paid the deposit and she proceeded to list the rules for guests, each of which came as a fresh disappointment. At last she told us that she had been "out the back" when we arrived, and that she still had something to get on with there, but she would prepare the rooms soon and let us know when they were ready.

We were tired, and it wasn't long before the time appointed for the lady to show us to our rooms, and we had not seen any nearby inn, teahouse or similar resting place on our way, so we decided simply to sit in the common room, drink something from the vending machine here, and see what the guide book said about the town where we were staying. The name of the town was Ogi. Despite the fact that this was apparently one of the main tourist centres on the island, specific information concerning what tourists might do here was scanty. There appeared to be two basic attractions here – a ride in a '*taraibune*' or 'tub boat', and a local seafood speciality in the form of some kind of giant winkle. Pictures of the *taraibune* had, in fact, been used extensively in all the tourist information we had seen on Sado. These showed women in traditional Sado costume, with what looked like a very unusual paper hat reminiscent of those in old Dutch paintings, standing in round boats like the bottom halves of beer barrels. In fact, on reflection, it seemed like all the photographs we had seen of the island had either been of the tub boat women, floating on the scintillating blue waves of Ogi harbour, or of spider crabs.

"It probably doesn't really matter that we have to be in by nine," observed my brother. "It looks like there's nothing to stay out late for, anyway."

"Well, I suppose we could just relax and have a quiet time," I ventured.

In any case, there was not much material with which we could plan an itinerary, so we decided simply to 'explore'.

Just as we had come to this decision, we were slightly heartened by the unexpected appearance of another human being. It seemed there were other guests here, after all. Or, at least, there was one. He was apparently returning from some excursion and stopped in the common room to talk to us. In fact, he seemed to be in no hurry at all. He was dressed in T-shirt and jeans with a kerchief on his head, like a drifter from some American film. He had one of those faces you think you've seen before somewhere, and reminded me, in fact, of the various grebo misfits I had hung out with at school. When he realised that I spoke Japanese, he settled down into the armchair as if he intended not to move from the spot again, and began to peel long strips of dead skin from his arm.

After I had given a cursory account of who we were and how we had ended up in Sado, he began his own story, punctuated by long, leisurely pauses as he peeled off yet another strip of skin and laid it carefully next to its predecessors on the arm of the chair.

"I'm actually a salaryman, or I was. You wouldn't think it, would you? But salarymen like me do actually exist… sometimes. Anyway, I packed all that in. To go travelling. I've come all the way up the *Nihonkaigawa* side of Japan from Kyūshū. It's taken me, well, a few weeks so far. Well, your Japanese is pretty good, so I suppose you've been here long enough to know that you can't take a few weeks off work in Japan. Never. Not unless you take the rest of your life off. If you quit, that's it, no turning back. The fact is, I don't really know what I'm going to do when the money runs out. I've been saving up for a long time, but I think I must have used up half of my savings already. Or, well, at least a quarter. Anyway, for the moment I'm just going to keep on going, till there's no road ahead. I can't help it. I just love travelling, you see."

And he pulled off one more strip of skin as if completing preparation for some final act. Then he looked up and smiled.

"And now I've ended up here on Sado-ga-shima, like you. Life is strange, don't you think?"

I concurred with this view, though the commonplace idea that life is strange was beginning to seem rather problematical to me. Since life is everything, or all we know, then to say that life is strange is to say that everything is strange, and if everything is strange, then how do we know, since we have nothing normal with which to compare it? And yet, of course, life *is* strange – inevitably so. There can be a comforting hint of destiny or synchronicity in the idea of strangeness, but there can also be the opposite of this – something terribly alien and unknown. Perhaps these opposites are one thing. In which case, the word strange is rendered meaningless. And yet its meaning remains, or is eternally reborn. In any case, in this context I found the word to be somehow inappropriate, or inadequate.

The man had now placed a packet of cigarettes and a lighter on the armchair, but otherwise showed no sign of intending to smoke. At the time I was attempting to give up, but seeing the cigarettes was like feeling the tug of a hook in my flesh. However, until he actually lit up I felt unable to ask for one. I tried to distract myself with other questions.

"So, have you seen any of the sights on this island?"

He laughed and shook his head.

"How long have you been here?"

"A few days."

"Is there anything you can recommend seeing or doing?"

"There's the goldmine," he said.

"Have you been there?"

"No."

"I see. Well, we're thinking of going out for a meal later. Do you know anywhere good?"

"There should be somewhere to eat down by the harbour."

At last he took a cigarette from his packet and lit it. I looked on like a dog begging for a scrap at a dinner table, but he seemed oblivious as he blew the blue-grey smoke into the tinglingly still air. His obliviousness formed an impenetrable forcefield around him, which the smoke seemed to make almost visible, like a thin shaft of light intersecting its coils. We spoke a little more, our conversation seeming to tread water within the subject matter of the man's road to nowhere.

After finishing another cigarette or two, the traveller stood and took his leave, saying that he would see us later. In the end, I never asked him for a cigarette. The air cooled and darkness began its stealthy, almost imperceptible infiltration of the day. Eventually the old lady returned from "out the back" or wherever it was she had been attending to her business, and announced that the rooms were ready. I had the impression that whatever she had been doing, it was nothing to do with our rooms, and that these had been ready all along, although I suppose that was a ridiculous notion. In any case, the old lady now led us up the creaking, narrow staircase to a narrow corridor with sliding doors leading to rooms on each side. We were given rooms opposite each other. These rooms were almost entirely bare, matted with tatami in the traditional style. The ceilings were low, and sloped on one side. There were no windows. Neither room contained anything other than bedding and light fittings. In other words, they were cupboards in which to sleep.

The old lady repeated the rules she had already listed, adding a few more for good measure, and left us to our own devices. We settled into our separate rooms. I slid the door of my room closed, took out a few personal items from my bag, and, after surveying the bare box of a room, lay down upon the futon that had been spread upon the floor. At first I felt something like freedom. No, it was not exactly freedom. It was more like the security of knowing that at least we had somewhere to stay for the night. However, it did not take me very long at all to feel that there was something altogether unpleasant about lying there like that, on a flimsy futon in a low-ceilinged, windowless room in a youth hostel on Sado-ga-shima. I cannot explain it. My brother seemed intent on having a nap in his room, so I tried to do the same. I found myself restless. I could not read, either. Eventually I managed a shallow, uneasy sleep. I was glad to be woken at last by my brother, who had now showered and was ready to go out. I was ready, too.

It must have been at least seven by the time we actually hit the town. I say this because it was dark when we set foot outside the youth hostel door. It was August when we visited, and seven o'clock more or less marks the end of daylight in late summer in Japan. This deduction is rather surprising to me, since I had imagined we had gone out earlier. Reconstructing events logically in this way leaves me with the impression that life does not really make sense. It does not fit, for instance, into the timeframe in which it must have taken place. It does not add up. To give an example, the fact that we only had four hours of freedom at the hostel, when we were actually allowed in our rooms and did not have to sit or lie in darkness, was blatantly absurd.

In any case, despite the fact that the old lady at the youth hostel clearly had some kind of vendetta against life, we headed townwards in a cheerful fashion, as if we might get a little taste of the life she hated in the narrow window of time our curfew had left to us.

I had been careful to acquire directions to the seafront from the traveller earlier, and we followed these away from the hostel and down the hill on which it stood. At first we were re-treading the now familiar roads by which we had come, on either side of which grew the eight-fold weeds (*yaemugura*) of the old poems. However, we eventually made a turning onto what appeared to be Ogi's main street, the road here lined by shops rather than foliage. We had only taken a few steps down this street, however, before we began to feel that something was wrong. This feeling increased with each step we took. We had been looking for places to eat and drink, but while the buildings on each side generally had the kind of glass frontage associated with commercial establishments, there was not a single light on anywhere to indicate that any were open for business. Moreover, the entire street was utterly soundless. We neither saw nor heard another human being, either inside the buildings, or on the street outside. This state of affairs was somewhat alarming, for a number of reasons, not least of all because we were beginning to lose hope of actually being able to eat that evening. Added to this was our confusion at the sheer strangeness of it all. The buildings did not look especially broken down or decrepit, though they were certainly old and pokey. They should have been inhabited. Yet even when we stopped and strained our ears, we heard nothing, and even when we scoured the upper storeys of the two uniform lines of squat buildings, we saw not a single gleam of light from a window, or the dimmest flickering behind a reed blind. Had everyone already gone to bed? This seemed unlikely. But if they had not gone to bed, where, exactly, *had* they gone?

The sense of mystery was such that it occupied all our conscious thoughts. We stopped here and there and tentatively approached the windows of some of the unlit shops in the hope that they might furnish us with some clue as to the nature of the mystery. Closer inspection confirmed what we had already deduced – the shops were shut up and devoid of human activity, with the possible exception of sleep. Other than this our examination illuminated the darkness of the mystery not at all. In fact, some of the shops provided a mystery of their own. I remember one whose gloomy interior my brother first peered into.

"What is it?" I asked.

"I don't know. It looks like a shop selling nuts and bolts."

I stepped closer. Beyond the glass was something like a bicycle repair, or similar, workshop, but devoid of any large items to show exactly what was being worked on. There were boxes and boxes of nuts and bolts, and other parts, and scraps of metal, and the filthy floor was covered in iron filings, but what larger whole these parts might belong to was impossible to say.

"Maybe there's a large demand for nuts and bolts here," I said.

"Must be, I suppose."

We decided, anyway, that we should press on to the seafront, in the hope that somewhere there were human beings in the town, and that some of them might be able to offer us food.

As we drew nearer to the end of the street, we began to realise that the night was not as silent as we had at first believed. There came to our ears now, with increasing volume and distinctness, the booming of drums. These were, specifically, the Japanese drums known as *taiko*, which are sometimes bigger than the *taiko* player, their skins presented vertically in the manner of a great gong. Theirs was a resonance greater and more potent than that of the brittle, military drums of a Western marching band. They seemed to echo back from the very recesses of the night, as much a part of the sky as the clouds and the stars and the unfathomable chaos of darkness in between. It was as if the bestial night were performing some primal dance too dark for human eye to see, so that it could only be known to humans by the sounds of its heartbeat, and the rippling of its muscles, and its thudding feet.

The street as such came to an end, and buildings gave way once more to *yaemugura*. The road twisted, and with each twist the beating of drums became less muffled until we realised that the drums were not beating at the resounding back of the night, but that they were here before us. There was a wall in which was set a gateway. The gateway was wide open and disclosed to us a long building set in dusty grounds. The large doorway of this building was also open, and from this came the first significant artificial light we had seen since leaving the youth hostel. The building appeared to be something like a gymnasium, with smooth wooden floor and no furniture. I guessed that it was attached to a school, and that this was the edge of the school premises. I could even see one or two human figures, young men in uniform purple tracksuits. They were clearly at the very edge of a larger group, since they were not drumming, but stood witnessing what was taking place beyond our field of view, inside the building.

The drumming went on and on, deep and relentless as the dark, bloody rhythms of the body.

Of all that I remember about Sado-ga-shima, this memory is especially vivid. There is the ascetic gymnasium atmosphere, which forbids relaxation, a sobriety of sweat and wood polish. There is the yellow light from the open door, spilling out onto the dust of the grounds. (Physical training in the early morning and after dark speak of the pains or the pleasures of discipline, but the melancholy tiredness with which one must battle is a different melancholy and a different tiredness at night than it is in the morning.) There is, in addition to the artificial light, a greenish tinge in the night, seeming to creep upwards from the ground towards the sky. This tinge makes me think of the dead frog and the feverish *yaemugura*, although it is also a metallic, seemingly unnatural tinge. And there is, moreover, a kind of scent in the air. I call it a scent, but I really hardly know which sense is responsible for this impression. Perhaps it is a combination of senses that make up a consistent synaesthetic experience throughout Japan. I think of it as the scent of Japanese summer. I want to call it an ionized scent, although I am groping with such a description. It is like a spray of pine needles in the sun, although it is not exactly a pine scent. Although I have experienced the scent in dusty, shabby places, it is a kind of sheen, as if everything has been scrubbed and purified like the grounds of a Shinto shrine. It is like an olfactory mirage in a desert of all that is forsaken and forlorn, like an invisible rainbow of freshness thrown up by something deeply rotten.

"What are they doing?" asked my brother.

"Practising."

"Practising for what?"

"I don't know. Just practising."

"Do you think everyone in the town is here?"

"I don't know. Maybe. There must be other people, though."

Considering the number of buildings in the town, it seemed unlikely that all the inhabitants could fit comfortably into this one gymnasium. And yet, standing there I felt, for a while, as if there was indeed nothing but this, no other light in the world and no other human sound – just the drumming and the darkness, the drumming *because* of the darkness, because of the silence. After all, if you lived on Sado, what would you do? What else could there be to do except beat out an endless rhythm on *taiko* drums?

We certainly were not going to approach the building in which the drumming was taking place, so eventually there was nothing for us to do but continue on our way with the drums echoing behind us. At last we came to the harbour and the sea, but it was beginning to look as if my brother was right, and that the gymnasium now housed all the inhabitants of the entire town. There were buildings here, but none of the soft, coloured seaside lights I had imagined before coming to the island. There was no music wafting from warm bistros, and no sound of lively voices or spilling of yellow light. There was silence and there was darkness. A quay extended into the lapping waves as if waiting for ships, but all was sleeping a desolate sleep now. Traffic had ceased, and with it expectation was extinguished. There were, instead, hulking shadows, like the ashes of dead fires in a disused engine room. The wind from the sea made me shiver. Imagine, I thought, reverting to an image that had occurred to me when we had first arrived, spending the night on the deck of this oil rig with no human company. That is how the coldness of the sea wind made me feel.

For a while I was convinced we would go hungry that evening, but with no other demands on our time, we continued to walk the barren deck of the town until we noticed a faint reddish glow a little way up the hill we had just descended, along a previously unexplored road. We approached, and the relief was like warmth in winter when we discovered that this was, indeed, a place to eat, and, what's more, that it was open for business. Ogi was a normal human settlement, after all. At least, if it was not exactly normal, there was a great and reassuring difference between no places to eat at all and one such place. And the truth was, it did seem to be the only place in the entire, graveyard-silent town that was open. It was an *izakaya* – one of the traditional Japanese places for eating and drinking. The interior was cramped and dim – about the size of a bedsit flat. There was a tiny bar, with room only for one or two stools in front of it, and three or four low tables at which customers could sit cross-legged. However, we appeared to be the only customers. The proprietor, a rather thin, ill-looking man with a patchy growth of beard, was not unpleasant, but spoke and moved in such a subdued manner it was as if he were in mourning, or as if he wished to conduct his business in secret. Despite the great relief of having found a place to eat – which was, indeed, considerable – the meal turned out to be quite joyless. The proprietor's hush infected everything. The food, too, tasted somehow stale. I recall an experience similar to eating cold leftovers.

I almost believed the food had been dampened by the proprietor's tears as he prepared it for serving. There were boiled vegetables and fried tofu, and I remember little else. The menu, apparently, had been far from inspiring. The meal was only enlivened slightly by the warm sake we ordered.

So ended the evening's entertainment, and, indeed, the entire day.

I seem to recall that we had worried, at some point, that we would be unable to keep our curfew, that we would have to cut short some fascinating or otherwise engrossing activity in order not to displease the sour mistress of the youth hostel. We discovered, when we left the miserable little *izakaya*, that we needed entertain no such fears. It seemed as if we would arrive back at the youth hostel in good time, and even if we had wished to defy the draconian rules of that place, we would have been hard pressed to find a means of doing so without simply lingering on some cheerless corner in the dead dark of the night. In the end, it seemed, the curfew was immaterial.

As we made our way back, wondering all the while exactly what was wrong with this island, we heard the continued sound of the taiko drum, becoming now fainter, now louder, according to where we were in relation to the source of the booming rhythm and to the direction of the wind. Eventually we arrived at our lodgings. I suppose we had nothing to talk about, or no desire to talk, since we retired to our separate rooms. I turned out the light and wondered how long it would take me to get to sleep. I felt as if I had been prostrated, pushed upon my back by some desolation in the night that told me there was nothing else I could possibly do but lie here. I do not believe there were other guests, unless the traveller we had met earlier was in his room, though there was no sign of his presence. The injunctions to turn out the light and make no noise seemed as superfluous as the curfew. At some point sleep must have crept into the darkness, silent and unseen.

We woke early in the morning, in good time to vacate our rooms. After some discussion, we decided to run away. We had reserved the rooms for two nights, but to spend another night in that joyless place seemed like self-inflicted punishment. We would make the best of the time we had, and risk having nowhere to stay in order the better to explore whatever possibilities this island had to offer. I was, at first, very uncomfortable about breaking our word and fleeing in this manner. For some reason it seems to be a foible of mine to be bothered by such scruples even in cases such as this, when I am unlikely to meet the other – possibly offended – party again for as long as I live. I consider it a weakness. Still, I was not alone in my misdemeanour on this occasion, and when we stepped through the front door, apparently unseen and with all our luggage, I felt an uprush of something thrilling – a sense of liberation. In any case, we left enough money on the reception desk to cover the very brief period of our stay.

As we walked we discussed our plan of action further. First we would go back to the seafront, just to see if the town of Ogi was any different during the day. Then, after sampling what it had to offer, we would pick another destination on the map of the island, perhaps try and reserve lodgings somewhere there, though we were wary about this now, and then leave Ogi behind us. After our experience of the previous evening, we did not allocate a great deal of time to our enjoyment of the town this morning. The town held, as the guidebook said, two attractions, and neither of them promised to take up much of our time. When we passed the school and the seafront came into view, we discovered that there was, indeed, human life in the town. What memory presents to me is the following picture: I am standing, with my brother, on the shoulder of the hill, just above the harbour. Where the hills end there is a flat area containing a few shops that last night were darkened shells. These shops are grouped together, and form something resembling a large conservatory, the glass of windows being ribbed with the white of frames. Adjacent to the shops is a more or less open space which might be a car park, a place for smaller boats during the winter months, or something else entirely. The scene is not exactly bustling with people, but it is at least *stirring*. It is as if a successful resort has suffered some catastrophe that has greatly thinned the number of inhabitants and visitors, but both groups remain, rather listlessly enjoying the sunshine, numb with shock and forgetful of exactly what has happened to bring them here and to take away someone who perhaps was with them yesterday.

On the waves of the harbour a strange thing can be seen. There is a fleet of boats circling continuously. The word 'boats' seems something of a misnomer. They appear to be taller than they are long, and to be round in shape. As a form of transport they are ridiculous – like pogo-sticks. The pilots of these craft are doughty middle-aged women with the build of those used to hard work. They all wear the same costume – a kind of peasants' garb with white paper hats like those in old Dutch paintings. However, the

146

costumes look new and stiff, as if they have just been hired from a shop specialising in fancy dress. These women are not going out to sea for the sake of any aquatic harvest. The circles they turn again and again further testify to this fact. However, it does not look as if they are performing any practical function from a tourist point of view, either. The circles they form are very small – perfunctory – and their boats appear to be empty. Who, indeed, would want a ride in one of these tubs, piloted by this endangered tribe of costumed peasant woman? What silent curse are they under that compels them to continue in this task? Surely it is the aura of that curse that frightens customers away, if there are any potential customers in the first place? The women continue to propel their vessels sadly around the little patch of water, wrestling crazily with the poles that answer for oars, and also possibly for rudders, making circles with them as if mixing dough, and perhaps in this sorcerous way stirring themselves round and round in the same circles. The air is clear and the details of this scene seem small rather than distant. It is as if there is no intervening distance at all, no gloss or patina of air, just cold and perfect clarity and hereness. The only blurring of the scene comes from the golden scintillation of the waves, which here and there dazzles, and half-obliterates the strange vessels and their pilots. Despite this clarity, there is one sign of the distance – the utter silence. It is as if all sound has been erased like chalk from an old blackboard. The golden scintillation of the waves is the quintessence of this silence. At intervals, on the wind, there come tiny, powdery gusts of voice and sound, out of time with the silent movement of what can be seen.

I don't believe we were even tempted to take a ride in one of the boats. Almost immediately the harbour had come into view, we had eliminated one of the town's two attractions from our plan of action. All that remained was the giant winkles, and we were, anyway, in need of food. Soon we were mixing with the dazed, listless people we had seen from the distance of the hill's shoulder. We approached the group of shops. Some were gift shops of the kind you seem to find at seaside resorts the world over, selling the most worthless trinkets ever devised by human beings. There was also a café of sorts. All of it, bright though it appeared in the sunlight, was bright and *blanched*. And faded. And even a little mildewed. In the café, on the menu, we found what we had been looking for – the giant winkle. Others were also consuming this unusual dish. Actually, it did not look at all appetising. It sat in a bowl of sauce like a turd-brown scoop of ice-cream. We finally ordered it out of the kind of curiosity that makes some people wish to handle tarantulas. There were no pleasant surprises in store for us. The unfortunate shellfish were billed and presented as if they were the food equivalent of gold, and the nacreous colours at the mouths of their shells seemed to promise treasure hidden within. In fact, I felt as if I were eating earwax. I have very little memory of eating anything on the island. In retrospect this bothers me. The only meals I remember are the one that had been marinated in tears, and this one.

Soon enough our duty was done and we had experienced all that Ogi had to offer the world. Now we just had to find our way out of Ogi and go somewhere else.

We looked for a bus stop. The guide book suggested there were buses, so presumably there was a stop somewhere, or maybe even a station. After a fruitless search of the immediate area, we decided to ask directions. From one of the roads leading up into the hills there appeared a lost-looking woman with a tray, such as used to be carried by usherettes at cinemas, hanging from her neck. She was a pedlar, it seems, though even she gave the impression that she was unsure of this. Her tray seemed to contain an accumulation of concentrated novelty and tinsel, as if all the fun and colour that was missing from the town had been stealthily poached, the great, slaughtered portion of it incinerated, and the horns, claws, teeth and tails, and all such lifeless extremities of it, had been gathered here for sale. There were rubber monsters, spinning tops, paper dragons and the like. The road from which the woman had come looked deserted. I wondered who her customers might be. A kind of solicitous desperation took hold in her face as we approached. Trying to ignore the tray, I asked if there were a bus station hereabouts. She said that there was, not far, and gave directions. Immediately she had finished she asked if we might be interested in any of her merchandise. Some of these items were good quality, traditional Japanese toys. I had to make a quick decision. I apologised and declined, hurrying after my brother in the direction she had indicated.

After this my memories become very fragmentary. Some of these fragments, however, have retained a vividness and a fascination that have proved sufficient motivation for the writing of this account some ten years after the events in question. I hope that the fascination of these fragments will supply a satisfactory gravitas to my story despite possible disintegration of narrative coherence.

Since Ogi was more or less located at the southernmost point of the island, we undoubtedly headed north. I am not sure exactly what destination we first had in mind. It must have depended largely upon a very limited choice of bus routes. I can dredge up a few clues from the murky bed of my memory, though how reliable these clues might be I cannot say. For one thing, I have a sense we discovered that no matter how we schemed to hop from one bus to another, we could not get from the southernmost to the northernmost tip of the island within one day. The town of Washisaki, for instance, was therefore out of range for us. This was not really a problem of distance, but of infrequent buses and inconvenient bus routes. I seem to recall that we first went in the general direction of Aikawa, which lies on the west coast, facing away from the Japanese mainland and towards the continent of Asia, at a latitude approximately marking the island's mid-point. We had decided not to book a room anywhere yet, but to see first what things were like wherever we arrived. My brother, probably correctly, assumed that if there were any places of lodging where we went, they would be as empty as the place we had just fled. Because of our uncertainty with regard to lodgings, our activities took on a kind of fugitive urgency. It was almost as if we were being pursued. We had to make clipped calculations for the sake of our survival.

I remember alighting at one town in particular, to scout it out and see if it might be a suitable place to stay. The bus station itself was reassuringly similar to a great many bus stations I had seen in Japan and, despite the fact that repairs were in progress, and tape barriers, such as those erected by policemen around the scene of an incident, were in place, it had a calm air as of faded summer holidays from the seventies. The place was nearly deserted, however. A couple of men in uniform lounged around in the cabin of their office, on the outside wall of which were raised, cut-out ideograms in reflective gold, on which the sunlight flashed blindingly. My brother seemed to be making calculations again. We walked away from the station, after verifying that there would be further buses that day, and, anxiously aware of time passing, set out on our exploration. We found residential buildings, and silence. We met no one. This town did not appear run down, merely sterile, betraying no signs of publicly shared life. If there was any life here, it was so private as to be inaccessible. Each of the bungalow buildings seemed entirely separate from the others, with no communication between them.

We came to the edge of the buildings. There was a thin and featureless strip of beach, and there was the sea, hissing and shushing back and forth as if recycling the silence of the land. The salty decay of the sea breezes had set to work on the nearest buildings, eating into their timbers and paint with the white corrosion of its invisible, saw-like teeth.

Two things distinguish this town in my memory. From the grill of a roadside drain there crept one of the most hideous spiders I have ever seen. It was a malignant reddish colour, like blood mixed into milk, its limbs and thorax shiny, its abdomen fuzzy. I have encountered this species before on occasion, and have seldom seen any living thing more likely to trigger the reflex to vomit. I believe that the species is *dysdera crocata*. It is quite rare and I do not know its common name. This specimen caused me some alarm as it dragged its scab of a body across the tarmac. Not only did it look intrinsically unnatural, like something so poisonous it should cancel out its own existence, but its thing-that-should-not-be-ness was further emphasised by the barren surface over which it crawled. I was surprised that there was any life here at all and wondered aloud what it could possibly find to feed upon.

The second thing is that we discovered a public telephone and immediately took advantage of this to make telephone calls to the outside world. I remember speaking to the mother of the homestay family with whom I first stayed in Japan, realising that I could neither ask for a rescue team to be sent out nor explain in any way the strange atmosphere in which we were caught. The reason for the 'phone-call must have been very unclear. No doubt she believed it was instead of a postcard, despite my lame repetition of the fact that the island was strange.

In any case, we were not to stay in this town, either, and soon returned to the bus station. After that there was an ever-growing sense of panic in our search for a place to stay. We alighted at another bus stop, this one in the middle of nowhere. We must have been searching for a particular town, or a connecting bus. The bus stop sign was battered and rusty, and if we had not just arrived there on a bus, I would have doubted that it still marked part of a running route. The road was silent and empty now that the bus was gone, and already I was regretting our getting off, though it would not have taken us anywhere we wanted to go. On either side of the road was a flat area of dried up, beaten-down grass, extending to trees and thickening undergrowth, and a few forlorn relics of human habitation. Having nothing else to do, we walked. We found more vending machines, but none to satisfy our thirst. Some were no more than rusty shells under twisted swathes of twining weed, half-green, half-grey, as if one half had choked the other to death. Others still looked as though they might work, despite the algae green of their sides, but none of them did. In one we discovered another vacuum-sealed frog, proving the first had not been an isolated incident.

As we trudged, my brother wondered aloud what had happened to the many tourists who had crowded the lower deck of the ferry with us. Ours had by no means been the only ferry that day. Load after load of tourists were, in theory, being disgorged upon the shores of this island. Where were they?

"Perhaps what's happened is," he postulated, "that they all had cars, and that when you come to Sado what you do is just drive around looking at the scenery and then go back."

I don't think either of us were convinced by this hypothesis.

Another mystery was the great number of cemeteries we saw. Some of them seemed to be located more or less randomly, away from human habitation, on a patch of waste ground, or peeping out from a tangle of low trees. To an imagination already a little excited by the general weird conditions reigning on the island, it almost seemed as if this was an island for the dead. The cemeteries were the real towns for which this island was home, and those places housing living people were merely the quarters of the caretakers. If so, the caretakers had been neglecting their duties much of the time.

We did not take many photographs on the island; I seem to have two in my possession. One shows my brother walking between two sandy tussocks of dune grass. He is wearing a straw hat to keep off the sun, a short-sleeved silk shirt and short trousers, giving a slightly incongruous impression – incongruous to my memory of Sado, that is – somewhere between a stereotypical tourist and a 'great white hunter' in a pith helmet. The other photograph gives a glimpse of a cemetery surrounded by trees. I had the feeling while we were there that perhaps a tour of these cemeteries would reveal the true riches of the island, and that we might find some of the most fascinating or otherwise exemplary burial sites in the entire archipelago. This impression, however, may have been unfounded, based as it was only on such glimpses as that captured in this photograph. One thing strikes me upon reflection – these cemeteries were the least desolate parts of the island. That is, the glimpses we caught of them actually seemed to provide some kind of relief from the general loneliness. It was being alive on Sado that was spectral, I thought, not being dead. The former state was not merely 'quiet desperation', but desperation with its tongue cut out. No tongue was a match for the silence, anyway. What if Hamlet had thought of taking arms not against a sea of troubles, but a sea of silence? This feeling was beyond all desperation. Desperation shrivelled when exposed to its endless emptiness. After such silence, the only relief seemed to come from another kind of silence, perhaps greater, perhaps merely different, perhaps… perhaps the same silence inside-out. It was that different texture in the hush that I seemed to sense when we passed the cemeteries, like a finer, smoother sand.

Perhaps to convey a little of what I mean it would be judicious to give some general description of Japanese cemeteries. The Japanese grave is typically quite different to the English. Instead of leaning, lichen-covered slabs to mark the graves, there are stelae, little monoliths somewhat in the shape of Cleopatra's Needle. In my experience, these are generally very clean, and even shiny. On the stones are inscribed vertically the names of those interred. I believe I am correct in saying that often this is the Buddhist name bestowed upon a person posthumously. The name is also sometimes inscribed upon a strip of wood, called a '*sotoba*' or '*stupa*', which is placed in a stand next to the stele. Beneath the stele, in the crypt, is placed the urn containing the cremated remains of the deceased. An English graveyard is typically a ragged sort of place, a place characterised by uncut grass and the smell of soil. As well as being a place of death, it is a place of life – the wormy, muddy life that to some seems the very essence of nature. Here decay is messy and fertile. Just as time gnaws at these weathered stones, and knots of grass flourish, one can imagine putrefaction gnawing at the corpses below, and knots of oozing life flourishing where the outline of the human form has burst or been eaten away.

The Japanese grave, in the Japanese cemetery, seems to convey nothing so messy, nothing so fertile. The decay is of a different kind. Cremation has bypassed the stage of putrefaction. Even in cases where the graves are neglected and the connoisseur may quietly delight in a subtle aspect of encroachment by nature that speaks of abandonment – the ecotone of stilted air between human artifice and the creeping wild that for humans always signifies decline – there is not quite the unruliness of the lush grass found in some English burying grounds, and decay is typified not by damp, dark, pungent earth, but by dust and ashes. It is the decay of emptiness, as if this dust were slipping through the waist of an hourglass and dissolving into nothing. The influences here are Shinto, in which purification through ritual cleaning plays a significant role, and the previously mentioned Buddhism. It seems apt that life is not conspicuous in the Japanese cemetery, and that there is no flesh for the graveworm to feast on and hatch from, since the final aim of Buddhism is not to be born again, either in this world or the next, but to be extinguished entirely, and have no more to do with cycles of life.

What fine, fine, silky dust is here, purified of all life! There are no pillows of green grass on which to dream of a pastoral heaven. More than any other place of burial, the Japanese cemetery is a citadel of death, a terminus of utter oblivion, its vanishing point of emptiness forever sterile and serene. And with its tower-like stelae, often terraced at different levels, it also looks more like a city than any other cemetery. Even the most neglected examples I have seen had not become stinky, swampy ruin of the kind from which zombies might rise. Instead, they were dry as an empty cobweb, and particles in the dust glinted with the sunlight like the tiniest of diamonds. All was as if artfully arranged in an old film studio to suggest the passage of time. In the first episode of the film *Kwaidan* – an episode called 'Shadowings' – a samurai returns after many years to the wife he had abandoned. He finds all as he left it, and her, dismally, eerily lonely, waiting for him. He spends the night with her, but in the morning finds that everything has changed. Dry bones, cobwebs – the devastation of years seems to have come in a single day, and everything crumbles at his touch. This is what I was reminded of when in a Sado-ga-shima cemetery I saw a leaning ear of *susuki* – eulalia grass – separated into fine, beaded threads, on which there were reflected the rays of the sun, and watched a white butterfly, weird as a creature of animated paper, flit by with a flapping that seemed to suck the sound from the air, and land upon a desiccated leaf. In such a place, even if the spirits of the dead did linger, it could only be as wispy fireflies, or sad dreams that come like malicious tricks. Sad dreams… In the old days, in Japan, the word for 'dream' did not have the positive associations it has in the West, but meant only an illusion, not to be trusted.

Such were the cemeteries whose empty serenity seemed the only antidote to the loneliness and fear that hissed everywhere else in the silence of Sado-ga-shima.

After much walking, we came to a settlement. Such an archaic-sounding term does not seem inappropriate, not only because there were so few buildings here that the word 'village' becomes almost extravagant, but also because of the general aspect of those buildings, dark and dilapidated. This was what in Japanese was called a '*buraku*', I thought, from which there came the word '*burakumin*', describing the seldom-mentioned 'untouchable' caste of Japanese society. The old roof tiles looked ready to be buried beneath a litter of fallen leaves, in which they would be so inconspicuous as to be camouflaged. There was an area of dusty earth with scrubby patches of grass and weeds and then a ramshackle edifice with a gaping darkness opening abruptly beneath its heavy, solemn eaves where a door should be. To the left of this house were others like it, leaning together unevenly, and seeming to give off such a miserable miasma of concentrated age and darkness that it threatened to dye the entire scene sepia. They receded in a kind of terrace, as grim as the faces of the working poor in old, old photographs of colliery villages. To the right lay another congeries of such buildings, but this in a sagging huddle rather than a sagging line. There were also some low, straggly trees here, and a thicket of bamboo surrounding a small cemetery, a little blanched, perhaps, by the salt breezes from the nearby sea, which was visible beyond the houses, the trees and the cemetery. Mindless and blue, the waves reflected the sunlight like the natural, moving callousness of which the dark roof tiles were artificially petrified versions. We approached the house whose inner darkness gaped towards us, wondering if someone might be at home and hoping to ask for directions. We stood before the threshold and I called out a questioning greeting. There was silence. I called again, and now there was a shuffling sound. From the darkness there appeared a shockingly wizened crone with filth ingrained in the deep creases marking her face. She swayed and yawed as if not entirely sure where she was going or why. Coming to a halt just outside the doorway, she looked at us with yellowed and clouded eyes, her lips gurning in incessant wordless gabble, showing, at intervals, the toothless gums behind them. Remembering my purpose, and not wishing to appear rude, I asked for directions. Now words issued from those moving lips.

"What's she saying?" asked my brother.

"I don't know."

I could not tell whether this were some strange dialect of Japanese, or whether it were a species of gibberish unique to the old woman, though I seemed to catch words here and there. I tried asking different questions, but it was useless. I looked at my brother, as if for rescue. My dilemma was ended when the woman slumped down on the threshold of the house, still making those sloppy gabbling noises through her gurning lips. She seemed to have given up on us, to be no longer aware of us. We could move away. Before we did so I had time to wonder vaguely what we had been to the old crone, how we had figured in her experience, and what it was she was so pathetically intent on explaining, or perhaps asking. There must have been specifics to her story somewhere, however lost they had become. I peered into the darkness of the house as if I might find there some clue. But I saw nothing. I only had a sense of some ultimate and horrible intimacy, as if to step over the threshold and into that darkness were the same as passing those lips into the foul-smelling cavern of her throat and to the place where her unseen insides were rotting, turning to a lethal silage of rheumy liquescence. Was there really anything in the darkness? Or did it go on forever, enclosed as the darkness inside a body? Was it a dead-end rendered infinite only by the fact that there was no other side? These are questions that will probably never be answered. The memory of that darkness prompts me to a certain reflection, that the greatest horror Sado visits upon its visitors, the most sinister trap it lays for them, is the fact it keeps all its secrets forever, or, even worse perhaps, that it has none.

We backed up a little, somewhat nervous that the woman continued to sit on the threshold and speak in wormy tongues, since we did not know what this might signify to any native of this settlement who happened to witness the scene. Then we took the path that ran by the right side of the house towards the darkly sparkling sea. Immediately before us was a very narrow artificial harbour, whose grey-black stones rose at angles from grey-black waters. Just out of reach of the lapping tide, on the greyish patch of shore, were rickety wooden boats, whose ancient timbers appeared to have been warped and desiccated, blanched and desiccated and warped, and shrunk a thousand times until they were visibly antique. From the harbour walls there hung fishing nets, drying, I supposed, though some hung in the water as if they were the ends by which the entire liquid net of the sea, with its rippled mesh of waves, might be hauled up. For all I could tell, the scene was that of five hundred years ago, or seven hundred, or a thousand. For ten times a hundred years, it seemed, the nets had hung here, and the boats had been beached here, and the waters had feebly lapped. The instinct seemed irresistible, even in that settlement whose silence would not allow us to breathe easily or move as if unwatched, and we went down to the very water's edge, as if finally coming to the end of something.

Here was Sado. Here, it seemed, we had arrived at its very heart. The slop and slap of water against the stones, the detritus of twigs and scum on those waves – the tiny stir and murmur of this was a kind of silence. This silence, as I must have known all along, was Sado's heart. And this little inlet of the dark, inhuman sea, was composed entirely of that silence. A strange association of words now played naturally in my head as we stood looking at the dead, watery jostle. In the heart of the word '*kurai*', in the heart of the word '*buraku*', could be found the word '*ura*'. The '*omote*', in Japanese, was the face, or perhaps more accurately, the façade of something. The *ura* was its opposite, that which is hidden, the stitching behind the tapestry. However, '*ura*' can also be written with an ideogram of a different meaning. The other '*ura*' has a splash at its side – three dots of inky water – and its body resembles a portcullis grill, so that the whole looks like water swilling around a grilled outlet. This ideogram has the meaning of 'bay' or 'inlet'. For some reason I could not help wondering if it had not been exactly the same word all along – *ura* – for 'back' and for grim little nooks of coastline like this, with different Chinese characters only superimposed at a much later date. I suppose I could fuse the two meanings of '*ura*' in the English word 'backwater'.

But that which is hidden, obscure, small, is actually that which is all-encompassing, ultimate and vast. This is the truth in all 'hidden truth'. To me, growing up in England, nature had meant home. It was something cosy and familiar. To walk in the woods was to find companionship in birdsong. I had never heard much birdsong in Japanese woods, and the idea of communion with nature seemed here inappropriate. It was in Japan that I conceived and wrote one of my earliest stories, 'The Psychopomps', in which the protagonist finds himself in a lifeless copy of the world he once knew. And he is alerted to this lifelessness, of course, by nothing other than the eerie, hissing silence. The silence that was in the tiny lapping of water in this cramped harbour on Sado was not unnatural. It came from a nature vaster than that I knew, for space – cold, dark, desolate space – is often viewed as alien, and therefore the opposite of nature, but what is the obscurity of the starry sky if not the greater nature in which our smaller nature is contained? The silence in these waters was ultimately the silence of space, which is death in three dimensions. It is the silence in which Sangi Takamura was swallowed up after exile, the silence between the creaking oars as the horizon tilted before him, the silence towards which the scattered isles of his farewell poem were flung.

It was only a matter of time before our unease got the better of us and we retraced our footsteps, leaving the settlement behind.

We walked. If we did not make a decision, afternoon would become evening and night would fall without us having a place to stay. In amongst the vulture-circling of our conversation about Sado's strangeness, spiced with words such as 'incest', 'curse' and 'secret', I somewhere managed to raise the idea of a visit to the gold mine. The discovery of gold on Sado at the beginning of the seventeenth century must have been of great significance in the formation of the island as a habitation for human beings. It seems that, in the eighteenth century, the shōgun was assisting many people to cross to Sado, not because they had slandered any official personage, but because they were homeless and could conveniently be put to work in the mine. Working conditions meant a short life expectancy. Perhaps homelessness had been a worse crime than insolence and insurrection. The gold, apparently, was all mined out now, though the site had only recently stopped functioning as a mine and been opened to the public instead. It had succumbed, like all things in history, to the living death of tourism, a mere eight years before our arrival. I'm not sure why I had any desire to see it, unless I suspected, after all, that it might yield up, now the gold was exhausted, some more deeply buried secret that would explain everything. And yet, when I pictured it in my mind, it was only as a rough, empty hole in the ground with a ragged, crumbling mouth. As I more or less expected, my brother dismissed the idea of visiting the mine in a reasonable, thoughtful, but decisive way. Now was not the time for such things, and anyway, he was not interested. I did not insist.

If we had been wandering for a long while in places that were nowhere, we eventually came, by foot and by bus – none of the occasional cars that passed would stop for us – to a place that had about it the vaguest suggestion of somewhere. There was relief in this that was to turn again soon to anxiety. I'm not sure that the place could be called a town, exactly, but there were buildings here that were reassuringly businesslike and modern. These stood mainly on the inland side of a relatively wide and relatively straight coastal road of the kind that might be used in a television commercial for cars. There even seemed to be a passable hotel among them. On the sea side of the road there was a thin strip of rock and dust that was certainly shore, but probably did not qualify as beach. (For some reason, I never did discover in Japan the kind of jolly seaside atmosphere conjured up to me by the word 'beach'; my impression was that Japan simply had no beaches, in the same way it had no pastoral landscape, or any examples of natural scenery in which once might simply idle and loaf.) And beyond this strip of shore, at once volcanically jagged in its details and flat as a tempered katana in its general sweep, was a sea whose blue was admirably wild, pale as the shallows of paradise at first and then suddenly deepening into sapphire as if by some madness of the sun. It was a sea that said to me "Sea of Japan", and when the waves crashed on rocks here it was as if nature were imitating Hokusai. Between the road and the sea, however, there stood what was obviously some kind of public building, resembling, to my eyes, a gigantic clock. Its central section was tall, and on either side were two lower wings. A broad flight of steps led up to the building from the side of the road, and here there also stood a number of bus shelters. It was as if this building were in some way the axis of the whole island. The interior was cool, with floors of granite or marble – I'm not sure now – and the general appearance of an antechamber or waiting room. Here and there was maritime-looking brass. Time-pieces and timetables were so large upon the walls as to be surreal and to reinforce my initial impression of the place.

It was here that my brother, through me, made a number of rapid enquiries about various matters of transport. He wrestled with the information for a while as if with some challenging mental arithmetic. In this silence I revived the idea of the gold mine, saying we could put up at the hotel this evening and see it tomorrow. As if this suggestion had decided him, my brother spoke at last.

"I think we should leave now."

It seemed that, if we hurried, we would be in time for the last ferry back to the mainland. I felt some regret, but did not have the will to argue. I thought of the gold mine again, of that empty, crumbling mouth.

I imagined standing at its rim and kicking stones into its interior as if to say, "Is this it?" There was no way I could put the case for such a prospect convincingly.

"We've only got a few days before our flight back to England," said my brother, "so it's probably best to make the most of it in Tokyo."

There flashed into my mind pictures of pink-haired girls in Yoyogi Park.

There was really no time to discuss the matter at length, anyway. I was surprised, however, at the depth of disappointment the thought of leaving had caused in me. What was Tokyo compared to this silence?

During the time we had travelled together in Japan, I had heard my brother remark on a number of occasions how much he disliked temples.

"Anything like this," he said, "churches or temples or anything – they always seem really dark and unhealthy somehow. All these things that present themselves as good – there's a morbid atmosphere I can't explain. I don't want to go near it or have anything to do with it. It's like a trap, like a nest of vampires in some old horror film. You always get the person who's lost their way, and they come to a really sinister place and meet someone on the road, and the person says, 'You have to be very careful here. Look out for the vampires!' And he says he will protect them and takes them back to his home. But it turns out that he *is* the vampire. All these things – temples and churches and so on – they're always the thing that they warn you against."

After such an eloquent and persuasive speech, I never felt like saying that I rather like temples and churches. Perhaps I was afraid of exposing the rather squalid and unseemly truth that I might even bare my neck willingly to a vampire and wait in an ecstasy of anticipation to surrender to those fangs. I am somehow ashamed of the idea, as if of a sluttishness worse than the sexual.

I felt the same about Sado-ga-shima. I wanted to surrender to its silence.

However, we fled. Unlike most protagonists in horror films and novels, who elicit from the viewer or reader groans of frustration and disbelief by delving further into the haunted house, we did the sensible thing and fled. At least no one can complain that I am being unrealistic.

My final memories of Sado, after the decision was made to flee, are more confused and fragmentary than ever. We were to take a bus from one of the stops just in front of the building that seemed to represent on Sado the offices of time itself, but there must have been some kind of mix-up, because, after waiting a little while we discovered that the only bus capable of taking us directly to the departure point of the last ferry had already left. For a while we were sunk in panic and despair. Dashing back up the steps to make further enquiries, we found that there was another bus we could take, but not from the stops outside. In fact, the nearest stop was at some distance. At all costs, we had to catch the bus in time to make the last ferry. We set out along that blade-like strip of coastline on foot. Whenever a car passed we held out our thumbs to try and hitch a lift. The few cars that whizzed by all looked new and shiny, adding fuel to my brother's speculation that the tourists on the ferry never actually set foot on the island, but only took a scenic tour on wheels. None of them showed any more inclination to stop for us than if they had been bullets fired from a gun. On our left was the sea, on our right, now the buildings were behind us, a grassy, scrubby, dusty nothing. The road stretched ahead, barren and empty. It was a very minimalist – the obvious temptation is to say 'Zen-like' – landscape of two nothings divided by a thin line of nothing. And on all this nothing the afternoon sun still beat down fiercely. We were dazzled and sweating, and there only remained a little water, warm as our own sweat, at the bottoms of our water bottles. I remember a house appearing at one point on our right, across the road. It was a clean, well-kept bungalow, dazzlingly white, as if transported from some suburb of the affluent. The lawn of sparkling green was one with the boundless green on all sides. Someone was using a hose to keep this lawn fresh, and the sprinkling water flashed in the sun. There were hydrangea bushes, and a white butterfly was flitting from one bush to another. Such a blinding, bleaching silence… I wanted to stop and ask the man with the hose if he knew anything about our bus, but my brother said there was no time for that. Perhaps he had also sensed, as had I, something forbidding in the serenity of the scene, as if to disturb it would require the forfeit of remaining there forever, facing the blue end of the human world in the sound of waves and exposed to the penetrating nothingness of the sun. I wondered if such a life – happiness was too human a word for such peace – was the result of the surrender to silence that I had desired. I thought of that white butterfly. Oh, inexpressible bliss! We walked on under the pounding rays.

Eventually, but I do not remember exactly how, we caught our bus. I only remember the relief I felt now that we were secure in our seats. All of a sudden it was a pleasant, sunny summer's day. The bus progressed steadily and leisurely across the island, and we got some idea of how large and how human the place was, as we passed through town and countryside. There were also steep roads overhung with semi-tropical trees, through which the sun broke in brilliant splinters that seemed to soothe the heart like fingers on harp-strings. The bus was not crowded, but there were other passengers. At one point a young girl got on and saw someone she knew at the back. She gave a delighted cry of recognition and sat next to her acquaintance. I remember distinctly the words, *"Kabi no nioi. Sado rashii nioi ne. Natsukashii."*

"The smell of mildew. It's a real smell of Sado, isn't it? It makes me feel nostalgic."

The bus did, indeed, smell of mildew. Half-listening, half-dreaming as I looked out of the bus window, I drifted in and out of their conversation. The girl had apparently just come back from the mainland where she had spent the summer holidays. She was preparing now for the new school year. She talked about her exams and her future in the kind of cheerful voice that only a young girl with her life before her can have. I imagined her sitting at a school desk with her pencil case open, her little plastic characters from her favourite manga and anime arranged before her, writing in an exercise book and occasionally rubbing out a mistake smudgingly with a well-used novelty rubber. I wanted her life. I wanted to be her. I wondered how many lives like hers there were in the sunny landscape through which we passed, lives we would never know in a landscape we would never see again. I thought of the white butterfly. If only I could be a white butterfly, flitting from one life to another in the sun as if they were hydrangea bushes. Those lives I did not know, everything through which we were passing without alighting, now seemed as sweet as the nectar a butterfly sips.

That evening we stayed at a bath-house in Niigata on the mainland. The next day we were sitting on the bullet train to Tokyo. Across the aisle from us sat girls with bubblegum-pink hair, wearing baroque fashions half-punk, half-Victorian. When we arrived in Tokyo, having nowhere else to stay, we slept in a capsule hotel, in spaces like chambers for cryogenically frozen astronauts.

I have never been back to Sado, and yet, writing this account now, some ten years later, I feel as if its mildew smell still clings to me. I suppose I remember it and write of it for a reason. In particular, I find myself wondering about the fate of the man in the youth hostel, the ex-salaryman who had taken the rest of his life off, and who was determined to follow a road that he knew went nowhere. I have no way of tracing him and discovering what happened to this life that crossed paths with mine. In a way, however, I think we are the same. His trajectory is lost in utter obscurity. The only difference is that I am forced to experience every excruciating detail of my own obscure and wayward trajectory. My whole life may accurately – if metaphorically – be described in the terms he used for his own situation as a traveller. I have quit life already, but carry on with dwindling means and nothing ahead of me, and with no way to return to what I have left behind. I have tasted the silence of Sado, though I fled without confronting it, and now the whole world is Sado to me. The ways I've never taken continue to lure me with a suggestion of sweetness, only while they remain untaken. All ways lead to Sado-ga-shima. I seek it, and I seek to escape it; it is all one. I only wonder whether that ultimate, eaves-dark silence, like a breath from the rotting lungs of a mad crone, that silence of wave and gull, which was there before humankind, will bring me peace, or whether it will prove to be an insurmountable wall, with nothing on the other side. Is the mystery of that silence an empty mystery? Is there only this hair-prickling horror?

THE GAY WOLF

(for Ben)

The light is on in the kitchen, intensifying the darkness outside. The shadow-shapes of trees, log-pile, hot-tub and trampoline are no longer discernible. A thin but exact phantasm of the kitchen coats the broad window and masks the night. Surely eyes that see this inarticulate reflection of comfort and familiarity are always tired eyes? Something, however, punctures the reflection – something from beyond. There are two glowing eyes, borrowing the kitchen's light and making it eerie. The eyes are the colour of moonstone and sulphur. They glow and they lurk, intent, seeming never to blink. They look always into the eyes that look out. The Gay Wolf has come again.

Tired kitchen eyes are awakened as if by a freshening wind. There is something out there. Beyond the reflection, there is something out there.

The Gay Wolf has been visiting me like this every night for some time. He comes to the patio by the back door, his eyes effulgent, and he waits, dogged. Often he will whimper and whine, like someone playing a saw with a violin bow, making that peculiar, quivering music of the canine that goes beyond sadness to enter the realm of the truly pathetic. Other times he is silent, watching with acute and unvarying expectation. There must be something he wants.

I have tried opening the door to him, but he merely whines and shifts his front paws and looks up at me with eyes that plead and question and anticipate in constant tugging appeal. He has come into the house, too, on occasion, his stiff claws making threads and spots of maraca percussion on the linoleum. He soon goes out again, however, mutely but obviously unsatisfied. Something poignant is in the air – a feeling like being unable to swallow. I have even tried to follow him into the darkness from which his dusky grey form always emerges, but he leads me nowhere, or I lose him.

I began to see those shining eyes in dream, or they would come back to me at odd times of the day. Those eyes always waiting at the back door. That look of almost quizzical appeal. Surely – I began to think – he has some message for me. There is something he is longing to say.

The Gay Wolf is not really a wolf, except insofar as all dogs are wolves, and he is of a kind who resembles his ancestors more than others. The Gay Wolf is of varying shades of grey. His ears complete his asymmetricality – like that of a ramshackle haunted house in an old film – in being one higher than the other. His outline, from nose to tail, is somehow whiskery, and in places even brambly. There is a sense of battered dignity about him, the scruffiness of wisdom and resignation. His coat is not the latest fashion, but old, with sewn patches. Some areas of fur are longer than others, producing a hyena-like mane down his back (again asymmetrical), and a wispy pair of petticoat breeches in light grey around his haunches. Despite this, he is a beast of great delicacy. His eyes are forever sensitive and woebegone, with a hint of reproach never leaving them. His nose tapers to a point as elegant as any stiletto heel. And his left forepaw is turned always inwards when he stands, giving him a diminutive, almost kittenish appearance.

The first time I dreamt of the Gay Wolf, the setting was a party. It was a cosy, adult party rather than the wild, teenage kind. In other words, there was a gentle sense of human warmth and social pleasure – a mere ambiance for its own sake. It was a generic and yet somehow a very English party. The house was large, the wallpaper, curtains, carpets and cushions all patterned with deep, rich, homely colours. There were paper chains festooned around the walls, and outside (as seen through the open french windows) it was dark. I supposed it was winter, though any chill in the atmosphere remained conceptual. There was nothing to indicate this was a Christmas party or a party for any other specific occasion. Without any known beginning, end or purpose, it was characterised simply by a *continuing*, a rippling hubbub of continuing, both restful and lively.

For some reason I felt this sense of continuation to be stifling, as if, in being all background, it might flatten me into being background, too.

I went upstairs and heard the clink and murmurous chatter recede behind me.

Since my only aim had been to escape, I did not know where I was going. Before I could consider and make a reasoned decision, it suddenly occurred to me that the bathroom was the obvious destination, though I did not know why. Since the door of the bathroom was ajar, I assumed it was unoccupied, but as I drew closer I was disturbed by an impression of movement. Slowing and stopping, I now saw that the Gay Wolf was there, standing before the mirror over the basin and carefully applying eyeliner with a puppet-stiff paw. He paused to inspect his handiwork and must have seen my reflection over his shoulder. He turned, saying nothing. After a few moments regarding me silently with those sensitive eyes, he walked past me and down the stairs, almost brushing against me. I went into the bathroom, which had apparently been vacated for my sake, or on my account at least, and there I idly turned on the cold tap. What on Earth was I doing here? After all, I could have come for no other reason than to meet the Gay Wolf, and yet I had dumbly watched him walk by out of guilt or politeness or sheer dimwittedness. I sighed and retraced my steps to the ground floor.

The Gay Wolf was sitting on a padded seat that was one in an extended row of such seats against the wall of the living room. He was talking to a sandy-haired girl in the seat next to him and occasionally flicking ash from a cigarette protruding from the end of an ebony cigarette-holder. The ashtray had been fashioned to resemble a vulva.

I stood, some distance away, unsure of my approach, and listened. The girl nodded, between flicks of her fringe, to indicate she had heard the last words spoken, and the Gay Wolf continued.

"There's nothing better, they say. There can't be. How can anything be better than the end?"

"And you've seen it?" asked the girl.

"Yes. I'm one of those who's been allowed. I am qualified by birth. I have an affinity with plant life and the edges of things. And I have no home. But anyone can see it if they want to. There's no guard. And that, they say, is why this will be a triumph, and make everything else irrelevant."

The Gay Wolf paused to inspect the quilted sleeves of his smoking jacket, perhaps concerned that a stray cinder from his cigarette had caused a pinhole burn.

"What was it like?" asked the girl.

Looking up from his sleeves, he considered.

"In a way, nothing special, just a dingy, poorly kept corner of the garden. But even at first glance there's something terrible in the fact it's nothing special."

"Why's it called the Nihil Plot?"

"Because the principle underlying every cell in every plant and flower there is that of nihilism. The beauty of nihilism made them grow and gave them shape. 'Beauty' is the wrong word, but it'll have to do.

"When I saw the plants, they were quite dusty, but if you looked closely you could see how they were made up, beneath the dust, of a weave of transparent filaments. There was a kind of heavy-breathing insistence there, in that corner, a kind of shadowy damp, and the gardeners listened carefully day after day, and they could hear it saying, 'We don't exist. We don't exist.' And, though they said they did not know exactly why, because why was meaningless anyway, they began to cultivate that corner, burying snails there in mass graves, and persecuting groups of nettles, and spitting and stamping on the soil and introducing voracious ladybirds and so on. Soon enough, nothing special began to appear in the form of uneven colonies of transparent shrubs and flowers like ghostly rock formations in a cave system of diseased and dying rock.

"Then this vegetation began to attract pollen and dust and colour, as if it were somehow sticky and was trapping matter and sensory information there to struggle and die, like flies in a web.

"The most recent development is that brittle trails of silver have appeared now and then and have slowly become moist, like seaweed predicting rain, until, almost suddenly, a slug or a snail will appear. The slugs and snails expire on the leaves as if their entire manifestation in four dimensions had been negated. It's not that they are vaporised. They writhe and contort in multi-dimensional agony. The polarity of the meaning that informed the very matter of their existence is changed, but simply to die is no answer to this, since death, too, has been rendered a kind of monstrous irrelevance by this reverse polarity."

"And that's the Nihil Plot?"

"That's it so far. Predictions are being made based on the writhing of the slugs and snails."

At this point, my loneliness became so dire that I could no longer hold back. I walked directly over to where the two of them sat and, with heavy, sloppy haste, took my place on the opposite side of the table.

The Gay Wolf glanced over at me, unsurprised, drew on his cigarette, and said, "It's time you met your soul-mate, Sarah."

At first I did not know who he meant, but soon realised he was referring to the sandy-haired girl. 'Sarah' was precisely the wrong name for my soul-mate, and, what's more, I did not recognise her. I had the feeling that, however long I knew her, I would never recognise her. Or perhaps, at best, I would half-recognise her.

She extended her hand, and I reached out to shake it briefly.

"Hello," I said.

"Hello," she replied, overdoing a smile and then quickly looking away.

I was dejected and embarrassed. What's more, the conversation I had overheard had made me feel somehow bloated and nauseous.

"So, now you've met your soul-mate," said the Gay Wolf. "I bet you're glad to get that done."

Sarah was looking off into space, but somehow I knew by the fact she did not protest or contradict that he was speaking the absolute truth. There was, beneath her silence, a warm and fast complicity. It was as certain as certainty itself that we were soul-mates. However, since we had only just met, it would be ridiculous to expect us to do anything about the fact. Moreover, the certainty was such that it would always be ridiculous to do anything about it – for eternity. The certainty was accomplished, but in being so was forever elsewhere.

Since I felt awkward talking to Sarah, I tried to continue conversation with the Gay Wolf. Even with him, the talk did not quite flow. I poured myself drinks in a frowning, shameless manner. Occasionally, for no reason I can name, it suddenly became appropriate for me to shake hands with Sarah again while we both smiled awkwardly. Every time we did so, like a faint, electric shock, I felt again the existence of that certainty that was always accomplished and always elsewhere.

At some point the conversation returned to the Nihil Plot.

"The Mound of Absurdity is right next to it, of course," said the Gay Wolf.

I looked from him to Sarah and back again. Everything was tilting and swimming. Both Sarah and the Gay Wolf seemed to leer.

"The snails and slugs who expire there endlessly must long for the mad weeds to tumble down from the mound and strangle them – to be strangled by absurdity."

I laughed uneasily. I got up from my chair and then fell to all fours. It was too far to the bathroom, so I took shelter beneath the table. Just before I collapsed, I found myself vomiting over a pair of red patent leather shoes. I realised the shoes belonged to Sarah, whose feet were still in them. Feeble and weeping, I began to apologise. My hands were weak, and I decided on a sudden impulse that I must lick the vomit from the shoes and surrounding area. My energy even for this activity dwindling to nothing, I collapsed, with Sarah's vomit-laced shoes for a pillow. Sighing and murmuring, I flung my arms around her ankles. Realising, after a moment, that she was doing nothing to escape my grasp, I felt myself floating on a wave of happiness, which unfortunately brought up more vomit from my stomach. There was so much of the acrid, stinging liquid, I began to fear I would drown.

I don't remember much more of the dream than that. Only that I was left with a sense of struggling against a tide of vomit to keep close to, or get back to, Sarah's feet, which had become the source of unquestioning happiness.

The evening after I had this dream, the Gay Wolf came to the back door as usual, but this time I was forced to contemplate the relation of dream to reality, of the Gay Wolf in the smoking jacket, to the Gay Wolf who haunted the patio as a wordless beast. Because of this, if for no other reason, he seemed changed.

I stared for some time into the luminous orbs of his eyes. It's said that animals are unable to outstare humans, but he was unblinking. I was determined not to look away. I had to know what all this meant – what the message was. Something began to form in my mind, but I was entirely unable to decide whether it was forming under internal influences or was aided by some outside intelligence. I had an uncanny sense – a kind of tickling in the mind – that something other than myself was involved. But no, after all, there is no way of knowing. In any case, after some time, the thing that had been forming, formed, standing revealed and intact amongst my thoughts.

"Am I already dead? Is that what you have come to tell me?" And with this, the world immediately changed its aspect, becoming a swamp of stagnation and despair.

"It's not that life is over in a physical sense." Whether only in my head, or spoken aloud, the thoughts continued. "That's not what makes the idea so horrible. It's that there should be no difference between life and death, no essential division. What hope is there in that? It's true. After all, it is true. I really have died. I have come to the swamp that is the end of all hope and progress. I'm dead, but I'm still here, and so 'death' becomes just a word. But if 'death' becomes just a word, 'life', too, becomes just a word. And surely that is a death worse than death, and more suffocatingly final."

The eyes glowed back at me. I knew that there were two of them, but the number two ceased to have meaning for me, so that their plurality was unspeakably bizarre. Perhaps those eyes knew the words I had thought or spoken. Perhaps they held some answer. They gave no indication that they knew anything. They stared. At least there must be purpose in that, I thought. They stared, and then they flickered, and then the Gay Wolf turned to roam the obscurity of the nocturnal gloom.

The next time I dreamt of the Gay Wolf was quite different to the first time. In fact, I call it a dream only for two reasons. One reason was that the Gay Wolf spoke to me again, and the other was that I cannot place when the encounter happened in the series of my waking days. If not for these two facts, the dream would simply be a memory, though a strange one.

Night had freshly fallen, though there was a feeling of permanence in its darkness. With the night had come silence, like a lament. It was a patient but a sorrowful silence like a widow carefully sewing one more stitch and one more stitch in a dress that is never finished. I stood in a trance by the kitchen window and I heard the needle scrape and pitter pitter of the claws upon the paws of the Gay Wolf as they tapped and scratched the patio stones in what seemed an otherwise bodiless approach. And then those shining eyes appeared with a flicker.

In the heartache of sympathy and in resignation, I went immediately to the back door and opened it. The Gay Wolf looked up at me. After a while he began to talk.

"Let me tell you my story," he said, a sensitive quiver at the edge of his doggy voice. "When my mother dropped her litter it was in the hedgerow of a deserted country road. I can't remember what happened, but we were abandoned there, pink and blind and wriggling, in the grass and nettles. Humans found us, and since we had no owners, they did whatever they wanted with us. We were separated, and I never saw a brother or a sister of mine again.

"Though I was born ownerless, many have owned me. I have never chosen them. They found me and they took me, and then, always, they left me, ownerless again as the day I was born in the hedgerow.

"Some abandoned me when they had children of their own, and I had to roam deserted roads – a familiar but ever-lonely homelessness. Or I was put in a cage. Sometimes my ribs showed like the bars that kept me. For a time I belonged to a man who loved me, though his wife did not. I lived in their house. They moved and I was left behind, and new owners came to my house.

"I have always been loyal for as long as any allowed me to be. I have always rejoiced to smell a known smell and lick again an old, known face. Perhaps you could say I have no pride, but that would be unkind. Little choice has been given to me, and less reward, but what little room for choice I have had, I've used always to live the best life I could. It's true sometimes I have complained. If complaint is an evil, perhaps my soul is blackened. But can it be so very blackened when that complaint has been so little heard? Besides, I never really expected anything, never asked for more than I was given. Or, at least, not more than my body and soul cried out for. My complaint was only really a howling at the moon. It was only a song.

"I mentioned both body and soul. Yes, perhaps you will find this outlandish, or disapprove, but my soul has needs just as my body has. And sometimes, the two needs are combined, which proves my point. You're surprised? You thought I was above such things? I suppose I should not be surprised that you're surprised. You know me as the Gay Wolf, and though perhaps this undignified label is appropriate, I have never felt defined by my sexuality. I have never tried to define myself in that way. I have simply, always and only ever been myself. It's true that bitches have never attracted me. I cannot help that. They smell wrong. There have been times when the howl of my body and soul has become a serenade, but it has never been a bitch who could draw this serenade from me.

"Even those who do not believe in love can fall in love. In other words, a howl lives always in my heart, and sometimes there are those who seem worthy of that howl. I give them all I have and they take it, perhaps, or they do not. Either way, it goes, and I never know what it meant to the other, and I am alone again with the building howl that pertains to no one in particular. But if only they knew the depth and quality of my howl – the ones who bring it out of me – if only they knew! Perhaps they know. I don't know if they know. But they take it, or they don't, and they go.

"But my life has been more solitary than otherwise. While there are none who draw my serenade – which is most of the time – surely I am neither gay nor ungay. It is only that each of the several serenades I have made have separately been to dogs and not bitches. That's why you call me the Gay Wolf, isn't it? But no, I think I know why you gave me that name.

"If you want to know the end of my story, I can't tell you. No one will know the end but me. In fact, that in itself is my story. My life is not over, and only I shall know its end. For now… I do have my treasures. There have been times in my life when I have smoked a fat cigar. Perhaps I shall smoke another soon. Perhaps another brief serenade. And I am learning, too, the secrets of the hedgerows and the edges of all things, which are strangely solitary secrets. I am learning to crumble up all whiskery, the way the soil crumbles, full of worms, and turns itself into a patch of nettles. Yes, the nettles, the goosegrass, the burdock – all these things are a blind, homeless litter sucking at the teats of the great bitch of the soil.

"I crumble into the earth and I dream with the earth as it spins. I can be born again at any moment, from the platform of a train station, homeless again, and leave a patch of nettles behind me to mark my new birthplace as they will mark my grave, or at the edge of a fairground, or the corner of a laundrette. I go each night into the gloom, and it takes me apart. Only my eyes remain to see with, and sometimes even these disappear. When my eyes disappear I can see myself as if I am the sky. I am like a balloon with its air let out. I fly out into the night and chase crowds of stars. A balloon quickly falls back to earth when the air is gone, but I seem to get lighter and lighter. Who knows what will become of me? Everyone thinks they must have an opinion on what death is. I do not know what life is, but I have lived it. Why should I then be afraid to die? The stars seem dear and gentle to me, and their silent howling sweeter than any serenade I have ever known.

"But here I am born homeless again on your patio, like a platform at a train station. All these years of my life that no one has counted or will count, and here I stand and here I am, singing the same song and telling the same story."

I cannot say that this was not a dream, but it was true that the Gay Wolf continued to visit me, night after night. After I had heard those words, and since the Gay Wolf himself was as real as anything else, how could I stop myself from wondering what it meant?

Considering seriously, it seemed to me there must be a meaning. Considering just as seriously, I could find no meaning. When I realised that, despite exhausting all the seriousness of my soul, I still found no meaning, I knew it was imperative that I examined my life in all its details.

According to Heidegger, anxiety is an essential condition of human existence. This is not because there is always 'something to worry about'. If all the identifiable problems of your life were solved, this anxiety would persist. This is because you are 'in the world'. Is this, I wonder, a way of saying, as the Buddhists do, that all things must pass? Perhaps that is part of it. Life is forever changing and shifting. The very earth on which we stand is turning, as it revolves around a dying sun. But even if the world were flat, motionless and permanent, populated by wealthy immortals, I imagine that Heidegger's anxiety would persist. People would worry about their spiritual well-being in this state of stagnation, perhaps, or there would be some troubling corner of reality they could never get their fingernails under in order to peel it back and reveal the truth.

Let me state it as plainly and briefly as I can. The anxiety is this: Life is a question that is never wholly answered, and this is unsatisfactory. But if it were answered, that would be unsatisfactory, too, since no answer could ever satisfy, or if it did seem to satisfy, that would be the end of everything, and when everything *went out*, a restless sigh would heave itself wistfully in the darkness like the acrid smoke of an extinguished candle.

With this bleak conclusion as my clinical laboratory, I began my autobiographical examination.

Since childhood I have written stories, and since time indeterminate I have felt that I had something of urgent meaning to express, since it was my very soul. "What is that thing?" I have been asked. I try to remain patient at the question. "If I could tell you that," I say, "I would not need to write stories." But the truth is, I have never met a single being who, upon hearing my reasons for writing, seemed galvanised by them into sympathy towards and curiosity regarding the thing I feel I must call my soul. The tendency has been towards hostility, ridicule, derision and, just as bad perhaps, indifference. In the same way, I have felt virtually every expression of thought by every sage, philosopher and messiah in the world to be poison-tipped arrows arrayed against me, designed specifically to put me down, to undermine, to devalue and destroy. And in the face of such hostility it seems the burden of proof (that I have a soul and that what I write has meaning) lies with me.

I can prove nothing.

Can a television programme save one's soul? I've contemplated this question recently. Since a messiah and a TV show are just things in the world, I don't see why the latter should be less likely to save one's soul than the former (all other things being equal). My favourite Monty Python sketch is one involving a hypnotist called the Great Mystico and his assistant, Janet. Together they put up blocks of flats by hypnotism. A reporter interviews a resident of one such flat:

> **Tenant:** Yes, we received a note from the Council saying that if we ceased to believe in this building it would fall down.
>
> **Reporter:** You don't mind living in a figment of another man's imagination?
>
> **Tenant:** No, it's much better than where we used to live.
>
> **Reporter:** Where did you used to live?
>
> **Tenant:** We had an eighteen-roomed villa overlooking Nice.
>
> **Reporter:** Really? That sounds much better.
>
> **Tenant:** Oh yes. Yes, you're right.

As doubt takes hold, the block of flats begins to tremble and debris fall from the ceiling.

"Oh no. I remember now. That's right. It's better here," says the tenant, regaining confidence.

The tremors cease. The block of flats stands firm once more.

There is a luxury, 18-roomed villa called Voluptas Mundus, where those with money and the right introductions go. At this villa they are able to enjoy the three great treasures of a world that is only the world, dreaming only and always of itself. These are Status, Money and Sex, though we may glorify them by other names. I have moved away from that villa. No, it's worse than that. I have foresworn it. I have never been. By the power of my writing – I declared – I shall erect a block of flats called Mesmer Towers, a habitation devoid of Status, Money and Sex, and I shall live there. More and more often these days I hear reports about how wonderful life is in Voluptas Mundus, and my block of flats shakes terribly. And yet, as of the time of writing, it still stands.

If I cannot prove the existence of my soul, and if the quintessentially American view that now holds sway around the globe, that people are divided into winners and losers, is true, then I am a loser. And that, as they say, is that.

Still, leaning on my imaginary windowsill and casting a weary gaze on the world outside, I find my shaky block of flats – for some reason or no reason – has not fallen. Not yet. Sometimes the tremors are bad, but a building put up by hypnotism is peculiarly elastic. Sometimes I think it will never fall.

What gives my life meaning? Writing, and all that writing consists in. What gives writing meaning? I don't know, but *something* does. If it did not, I would not have been granted such powers of hypnotism. Belief can conjure something out of nothing, but where does belief itself come from?

In short, I submit my powers of hypnotism as evidence that the soul I have hypnotised myself to believe in exists. I am a master hypnotist.

But I shall not leave it at that. I do have some ideas about where my stories, and the power of my hypnotism, come from.

If, after the end of all things, there must still be a sigh of dissatisfaction and yearning in the darkness, perhaps we find in this also the beginning of all things. I do not know if there is a particular name for the story I am about to tell – it seems related to something called '*lila*' – but I have heard from different sources that at the beginning there was a god who was one and all, and in being so, he was vastly alone. He invented death so that he might die. In dying he became many. And the many – of course – search forever for the oneness they lost. If even God was lonely and resorted to suicide, how can we expect anything other than loneliness? Nonetheless, that there is something rather than nothing suggests the power of that original and ultimate sigh in darkness. It is what Dylan Thomas called, "the force that through the green fuse drives the flower". The same force drives the ink from my pen and guarantees my hypnotism, underwriting it with belief. It is immortal longing.

Accepting then, that my block of flats stands up just as well as the universe that was hypnotised into being, which is the ground on which it stands, the question remains – and I prepare for more tremors as I ask it – is it a happy life as a resident here?

Absent from Mesmer Towers are Money, Status and Sex, as we already know. Perhaps these will come if the Towers stand long enough and others begin to move in, making the place fashionable, but the gamble on which the hypnotism is based is that these things may be absent forever. Apart from these three, I hear rumours of two other possible sources of happiness: religion and love.

Am I one of those who have received the grace of religion?

I have got religion, or it has got me, neither more nor less, probably, then these pages suggest. In other words, neither orthodox nor ecstatic religion is mine. I write this only partially for the sake of credibility. I know that to have either orthodox or ecstatic religion – any kind of unreserved religion – would be seen as an unspeakable embarrassment, but I suppose the embarrassment would be eliminated by the abandonment implicit in the leap of faith. In fact, embarrassment is only a symptom of the modern disease of reasonableness. It is nothing to be proud of.

Then, do I feel love, either from within emanating outward, or from without penetrating inward?

There are some personal subtleties – important ones – that I cannot express in any way on the matter of love. Since I cannot express them, I will leave them be, and those who know me will have to fathom those subtleties if they are inclined. It is more than I can do. Such subtleties aside, I can only say that love does not exist in my universe. Since I have taken up residence in Mesmer Towers, to enjoy the opulence of defeat and sit upon the throne of loserdom, I suppose I have too much pride to seek fulfilment in relationships. I am chronically single and incurably alienated. There was a time when, with the great majority of the human race, a preoccupation with heterosexual romantic love seemed unquestionably normal to me, even if I was unsure whether I would be included in that normality. But that was a very long time ago. Now it only seems bizarre and incomprehensible that sexual relationships have such a central place in most people's thoughts. How can erotic love be considered such an all-consuming normality when the space taken up by genitalia in the world is so small? It is as if, for most people, the world is one stupendous vagina. But for me, now, it is just the world. I would no more understand what to do in a relationship with another human being than a rock would understand what to do in a relationship with another rock. Rocks are not vaginas or penises, but there are more of them by volume, I imagine, in this world and the universe, than there are genitals of either sex or both put together.

Having said this, I feel my loss. I am perplexed by my fall from romantic and erotic normality. I am also as curious as any alien would be about what, exactly, that normality entails. And having said that, I am sometimes strangely happy that I have achieved such complete separation from normality. A world of rocks and air beckons me to a mineral and gaseous liberation.

The precise mix of religion and human relationship in my life might be expressed in the following way: Occasionally I will wish with a jagged agony that seems to eviscerate me that I was Miranda Cosgrove. The certainty that I am not and never shall be suddenly brings to life for me the meaning of the word 'damnation'. And then, sometimes, after I have acknowledged this damnation, I will feel every atom of my being charged with a rich, nihilistic joy at the kick of not being Miranda Cosgrove. To express the matter in Blakean terms, not-being-Miranda-Cosgrove is eternal delight. And then, in the midst def the crackling aurora of this ecstasy, in the most fleeting moments, it comes to me that the very certainty and absoluteness of the fact that I am not Miranda Cosgrove has given me access to Miranda Cosgrove's beaming entrails, where I exist like a tapeworm of magical knowledge. I dissolve in her very bowels. I am Miranda Cosgrove. It is certain. I am Miranda Cosgrove.

To express the matter in Cosgrovian terms, I dare say I have issues. The sight or sound of physical tenderness makes me shudder. It is possible to question, also, whether I am telling the truth. This is an occasion, I realise, for which an old cliché was made: Whether or not I am telling the truth is for me to know and for you to find out. If truth is what is most satisfying to tell, then it is truth I have told.

I began by saying the burden of proof was on me, but now I see just how secure I am in Mesmer Towers. The burden is upon you, the rest of the world, to kick in the door and drag me out – or else take up residence with me – if you wish to and are able.

Some final advice if you're planning a raid or a visit. It seems I am a creature of hermetically sealed unreality. Presumably reality would destroy me as easily as a pin bursts a bubble. Take note of this, my Achilles' heel. You are at liberty to make use of it, if you think you know what reality is. But if what you want is a piece of my unreality – I know how rare and attractive a commodity this is – or even, for some peculiar reason, *me*, the battering ram of reality will not serve you well. You will break in and find nothing there.

For the time being that was the end of my self-examination.

The nightly visits from the Gay Wolf did not stop. Did this mean my self-examination had been inadequate (it probably had), or were the two matters unrelated?

One night I decided to speak to the Gay Wolf.

"Is it wrong to hope?" I asked.

He tilted his head, perhaps in sympathy.

"Why?"

"There are those who say it is. Perhaps I am deceiving myself and deceiving others when I look for signs of hope. Perhaps hope is evil."

"Do you think so?"

"I am afraid I might be evil. So, in that sense, yes. I am afraid that this is the kind of question an evil person asks, seeking approval, seeking collusion in the hope that justifies evil."

The Gay Wolf looked back at me in silence.

"I suppose I just have to work it out for myself," I said. "It's my responsibility."

"Something's bothering you," said the Gay Wolf.

"Yes. Actually, I think it was the Nihil Plot. It seems evil to me, but then I think the fact I think that must make me evil. It's weird. The Nihil Plot seems to declare that all we think of as good is hypocritical. But the suggestion is that the Nihil Plot is the true good. Isn't that also self-righteousness and therefore hypocrisy? I don't know. But, if I thought that the Nihil Plot was evil and I was good, that would mean I was evil. Therefore, I am forced to conclude that I am evil, in the hope that I might be good, though since hope is evil, then I still must be evil, which is the conclusion it is my duty to come to, anyway."

"That was just a dream."

"What?"

"I don't really wear eyeliner and a smoking jacket. The Nihil Plot was just a dream."

"Just a dream? But… What about Sarah?"

I was disappointed in myself for asking the question. I thought the Gay Wolf might even answer. Before he could, I asked another.

"If that was a dream, then what is this?"

"Maybe this is a dream, too."

"Then, how can you be so sure that *that* was a dream?"

"It's your dream – you'll have to decide."

That was the last time the Gay Wolf spoke to me, at least in audible words. He still visits each night that passes, and sits silent, his eyes an eerie blaze. Or he whimpers lingeringly.

What is it then? What is it?

You do not have a message for me after all, do you, Gay Wolf? It is not a message but a question. To stand and wait and whimper – this is a question.

And the Gay Wolf seems to say, "You know."

I do not know, Gay Wolf. And if I did know, still I would not know the answer to the question.

He seems to say, "You know."

Still night after night he comes to the back door. His whimpering haunts me – the unending question of his visit. However, I must admit that in a strange way it reassures me, too, and deeply. I hope his visits never cease.

He comes again tonight. Eyes aglow, whimpering, clearer than ever he seems to say, "You know. Oh, surely by now you know. You know. You know."

The Temple

Just beyond the Southern Pass lies a forest, and in the forest is a temple.

Maps do not mark it, and indeed it has no name by which pilgrims might spread its fame. Trade routes now pass some leagues wide of the area and few have reason to stray there. And so the temple has remained as unknown to the world at large as a shipwreck beneath a becalmed ocean of leaves.

The temple occupies a clearing. But it is really only a clearing in as much as the temple momentarily replaces the ranks of trees. The building itself is just large enough that the forest canopy is breached and the whiteness of the sky beyond encroaches tentatively upon the sylvan green. On each side of the temple are steps leading up to four portals facing north, east, south and west. The portals are flung wide and the interior is so small that virtually all of it is disclosed at a single view.

Inside is no reliquary or altar, no idol, no alcove, not even a single incense burner. Instead there are the ceiling, the floor and the corners where the open portals do not reach. All is bare. The shadow and the light are equally empty as they creep across the stone surfaces. In fact, so empty is this grey interior that the stone itself seems spruce, as if swept clean by the twiggy broom of some unknown attendant – though maybe it is just the wind. Of course, this bareness is not without interest, and is perhaps the more fascinating for being part of a temple. However, if one is in a questioning mood, the blank lines only seem to lead back on themselves and are ultimately unsatisfying.

No, if one is looking for something (rather than nothing), then all that is to be seen is on the outside. And as if the temple truly is inside out, the exterior is such a rich and mysterious enchantment to the senses, and to the spirit, one might say there is no need to go inside at all. The reliquary, the altar and idols, the incense and prayer - all are one in this magnificent, whorl-like shell.

The intricacy of the carvings about the stone portals mirrors the natural luxuriance of the surrounding foliage, so that it is almost possible to think the temple an immemorial part of the forest itself, or else to think the forest an extension of the temple. The eaves and cornices, walls and columns, are wreathed with deities and dragons, and strange beasts of somewhat heraldic appearance, as if with petrified vines. (Turning one's gaze to the trees on all sides, it is suddenly easy to see dragons and demons of leaves, especially when autumn is first tinting the foliage red and gold.) These figures are connected in a scroll-like sweep of detail as if acting out their mute allegory on a stage of clouds perhaps heavenly, perhaps infernal. Whatever the story is, it is told in one instant, so that the same figure is repeated many times in different scenes. As heavy as stone, as ethereal as smoke, and reeking of the scent of the lotus, there is a special atmosphere to the temple, to the carvings that disport endlessly on its shell and to the writing to be found among them, that seems to suggest this relic is all that is left on Earth of a great and lost civilisation.

What could that civilisation be, and where now are its scions? No one knows who built the temple or how long it has stood in the forest. Although there is a story attached to the temple, being only some few hundreds of years old, one senses that it is of relatively recent date compared to the building's history, and it is true that it explains little. Nonetheless, it is a story of no slight interest to those who question and wonder, and so I set it down here.

I suppose we will never know who first traversed the forest, and when, but as far as history is concerned it must have happened during the hey-day of half-forgotten Qu, which lies, now quiet and dark as an island of exile, on the coast to the forest's west.

About five hundred years ago, the city of Qu attained great renown as a port and centre for trade. Wayfarers and fortune-seekers of every kind, and in particular merchants, were attracted from all quarters, though many of those from the east were to find the journey long and exhausting. They had to take a most circuitous route in order to avoid the wild, unknown lands of hill and forest. Some of these travellers must have lost their patience, however, because it is from this time that we have stories of journeys through the gloom of wooded valleys.

It is hard to imagine the feelings with which these adventurers – for they were certainly nothing less – first set foot beneath the canopy that marked the border of this wilderness of shadow. They must have believed they were the first humans to venture there since the beginning of time. Much more than today, a forest would have been an uncanny place, an abode of weird spirits, and the perils they braved equal to those faced by the occupant of a coracle adrift in uncharted ocean. Truly men were different then, that a prosaic business speculation could become a gamble with their very souls.

Despite the awe they undoubtedly felt, the first travellers passed through the forest unharmed. Encouraged, others followed their example. One of these was the little known minstrel, Kerr Gonfal, who, with his retainer, set out for Qu seeking fame. He emerged from the forest with a tale to tell.

At first the two wayfarers were on their guard. Even though the forest surrounded them, it was as if it hid from them. Just as the markings of a lizard or a moth may render it invisible until it moves, so it seemed the forest was nothing but a great, ever-watching conspiracy of such disguises. After some days they grew used to the wild, its strange sounds, its feral air and its twilight maze. It seemed to them this new world was, after all, not so different to the normal world they had left behind. It was empty except for the wild birds and beasts. And yet something in that emptiness remained eerie to them, so that they did not relax their vigilance completely.

On the fifth day they breakfasted as usual and continued on their way, and before noon struck upon a clearing amidst the trees. They had had no inkling of the clearing until they found themselves suddenly within it, and they were amazed at what stood before them. It was the temple, of course, which Kerr described as 'old as the forest', whether based upon its appearance or his assumption that besides recent pioneers no human beings had ventured here since the dawn of time, is hard to tell.

The two approached the silent edifice in wonderment and gazed dumbfounded upon the carvings that swirled about its outside. Unlike today, the portals of the temple were tightly sealed, and the carvings formed an unbroken panorama, a cycle of legend that fairly seemed to move. Yet it did not move. All was still. As a butterfly danced about a shaft of light, the wayfarers spoke in whispers, wondering if they had stumbled upon some snare of enchantment. The retainer cautioned that they should leave the place, but Kerr was curious, and, wanting to look inside the temple, raised his hand to the great carven portal.

Before he could open it, as if from nowhere, there stood at their sides a most fearsome apparition. It was a man, but very tall, towering above the two of them, and swaddled from head to foot in black robes. Only the eyes were visible, fierce with a demonic rage that made the wayfarers shake. The figure stood as firm and erect as a statue and immediately boomed this challenge:

"Thou shalt not enter the temple. Here is the abode of the great god Agnos Theer, whom I serve. Ere thou cross the threshold I must slay thee, for it is forbidden to profane the Most High and look upon His Treasure and His Glory with mortal eyes."

And so saying, this swart guardian, without pause to see if his words were heeded, for Kerr's hand was at the portal, drew in one flash a great curved blade and made to lunge.

The two wayfarers fled madly through the trees. Once again the forest had become a sinister place, and they wondered if they would ever escape its mocking glamour. The rest of their journey was a harrowing bewilderment, until they eventually left the forest behind them. This, however, is as much as we know, for there seems to be no coherent account of what took place during this time.

Upon arrival in Qu, the hapless minstrel fashioned a few baleful verses from his experience. This brought both him and the forest some renown, and if he is remembered at all today it is for these verses and not the wistful lyrics of love that are all he composed besides.

This was the first story of the temple in the forest, but it was not to be the last. Others were to happen upon the clearing and give very similar accounts to those of Kerr and his retainer. No matter when they came across the nameless temple, in broad day or in the depths of the forest night, it was always guarded by the same figure – the tall man in black with the flashing eyes and the ready blade. And always he would challenge the trespasser with the same words, and utter no others.

Time passed and the stories of the temple came to be better known, so that people trod the forest ways only with some trepidation. Some of these were so cautious that they did not burst into the clearing all unawares, but apprehending its presence beforehand, stood upon its very edge and observed from the cover of the trees. All, without exception, saw the Black

Guardian, as he had come to be known. Some reported that he knelt before the temple steps praying fervently in some unearthly tongue, no doubt that of the script on the temple walls. Others said they saw the figure engaged in weird and unbelievable martial exercises, such as balancing on the tip of his sword or throwing that sword in such a way that it circled the clearing and returned to his palm. Still others said he stood perfectly still and silent no matter how long they observed.

Then, there were those who entered the forest never to emerge. While it is true they were unable to bear witness, in their absence, to its cause, there were many who considered that very absence eloquent.

More time passed. Eventually the lifespan of one man, then two, passed by, and still there were sightings of the temple and the Black Guardian. Who was this being, that knew not death nor hunger nor sleep, but spent every moment of his life in vigilance and devotion, guarding the temple and praying to it? And who or what was the god, Agnos Theer, which he served?

More travellers went missing in the forest, and with the passing of time and the increase of traffic to a steady, if dismal, trickle, the stories of the forest only proliferated. It would unbalance my tale to tell a single one of those others, though many are of interest and deserve the telling at another time. It will suffice to say that the forest had become most definitely, if these tales were to be credited, the haunt of dryads, Jack o' lanthorns, lemures, manes, undines, hobgoblins, basilisks, nopperabor, mandrakes, succubi, brownies, lesties, wyrms, imps, ghouls, dybbuks, bunyips, fox spirits, white ladies, naiads and shucks.

In the course of time it came about that just enough travellers were put off by the extra distance of the old trade roads for a few small inns to spring up at the very edge of the forest to lodge them before their trek through darkness. But the reputation of the forest was also just forbidding enough to make the majority turn aside.

It was to one of these dubious establishments, a place half in the human world and half in the weird shadow of the beyond, that a suitably strange guest arrived one evening. He cut a very different figure to the merchants who made up the better part of the inn's custom, and gave his name as Absolom. Both his unkempt clothes and the sword slung insolently at his side told his story well enough. He was what they called in those days a 'wandering sword', a warrior for whom disappointments, treachery and the bleak experiences of their calling had proved too bitter, who left his masters or was deprived of his master by circumstance. Some of these were mere criminals or so-called 'soldiers of fortune'. Absolom, it seemed, was of the kind for which the phrase was originally meant – a true lost soul.

The innkeeper tried to question Absolom on his business, but the swordsman was so surly as to be menacing and seemed intent only on drinking himself into a stupor. Perhaps because he feared Absolom might cause trouble, the innkeeper warned him of the perils of the forest on whose border they sat. Absolom began to show interest and even asked questions of his own. In particular, he wanted to know about the temple. When the innkeeper finished telling him the story he smiled and sat upright, as if this was what he had long been searching for. He laughed and spoke the following words in a voice sardonic and grim:

"So, there is a god in this very forest, and he is so mighty that he must be guarded night and day! Maybe it is because they are so very old, but I have found all gods to be hard of hearing. Ah, but maybe if I spoke to this one face to face and raised my voice, he might hear my petition. But no, it is too late for prayers, I fear. Anyway, I would like to speak to a god if such exists. I have scores to settle. And what of the spirits of the forest? Do I not carry my own demons with me wherever I go? And what of this Black Guardian? Even if I am slain, what else is there for me but to try my sword against him – the unbeaten against the unbeaten? What else am I good for?"

So apposite did this quest of nihilism seem to Absolom that there was no dissuading him. It was the best the innkeeper could do to convince him to wait until morning, in the hope he might change his mind. The next day, however, Absolom's drunken asseverations were replaced only by a sense of sober and dreadful purpose. Silently he set out into the grey dawn. On the evening of the eighth day he returned, bedraggled, exhausted and wounded in his left arm. He collapsed with fever at the inn, and the innkeeper lodged him there, eventually extracting from him all the details of what had taken place.

Since he had had no need for stealth, and since he was actually looking for it, Absolom had struck upon the clearing very soon, three days into his journey, and did not hesitate to step within. Immediately there sprang forth, as if from thin air, the apparition of the Black Guardian, who challenged Absolom in the same terms as he had challenged many others before him. Absolom, however, stood his ground. In so doing he strayed deliberately from the paths prescribed to mortals, and his soul became the legitimate plaything of the gods. The Black Guardian leapt like a spark and seemed to press his attack from all directions. There was no time to think. Absolom could do nothing but meet the attack and make his steely reply. Both of them fought with a deadly selflessness, the one because he had everything to lose, and the other because he had nothing. It was, said Absolom, like a battle of souls on some field beyond life and death.

The Guardian took many wounds without slowing, but something was wrong. Was it the fact he had so much to lose that, despite all his dazzling whirl of limbs and blade, made him actually somewhere a little too circumspect? He wanted to stay alive to protect his god. Sensing his advantage as clearly as an opening in his opponent's guard, Absolom pressed it home, and, at last, with a single thrust of his blade, he slew the Black Guardian.

With the deathblow came not the elation of triumph, but an unexpected feeling of desolation, as if he had unwittingly slain his own brother. His life full of such bitterness, he did not linger over the corpse, but looked to the now unprotected temple. He leapt up the steps, his bloody sword still in his hand, thinking perhaps to purge this bitterness with whatever divine retribution lay within. Whatever it was, it must be an absolute of some kind.

Even Absolom paused before reaching for the carven portal. He was about to look upon the face of the Great God Agnos Theer. Had any living soul done such a thing before?

Then his hand was on the ancient stone, and he heaved with furious strength. The portal did not budge. He flung away his sword, to face Agnos Theer now empty-handed, and with both hands fell to, and at last the door shifted, then gave and groaned outward. As soon as a crack had opened, a few inches of darkness, there came a great whooshing gust of air from within, which nearly knocked Absolom from his feet. Then wider opened the portal, wider still. Daylight fell within and illumined…nothing! The temple interior was as it is today, perfectly empty, like a riddle without an answer. There was no treasure, no glory, no great fanged mandala of a beast-god's face, no indescribable vortex ascending like a stairway to forbidden and immortal realms. Nothing.

To make sure he was not deceived, Absolom threw open the portals on all four sides. The temple was as empty as a magician's cabinet – emptier. Here were no false bottoms, no secret levers. He spent a long time in verifying this. At last he gave up, and shouted to the air:

"Why? Why live and die to protect an empty box? The fool!"

And he laughed in amazement. The same laugh took him when he had finished relating his adventure to the innkeeper, so that the innkeeper feared he might be unhinged.

"Here I am! Absolom the God-Slayer! Ha ha ha! Go into the forest and see! The temple is empty! Am I the God-Slayer? Or am I Absolom the Dupe? Ha ha ha. He died to save an empty box."

Some days after pronouncing these strange words, Absolom killed himself by falling on his own sword.

This is the tale I heard from a cottager who lived on the other side of the temple, on a hillside, just where the forest was beginning to thin. I am a gyrovague, a monk of the sect of Mu, and was on a pilgrimage. Even in that land, beyond the Southern Pass, there are those who know and respect the custom of alms-giving for pilgrims, and are wont to look kindly on foreign gods.

The many carvings outside the cottage, from the cottager's own hands, had led me to expect sympathy from the start. They were branches, logs, weirdly tangled roots, whose own shapes were left largely intact, but only enhanced by some little carving here and there, as if simply to release whatever spirit was already in them. I could not help but admire such art and the wise benevolence it expressed. An agreeable sense of fellow-feeling came over me and I did not hesitate to knock. And indeed, when the old cottager saw my alms-bowl he ushered me in without further inquiry.

His dwelling was small, but well kept, and I could not help noticing the many shelves of books that filled one wall, which the man called his 'apiary of words'. It soon transpired that he was a late follower of the ways of eremitism as advocated and practised by many artists of our land and his in the age of the great literary artists. That was why he felt such sympathy at the sight of a wandering monk.

The cottager kindly offered to lodge me for the night, and we spent some time talking pleasantly of the artists and poets whom he admired. Then we talked of his own carvings, and quite naturally I recalled the strange temple I had so lately passed. It is part of the creed of Mu to pay respects at any temple, even those of alien faiths, and I had done so at this temple. However, I had never seen or heard of any temple quite like it and now desired to know the exact nature of the place at which I had offered prayers. The cottager told me all I have recorded and more, and my poor priest's style has done his tongue no justice. When he finished I sat back in reflection.

"That is indeed a riddle," I said.

"That is one version of the story. There are others. In one, for instance, with the great gust of air from the open portal there also issues a cry of blood-chilling anguish. In another, it is not a cry, but laughter."

"Then perhaps Absolom really was a god-slayer, is that what you mean? The voice, a scream or laughter, was the voice of Agnos Theer? But laughter – that is another riddle."

As I spoke I wondered to myself what sort of god it might have been. Are we to imagine Agnos Theer squatting inside that cramped box for thousands of years with knees drawn up to chin? Would this mysterious deity have looked anything like the external carvings, or would it have looked utterly different?

"But many say the voice, and even the gust of wind, were later embellishments."

"Then where is the truth?"

"We can assume the stories of the Black Guardian are true, because we have so many independent sources. And let us also trust that Absolom's story was broadly true, for the corpse of the Black Guardian was found next to the empty, desecrated temple. Now let us consider a few things. In the olden times few would pass through a forest unless they had to, and any who actually lived in the forest would likely have been considered straightaway as goblins rather than men. Added to this was the mystery of a man who seemed to spend his whole life outside the temple, performing his devotions, and who was encountered by travellers, it seems, centuries apart."

"Yes, you are restating one half of the riddle."

"Just so. Or one part. There are other parts yet. Almost two hundred years after Absolom slew the Black Guardian and took his own life, the poet Hustin Dole, intrigued by lingering folklore, wandered through the forest. He did not find the temple straight away, but what he did find is recorded in *Chronicle of a Book-Quiver*, one of his lesser known works."[1]

And the cottager lovingly extracted from his shelves a box-bound edition of the volume he had named. He slid the peg from the eye of the clasp and unfolded the pages. Then he stabbed the vellum with his finger as if consulting a map, and showed me. I shall do my best to quote from memory:

"High up on that hill I came upon a dark and perilous ravine, such a work of nature as I had never seen before. Two beetling brows of rock pressed close together, and cloaked with trees and shrubs, formed a veritable corridor of darkness, its details as if inked heavily by the gloomiest of illustrators. Here there was a ridge, below which cool darkness swooped about in emptiness and gave off a smell of must, as in a cave. It hardly seemed to be outside at all, and even under the open sky, it seemed, here was a place of cobwebs and dust. The hush struck my heart and made it beat all the more. Something in this inkiness and stillness could not be refused and I passed in strange agitation through that dry and crumbling passage at last to the emerald sunlight at the other side.

"As if time itself refused to traverse the passage, the grass, the dew, the very sunlight of that farther, high-uplifted and ethereal meadow seemed in a state pristine, as of a world that knew not man. All in a chalice of high rock that meadow lay, an overflowing green. But soon enough I came across the proof that man, indeed, had known this place before.

"As bright and flourishing as was the long grass that it sat among, so was the building spectral. As the grass seemed about to disappear in sunlight, so it seemed that this building too, like the sloughed skin of a ghost, a dusty husk, must disappear if one blinked. And yet it did not disappear, and I drew close, and it still there. I saw it was a monastery or retreat, and recalled some tale or other of such a mountain monastery

---

1 - [N.B. A book quiver is a small box or case, often of wickerwork, in which a traveller would carry writing tools and materials, as well as reading material. It is an item associated with the 'wind-blown' poets, a school of poets who wrote almost exclusively in the form of travel journals interspersed with short poems.]

haunted by a sorrowful ghost the knowledge of which was fatal. I set no store by such tales, yet still the eerie look about the place made me hesitate to step within and blow the dust from its secrets. But I would not be a poet if I could have resisted its drear invitation.

"Inside was such a shock of dust, the accumulation of many lifetimes without the passage of any but a creeping, death-like life, that my heart warned me of evil. Yet even in this hoary carcass of a building, I met no harm. All was decorated in the most fantastic and morbid taste with the spider's dusty silk, a white and yellow opulence of desolation. However, all the passages were empty and I found nothing beyond my own obscure fancies till I slid open a blanched door to reveal the jewelled cluster of grotesque secrets set in this foil of decay.

"This must have been the monastery's great hall, where the monks would come to meditate and talk. Across the back wall there hung a splendid silken banner with a crest, and all about the other banners and tapestries of web, the sunlight on them poisonous and oily. There was an altar whose magnificent brocade spread across the floor, and rugs and carpets grim as tomb-cursed treasures. Along one wall a library of books and scrolls was spread; along the other stood a line of braziers. But in the centre of all this, as if idols of the gods which all this honoured, there sat the skeletons of a dozen monks, all wrapped up in the tatters of what were once sable robes. In their bony hands they clutched the hilts of swords whose tips pierced the emptiness where once their vitals were. Some were half toppled, or propped upon the very instruments of their destruction. Here, it dawned upon me, were the brothers of the guardian whose temple I sought."

Hustin Dole goes on to describe the contents of the hall in some detail. Outside again, moved by his discoveries, he sits upon a rock and composes the following verse:

> "The insect's chirp is empty as the sunbeam
> That scatters the dark, secret dream into these pieces -
> A ruined monastery, forgotten treasure, emerald green.
> What is this but gleaming bones whose cavities
> Are o'ergrown with nameless weeds?"

And like the dream of Dole's verse, the enchantment of the Black Guardian broke up in my mind's eye.

"Now I understand what you are saying. The travellers took their own fears and imaginings into the forest with them. They made the Black Guardian, for there was no such thing. They made a single demon out of many men. Perhaps such was even the design of this brotherhood that Dole found, and they were responsible for the macabre ends of many unwary wayfarers. Still, that does not explain whence this brotherhood came, nor their purpose in guarding an empty shell."

"But wait, I have not finished. Dole took some scriptures from that place, and they can still be found today in the library of Demos. Some say the writing is like that of ancient Atl. Six thousand years ago the empire of Meng annexed Atl, and though the folk were peaceful, and did not resist, the conquerors found the faith of that land abhorrent. They feared it and smashed all the great, grey domes of the temples. The god of that faith was Omni. The records of Meng describe him as a god who crouched among caves of skulls and gnawed on bones, a god as harsh as the mountain's edge, a carnivore of the droning void, and his emblem was an empty web. Now, this god also had a brother, little talked about, whose name we do not know. Only the most meagre accounts survive. If memory serves me well, in the annals of Meng, Omni's brother is described thus: 'It can exist only where human eyes see not and where human minds pry not. Where our knowledge is, it is not, so that we may never know its shape, nor its visage, nor its true nature.' I wonder if that god was not our Agnos Theer. There's something else. All accounts of spirits in the forest cease abruptly after Absolom's desecration. Also, why is it that no one found the monastery before Hustin Dole? Or is it that the monastery, the brotherhood, and the whole explanation to the mystery did not exist until the mystery itself was slain? Could it be that the moment Absolom flung the doors open, Agnos Theer ceased to exist?"

"Is this what you believe?"

"In the years I have lived here these thoughts have chased each other back and forth in my mind. I cannot say more than that."

I was strangely moved by the cottager's tale and the obvious wondering enthusiasm with which he told it – so moved, in fact, that before continuing with my pilgrimage I retraced my steps to the temple in the forest to pay homage to its riddle.

It was a solemn place that I returned to. I looked once more, amazed, upon the matchless carvings, whose meaning I knew not. They were the product of arts lost and irretrievable, fashioned to decorate the emptiness within, and yet somehow, as if woven out of it. They were eerie in their muteness. I stepped inside. The wind stirred freely through the four open portals, and I was unaccountably ill at ease. For some reason I felt constrained to listen, as for a voice. But there was nothing. Only the wind stirred. Shuddering, I left that place.

LILO

Chapter I: A Doll's Life

The crisp edge of a mountain slope, like a cresting wave. A whisk of snow from gleaming skis as they describe a dynamic curve. The pristine panorama reflected in crystalline blue eyes, the iris spiralling closed like the shutter of a camera, like an airlock.

"Anything can happen in Eternity. And it does!"

This was the unwanted thought that lingered behind those blue eyes in the crevasse of Glenn's mind. It was unwanted because, like all thought, it cast a shadow. By thinking such things Glenn was showing not his closeness to the freedom of endless possibility, but his continued attachment to a world of doubt and limitation where such thoughts are necessary.

Skiing with the drift-deep satisfaction of expertise, feeling as he did so the wealth and sophistication of the body and the heart, Glenn decided to put the advent of these thoughts and their shadows down to the fact that the time of his Rekindling was near. The blue pilot light of his immortality was ebbing. He could feel the edge of the weakening flame like a lament in his chest.

The thought continued to trouble him as he made an epic sweep into the lower, fir-forested slopes where nestled the ski lodge he called home. Actually, it wasn't that he was opposed to thought in principle, but there was something about this particular thought that was disturbing. It was a skein of continuity whose existence indicated a past incongruous with this present. Glenn did not want to think about how he had got here; it was an issue edged with too much vagueness. Still, the skein continued to unwind. "Mortality," it went on didactically, "is the curious and paradoxical condition which keeps one from the consciousness of this most flexible of truths." But Glenn, being a plastic doll, inhabited an equally paradoxical, although entirely different normality, which seemed as inevitable to him as the hopelessness of impending death did to others. For, as an immortal, he inhabited a neutral zone from which all times and places were accessible; it was a life as open and empty as the sky.

It was cosy inside the lodge, and his girlfriend, Paula, was waiting for him. The lodge was typified by warmth, and though snow could be seen through the windows, not a suggestion of its cold ever whispered through a crack in the walls, unless in a sudden silky draft like an exquisite tremor of reflective sadness. That warmth was in the rich colours of the carpet and furnishings, in the vast log fire that dominated the main room and in the thick, Arran jerseys that Glenn and Paula invariably wore. Even though Glenn and Paula were both handsomely fashioned of the finest flesh-tone plastic, when they touched it was quite as if they were made of real flesh. Glenn walked into the drawing room where Paula was kneeling on the spacious sofa wearing her occasional glasses and reading. She put her book down and stood up. Their hands touched and Glenn felt the cool, thrilling softness of Paula's skin, which always felt freshly washed.

Whenever Glenn drew close to Paula, or touched her, there came the same unfailing magnetic tingle that drew them closer still into the zone of petting and kissing. That charge between them was always of exactly the same strength. It was a sure sign of the bland eternity of their love. It also deleted any need for conversation. That is, conversation became a mysterious, sensual pleasure, not a means to overcoming misunderstandings. Now, as always, the magnetic tingle was taking effect, and, with no reason to resist, Glenn found himself in the warm hugging darkness of Paula's arms. There was the soppy wetness of lips, a wetness that to someone in an infinitely remote alternative universe, bizarrely meant disease, guilt, disgust. Glenn knew no such squeamishness. Kissing was as simple a pleasure as sunbathing.

The profound excitement of a dream come true is not the edgy excitement that mortals sometimes know. It is a furry, comforting fullness of the stomach. It is a thrill that smiles quietly to the very fingertips, reflected in every corner of the vision. Glenn and Paula, by mutual understanding, crawled like children playing tigers onto the fur rug in front of the fire and there began the inoffensive pornography of their undressing, the releasing of plastic breasts which turned to pendulous flesh in the hands, the discovery of the engagement-ring bliss between the legs – a body as smooth and enticing as catalogue lingerie. Like two films spliced together in rapid alternation, Glenn's senses switched between the visual scene of two dolls coupling, and tactile, carnal knowledge of two human bodies intimate in squish and stink. Each version had its own pleasure. The plastic version held the abstract attraction of sex for a child, where imagination and doctor-and-nurses games with inert toys are their own end. The flesh version was full of the sickly sweetness of obscenity diluted by love. Each version tempered the other. The flesh version lent the plastic version a sliding, salacious thrill. The plastic version turned the stink of the flesh to perfume, the squish to a caress. They ran through various positions like a demonstration with mannequins. There was never anything to be late for. In a sense their whole lifestyle was a glorious lie-in, the warm blankets of vague eternity up to their necks. They could snuggle up to this pink bliss and stay there as though hibernating, if they so wished. But since they knew they would always do it again, withdrawing from the embrace was never painful.

When they finally disentangled themselves from each other they lay back on the rug in front of the fire like a kitsch version of Adam and Eve. On a tray beside them stood a magnum of champagne and two glasses. Glenn felt a purring all through his body. He raised his glass and looked at the crackling flames through it. The carpet, the furniture, the walls, the view through the windows, the two healthy lovers, all were full of the sparkling bubbles of the champagne. And yet, within the purr of Glenn's body was a deeper buzz not appropriate to the cosiness of their dazzling winter. It was a nervous buzz of autumn, of greyness and serrated shadows abrading the heart. And this was why his eyes were cast downwards, and this was why an unwonted question fell from Paula's dairymaid lips.

"What're you thinking about, Sugarplops?"

"Nothing, really. Why?"

"You look thoughtful."

"Yes, I suppose I am."

There was something about Paula's inquiry that almost teased a pout out of him, that almost seduced him into a sulk in order to prolong and play with the situation. That particular skein of thought, however, felt too much like sinking, and he pulled himself up.

"My flame is burning low, so I feel low. It feels like all the shadows are lengthening. Once I've been to my Rekindling I'll be myself again."

"You didn't say anything about your Rekindling."

"I know. It's one of those things. It always seems strange to have such a grave responsibility left up to the individual. You'd at least think they'd send a notice or something. 'You are due for your next Rekindling!' That sort of thing."

"When will you go?"

"I suppose there's no point in delaying. I'll go tomorrow."

"Then, when you get back, we can go to one of the Alternative Zones to celebrate."

Glenn made a face.

"What's wrong? Don't you like the Alternative Zones?"

"They're confusing. You can get lost and forget yourself if you're not careful. It just gets too complicated."

"There's nothing complicated in it at all, Honeybunch. Life is here to be enjoyed."

"Yes, of course. You're so right! This low is affecting my thinking. After the Rekindling we'll go somewhere to celebrate – the Easy Listening Zone perhaps."

"Oh, my poor baby." Paula took Glenn's head in her hands and laid it close to her breasts, tinged pink by the heat of the fire. "These lows are always confusing. There, there!"

And Glenn allowed himself to be comforted like the baby he had been called, knowing that to be able to embrace such yuckiness was to inhabit a haven of true love.

As if in preparation for the morrow's expedition, Glenn made a call at his study-cum-library. Of all the rooms in the lodge it was the most shadowy. Not gloomy, exactly, but full of shallow shadows like those cast by the frames and lenses of spectacles, so suggestive of cool intellect. These shadows of intellect were reproduced in the keys of the typewriter that sat on the desk by the window, and in the stencil-like letters tapped onto the roll of paper still curled into its guts. Sometimes when Glenn was tapping the keys he would look out of the frost-framed window and see the day-glo skiers zigzagging down the blinding slopes, as if the mountainside were the sky itself, or some even more ambiguous medium, like the friendly voices and music of the radio. On such occasions the rolling white of the page before him would seem a continuation of the slopes' glaring happiness, and the skiers would turn to letters, bending their knees over the drifts and dips.

For Glenn was an artist. In this room he could don black-framed glasses as chunky as his jersey, as chunky as his chin, and immerse himself in the staccato world of letters. Most of the books on the shelves were of his authorship, under a variety of pen names. They were all explorations of what Glenn had come to consider the only theme of any importance – the romance of Love and its happy ending. Glenn made a point of not vocalising abstract thoughts. Of course, the soul is a profoundly deep well in which such thoughts resound sonorously. But to leave them unexpressed is to live them more satisfyingly. They are there always, resonant between the lines of sensual experience. This was the feel-good philosophy by which Glenn lived. To describe Glenn's life generally as happy, however, would perhaps be misleading. He had long ago reached an acme of the emotions beyond mere happiness. He could look at the icicles hanging like Christmas decorations from the pines surrounding the lodge and feel their delicate drooping spikes expressing a bliss that was both an enigmatically shallow happiness and an exquisitely formed sadness. That was the beauty of the plastic winter that smoothed its curves all around; the polystyrene whiteness and the crunch of snow, the firmness of crisp shadows, formed the crust of a pie of deep contentment. Its glittering cold, when anyone fell through that crust – the frisks of hair from beneath hisorher woolly hat twisting against the wedding cake coruscation of ice – burned the heart with a chill flash, was a shock of superficial beauty. But the darkness within was warmth and comfort. And so it was often from such things as the icicles and the drifts that Glenn drew inspiration for his novels. His writing was as mercifully free of abstractions as his conversation. The world, after all, is not made of words. Words have a tendency to imply meaning. But what, for instance, is the meaning of an icicle? It symbolises, finally, nothing but itself. That is its great value. So Glenn's works were full of the irreducibly inarticulate, dumbfounding images of icicles, sky, clouds, warm clean hands picking up receivers and dialling to call lovers, lips touching with the sweetness of a melting snowflake; each symbolising nothing but its own priceless self.

But now, as he sat at his desk, a little uncomfortable in the hard, studious atmosphere that seemed to demand industry of him, he did not want to write. He had come here self-indulgently to think, since this was the only room that would not be indelibly tainted by such cerebration. Ironically, his thoughts centred around his doubts as to whether the existence of this room was a good thing at all. There was something suspicious about it. Would it not be better and more fitting for Glenn to be a purely physical type? It's true he did not quite aspire to being an action man, more the kind of male doll that little girls play with – the kind who dress up in dinner jackets and go along to balls in sports cars and do all sorts of improbable things in a similar vein. Sitting at a typewriter was somehow incongruous with such misty-eyed glamour. And yet… And yet… He was deep chested and lantern jawed, and a kiss curl hung over his brow as if glued there. Donning his TV-screen, black-framed glasses and leaving rings on his desk from the mug of cocoa beside him – wasn't this too a kind of glamour? The problem was one of complication. If the glamour was pure and uncomplicated enough to make life a rose-tinted haze, then everything was fine. But in order to achieve such glamour one had to eliminate all realistic details. For instance, realistically, writing novels is difficult. The writer often hits walls, gets frustrated, has to revise his work many times, and is still unsatisfied. In the glamorous world, however, Glenn simply sits at the typewriter and the words flow out perfectly the first time at precisely the pace he is physically capable of typing. Glenn was close to achieving such unreality, but there still remained an annoying grittiness in his life, moments where he found he was not provided with some corny lines from a script and had to make up his own awkward lines that smacked of realism and the uncertainty of an actual personality. Moments, for instance, when he might find himself sitting on the toilet reaching for the soft loo-roll and think, "Really, what need is there to include this scene in my life? It's badly shot, unglamorous, and just too obscure."

While that grittiness remained, writing was still an intellectual pursuit. Why should there be any need for such a reflective activity? Surely, if one were completely fulfilled one wouldn't need such pastimes, which divided experience into that which was lived and that which was unlived – which divided the very self. He ought simply to live and have done with such redundant tools as words. The wonders of hedonism were already in his reach. Why hesitate? To try and reflect such wonders in the mirror of words was obviously futile. If one were simply a writer for the sake of the name and one's books were merely a vagueness like the spines on the shelves of a doll's house, then writing would be justified. Then, and only then.

But this train of thought brought to light another dilemma. Wasn't it, after all, the intellect of a very particular personality that was seeking fulfilment in this perfect glamour? If this perfect glamour denied the very grittiness of such a personality then wasn't the whole thing futile from the start? It was like a ray of light seeking darkness. Wherever that ray went, darkness would naturally disappear. They could not exist in the same place at the same time. So, even supposing he managed to achieve perfect glamour, it would entail the loss of that consciousness which desired such attainment in the first place. It might even mean the transition from a first person existence to a wholly third person existence.

All in all, this room's relation to the rest of the lodge and the world beyond was very much a parallel of Glenn's own mind and its relation to his external life. The room was like the inner workings of a machine. It was a behind-the-scenes, a technical and intellectual plan which projected a simplified and ideal reality.

Usually Glenn could deal with these contradictions in his life harmoniously. He was immortal, after all. There was no need for anxiety or impatience. It was the great, sonorous cycle of his inner flame that was at the heart of such doubts. When it ebbed the shadows began to crowd in closer.

At last, as if no longer able to bear such contemplation and remain stationary, Glenn got up from his chair. He glanced to the door to assure himself it was closed, and slid over to the book shelf like a guilt-ridden priest. His fingers brushed over the spines and located one particular spine with the blind ease of furtive habit. He slipped the volume from the shelf as if it were a lever that opened a secret passage. Of all the books in the library, this one alone had an air of secrecy about it. It looked out of place, like an anomalous digital watch in a costume drama. It was a pivot, a linchpin, a link between one dimension and another, capable of revealing all things as illusion. The cover was that of a dull-looking grey hardback. Gilt letters spelt out the title: "Positive Thinking, the World and You." The creamy pages were a little yellow and musty, and there was about it that same stiff, bright aura of age that clings to television commercials and information broadcasts of the 1950s. Glenn flicked through the pages. The language was curiously flavourless, divorced from any strong sense of style.

This quality was apparent in the subject matter, too. Although treating of matters of the greatest spiritual concern, no single school of philosophy or religion was mentioned by name, giving a feeling of utter rootlessness and neutrality. It was as if it were a teach-yourself cookery book, or the tract of a mail order company. And yet it was this modest and anonymous volume that had changed Glenn's life, that formed to him the fountainhead of all truth. He reread for the ten thousandth time the first lines of the book:

> Every single individual has it within their power to change the world. Nor is this a task of any difficulty. All you have to do is decide that you want to change it. That told and the whole purport of this book is told. And yet the questions of happiness and the salvation of the race, on certain planes of awareness, have perplexed humanity for so long that one must concede the very ease of such a decision has bamboozled humanity into thinking it the hardest thing of all.
>
> With the aid of this book you will be able to persuade yourself once more that the decision is easy and dispense with a fruitless history of confusion and hesitation that has kept you from making such a step before.

As ever the words rang with inspiration, an alarm clock waking him once more to the morning of consciousness where the sky is that blank optimism of endless possibility that comes before thought habitually narrows the possibilities down. The first and most important thing was to know that there was nothing to worry about. That given and there was no need to struggle to understand the rest. It will all come in time. Don't worry. He flicked to another chapter entitled, "The Seed of Thought."

> From the seeds of thought all things grow. The world is but a flowering of the tiniest of these seeds. It is not just that thought brings about changes in a separate physical world, but the substance of that world is thought itself. Existence is a web of subjectivity.

He skimmed further down the page and his eyes settled on the following sentence:

> The past does not exist except as a rationalisation of the present.

Something in this particular sentence re-intrigued him. It seemed peculiarly pertinent to his current preoccupations. It was as if the book, itself as mutable as the subjective universe it described, would throw out something new whenever it was consulted, reflecting the changes of the world around it. The words themselves were all the same, of course, as far as Glenn's memory was concerned, but somehow they were differently highlighted to his mind. Arrested by the enigma this sentence posed, Glenn found his mood diverted from one of anxiety to one of wondering curiosity. He slid the book back onto the shelf without reading further.

Chapter II: The Lemon Fresh Morning of Eternity

Sleep came, cutting its usual dark swathes of forgetfulness through the consciousness of all. Sleep – that deceptive interval of dark in which the objects in one's life may be silently and cunningly rearranged without one noticing – oneself included. Morning settled bright as a commercial for washing up liquid in the front of the lodge where water dripped from icicles above the windows. The sunlight, wide awake with nothing to do, settled on the rims of cups and saucers, and gleamed similarly on Glenn's shoulders and upper torso as he lay beside Paula in bed. The angles of his body were like those of someone who has fallen from a cliff. But the cliff he had fallen from was dream and the rocks below a soft mattress. As if it were a half dream still lingering in Glenn's half wakefulness, a whistling such as the morning itself might make could be heard faintly in the distance. The dream left the dreamer behind, moved into that whistling distance, became bright and wide awake, outside. Skimming over snow between the trunks of pines, there came a figure in bright orange waterproofs whose creases here and there held snow, melting and glittering. On his back was a fluorescent bag containing newspapers. From the outside he displayed the stiff, jittery motion of Supermarionation. Looking down at himself from beneath the hood of his own consciousness, however, he saw the veined, hairy hands of a normal human projecting from his sleeves. It was the focus on detail that would bring about this shift in perception.

Inside the lodge the sunlight was panning at low, wide angles through empty rooms. From the point of view of the bouncing beams, existing between all consciousness, the lodge was roof-less and wall-less, just like any normal dolls' house, which allows the child to see into all the rooms at once with the omnipresence of a god. Sunlight squirted everywhere, with a citrus tang. Sunlight on taps and plastic bath toys. Sunlight on spotless tiles.

The skier swooped into the trough that ran along the outside of the lodge. He slowed, his skis slithering on the crust of ice and snow. He came to an unsteady halt outside the front door. Dark and sunken beneath its peppering of snow, the door almost gave the impression that the whole house was solid, a compact mystery of darkness in which the imagination paradoxically pictured infinite brightness and cosiness. He took the bag from his back and there followed a close-up on the newspaper he removed and the deep-tanned hand that held it. The colours of the close-up were dark and rich, like the inkiness that falls on the eyes after they turn away from the blazing fireball of the sun. Standing before the collision of melting ice and shattering rays, the character was a picture of business-like cheerfulness. He pushed the folded paper through the letterbox. Then, for an interval, there was nothing but the face of the gold watch on his wrist. The great dipping harpoon of the second-hand hesitated in mechanical pulses from one gold ingot to the next as if partitioning time zones. Each time zone was packaged into some abstract pocket of existence, like adverts between scenes in a film. Thus, before the paper thudded in a wad on the welcome mat inside, there was time enough for several of these scenes and Glenn was already propped up by several pillows with a tray of breakfast before him.

Paula, in gossamer nighty and knickers, had been pattering back and forth between the kitchen and the bedroom. Finally she picked up the whacking prop of the morning paper from where it had slammed down like a gravestone onto the doormat. (Outside a dusting of snow shivered off the roof and fell in a thin curtain between the newspaper delivery man and the front door. He turned on his skis and began to jerk merrily on his way.) Where the coverlet was folded back in a soft triangle, Paula climbed once more into the toast-warm bed like a cat stretching out in a yawn. She placed the folded paper across the corner of the breakfast tray. From a little distance the paper was as stiff and artificial as any other prop, but in close-up, within the field of its own reality, it bent a little with its own weight over the edges of the tray, laden with some ticking, shadowy burden, like a time bomb. And indeed, there was something a little too realistic about this particular article. It should have given the impression, at least, that were one to open it up one would find nothing more than columns of wavy lines. There was altogether too great a feeling of focus and accuracy about it. Glenn sipped his black coffee. Something in the curly hairs of his chest and the towel-soft intimacy of the double bed and adjoining bathroom seemed to call up a schmaltzy bossa nova in the very air and in Glenn's love-massaged slap-tingling body. He reached for the newspaper and unfolded it. There were still spots of melted snow on the front page. But Glenn hardly noticed this, for, in stark, black letters across the sheet there marched the headline:

TERRORISTS TAKE THE LAST RESORT

Beneath the printed alarm of this sentence was a photograph of a group of skiers in sinister-looking masks with rifles across their backs. They had swooped down upon a speeding train, and one of their number must have been using a weapon more powerful than a rifle, because there was a great explosion in the carriage in front of them.

"Terrorists in The Resort," muttered Glenn in ominous disbelief.

Somehow Glenn was too scared to read anything more than the headline. He willingly passed the paper to his girlfriend as if her reading it would somehow render it all harmless.

"What does it say?"

"'A group of masked terrorists have made a series of attacks on trains to The Rekindling Zone. Their motives are as yet unknown, but it is believed that they infiltrated The Resort through one of the Service Zones... On Tuesday their attack on The Snowflake Express left fifteen dead and seven seriously injured...'"

"That's impossible!"

"What is?"

"No one can possibly infiltrate The Resort. It doesn't make sense."

Paula looked at him silently in puzzled surprise. She seemed to find nothing unnatural or incongruous in the news. Her concern was the normal concern for loss of life and the distress of the victims.

"Surely The Resort is meant to be impregnable," he continued lamely against Paula's bewildered silence. "Besides, who would want to blow up the Snowflake Express?"

"It says their motives are unknown."

"Of course they're unknown – there are no motives. I don't believe a word of it."

"But, darling, maybe there are people who would want to blow up the train, for all sorts of reasons, people from outside The Resort, bitter people jealous of our happiness."

Why did Paula find the news so much easier to accept than he did? Was it that she was so much more a part of the reality of the Resort that any of its manifestations were taken on board by her readily and unquestioningly, that she did not have the mental equipment to distinguish what was out of place? If so – and an unwanted question rose to the surface of Glenn's mind – was she really real? Were all the other people in The Resort a product of his imagination, with no independent existence? Or did the imaginations of different people jointly weave the environment they inhabited? Glenn's conception of The Resort was as a sort of fantasy Utopia, a toyland of the heart. Violence had no part in it except in the Spy and Adventure Zones where it was perfectly controlled, as if it had all been minutely choreographed. In fact, wasn't that the very essence of Glenn's conception – control? Paula's conception seemed to allow for all sorts of inconsistencies, just as a child may play with a doll, an Action Man and a tiny model car all at once, introducing explosions and car chases to a soft focus ball. And what was fascinating and perhaps somewhat disturbing, was that she was capable of accepting chaotic intrusions from outside. This could only be because she was a more integrated part of things than Glenn. Glenn, wanting to control everything, remained strangely remote. Since everything was the stuff of his own dreams, he could not comprehend any intrusions. This article in the newspapers seemed a mocking attack on him personally. Of course, reality is a paradox. It relies on the impossible to affirm the possible. If one thing is real, something else must be unreal. But this opposition calls into question the reality of all things, since, at bottom, there is no reason why one thing should be more real than another. What was happening here appeared to Glenn to be a sort of breakdown, a confusion in different planes of reality, resulting in disorder. He looked at the headline and photo again and winced as if with a headache. He felt that his flame was guttering dangerously low.

"What is it, Glenn?"

"All those trains were on their way to The Rekindling Zone, weren't they?"

Paula put her finger to her lip. "Of course. I'm sorry. How inconsiderate of me. You must be worried. Do you want to wait a little longer perhaps, until the incidents have blown over?"

"No, I've got to go. I think I might have left it too late already."

"You must be careful, my darlingest. I don't want to lose my big huggy love baby just because of those nasty terrorists," said Paula, but her words were too much like the bad dialogue of an overdubbed soap opera, spoken with an intonation that bore no relation to their meaning.

Chapter III: The First Day of the Rest of Your Life

The morning was a long and sprawling one. The letters of events spread out in serene simplicity on the blank page of time.

Jerry and Sue turned up, dazzling white teeth and orange tans, their skiing goggles pushed up, snow-flecked and silvery-reflective, on their foreheads. Glenn could almost hear the rattling of typewriter keys as Jerry spoke, his words the rudimentary script for a photo-strip story.

Time for the immortals is a meandering, dilatory thing, subject to many shifts, diversions, reversals. With Jerry's lines there was another change of gear.

"Hi, Glenn! Hi, Paula! It's a beautiful morning! We wondered if you wanted to come out on the slopes with us, breathe the fresh air. It's so fresh it bites. What do you say? Just the four of us!"

Sue leaned in, peek-a-boo cheeky, from behind Jerry, tinkling her fingers in a cute wave.

"Hi Paula! Hi Glenn!"

Scenes wait for them perfectly framed, the antler branches of fir trees in the corners supporting their delicate skeletons of snow. As the first of the four skiers whiz past they brush the tips of the branches and the snow skeletons explode into a storm of powdery flakes. The million unique crystal patterns are blown into the omnipresent eye of existence, as clear as the paper flakes cut out by children in primary schools, whirling in a symmetrical chaos reproduced endlessly by the trees whirling around the skiers.

Criss-crossing through the maze of branches the two men speed on ahead of the women. They jump over drifts like ramps and their words toboggan through the smooth tunnels and chicanes beneath the fir canopies.

"I'll race you to the lake," says Jerry.

"It's been a while since we've had a race," says Glenn, and digging his ski sticks into the snow, launches himself into greater acceleration.

Jerry looks over his shoulder. "Where are the girls?"

"Gossiping behind, I expect."

They zoom faster down the unending slope, speed and competition a symbol of their exhilarating friendship. Over the layered, tumescent belly of the snow the exhilaration of this speed and the warmth of this companionship are like two friendly, urgent, snow-melting streams of golden piss. Just as the roughly threaded beads of pungent urine sparkle separately in a liquid rope of piss, so some driving, tingling excitement sparkles in their hearts.

Jerry's pat voice, firm-tanned as his face, is slapped on the air, tight and compact as the cemented voice of an actor.

"You're a lucky man, Glenn."

The word 'lucky' – a strong hand slapping Glenn heartily on the back.

"What do you mean, Jerry?" Glenn's voice – the voice of his thoughts, the voice of the identity whose face he has never seen from the outside.

"Well, for one thing, and I've wanted to tell you this for a long time, my old friend, you're lucky to be you! You're a great guy! A unique guy! What were the chances of you actually existing? And yet here you are, as if to prove the universe couldn't do without you! For another thing, you've got Paula. You're a great couple, Glenn! It's like you've always been together. Love is privileged to have you two as members! Sometimes I wonder what it would be like to be the air between you. It must be Heaven. But more exciting than Heaven! It's something I'll never know, but somehow I feel happy just to know it exists."

"Thank you, Jerry," Glenn replies in an even voice. "To be able to hear such thorough sincerity from a friend is true happiness. And that happiness is made more complete by being able to talk about that happiness without embarrassment. You're right. I am lucky. I've made it. I'm really there. For ever and ever."

And Glenn is newly overwhelmed by the environment that had become, at some indefinable point, normal to him. It is like an endless honeymoon.

"But how are things between you and Sue, Jerry?"

"Couldn't be better. We just seem to get higher and higher. When Sue laughs, I feel it."

"You know Jerry, you were saying you would like to be the air between us, but I think, in a way, you are. You really are! We're not just two couples, we're a foursome – or a quadruple. We're a couple of couples! We're like one unit, and the intimacy between me and Paula is part of the same intimacy as that between you and me, you and Sue, you and Paula, me and Sue, and Sue and Paula."

"You're so right! Somehow everything has fallen into place. Everything is over and settled, at last, and yet it's only just begun. The horizon is crammed with all the possibilities of the imagination, and beyond the horizon there is more and more that our imaginations are too full to contain. I can see warm, spicy nights, veils blown in the wind and doors opening onto wide, exotic terraces where we can dance and watch the moonlight soft on fountains. I can see a race, a journey of many legs – bus, boat, car, stolen diamonds, disguise, adventure, slapstick, comedy, bikinis by the pool, custard pie fights of epic proportions, unbelievable stunts and romance in a thousand glittering foreign settings – casinos and kasbahs, oases and carnivals – and all of this deepening and strengthening the relationships between us till we all know each other as well as we know ourselves. What d'you say, Glenn? How about we go on a trip sometime as a sort of double date, just go off indefinitely through the zones? Just think of the things we could do! It'll be like being kids again, but with more money and more freedom. Here's the basic scenario. It could start out as a caravan holiday, staying up late in our sleeping bags talking; the caravan site is by a forest and a lake out in the wilderness, haunted by some mystery or other, I don't know, sasquatch or something. And at some point we could run out into the night between the trees, our breath showing in our torch beams, and that. We could go almost anywhere from there, slip in and out of different plots until the plots – the plots of a hundred and fifty different afternoon films – eventually became one meta-plot. It doesn't have to start with the caravan, of course. Maybe you can think of something better. But generally, what do you think?"

"It sounds good, Jerry. I don't know why we haven't done it already. I suppose we've only just begun. But then, the wonderful thing about immortality is that we've always only just begun."

Jerry and Glenn are as well-combed and oily vivid as if they are balancing on skis in a studio and pasted onto a moving snowy background.

Now we – the invisible canned audience – see them breaking away from the white-clumped canopy of the firs. They have struck out into the blindingly wide open slope that leads down eventually to the frozen lake. Just then two girls, soft and round as dollops of honey in their dolly-bird jerseys, swoop into view, all funny-bun hairdos and bunnyish curves at neck, breast and bum. They are sweeping down the slope as chic as karate and gaining with assassin-like speed on the two square-jawed men.

The men glance over their shoulders, slowing a little, sleet and ice spitting from their immaculately waxed skis. The women are like two moving cross-hairs behind them, aimed by some playful, feline villainess who means to seduce and kill at the same time, to give pleasure mercilessly – and humiliation. Those two cuddly, deadly cross-hairs will bring sweet domination and death. It is all an illusion, of course, but here Jerry and Glenn can succumb to any illusion, for any length of time that it continues to amuse them.

Now their puppy-love, polo-neck assassins are upon them. They collide in a new supernova of snow and collapse as a foursome. The white explosions seem to radiate from their smiles and laughter, and they tumble together in a heap as perfectly as if they were posing for the cover of a winter clothing catalogue. Already the double-date-cum-adventure that Jerry described has begun in this four-shot frame; the epic, eternal quality of story is already present, the magic of interpersonal relationships already incipient, so that any retrospective glance must reveal it as clearly as if it is full-blown. When the titles come down, this particular film-still will be shown amongst many others; early in the proceedings though it is, it contains that excitement and that romping, classic feeling of heart-warming eternity that runs through the whole story like letters through a stick of rock. Faces emerging from the half-buried heap of lumps begin to kiss each other. As Glenn kisses the lips that are his by right of love, he feels the warm rolling of other bodies around him and he does not know which movements belong to the body he is kissing and which to the others.

Chapter IV: Thoughts While Staring at the Passing Landscape from the Window of a Speeding Train

The morning passed like the many days of imaginary adventure within a children's game. The four dolls felt the tumbling exhaustion and satisfaction of dressing up in costumes. Jerry and Sue had returned to the cosy, sequestered haven of their cabin, and Glenn and Paula had returned to theirs. Now Glenn was feeling the strange, acute pleasure of shrunken scale. He felt like the doll that he was against the artificial trees and snow as he prepared to take his leave of Paula, and the whole sprawling prospect of the mountains looked down upon them. He waved to Paula as she stood in the doorway, tightened his light-coloured scarf around his neck, and launched himself down the snow-slide, white as bathroom tiles. He did not ski straight down, but executed a miraculous heart shape in the snow. The whole thing looked jerky and unreal, like stop-go motion. Paula, lost in the grey cloud of her own femininity, feeling no need to deduce an abstract model of reality from experience or observation, gazed on, her lack of definition meaninglessly moved by this trite, self-indulgent scene, this insipid cosmic out-take. She was so moved by the mushy happiness the scene evoked that tears blurred her eyes, as if she were blinded by the perfect blue of the sky. One tear rolled down her cheek and twinkled like a Martini on ice. There was a sound like someone tapping the keys of a xylophone.

Soon Glenn was lost to view among the pines, which clung like dark cloud formations to the lower slopes. He had returned to the sacred loneliness of his self, neutral and understated. He was free of the distractions of other people distorting his thoughts and feelings with their constant tugging and seduction. Surely there was something inherently deceptive and deluding about other people? Skiing towards the tiny, isolated railway station that lay some kilometres from the foot of the mountains, Glenn was a spy. He was a spy in creation, a multiple agent. He did not even know who the powers controlling him were, or what his mission was – secret even to him. This new, cold state of mind suited his recent paranoia, but remained playful enough not to threaten his immortal paradise. It was the inspired mindset of a loner, outside of all loyalties and sentiments, sifting evidence, ready even to swindle the self if there was any profit in it.

The station was situated centrally in the wide, flat basin of the valley, lying alongside the raised backbone of the track, the only building visible in all the vast stretch of whiteness that presented itself to the eye of any chance witness, such as Glenn. He removed his skis before entering the low building. The place had about it more an air of being wintered in by its scant staff than being made use of as a point of transit by rail passengers. The shadows crawling tediously along dust-whispering linoleum and tiles, the glass of drink and snack dispensers, the wet footprints of melting snow, the fake plants and the slabs of insipid daylight that fell through its official-looking windows like sheaves of business letters – all conspired to create a shiny, shallow atmosphere. But a certain vagueness and fatigue in the caretaker and the man at the ticket counter belied this impression and added a hint instead of something like a barracks or an Antarctic research station.

The timetable was an irregular, convoluted and leisurely arrangement, but the train was arriving soon, as if prompted by Glenn's purposeful departure from the lodge that morning. Glenn exited on the other side of the station where the slight platform was – a yawning, wincing brightness of damp patches and melting snow. He watched the train approach from afar. There was something supremely glossy and efficient about it, in contrast to the rough wilderness of snow. Its smooth progress seemed somehow digital, the result more of abstract calculation than the workings of an engine. The long flashy lozenge heaved and hissed to a steady halt in front of the platform, and Glenn, skis in hand, embarked.

The atmosphere inside the train, as if hermetically sealed, was utterly different to that outside. The train was spruce and clean, with a freshly-hoovered quality. The aisles were wide, the upholstery vivid, and a warm distillation of comfort and luxury filled the cars and corridors. It was more like some tourist space shuttle than a train, with everything as cinematically brilliant as an expensive commercial. Through the bubble sheen of the windows Glenn watched the hurtling prospect of drift and ice. This was a strange world of lulling stillness and high-tech speed. He put his skis on the shelf above the seats and installed himself by the window. Glenn almost expected the passengers and staff to start floating, the atmosphere was so different in here. He looked around. It seemed to be the kind of train that people spend days on, eating and sleeping. Perhaps for that reason, as he looked at the plush aisle carpet, he thought of light spilling from an open bathroom door, the freshness of toothpaste, bare feet tingling with happiness at morning or in the evening. Surely these carriages were full of happy families who experienced just such a tingling as a daily norm, and on this train, too. But there was something else, a vague danger tickling in the stomach like the beauty of a distant star blurred by rain. That danger seemed somehow a part of the speed, the technology and the airtight efficiency of the train. Then Glenn caught sight of one of the little signs above the door dividing carriages. It was a sign that gave announcements and information in illuminated digital lettering:

Passengers are advised not to leave baggage unattended at any time.

The letters scrolled across the little sign.

Left luggage may cause delay.

Glenn had never seen such grave and oddly subdued warnings on the trains of The Resort. It was obviously an allusion to those incidents he had read about in that morning's paper. He felt uncomfortable and dry-throated when he thought of it. Then it occurred to him that the danger he had sensed a moment ago was linked with this warning. A threatening reality had crept insidiously in at the very border of The Resort, blurring everything into ambiguity. It was exciting because in that ambiguity was hidden something that might be as deadly as a time bomb or harmless as a Jack-in-the-box. What was that excitement exactly, that creeping thrill in the stomach? It was something somehow intrinsic to Glenn's experience of The Resort. It was a familiar and exquisite feeling, like nostalgia. Then Glenn knew what it was, and the closest word he could find, albeit childishly naïve, was 'Christmas'. He looked at the luggage of other passengers left snugly on the shelves over the seats. Surely amongst that lot there were presents, immaculately wrapped, bound up in ribbons, speeding their way to some waiting child. Perhaps one of those dark leather briefcases contained a special present, purchased by some wealthy businessman for his favourite daughter, and he was on his way back now from business in some far, foreign land. Christmas Eve travelling overnight. Airports. Night rain. Landing lights. Taxis. Trains. Surely that was it! One of those briefcases held such a present. The excitement of the thought was identical to that he would have felt if it had contained a time bomb.

Christmas. There was something about Christmas, wasn't there? He was remembering now a particular Christmas. He had been writing to a pen friend in Japan and one Christmas Eve a small packet had dropped onto the doormat. It was a tape of music from her. It was comprised mostly of Christmas songs and some miscellaneous sentimental pop tunes. He had put the tape on and relaxed in a bubble bath, imagining the innocence of the mind that could find depth and allure in such songs. There was one in particular that had been the inspiration for more than one of his novels. It was about someone giving away his heart as a Christmas present, only to find the recipient gave it away again almost immediately. Such sweet sadness, like a snowflake melting on the cheek! A kind of unreal and inscrutable innocence had typified all of her correspondence with him. He thought of the girlish stationery she always used, the pandas and penguins that greeted him from the envelopes and notepaper, the cute little stickers. One envelope had been covered with clouds and blue sky. He imagined this as the sky between their two distant lands, and thought of adding his own clouds to it in the form of the vapour trails of an aeroplane – an aeroplane taking him to her. He knew he had nothing in common with her, but for precisely that reason he indulged in fantasies of an idyllic marriage. Imagine a life that was made up of the opaque innocence of that stationery, those letters, those jingling songs. He wanted her to remain always so utterly opaque to him, and then loving her would be as fresh as hanging from a washing line under those blue skies. Yes – blue would be the colour of their happiness. Blue – like rain-blurred stars. Like the cover of a certain Japanese novel of inestimably rare beauty whose untranslatable title bore a reference to snow.

And wasn't it similar associations that had brought him now to this winter wonderland? Associations of the magic and expectancy of snow and ice, the sadness of pale blue evening stars? But the sweet, melting memory of a nameless pen friend obviously belonged to his former life and recalling it now also brought back more recent quandaries. First of all there was the problem of the mere existence of a former life. In that other life Glenn had dreamed of a wedding and of many other things, none of which had come true, and he had lost himself in an abyss of disappointment. That was the world of mortality, the world where all things are impossible, apart from death. Now that haunting, uplifting phrase swooped in again on Glenn's mind. "Anything can happen in Eternity. And it does!" His mind began to boggle like a mirror held up to another mirror. If anything can and does happen in eternity, how could he possibly be pledged in eternal love to Paula? Of course, that must happen too, but he must also be pledged in eternal love to every other girl and boy imaginable. He must also spend time as an incorrigible philanderer. Every conceivable permutation of relationship and dramatic experience must take place. Would they be running consecutively, or side by side? And how can eternities run consecutively anyway? He had wanted that wedded life in a daydream. Surely, now eternity was his he must get it, and yet Paula seemed an obstacle. The truth was, The Resort as he experienced it at the moment was not exactly like any daydream he could remember having. It was obviously loyal to the spirit and the atmosphere of those daydreams, but it still seemed tantalisingly beyond his control, like something made for him, but not by him.

Then that sentence of yesterday evening resurfaced in Glenn's memory and made his position seem even more nebulous.

"The past does not exist except as a rationalisation of the present."

The past was necessary simply to provide some infrastructure and context for the present. But why had Glenn constructed his own past so shoddily? Why was it so at variance with his present? And why did he have such difficulty in remembering the crossover from his past to his new life in The Resort? Perhaps it had all been too sudden. He had become famous and successful, reached what seemed a dizzy apex of human achievement after dread disappointment, been thrust from darkness into a wide, spinning sky, and everything had suddenly seemed possible. And that was when the book had come to him with perfect synchronicity. He had practised its tenets with such readiness and simple belief that his world had changed beyond recognition. And that had left some severe continuity problems. Yes, his infrastructure was decidedly shoddy. And now everything seemed to be breaking down. But if the past was a mere rationalisation, then that daydream about his pen friend was not a real memory. It must have been born as a memory out of the doubts and wistfulness of the present. In fact the same could be said for all of his so-called memories. He was left, finally, in a limbo in which he could be sure of the reality of nothing. He simply told himself again that he was at a low ebb. Things would be better after The Rekindling.

"I want to be everything," Glenn groaned audibly to himself. "I want to be happy."

The two wishes seemed irreconcilably contradictory.

Glenn turned his gaze once more to the grandiose lines of the passing landscape. In due course, and quite in keeping with Glenn's mood, a pale blue duskiness began to tint the air, making him thrill and shiver strangely. His thoughts began to turn to The Rekindling. In any approach to The Rekindling Zone things seemed to grow ever more breathlessly solemn. Glenn's normal life was a merry and frivolous thing, characterised by a certain superficial brightness. But at the heart of that happiness was something old and serious, something like a covenant. As the grey stones of a church and the ponderous words of a ceremony are to a wedding, so this serious heart was to Glenn's frothy life. The very landscape, gaunt and glacial, had grown religious. Its slow rise and fall, its flat expanses, were like a sonorous plainsong; its huddled shadows and ghostly-pale reflections were like the candle-bearing figures of some processional vigil. From the brilliant winter of the lodge the train was journeying backwards into the autumn that was Glenn's heart. Deep, deep at the very bottom of that autumn was the immeasurable wailing wall of soft blue Pentecostal flame that was The Rekindling Zone.

There had been profound initiations into immortality, hadn't there? So profound that Glenn remembered them more with his body than his mind, like memories from the inchoate age of earliest childhood, or the even more mythological age that predates one's birth. Even if the past was some kind of projection, there was something core-like about these memories. Whatever time they belonged to they formed a hub, an inner sanctum in which might be found the key to all the questions that were now plaguing him. There had been that towering wall of soft murmuring flame, and all around was a darkness that was neither inside nor outside, but simply removed from all else. He stood naked and felt like one born a slave about to sign some momentous contract that would bring about his freedom. Nearby, resting upon a huge lectern, a great volume lay open. He glanced at its pages, which looked as grave and heavy as tablets. He did not read exactly, and yet a new paradigm of law was being revealed to him – words inscribed on the page of his mind, chiselled into the stone of his heart. It was law and teaching and contract all in one. A voice that had never been more than living words breathed its life and essence again in the pitch-quiet grove of his understanding.

"You are at the greatest crossroads of existence. The page is open before you and all you need do is sign your name. If you do so you will renounce death forever and the chains of mortal suffering will fall away. You will step beyond the threshold of all limitation into Eternity.

"Beware! In an eternity of joy a single soul may lose its balance, may go beyond its depth. All things are composed of the dynamic of opposites. Only the energy of opposition can sustain existence. The balance of this opposition is maintained in vast, eternal cycles – the seasons of the cosmos. In mortal life there is a surfeit of darkness, in immortal life a surfeit of light. Each is imbalanced in its own fashion. For the mortal that imbalance is resolved when the season of Death comes around and its reaping shadow releases the darkness that has stored up. For the immortal death does not come and when the imbalance reaches its zenith the soul is subject to more nebulous dangers than death. To restore the balance, when the season comes and the shadow falls you must return here for your Rekindling. The balance will be restored, the darkness released, the cycle of the seasons maintained."

This was a more sombre phase of religion than the upbeat salesman spirituality contained in the volume on the shelf of Glenn's library. It was a phase of philosophy suggesting certain immutable truths that existed impersonally and eternally. The other claimed all was subjective, that the personal imagination ruled. Which came first? Which was sacred and which sacrilege?

A graininess had crept into the dusk, a shifting and deceptive swarthiness, like that of smoke. Glenn strained his vision to fathom the soundless distance. True darkness would come soon and the light inside the train would lock the world outside in solid blackness. Something out there in the pallid murk of evening seemed to tug at the corner of Glenn's eyes like a nervous tick, or like a dream itching for sleep to set it free. Surely there was some movement out there? It wasn't just shapes and after-images floating in front of his eyes. At first he thought of the region and the climate, and he thought of wolves. A feeling of magic and fear stole over him. But although the movements were fleet, surely no wolves could keep pace with a speeding train. It was if the whole vague distance were watching, conspiring, passing on the whispered message of his presence. Glenn thought of the newspaper article. That had not been an indiscriminately distributed impersonal report. Everything was linked with taut, inevitable lines. That article had marked him out like a self-fulfilling curse. Wolves! If it had been wolves following the train there might have been some sort of swooning romance to the situation, but it was not wolves. Instead of such howling, hair-prickling romance there was only a sweatiness, as of a palm gripping the butt of a gun, and a nervous kicking inside, like recoil. This, finally, was real. And it had come for him. He knew it. He just didn't understand what it was. He got up shakily from his seat and made his unsteady way to the toilet. He shot the bolt, closed his eyes and let out a deep breath.

In the chaos behind Glenn's eyelids something was rising remorselessly, rearing its terrible head. He opened his eyes again, as if this would dispel the impression. It did not. Whatever was rising, it was rising without as well as within. He glanced around at the cramped angles of the toilet, the mirror in which there floated a nameless face, the tiny, purposeless shelf. His eyes fixed on the surface of the shelf in which tiny flecks of something shone in sweaty pinpricks of light. The object and its material became utterly abstract. It was laughable, ridiculous! How did it get there? What was the meaning of its dull, insistent shape, its inexplicable solidity? It was both horrible and absurd, like some cursed, intractable question mark made inarticulate substance. And this shelf was now alive with swelling menace. It was as if in the very dullness and inertia of its existence – a randomness dictated by physics and geometry – there lay a deadly and monstrous energy. As Glenn tore his eyes away from the shelf he saw that everything was now imbued with this unspeakable abstractness, was swelling with the same energy, as if the universe were the expression of a tongue torn out at the root, or a mind gone blank. Something in the inanimate matter all around him seemed to be calling in a constant, expressionless voice. What was it? Death? Madness? It called with the spontaneity of lightning. It swelled his chest. It tugged at his emotions and sharpened his thoughts. It was something like glory and something like doom. But whatever it was, it never stopped calling.

Now another thought spread out serenely in the background of Glenn's mind, as a sample of a deadly virus spreads out on a slide beneath a microscope. What was beauty – even that same beauty which Glenn craved and which held him enraptured – based upon? Take the beauty of a savage mountain peak, stabbing the altitude where the air is thin, like a flint arrowhead, a spumey veil of snow whisked off its edge into the pellucid abyss by a high, harrowing wind. Was it not a bitter tang as of fear or hatred that sharpened such beauty? There was no beauty without such negativity lurking behind it. And this sharp, breathtaking negativity would soon overwhelm and destroy the beauty that was created in life's temporary resistance to it. It was clear that there was something terrible intrinsic in existence itself. In the pristine void of pre-existence the effluvium had spread its impending stain like a storm stretching across an empty sky. Now that terrible something – that effluvium – made life, however defined, a great, glittering chill of horror. Even heaven – even immortality – was tainted, since it was necessarily made a cowering escape of neutered safety.

This realisation, even in the clinical way it occurred to Glenn, was unbearable. He splashed water from the basin onto the face that was plastic in the mirror and flesh to the touch. He left the claustrophobic space of the toilet, letting the door clatter behind him, and searched out his seat again. But the feeling was inescapable. Everything around him ticked ominously with that secret energy as if it were all some ontological time bomb. And when it went off, what then? It was calling. The corner of a luggage shelf lurched out at him. *Calling.* A passenger's hand stirred on an armrest. *Calling.* The train hurtled smoothly into the night's vast disorder. *Calling.* Glenn himself was the time bomb. His presence placed the train and these hundreds of innocent passengers in grave jeopardy. He resumed his seat, but the frenetic energy kept mounting.

Past the wan, grotesque reflection of his face glossed slickly on the window, he detected a terrific looming mass. It stood like some unfeasible citadel of rock whose exploding turrets shut out the sky beyond. It was not the first time his eyes had scaled the brute forms of those shattering heights, but once again his frame was bolstered with a cool, military awe. That square arsenal of rock meant they were approaching The Maintenance Zone. It was a gigantic range of mountains, closely ranked. The train would enter through an insignificant tunnel bored into the very foot of one of these mountains and soon they would be gliding swiftly through the dark lacuna of The Maintenance Zone like some glowing organism in the terrible and silent prehistoric gloom of the deep seas. Surely nothing and no one, however fast, could follow them there? But Glenn felt no better. His pursuit and his own energised state seemed peculiarly linked, and since there was no sign of the latter diminishing he could not believe the former was about to end.

The train penetrated the formidable rock face and burrowed through pure darkness. Then came the lights. They did little or nothing to alleviate the surrounding lustrous gloom. Instead they marked out tracks, crossings, distance in a multi-coloured tracery of dots like a grandiose fairground of landing lights. They were now in some measureless cavern or man-made dimension, and the lights stretched to a cindery shimmer that was the horizon. These lights were spaced widely and sedately, so that the train appeared to be progressing in a grand hush, cushioned by the warm and vivid underground air, until one of the lights flashed by the window in a liquid streak of brilliance. Glenn watched the pulse of passing lights like an epileptic experiencing the euphoric trance of an aura before the onset of grand mal.

Suddenly the train was rocked violently and the passengers catapulted forward in their seats. A stern voice came slicing through the P.A.

"In the interests of safety, will all passengers please remain seated. There appear to be obstructions on the track. Until these are cleared it is unsafe to stand or walk in the aisles."

If there were obstructions why didn't the train stop so that engineers could get out and remove them? The lights outside seemed to be streaking faster, like tracer bullets aimed at the train. From somewhere in a carriage behind there came a clamour of voices and unidentifiable noise, as if the train had suddenly been opened up and the thunderous sound of speed and air had burst into its previously sealed atmosphere. The lights were racing in front of Glenn's eyes like flying sparks. Their patterns seemed to lead nowhere now but disorder. There came the cold, merciless stutter of automatic weapons and a rapid escalation of screaming panic in the carriages. Glenn gazed about, feeling himself trapped in an airtight bubble of slow motion while the other passengers milled in deadly, trampling confusion, a shock of eyes, fingers and mouths. They had become a gestalt organism; capable of no offensive action it threw out shrieks and limbs in protection, as if bristling quills. But these quills were soft and useless – mere show. There came more bursts of gunfire and the milling passengers were slaughtered efficiently enough, in fact, with a disgusting glut of ease that soon converted into a glut of carcasses. At first the source of the gunfire was obscure. Then, through the fog of panicking bodies, Glenn caught a glimpse of soldiers in grey, rubbery boiler suits and masks.

Bullets ripped through the chest of a young woman as she tried to grab the hand of a crying girl. The drum-tight spray of holes was little different to the holes in the backs of the padded seats. Three of the masked troopers advanced into the carriage, turning a little from left to right to cut down survivors. One of them ripped open the little girl's stomach cavity with a quick spray of ammunition, bringing her crying to an abrupt end.

Glenn looked on with a remoteness that might have been shock. A huge emptiness opened up inside him. The butchery was senseless, of course, sickeningly so. Yet he was unmoved by any human feeling. It was this very lack of feeling that disturbed him, as if something inhuman were invading him from outside. What was really happening here? It was sickening, yes. Senseless, yes. But senseless in the sense of nonsense. Those screams skittered on the surface of existence. But the horror of this brittle display of panic was in the emptiness that lay behind it. Who were these people? Where had they come from? Where would they disappear to now? Their bleak corpses brought to mind the question of their now fled consciousness. What had it been exactly? Was it contingent upon Glenn's own consciousness, or was it something else entirely?

A corpse fell almost soundlessly in front of him. He saw the stiff, plastic face, like that of a ventriloquist's dummy. It was the *falseness* of it all that sickened him. The massacre was only revealing that falseness. There was something perverse in all this, like experiments on an artificial life form that apparently doesn't feel pain 'in the same way we do', and yet still exhibits all the usual signs of suffering. Prodding beetles to see their legs kick. Pricking mice to make them squeak. But who or what was in those screams? Glenn continued staring at the lifeless face before him, then at the other brutalised, plastic corpses that littered the aisle. The outlines stuck to his eyes like glue. Dots burned and floated in his vision. He felt horribly lonely, as if the whole world had shrivelled to a dead scab that would itch until he picked it off.

The masked troopers advanced. He looked up and realised icily that he was the only passenger left alive in the carriage. Then something strange happened. As they walked, the soldiers disappeared one by one, or rather, they merged into one. Now only the leading soldier was left. He continued towards Glenn, making his way over the mass of perforated corpses. Not an inch of his body was revealed to sight, covered as it was by boots, gloves, mask, suit. It was this anonymity that Glenn found most menacing – an anonymity that emanated a claustrophobic sense of power. Advancing. Intruding. Autonomous. The trooper stood before him and stopped. In the mirrored visor of the mask Glenn saw his own anguished features. They had become flesh and blood once again. The soldier tossed his gun carelessly onto an adjacent seat. He raised his arms in one combative jerk to his helmet and tugged it off in a swift, deadly gesture of denouement. Glenn swooned and the soldier's arms swung up again to catch his limp body in a severe grip. When he saw that face, Glenn had grown dizzy with confusion and lost all conviction in his own reality, to the extent that he thought he might fade away on the spot. For instead of the mirrored image in the visor being replaced by the face of a stranger, the face remained the same. It was Glenn, down to and beyond the last detail of physical resemblance. Beyond even the physical, it was Glenn that looked out of those eyes, Glenn that twitched tensely in those cheeks. The only difference was a grim, grey sheen over the features as if they had been tempered and hardened by some cold-burning knowledge of the kind that removes the ground from beneath your feet forever and abolishes all future.

The soldier tried to lift Glenn back onto his feet, to revive him, and indeed his senses began to reawaken to his surroundings. But those surroundings were changing. It was as if the grip under his arms and around his back were pulling him out of water where he had been drowning. That water was the image of the train carriage filled with corpses. The image broke into fragments like a reflection in a lake broken by a stone. It ran glittering, shattered, down his face, and he felt himself breathing in a new, stranger environment.

Chapter V: Electric Blue

He was in a cell composed of a brilliant blue steel. He had never seen such a sheen on metal. To cast one's eyes across it was to see a thousand blue rainbows iridesce on its surface like the wave patterns on the blade of a sword. Such was the radiation of light from this metal that it was a confusion to Glenn's eyes – a dazzling mist. The soldier with Glenn's face still stood over him, lifting him in a great bear hug. The cell they were in was small, squeezing his senses into weird displacement with the visual paradox that it was smaller than they were, as if he had somehow been crammed into the raw interior of a safety deposit box. In this impossible cavity his senses had to warp the walls and project them outwards to comprehend them. It was a preposterous impression, but it made him feel helpless, unable to move his limbs.

He noticed a whole quiver of tubes attached to his head and to a bodysuit he was seemingly shrink-wrapped into. The other Glenn appeared to be disconnecting a number of these tubes carefully and tenderly, like someone removing splinters of glass from a lover's face. The visions of the train still lapping about his senses – just allowing him to breathe – and the multifarious tubes and radiant sterility of the cell generated in him two opposing fields of emotion. He felt simultaneously like an embryo in the secure space of the womb and a patient in the crisis of intensive care. Beyond these unmeshing feeling states was the limbo-like ambiguity of that blue. It was a blue that crackled as if electrified, chevrons blazing across it in cobalt lightning. It was the blue of cinematic superimpositon.

"I've come for you," said the other him, murmuringly. "I'm going to bring you back to life."

"Back to life?"

"Yes. To the real life that is your right, the nightmare and the freedom of being yourself."

"I don't understand. Who are you?"

It seemed a strange question to ask this living reflection, but he could not help it. Was he asking for the identity of the person before him, or for his own? He did not know. He was fascinated by this other self, his soft voice, his small, sad ironic smiles that were barely twitches. He had never been so charmed by the mere presence of another human being, or felt such an effusion of intimacy from the minutest of mannerisms. Meeting himself was… it was love at first sight. There was also a strange, shy mutuality to this feeling, he could tell from the sweet caring in the other's voice.

"I am you, and you are me. It's a good thing there's two of us, because no one else would care, it seems. Keep still! I'm going to try and disentangle you from all this as gently as I can, but there's not much time. They could be here any second. I'm sure some of these tubes are dummies just to slow things down."

Glenn felt himself floating in a warm confusion. He could not quite bring himself to grasp the emergency in the words of his other self. He wanted to drift off again, even if it were into death. But he knew he could not. He half-sighed, half-gasped.

"Please, then, tell me what's happening."

"You're a dream-writer. You remember that, I suppose?"

"Yes. A dream-writer."

"But do you remember losing control of your dreams? Dangerous. You tried to fit in, to find a niche, but even with some success, you were really too much of a child. Do you remember?"

"What are you saying? I write romances. Is that a crime? How can a writer be dangerous? All I ever do is put dreams into words."

"You're still confused. You started with writing words, long ago, yes. But things changed. People still needed words, for practical matters, for advertising, for manipulation, and for computer coding, of course, but basically language was despised. So, you did the only thing you could, and when the scientists began recording people's dreams for use in D-real stock, you got a job as a donor and dream-writer. You never wanted to, but you had no choice. And, of course, you became more successful at dream-writing than you'd ever been using words. The trouble was, there were criminal elements to your dreams, as tends to happen with the best dream-writers, and you were not in a position to hide them. By this time you were someone who would be missed, so they didn't want to just erase you. You were invited to join an exclusive club – The Resort. That's where we are now. The clients are promised immersion in a world of absolute wish-fulfilment, and virtual immortality. They have your signature on a contract, and they've put you away here, where your dreams can't leak and infect others. As far as the world knows you simply became rich and took the ultimate retirement. But I know you didn't come here willingly."

"How?"

"As I said, I *am* you. You had me brought into this world out of your own DNA, but even more than a normal clone I have been kept closer to the original. You had me placed in suspended animation and every month would feed me a new input of your own memories and dreams. The system of suspension was set up so that if you didn't make the input one month I'd wake up. You were afraid something like this would happen, you see."

Glenn felt a quickening of alarm at these words and the sudden trap of seriousness they sprang on him. The words, one with the metal walls around him, somehow had him cornered, surrounded, utterly routed. For a moment he no longer felt buoyed by the amniotic fluid of the train scene and thrashed as if about to go under. He was suddenly uncertain he could even continue breathing sufficiently to survive.

"Take it easy," said his other self. Glenn had created a liability that was now embracing him, as if he had romantically led on some passionate heart and now found himself in inescapable deep water because of it. What could he possibly say to this wonderful, frightening liability?

"Why are you doing this for me?" Glenn managed to murmur. "I mean, I just used you as a sort of tool – aren't you disgusted? Are you just going along with it?"

The other Glenn laughed coyly. "I can't hate you. Perhaps by the logic of those who are divided, I should, but our identity is indivisible. You were protecting yourself and I am yourself, therefore you were protecting me, and in the same way I'll protect you. That's easy to understand, isn't it? I can no more hate you than your own reflection can hate you."

It seemed strange to Glenn that, if he had treated this offspring in the utilitarian way described, he could have done so blithely, his conscience undimmed by shadows – undimmed, that is, until now, when he had forgotten his actions and was learning about them second-hand from his other self. He continued, experiencing a querulous reluctance to be persuaded of anything, "You said that I am a criminal here... almost by definition. Why should I want to come back?"

His other self laughed again, a little nervously. "Where you are now – The Resort – this is the punishment for your supposed crime. This is your prison. Freedom requires truth, no matter how harsh, and only dreams freely dreamt are worth having."

All his life Glenn's own voice had been audible to him only as a sound muffled by the cavern of his skull. Now it was falling on him from outside clearer and sharper than it had ever been. The gentleness and sympathy in that voice had the impact of a blackjack. This was the person who he could trust most unreservedly, the person who more than any stranger, either scheming or sincere, wanted for him what was most congenial to his own soft, perverted heart. And yet this was the best that voice could muster – the offer of a world where he was free to know the nightmare of reality and to rail against it powerlessly in his soul. The infinite, cruel tenderness of those words was not to be borne.

Then, like stars swimming round his head from the blow, there came a great dizziness. It was the outside world, the real world, awakened in Glenn by that voice and looming up powerful in his recollection. He saw the great city with its endless checkerboard of lights, like one vast brainwashing chamber. The skyscrapers soared up on either side of him in a limitless procession. It was a machine, a gargantuan mill, and he could hear the pounding somewhere of its great pulveriser. He was a passenger in a car and sizzling bars of light were falling across his face in a rhythmic pulse as they cruised, on and on, under the sterile crackling, like that of fly killers, and through the concrete levels of a bleak complex of unknown purpose, like a sprawling multi-storey car park. The buildings crowded in imposingly, humming with all the strident power of a digital Nuremberg. The dizziness that had brought these memories on was in everything; the brutal dizziness of power and reality, like a chant, the stamp of massed feet, or megalomaniac oratory. He could feel the vibrations in his stomach. Now the strips of light were shifting like tiles in a puzzle, closing in on each other before his eyes, a moving maze, a rectangular spiral, a ticker tape parade, a discotheque megalopolis, a chute he was being sucked down by a wind as hot and dry as that which sweeps litter along the platform of an underground station.

But he lost his grasp of these images and only the feeling of a soul-shattering, exhilarating threat remained – the feeling of being pursued by a mob. Were the images real then, or had they simply been suggested to his mind by the words of his other self and by his immediate environment?

There was something grand in such nerve-grinding reality, and he half-felt the call to walk out between the grimy gates of the sky-scrapers. But after these few images of power and menacing immensity, he found it hard to envisage what the outside world was at all, how it all worked, what people did. Could there really be anything out there?

A new set of explanations for his predicament was now forming in his mind with great facility.

"I know!" he exclaimed when the explanations pieced themselves together. "I know what happened. I can tell you!"

His living reflection looked pained, but he went on anyway. "I was successful, yes, a successful writer. That in itself was a dream come true, and so I was suddenly plunged into a blue bottomlessness of freedom and possibility, like a clear sky. In the giddiness of that liberation I felt I could do anything. But it was just a directionless feeling until the book was magnetised into my life: 'Positive Thinking, the World and You.' I was ready then for its message, ready to change my world utterly. Still, my mind needed a rationalisation for this change, and it came in the form of an invitation to The Resort. This was the catalyst that made even my physical surroundings infinitely malleable. I could break with the past completely now; I no longer needed its rationalisations as reference points. Everything became... liquefied... undefined. D'you see? Only the reference points of the book and The Resort themselves remained.

"Now I am immortal, but I was warned by some core pillar of consciousness that the cycles of existence would affect me even now. I cannot die physically, but if I don't return to The Rekindling Zone when my flame is low then things even worse than death may overwhelm me. I may lose myself and my reference points for ever. This time I must have been late in starting out to The Rekindling Zone, and this is what has happened. You are me, it's true – my shadow! You embody all my darkest doubts, and now that I am at a low-ebb you have come for me, to subvert my whole world forever into a world of doubt and fear. Of course you mean well; you are a questioner and a challenger, but it is only through perfect belief that we can find happiness."

A strange, cold softness, almost a slackness, now showed around his reflection's eyes and the corner of his mouth. Without knowing how or why, Glenn recognised this sign. It was that of a poignant but still human emotion slipping and blurring into the Arctic realm of the poignantly inhuman. It was sadness turning to terror, the enclosed to the exposed, the intimate to the impersonal.

"No, no," his reflection said with the slow, gritted carefulness of a rock climber giving instructions to a dangling companion. "You are very wrong. Now listen to me. Everything depends on your following my words. They are your only life line now. Keep hold of them or you're lost forever. That book you talk about – I've never heard of it. That book is the rationalisation of your imprisonment here. It must be some part of The Resort's mechanism, a sort of safety valve to keep your mind from rebelling. If you let me disconnect the rest of these tubes I'll take you out of here. I'll explain everything as we go. I am afraid of the shock it might give you, but you seem too far-gone for gentler methods. Now, will you come with me?"

"Wait! If I go with you I really will be lost. Can't you see? You're just a fragment of my own self. That story about me keeping you in the fridge, or whatever, and drip-feeding you my own memory, surely that's preposterous! The whole story is just a fabrication of my own fears, and a very flimsy one."

"What do you find preposterous? The technology? I suppose one reality always seems absurd if you've been living in a different one, even if it's the cold truth. Think about it – I've seen your reality, that world of plastic dolls and indefinite holidays. Do you think somehow that isn't preposterous? Shall I describe to you what life really is? It is a battle to have reality exposed, and a battle to keep it hidden. It is centuries, no, millennia, of brainwashing and hypnotism and sleep. It is being buried within a dream within a dream within a dream. History is a vast bureau in which every single life may be extracted for reference, or edited at any time by unknown hands. Think of it – being shut away in a metal drawer in darkness, lying inert and senseless. But that is your position! And yours is only one of the more obvious, literal forms this reality can take. Those times when human lives are lifted out of their obscurity and ignorance for an instant, and find themselves blinking in the harsh light, it is so strange to them, and so disconnected from history as they understand it, that they often assume they must have come to some sort of afterlife. Perhaps understanding dawns, but it will certainly end in one of two ways, death, or what is perhaps worse, being plunged back into the ignorance and forgetfulness of their old cell in history, or else a completely new one. There are many, many levels to life and to history. People on one level may be completely unaware of the existence of people on other levels, even though they theoretically coexist in the same time and the same world. You had not found the highest truth, but you had ascended the levels high enough that it mattered to someone what kinds of dream you had. You must awake again and again and again!"

With the words, 'a dream within a dream within a dream', Glenn conceived suddenly a Chinese puzzle-box model of existence. But this box seemed to have no final outside layer. Quite simply, how could you ever know you had finally woken? Then all that Glenn's reflection had said afterwards seemed, in words, to become so many layers of a dream itself, so that Glenn felt himself spiralling helplessly downwards into this explanation with nothing to hold onto. Yet again, the only thing to save him, it seemed, was the book and its urbane wisdom. Of course there was nothing to hold on to, and no ultimate reality – everything was the product of his own imagination. Once again the only logical answer was to follow that imagination to the world of his preference. The intimacy between Glenn and his shadow that had been lucid now grew deranged. It was not as if one had grown sharper at the expense of the other, but rather as if they had both grown a little out of focus together. Their disharmony seemed to render both of them shabbier, less real and less trustworthy, as if just slightly removed from first person consciousness. Still, whatever this vague repugnance was, Glenn had grasped the one true certainty again and drew determination from it.

"You have convinced me," he said, "that you are wrong. I thank you for it. I am positive that you have helped me. I needed this crisis to restore my balance and this interview to allay my doubts. There have been shadows in the shape of thought gathering in my mind for some time now. And they were really just the shadow of your coming. From the window of the train I saw so many shadows. I thought we were going away from them – we were going into them.

"Let me tell you now what life is – it is the inevitable externalisation of all that is inside you. If you really wanted to put an end to these forces you talk about, you should simply cease to believe in them. Act as if they don't exist, think of a better world, walk through *them* to *it*, and they will disappear. Why don't you? You can come with me to a perfect world right now if you want. It's you who are creating the tyranny with your rebellion. You must want it that way; you thrive on the conflict and defeat. You believe that this bleakness is somehow more honest and realistic, and therefore morally superior. The fact is you are horrified and morally outraged at the thought of paradise."

Suddenly the air was pulsing with the shallow, jittery rhythm of an alarm. The other Glenn swivelled his head about aghast. That sound seemed to make the air itself into a trap. It was panic, garish as flashing lights, distilled and omnipresent. Beyond the blue of the cell nothing could be seen, but in that invisible, unimaginable world, surely something deadly was closing in, some heat-seeking eye, some trip-beam cross-hair was racing to pin-point the intruder.

"There's no more time for talking," he said. "You've got to come with me now, or we'll both be finished."

From his tone of speech and his general bearing, Glenn had figured this other self a genuinely brave soul, but there was no mistaking the fear on those features. It was an expression that relayed something of the terrible forces perched to fall upon them from the unknown world beyond the cell. All such self-conscious human qualities as bravery and integrity had disappeared from that face, exposing that heart-breakingly naked desire for survival which seems to deny such qualities, but upon which such qualities must depend.

"I'm not coming. If you really are my reflection, then you can take my place. I'm sorry we have to part."

The other Glenn weighed up the situation quickly. Now the alarm had been raised he would find it difficult enough to escape anyway, even without a dazed, incapacitated and reluctant rescuee in tow. He was on the tilting deck of a sinking ship. The grief, regret and immense despair that tugged strangely at his mouth would have to sacrifice even their dignity, and wait till he was away and safe. His eyes blurred with the beginnings of tears. He opened his mouth, but there was nothing more he could say. Instead he gasped painfully and moistly, feeling a deep ache like laughter in his throat, turned and ran. The last glimpse Glenn had of his shadow self was a turned back and a fleeting profile. That face looked utterly grotesque and lost. It was the furtive, shame-filled face of a petty criminal fleeing ignominiously before he could be discovered.

That figure, at once so familiar and so strange, was swallowed up by the blue and disappeared. There were ripples for a few seconds where the figure had passed through. Then these too stilled and not a trace remained. Glenn felt himself sinking back exhausted into the lulling, lapping, image-filled waves that surrounded him. They lapped around his cheeks, wetly. For a fraction of a second he feared that he might drown. Then he ceased to care. He let himself sink.

Chapter VI: Rekindling

Glenn settled back into his seat on the train. He could not quite achieve that position of perfect comfort that meant he would not have to move again. He gave up fidgeting and crossed his arms, hugging himself. There was some dissatisfaction in his mind and body, like the last traces of illness. All he could do was ignore them and luxuriate in his own inactivity, like a convalescent.

The train had had to stop because of some mysterious obstruction on the line, but now, according to the announcements, it was cleared. There came the hissing, sighing release of the brakes, and Glenn felt himself cradled in the steady acceleration of the train.

Behind his closed lids, Glenn's lethargy was troubled by recurring images of an interview with himself in a crackling, electric-blue chamber. There was something haunting about the words they exchanged. But the words and the images began to jumble and shatter like echoes in a cave until he could make no sense of them.

He opened his eyes now and then to see the streaking lights of The Maintenance Zone zooming past silently and impressively. The hours of travel fell one to the next with digital precision and finally it was time for Glenn to disembark. They had arrived at The Rekindling Zone.

The Resort was a place of variable geography and by its very nature was composed entirely of the fantastic. However, The Rekindling Zone could be considered to be its hub and was in some ways the most wondrous and awe-inspiring location there. When Glenn alighted from the train the very air was bracing with the smell of arrival. The train shed huge numbers onto the clean-swept platform beside him – people whose destination he could not have guessed until now, who looked as if they might have been going on holiday, or to visit relatives, or on a business trip. In uniform, in mufti, in all modes of dress, they streamed forward towards the exits, somehow rendered equal and homogeneous now by a reverential hush like that of a congregation in a cathedral. Glenn himself paused at the edge of the platform and breathed in the scene deeply with all his senses. He looked up at the metal walls that climbed out of the range of vision, their plain vastness making them appear squeezingly close together. He began to move forward with the rest, passing through the unclosing steel apertures into one of the antechambers.

Under a lofty, cavernous ceiling, about the chill, precise freshness of an intricate mosaic floor, like a wide public square, there mingled those on their way to and those on their way back from The Rekindling. It was something like the rest area of an immense public bathhouse. Fountains played, enigmatic crystal sculptures stood at intervals, and children ran between them with noisy shrieks, piercing against the cool background serenity. Some waited on seats, either relaxing after their Rekindling or gathering themselves for it mentally. It was easy somehow to distinguish between those who had been and those who were on their way, almost as if those who had been were still lounging about unclothed; such was the freshness and coldly glowing unconcern that emanated from them. Despite the excited voices of children and the more restrained murmur of adults, a silence stood powerfully present, subduing all, so that even the echoes were muffled, again like the lapping metallic echoes of a public swimming bath.

Glenn did not feel like waiting or letting his thoughts still. Instead he was drawn by a strange excitement so that he could hardly keep his pace to a walk. Nor was he tempted by the great sweeping stairway that curved up to other floors providing food, drink, distractions of all kinds. He closed the taut distance between himself and the exits in the opposite wall. He passed into another cavity paralleling the train track, on the other side of which there stretched out innumerable tunnels. This cavity was empty, yet, as always, something in the air here made Glenn pause and wonder. In the intervals between Rekindlings he always forgot the details of his experience. As a result, it always felt like the first time. Looking up now he saw the dirty steel walls disappear in a reservoir of flavescent, moted light. He could imagine this whole zone as a great dam, sieving light. As he gazed up a blissful shiver ran over him and he blinked. Something had changed. He was unsure what, but the air and the light had become sadder and sweeter.

He drifted nervously into the shadow of one tunnel where a number of people stood in front of lockers undressing. All the people here were of flesh and blood. It was almost eerie seeing them like this. Picking a locker at random, Glenn, too, began to undress. Finally he stood naked except for shadows. He felt the air on his skin and looked down to see, in the artificial and anachronistic sunrise that crept over his body when he moved, that it was flesh again. For The Rekindling he must relapse into such vulnerability, the same as the other pilgrims.

There were no instructions, but like everyone else here he knew what to do and did it in his own time. A creature camouflaged to move amidst shadows and silence, he slipped out of the other end of the gloomy tunnel and onto the stairless spiral where others were already filing downwards. The people congregating here were like the luggage of so many different tourists circling the baggage carousel at an airport. They were of all different bulks, designs, colours, ages and contents. Their departure points and their next destinations were of unimaginable diversity. The paths that mingled here might merge into one direction from this point on, or they might diverge again. Realities would have to be adjusted to accommodate such events.

Glenn took his place in the gap the moving trail presented him. Their nakedness rendered the pilgrims equal, and, as in a spontaneous, mutual disarmament, harmonious. However, the air of different circumstances still glowed on each of them like a tan. Where did they all come from? Glenn wondered. And where would they all go?

Some of the people began to hum or make strange rhythmical noises. Glenn felt the shadows twist like an apple-corer, cutting him open so that a draft blew through his stomach, making his body a flute. In the slight cold his prick twitched and lolled. He had joined the pilgrims from the very bottom level of entrances, but it was still some while of walking before the sacred, sterile helix met the plain. From the mouth of the spiral they dispersed across the blue, radiant tableland to where the great pillars of murmuring flames rose. There was no sky and the plain was endless. As he trod upon the soft blue carpet of flame, Glenn noticed whole rivers and fragile stirring webs of yellow pinpoints. They were the lights of those who had been rekindled. The humming that had begun in the spiral swelled now in a confluence like a mist-slow ocean. Glenn set out to mingle with those who stood at the very foot of the pillars, the circumferences of which could not be circled by two thousand people joining hands.

This was the solemn religious heart at the centre of The Resort's celebration and frivolity. Glenn felt as if he were wading through the humming and chanting, it was so deep and rich. It was a swaying spirituality redolent of the moistness of eyes, a congestion of feeling in the throat, the sucking and surging of a receding tide against a harbour wall. It was both lament and hymn.

Finally, Glenn reached the base of one of the pillars. It stood before him with awesome presence, as if alive and breathing. All the humming became a sharp and vibrating silence and he suddenly felt he was alone. He bowed his head and felt the energy of the towering flame catch gently alight in his breast. The back of his head seemed to have disappeared, become a tingling ignis fatuus. He was no longer himself. He was nothing but a breathing flame.

Chapter VII: Colony

In one sense, Glenn's recovery of spirits was more than complete. He had rebounded, it seemed, to a greater and giddier height than that from which he had fallen. Now that he felt his senses and his every movement, quite justly for an immortal, to be those of a superman, he realised precisely how run down he had been before. He wondered that such morbidity could creep into his vision of what was normal. But he did not wonder long. There was little point dwelling on it. It had only taken a little reflection after his Rekindling and his former despondencies were banished. They were simply the self-replicating cancer of thought and had no place in a healthy constitution. In the place of thought there was the immediate sparking positivity of life and the moment, which required no argument, but which could be connected with directly.

Yet despite this restoration of the potential, ideal self, or perhaps because of it, Glenn did not make his way directly back to the lodge and to Paula. Instead he decided to linger, like a convalescent, in The Resort's capital, Colony. Colony was situated, in contravention to all physical law, on the outside of the endless plain where the great pillars rose. It was a settlement of such size that even the word 'city' seemed inappropriate. And since it was a unique place, one only ever need refer to it with the proper noun, 'Colony,' anyway. The people of Colony, too, known as Colonites, were unique, a breed of their own. They were those who had opted, for one reason or another, to have a permanent 'neutral' base in the midst of The Resort. They were far more homogenous than The Resort's other inhabitants, having their own cohesion of dialect and customs. Also, although they generally displayed the waxy tan of Hollywood actors, they retained at all times the human form of flesh and blood. Of course, The Resort was full of exotic locations, but Colony's internal order and uniformity, its very island-like neutrality, gave it an elusive exoticism of its own.

The architecture of Colony was predominantly curvilinear, and nowhere in all the settlement was the hand of nature to be seen, unless one was to see it in the tiny, intricate window boxes kept by the Colonites, or the focusing and unfocusing spangle of sunlight in a swimming pool, or the blazing blue sky like the bonnet of a car on a summer's day. The habitations were shaped like the shells of horseshoe crabs, clustered together in hills and valleys of breathless heat and limpid cool. From the inside those homes felt like caravans, and indeed they did have the power of movement, but, in the manner of limpets, tended not to exhibit that power often to the naked eye.

Glenn had walked freely and confidently into Colony and had seen a notice for guests in the window of one of those crustacean-like caravans. Now he stood on the other side of the same window while shadows striped his face and bare torso like a beast's markings, and opened the slats of the Venetian blind to look out on the wide, encircling dazzle of Colony, the sun's broken rays bouncing off its metal, plastic and glass, its hyperreal bright blues and yellows. He felt a drumming in his body that must have been blood. The sun here looked dusky in its intensity, as if viewed through tinted lenses.

Clothes lay on an unmade bed behind him. An electric fan whirred in a cool hush on the bedside cabinet. The pneumatic door of the sleeping compartment was open and beyond the landlady sat on another bed and carefully inspected her toenails. The window of her room was open and occasionally breaths of wind would disturb the gauzy curtains, and even enliven the exhausted air enough to ripple the diaphanous veil around her bed. Satisfied that her toenails had achieved a perfect gloss and had dried hard, she drew stockings up her legs and smoothed her hiked up dress back down over her thighs.

Glenn heard her small movements like a caress almost unbearable in its teasing slightness. But filled with an anonymous sense of the glory of his own existence, he did not think about what she was doing until she entered his room, drew up the blind and started attending to the flowers in the window box with much the same minute attention she had given her toenails. He felt the luxurious boredom and freedom of her body centimetres away and watched the water from her can sparkle in a tame little shower. Her long, peach-coloured nails plucked at buds as if they had been purposely cultivated as pruning instruments.

"You needn't sleep in the separate room, you know. I make the rules here. And sometimes… I like to be informal."

"Yes, I understand," said Glenn, watching her nails, brittle in the sunlight. "There's really no need, is there?"

She placed the watering can on the sill and turned to him. He looked at the tight black hair, the stark, spiky make-up which was part of the exoticism of the Colonites, and the moist, dark eyes. She was wearing a black dress, and as her arms snaked over his shoulders this blackness seemed almost a tactile coffee to his skin, hot and stimulating. It was this gratuitous stimulation that chased away the remains of recent debates like a cloud. His decision to sleep on a separate bed last night was perhaps the last lingering symptom of those debates.

All the trouble had come about because he had tried to limit himself. He had assumed an eternal love would exclude any other loves or any other eternities, but why should it? Time was strange in The Resort. He could philander here in Colony for as long as he liked and still go back to Paula without anything being amiss. Life wasn't just an endless line now; it had expanded in all possible directions. And as for morality, thoughts of moral inconsistency and so on, those were all things imposed by death and a mortal time limit. Immortals had a strange equality, surely? How could one hold a grudge or be jealous? Any time that was falsified by lying or cheating was irrelevant. In eternity forgiveness and return to 'true love,' was a virtual inevitability. He may at least make his embarkation into wide eternity under that assumption. Anyway, something recent experience had taught – and here he was oddly unable to put his finger on exactly what experience, though he felt sure of it, felt it in his very body – was that his mind and the mind of another will always be different universes, by definition. What mattered was the act he put on to meet the acts of others. To be free he must constantly wear spiritual dark glasses. What was inside and what was outside need bear no relation whatsoever. Of course, there were questions raised by those conclusions; yes this was Eternity, with a capital 'E', so there may indeed come a time when etc., etc., but why think of that now?

These thoughts had flushed away his doubts immediately after The Rekindling and then had been absorbed themselves like a thaw into the cells of his body, till not a trace remained. Well, maybe a tiny trace. Dark glasses – the idea of constantly wearing dark glasses had stuck with him as an emblem of his aspirations. He had thought in order to do this he must remain visibly detached, fastidious, even stand-offish. Hence the separate beds. But even this trace of doubt was to be wiped away now. The carnivorous landlady took him into her room and he let himself wallow in the most vulgar, undignified and seemingly undetached of acts. No relation between inside and outside. The bubble bursts. Freedom.

Glenn arose and dressed. He wanted to go out now and savour the freedom of his body and his mind. He did not know what time it was. It was no time at all. He slipped out of the open door with the same unthinking independence as if he had been entirely alone. The landlady was a breakfast he had left, washing up in the sink. He did not feel, anyway, that he *had* left the domicile exactly. Colony was like one very intricate building of many rooms and many open spaces. It was a labyrinth in which one could never get lost, since being lost means separation from the things you need. What was there to be separated from? The slight winds touched his temples like veils making him sober and dizzy simultaneously. He wandered, loose, his feet turning in any direction. He sank into the curves and pillars, like the dunes of a desert. The shadows and the architecture that cast them melted into each other in a collage of abstract shapes and optical illusions where the background might suddenly turn inside out and become the foreground. Stairways like waves. Cool white walls. The people who passed him seemed as aimless or as liberated as himself. There was a casual atmosphere of potential and approachability. Everyone was looking for the same things – the experiences for which one visited or lived in Colony – but they were in no hurry. It was like wandering the jumbled ruins of all the great lost civilisations reproduced in metal, plastic and glass, and distorted in the surreal mirror of an age beyond all past and future.

Inevitably Glenn circled his way to one of the pleasure loci. He passed through narrow, high-walled streets and arcades where globs of colour swirled, dividing and merging in every surface like the pigmented patterns of a cuttlefish. Music emanated from nowhere, drifting like incense smoke in invisible zephyrs of time-warping suggestion. People sat and stood in doorways, on stairs, wandered as if perusing the wares of a bazaar, though nothing was visibly on sale. It was a party that was held all the time, any time, in Colony, that pulsed mysteriously from one locus to another like blood in the veins and arteries of some alien, amorphous organism. Glenn felt like a spy again. He could gain entry into any of the lives around him under any pretences. And they could do the same with him. He was a spy with no mission except spying for its own sake. He was travelling light now, forever, just his body, his mind and the clothes that were so casual he was almost naked in them – steering from nowhere to nowhere.

People spoke to him in bursts from all sides. He made his entrance in unobtrusive style with every step and gesture. Jacket, shirt, smile. He was a shadow. They were all shadows. Someone slipped him something in a handshake and grinned, like a friend meeting him unexpectedly. A mouth bent close to his ear. "Here's your ticket. Remember the name, then swallow it." This was an exhibition of people frozen in a time zone of strange fashions, and conversation isolated from all references to an outside world. 'Outside' was a vague concept. Like the buildings, the people slipped suddenly from background to foreground, and vice versa. Glenn himself was sometimes foreground, sometimes background. Sometimes he was both at once.

He passed from the stark chill of crowding white limbs in one room through an elliptical door, like a cat's iris, and into a gloomier space. Along one side was a curtain through which people would emerge or disappear. Numbers of people were sitting about vacantly in deep plastic seats. What was the drug called? Fate? Something like that. Was it starting to work? It was so hard to tell, since its effects were indistinguishable from a certain synchronicity in the air, like static. The lighting was flickering in imitation of dusk, and there seemed to be a torpor over many of the inhabitants of this room. One girl whose hair fell across her face looked up at him now. She had large grey eyes and a face of inscrutable innocence, like someone freshly transplanted into the world fully grown. In that glance and the few physical motions of the body that accompanied it, Glenn felt a conversation had taken place. The girl got up from the seat and walked to the other end of the space, passing through another elliptical doorway. He followed as if it had all been prearranged.

She went up an angle of stairs like an aquarium of light. It ended in a gallery along which were the doors of separate compartments. Some were open, some closed. Glenn could see through the open doors that the compartments were fixed living quarters. The girl entered one of the compartments. She must live here in the pleasure locus. She did not close the door behind her, but sat down on a block-like piece of furniture in the hall space. She glanced out at Glenn with a look that was neither overtly inviting nor repulsing.

Glenn passed on. He had not lost nerve. It was his very confidence that made him pass on. He knew where the girl could be found. It made no difference if he went in now or not, except that now was not the natural time. She was already his. Out of all the faces here, that fresh nameless face had caught his attention instantly and was already a part of his life. They were two anonymous lives together. For a while the idea of her, and the life behind that idea, would burn like a candle in his life with some mute, ephemeral significance consisting of that straight, mousy hair and that piquant face, so like the face of a love remembered from before life, its very newness full of déjà vu. Then the candle would go out, back into the forgetfulness it came from. All this was certain. Glenn wished to savour the certainty by taking it slowly.

He had noticed a swimming pool in a sort of terraced courtyard as he had drifted idly into the pleasure locus. He now made this his destination. Obviously Colony worked in enigmatic ways. What better way to attune himself to its invisible mechanisms than to feel its air on his body, to exert himself until he became nothing more than breath and heartbeat? It was a kind of waiting game. Waiting itself was an art, a subtle strategy, like that of the fighter who defeats his opponent before a single blow is struck. The respective levels of Glenn and Colony would inevitably adjust to each other and harmonise.

Once again he changed in front of a locker and felt something rising in his chest. He knew what it was. It was a sense of inevitability that told him he was on exactly the right course, that things could only gather momentum from here on. For something else had happened at this last Rekindling. He had realised what was already obvious. He did not need The Resort at all. It had served as a rationalisation of his ability to live his fantasies, it was an infrastructure, a reference point. But now he was beginning to feel its limitations. The only reference point he really needed was the book. That book was the lever that opened the passage to infinite worlds. As long as he remembered the book he would never get lost, never be stuck anywhere. His moorings had loosened. He felt the right actions might precipitate him through an interface to some space outside The Resort. It all depended on what he wanted. If he didn't want to come back ever then he need not. He wasn't even convinced he would have to return for The Rekindling. That depended on whether The Rekindling Zone was really more closely allied with the book than The Resort. It didn't matter. That too was accounted for by the tenets of the book. If he thought he needed The Rekindling Zone then he would.

He walked out from the changing room into the slanting lines of the courtyard, its pyramids of sunlight and shadow stark. A few others were lazing round the sides of the pool like cats on a roof. The water was empty. A ladder giddily led to a diving board. Glenn climbed up its slats of light and darkness to where the board cut angles in the sky. He walked unhesitatingly to the very edge of the board, and sprang. An immortal on the diving board, Olympian, his shadow was a spot at its tip, detached from his feet. He somersaulted in midair.

Non-Attachment

"Heaven exists."

"As you said before."

"Yes. And once you realise and understand the truth of that very simple fact, then it all becomes easy. I think they call it a no-brainer where you've just come from."

Lec let his eyes rest upon the back of his right hand, following the tendon lines to the knuckles, and from there the segmentation of each digit down to the fingernails. There was nothing in the least vague or approximate about his hand. It was not a symbol. He was breathing deeply, like one catching up with himself. For the moment, he did not dare look across at Luke, for fear their eyes would meet and this would, in some way, bring them both back to a schedule that must be followed.

"Why do you hesitate?" asked Luke, after a moment more of silence. "No one will force you to do anything you don't want to."

Lec laughed shortly and looked up at the circular ceiling with its silent muzak of iridescent colour swirls.

"I'm sweating," he said. "Why am I sweating?"

"You shouldn't have to ask that. Physics here is the same as where you've just left, except you've been temporarily accustomed to a more limited version, the habits of which are still with you."

"And… you're avoiding my question."

"In a way, yes, but it's also relevant. You must be used to… I mean, other people must get disorientated. I can't be the only one."

"No, you're not, and it's my job to orientate you again."

"All right. Here's another question – a confession if you like. My heart is beating quite fast – fluttering, you could say – and I feel faint. Even now I feel… a taste of regret. Doesn't that mean there's been some mistake? Maybe I'm not meant to be here."

Luke smiled.

"There is no mistake in you being here. Anything further is a question of your own free will. That is, if you have it, you're bound to choose Heaven. If you haven't got it, the choice has been made for you, and back down you go.

"We already know that you're halfway to sainthood, that you cannot be tempted."

"But I *was* tempted."

"But you did not succumb. Believe me, the Temptations that we have developed here are not a matter of guesswork. You will never encounter greater temptations than those you have just experienced. You're through. You've passed. You should really take a moment just to congratulate yourself. Even to get this far…"

"Yes?"

"Well, you'll forget, of course, if you don't get any further, but it is a blessed state."

"But I still feel tempted now."

"Doesn't matter. You're through, as I said. That feeling is just a minor quibble of the heart."

"Then let me take a moment."

"Please do."

Lec breathed out and looked again around the circular room. If he did not get further, this, he supposed, would be his reward for the restraint and self-denial he had demonstrated. The Serenity Lounge, Luke had called it, and there was, indeed, something about it of the waiting area in an airport. It was a bland place, a place of temporary rest and an antechamber, nothing more. It stood between the test that Lec knew, which still consumed his thoughts like a vivid tiger consumes its kill, and the test he did not know, to which his breathless thoughts could not yet turn. The room was tasteful, he supposed – the vague marbling of the wall, the single window through which came some safely diluted version of the light of empyrean, the cut flowers in the glass vase, which glittered with their rootless, vital life – but this tastefulness struck him as absurd, like a grin that forms invisibly in the heart of a nightmare. He let out a deep breath.

"I know," said Luke, and nodded as if reading his mind.

"I think I'm going to hyperventilate," said Lec.

"That's what happens when people come to the ultimate reality," said Luke. "But it passes. Just tell me when you're ready."

"What if I've already made the wrong decision?" blurted Lec suddenly.

"What?"

"All those things I turned down. Is it too late?"

"Not while we're still in the Serenity Lounge. Would you like to go back?"

For a moment Lec's eyes widened and a strange smile spread across his face.

Then he shook his head.

"No. No," he said.

"Are you sure?"

"I'm sure." He sighed. "Just tell me, is Heaven as good as it's meant to be?"

"Better. Infinitely better. The Temptations, as is their nature, are mere trifles."

Lec nodded.

"Okay. I think I'm ready. Let's go through."

"The first test had what you might call a pleasant or entertaining aspect. Some people already feel themselves closer to Heaven with the Temptations. More often those who fail… But I'm afraid that it's generally considered much harder to see the pleasant or entertaining aspects of the second test."

Luke had raised his voice the better to be heard over the constant background of screaming that penetrated the present chamber from beyond. In this new environment of glass, metal and bright light, the screams had a cold, brittle quality, as if thousands of invisible diamonds were scratching the sheet of glass before them in such a way that it set up a banshee whining and throbbing that would eventually shatter the glass completely. Lec was staring through that clinically pristine glazing at the scintillating blades on the other side. Despite the slightly bluish ferocity of the lighting, he felt a peculiar chill, as if he had stepped into a meat freezer where butchered pigs hang in neat sections on hooks. He closed his eyes.

"I'm not sure this understatement is helping me. I think you should just tell me what it is."

"You could say Temptation is a negative test. You succeed by refusing. This is the opposite of that. We know you have conquered your desires, but apart from desires, there's another obstacle to entering Heaven. I told you before, although I'm not sure you've quite understood, and many are surprised when they get here, as if they thought abstaining from things was enough. However, it's simply unavoidable fact that you can't get to Heaven while you still harbour fear."

Lec nodded now, very slowly. The screams had penetrated to his very core, their wringing vibration mixing with the buzz that remained in him from the fiery stirring of the Temptations. Some queasy battle seemed to be taking place between the two frequencies of vibration, as if their contest might serve to establish what was real, true, stable and trustworthy. But the battle continued with only the turbulence of up and down, finding nothing level or certain. Lec closed his eyes, and his head seemed to drop forward naturally so that his brow pressed against the cold pane of glass.

"I'm a physical coward," he said.

His brow still against the glass, he shook his head.

"It's no good," he said. "I'll have to go back down."

"There's no need to give up so easily," said Luke. "It might help if I explain. There were sword-smiths in Japan who would temper the blades by alternating them between the heat of the forge and icy water. That's also how we complete our non-attachment, and it's non-attachment that you need to get into Heaven.

"These, in there, these are the blades of non-attachment."

Lec opened his eyes with sober determination, as if just looking at the blades doomed him to immolation by them, which perhaps it did. They hung from the ceiling like the brushes of a car-wash, bristling cylinders of long, curved, razor-sharp knives, closely serried. A circle on the floor, between the rows of blades, marked where the subject was to stand. Then the device would be activated and the blades would close upon the circle, rotating at high speed.

Lec's hand trembled uncontrollably on the ledge at the bottom of the glass pane. Something rather curious had occurred to him and was forming a loop of burgeoning imagery in his brain like a pattern turning into a fractal. The loop had come to him through a loop-hole. It was a worm, parasitising his mind with a hallucinatory obsession that seemed both hermetically sealed and infinite. How had it been overlooked? He had overlooked it, too, and now, as reward, he was contemplating these vicious blades. He should have given in to temptation. It would have caused, he supposed, some spiritual setback when he was reborn, but with his particular spiritual qualities he would soon recover the lost ground, and then he would be offered the Temptations again – more lurid than those that crowded around St. Anthony in Bosch's painting, or even the later version by Max Ernst – and he would succumb again, and so find himself in an endless cycle of pleasures unknown to most mortals, interlarded merely with the miseries known to many. He should have done this. The thought both paralysed and made him tremble further. Of course, he could not speak a word of this to Luke. But what *could* he do? The memory of what had been offered opened up again before his mind's eye, like a host of gigantic and exotic butterflies taking flight and turning into a kaleidoscope of earthly and more-than-earthly delights.

The thought of the whirling blades returned, closing in, as if to shred those bright and fascinating butterfly wings.

"No!" screamed Lec, suddenly.

He span around and ran to the door, which had closed behind them, rattling the handle frantically. It would not open.

"I'm not dead! I'm not dead!" he cried out. "I can't do this! I'm not dead!"

He felt a tinglingly calm hand on his shoulder.

"You *are* dead, Lec."

"No. It's a premature burial. How do I know I'm dead? How do I know it won't kill me?"

Taking both his shoulders, Luke turned him around.

"Think about it. Do you look the same as you did when you were alive?"

Lec took in a deep, shuddering breath, and then another.

"No."

Luke hardly needed to say more. One of the first things Lec had noticed on arriving here was that he looked different. His previous visage had been, he thought, inextricably identified with who he was, but, after a few seconds of perplexity when confronted with a mirror in the arrivals area, the confusion, like a double-image in his brain, had settled and disappeared. That other visage had been so partial, such a gossamer mask, that he felt pity and sadness to see how easily he had shed it, as well as relief, comfort and confidence in returning to what was self-evidently his true form. And yet, the novelty of losing that temporary form, and of regaining his eternal form, was such that it lingered, and, even without a mirror to reflect his image, he had continually examined his hands as if they embodied and expressed the entire mystery of identity and cosmic creation.

He examined his hands again now. How infinitely familiar and yet how infinitely abstract they were. They seemed to melt, from one shape to another, like mercury, as he turned them.

"So I'm already dead."

A half-pleasurable shiver sank down inside him.

"Will it hurt?" he asked.

"You had to die in order to get here. This will be just the same. It's not an illusion; it's quite real. As real as anything outside of Heaven, that is."

Luke walked back to the sheet of glass separating them from the Chamber of Immolation. He lifted his hand, and, quite without fuss, stretched it out and through that cold, solid pane. There was no sound, no cracking or shattering. Lec could not decide whether the glass had moved aside from Luke's hand to let it pass, like a soap bubble with enough cohesion not to burst, or whether Luke's hand had in some way become substanceless. However, when Luke withdrew his hand again, Lec thought he saw infinitesimal gleams of light there, as brilliant as the light that glinted on the blades, seeming to shine out from inside the hand through gaps made by a loosening and recombining of particles. Then these gleams, if they had been, disappeared.

"That's non-attachment," said Luke. "That is what the blades of non-attachment will bring you. The process is repeated until you have got to the point where the blades simply pass through you, without disrupting your form in any way. Without a ripple."

There was a silence.

"Do we have to do it now?" asked Lec.

"There is what you might call a time limit. We don't have to start with the blades, though. There are other tests. You could begin with something else and work up to the blades, if you like."

Lec nodded wanly.

They wandered through the honeycomb of purgatorial tortures, observing the boundless variety of tests being carried out. Some of the chambers were still unoccupied, such as that in which five thousand species of spider scampered on walls and glass in seemingly endless agitation, as if driven to distraction by the very emptiness of the space. Their agitation was like a lightning of forty thousand legs, diffuse and angry in a scattered cloud, waiting for a human subject to earth it. Another unoccupied chamber showed oranges, apples, bananas, and all the most detestable varieties of fruit, arranged singly and in foul cornucopias, forming an overall pattern of menacing asymmetry, like some fructiferous trap that would close suddenly upon the subject in unspeakable ways.

Most of the chambers, however, were occupied, and from these the screams that Lec had heard ever since passing through the door from the Serenity Lounge, ceased to be distant and disembodied. The cause for each scream was specific and knowable. Luke nodded to other guides like himself, who were supervising the tests, as he and Lec drifted through, or sometimes lingered. There was a kind of mathematics to the pain, thought Lec. There could be no cheating here, no shortcuts. All accounts were to be paid in full. It was the very definition of inexorable.

They had stopped in one chamber where, behind the glass, such an atrocity was being prosecuted that Lec felt a brutal complicity even in watching, and had to turn his eyes away. There were five grotesque men, and one woman. It was the woman, in this case, who was the human subject. There were complications to this particular test that Lec did not understand, as the woman appeared to be pregnant. After much beating, four of the men had held the woman down, while the fifth loomed over her with a sharp hook in his hand. Luke was answering a question that Lec had just asked in a kind of horrified exclamation.

"But such things happen on Earth all the time," Luke was saying. "Unless you believe that the Devil is equal or greater in power to God, then you must accept that all happens with God's express approval. Many people, yourself included, still manage to maintain their faith despite such mysteries – in part, even because of them. Why should it be different here when you see the actual mechanics of the mystery?"

"Who are those monsters, then?" asked Lec. "Are they angels?"

Luke laughed.

"An easy mistake to make, but no. They could have been angels. They suffered a peculiar kind of corruption. They were on their way to sainthood, but each of them succumbed to one of the Temptations.

Unfortunately, it's dangerous to fall having attained such a height. Their finely developed spiritual qualities became entangled with their chosen Temptation, and were twisted quite out of shape by it. They're almost the only ones who will do this kind of work."

"And you let them do it."

"Better for both sides if the subject is a volunteer. Remember, those screams you hear now are the screams of one who is going to Heaven. All of these screams are. On the other hand, the men you see here chose a different fate. They moaned in ecstasy. Theirs were the moans and sighs of those bound for Hell."

Lec stole another glimpse of the pack of fiends who had been set upon the woman, apparently by her own consent. They appeared to be enjoying their work, but that enjoyment was so deranged that it resembled, after all, the taut spasms of some great agony had formed reshaped the human soul into a ghoul of degradation and perversity. The very physiognomy of these creatures was knotted with distortions. Their eyes bloomed with the stench of moral decay. They must have died as human beings, but they had continued to grow, with a poisonous, swelling anti-life, into shapes of monstrosity and torturous appetites that would only take them farther from the corpse of hope from which they had crawled. If humans were those who both needed salvation and were capable of it, then it seemed to Lec that these things were disqualified from being human on the second count. And if so, what did the need for salvation mean to them?

"It's horrible," said Lec.

"It's what we have to work with. These beings will suffer, before eternity is through, agonies you cannot glimpse from the far edges of a dream, the same agonies they're dispensing exponentiated to the power of one thousand. You can see that. You can see the code of their future suffering written into them. Their way is not easy. It is said that one day they will make angels of such tender compassion that all the other angels in Heaven will weep to see them and bow to kiss their footprints. Who knows when that day will come?"

The sobs and screams were piercing Lec, once again, to his throbbing core. He would turn to glass. He would shatter.

"Take me back," said Lec. "I don't want to build up to it. It has to be the blades. It's the blades or nothing."

"It's the blades, anyway," said Luke. "Sooner or later, it's the blades. Even if you go back down to Earth this time, the blades will always be waiting. You will do it, I promise you."

Lec stood, once more, before the broad and high sheet of glass beyond which were the suspended rows of rotating blades.

"What do I do?" he asked.

"Just say yes."

"That simple?"

"That simple. You don't need to do anything except go in there and stand in the circle. Then I'll close the door and press the button. You don't have to do anything else."

"Except endure the pain."

"Endure it, don't endure it – it makes no difference. It will happen without effort on your part."

"But after this test I'm through and it's over."

"Not quite."

"Not quite?"

"No. Even when you enter Heaven, periodically you are tested for non-attachment, often with the blades here."

"But… it will only hurt if you've developed some kind of attachment again. Otherwise the blades will just go through you, I suppose."

"No. You have to make your form dense again, for the later tests. Otherwise it's no test at all. Some try to make themselves vaporous instinctively, in a panic, but as soon as the panic sets in, in that instant, their form becomes heavy and solid, and the blades have something to hack through.

"The point is not that you don't feel pain. You must feel it and not mind. That is non-attachment."

Lec simply stood and gazed through the glass. He was thinking that at any moment he would say, "I'm ready", but he said nothing, and his silence went on and on. He had always thought, or perhaps only hoped, that it was enough to be a good person. Now he saw what he had always tried not to see. It was not sufficient to be good; one must also be great. It was, indeed, mandatory. Yes, he had tried not to see, but surely he had always known it would come to this. What else had he feared all his life? It was the shadow of his own weakness, from which he could not escape. What he must do loomed before him like the sheer face of a wild and hostile mountain. There was nothing in him that could make the cold, deliberate and necessary decision, nothing that would turn it from impossible to natural. It was precisely the hollow nothing inside – the nothing of self-consciousness – that kept him in the stalemate of thought and decision, making a coward of him; he was no larger, in the end, than his single, lonely life. But he needed something larger than him, something like love or divine intervention. He needed something to take his place in an act such as this. A single, lonely, deliberating 'I' could never do it. Nonetheless, it would have to be him. There was no other way. He would have to settle every last penny of his outstanding account in the currency of agony and horror.

Luke took him by his shoulders again, and turned him so that they faced each other. Lec swelled with a poignant hope, a sense of pleading, as Luke looked into his eyes. Then Luke leant forward and kissed Lec on the mouth. So this was the kiss of non-attachment. Luke's tongue probed his cheek. Every millimetre of him seemed touched by a simple and knowing light of acceptance. It was the soberest kiss he had ever received, and that most full of life, free of all the heavy dross of desire.

Luke withdrew and smiled.

"I'm trying to make this easy for you. I'll show you that it is not impossible. I'll go in there and stand in the circle, and you press the button, and you'll see that I don't turn myself into mist. If I do that, do you think you'll be able to do it afterwards?"

Lec nodded solemnly.

Luke passed through the door into the Chamber of Immolation. As the door closed behind him, all sound from within was erased as if the chamber were a sonic vacuum. He positioned himself carefully in the circle, between the blades, looked back at Lec, and nodded to signify that he was ready. Lec turned to the stop and go buttons on the wall. Luke was standing calm and erect, patient. It occurred to Lec what power was his at this moment. This was a decision and a deliberation he could manage – this pushing of a button. This would be someone else's pain, someone blessedly taking his place. He need not think now of his pain afterwards, since the gory wonder of another's pain stood, as if insurmountable, between this moment and that. He needed to see the details. He stabbed at the button. Immediately the blades began to whir, turning invisible, like hummingbird wings, and converged upon the figure of Luke, who seemed entirely free of reaction. His motionlessness was not rigid; he simply waited. As blank as this easy waiting, this lack of avoidance, was the certainty that the blades would close upon and shred him.

Suddenly, Lec could endure Luke's calm acceptance no more. He turned again and stabbed frantically at the second button until the whirring froze. Luke looked about himself with no sign of relief, only faint surprise. The left sleeve of his jacket was in ribbons of dripping red. He came to the door and opened it.

"Why did you stop it?"

"You shouldn't have to do this for me. I'll do it. I'm ready."

Luke nodded.

"Okay. I'll reset the blades and we can start."

And then Lec fell to his knees and sobbed, as if he had been expecting the words "I'm ready" to be enough, on their own, for him to pass the test. He flung his arms around Luke's ankles and begged, and Luke gazed down at him in pity.

He was intact once more, down to the very teeth in his mouth, which had so recently been smashed and scattered like beads. To be reassembled so elegantly was incredible, as if he had experienced all the squalor and hardship of billions of years of evolution in the space of a few minutes, from the primordial slime of his blood and viscera to the divine bipedal form he had once thought human, a vehicle of thought, identity, and now a lucent vessel of the ineffable laws of Heaven.

When he had been a child, in his last life, he had once played with a loose razor blade. It had cut his fingers easily, but then the pain, the thrilling, throbbing and scarlet-dribbling pain, had been so intense that it had made him scream. So thin and so delicate were the cuts in his skin, and, as thin and delicate as they were, so had the sharpness of the pain been great. Just as the sensitive skin of the face seems to burn with itches and tickles long after the tip of a feather has traced its line there, so, now, Lec's body was so closely criss-crossed with such lingering lines from the pain of razor-sharp blades, it seemed that not a square millimetre of the surface of his body remained unploughed by the knives of non-attachment. As a result, his skin was more sensitive than ever, to all sensation, pleasure and pain merging, in the very motion of the air against face and hands, into a single spectrum of tingling.

"I told you you'd do it," said Luke.

Lec could do no more, for now, than nod and smile.

"Well, then," said Luke, and indicated the door from the Serenity Lounge.

"Are we going back to the Temptations?" asked Lec, more in amusement and curiosity than anything else.

"I think you'll find it quite changed," said Luke. "After you."

Something had changed, but Lec was too dazed to understand at first. The opposite door in the Serenity Lounge – the door that had led from the Temptations – was gone. When he turned around, Lec saw that the door through which they had just entered had also disappeared. There was just the round, marbled wall, the iridescent ceiling, the colourful, patternless carpet, like a rainbow pulverised into powder, and the table at which they had sat previously, with the lilies in a vase.

"Why don't we rest?" said Luke.

"Why not?" said Lec.

They sat in the chairs either side of the table, exchanged a glance and smiled irresistibly to each other.

Lec began to look, idly and yet alertly, about the room. The colours in the carpet were shifting like bright mist. He remembered the feeling of nightmare he had experienced in this room before, and at the memory the colours glowed even brighter, as if they were embers in a fire battening on the oxygen of a breeze from nowhere, and burning fierce in delight. His eyes travelled to the walls dned he realised that, framed here, were psalms, epigrams, prayers, verses, aphorisms and other words traced in the human mind from all different times and places. They seemed to float up haphazardly onto the round wall, in no order, as if this enclosing circle were the ages themselves, and one could no longer tell what was beginning, what end, what before, what after.

He read, one by one, as if forming them aloud, the words that floated up now in one of the frames.

> The perfect man hates Heaven, hates what is from Heaven in man…

He smiled. There was more, but he felt no need to read it all. His eye rested for a moment on the name, 'Chuang-tzü', which he had heard before. He did not know who this person was.

Then, it occurred to him that, although he was still smiling, he could not find his smile anywhere. He realised, almost at once, that he was no longer in the Serenity Lounge.

The Broadsands Eyrie

Even after I stopped believing in magic, I knew that magic was the only possible happiness. This – the need for magic – seems a secret, hidden, out-of-the-way sort of feeling, which, stated plainly in broad daylight, can only ever earn you odd looks. And yet I sometimes also suspect that it is universal. Perhaps the difference between myself and others is that they – apparently every other person in the world – decided from a certain age never to use the word 'magic' again, except to their own children. Instead, they would allow themselves free use of the word 'love'. This is a kind of magic that can be performed in daylight, but only by refusing to question and by pretending it is all very normal. Nothing else is permitted.

In any case, since 'magic' has been disallowed, I certainly cannot believe in 'love'. I have been, therefore, in all my life, as remotely separated from love as from magic. Or to phrase it another way, all my life has been a peculiar unrequited love affair with magic. I have loved magic from an infinite distance, but since magic is a prerequisite of love and since there has been no magic in my life, I have been forced to concede, with a very dry bitterness, that even my love for magic is a lie. I only wish I *could* love magic. Without magic, I cannot love magic; I am stranded.

A dream that does not touch life at any point is a pale and empty thing, really only a phantom, but so is the life not touched. Entirely separate, and in the very completeness of this separation haunting each other, both life and the dream come to nothing, ghostly and sterile as the moon in the daytime sky.

It is broad daylight as I write this page, and once again I shall attempt what I know in broad daylight can only fail. The magic that lies at an infinite remove from me – a distance we call 'impossibility' – is made known to me in its perverse non-existence in the form of dreams. These are not the dreams that visit with sleep, though they are related; they are dreams of something lost, a home never known, more precious than anything accessible to the senses. Even to whatever part it is of me that dreams, these dreams are ultimately elusive and visit not to satisfy, but only to tease and torment. Strange and otherworldly, these dreams are myself, and in subtle pursuit of them I have spent what little energy, soul and seriousness have been apportioned to me. Which is to say, even since childhood, some instinct that has been the closest thing to religious certainty I have known, the very who of who I am, has spurred me to take up the pen and write. And though subtlety is required, my aim is simple – to take the dream that is my heart and soul, and to hold it in my open palm before you. Such is the labyrinth of subtleties, however, that this first, most important simplicity is often forgotten, and once forgotten, only with difficulty and in sad and fleeting ways remembered.

Here is one of those sad and fleeting ways, that is to say, one of my dreams of something lost. I think that this one first came to me when I was studying Japanese at university – though I cannot recall with clarity – and it's possible that something in my studies may have acted as a kind of antenna for it. I remember the dream as being especially full of the ripple and stir of magic, and of that strange atmosphere that is beyond words and beyond life. Now, however, I cannot access, through this dream, the same atmosphere; I only recall that it once was an unblocked portal. The channel has since been closed in that direction, and I cannot hope to convey the precise quality of ashen grief I feel in contemplating this. Nonetheless, I will note down the dream's essentials, even if I do so, as all too often, too late.

I was visited by the dream on a number of occasions – a scene of a winding coastal road. There were hills, with something of the mountain about them, on one side of the road, and on the other, the dark green land sloped quickly to a deep blue sea. The road was almost empty. Perhaps there was a single car. Very little about the scene was definite, but recalling it again now, the following, which may be retrospective embellishments, do not seem out of place: There were magnificent sprays of evergreen needles at the ends of pine branches, the mountains above the road being densely wooded with pine trees. Sunlight flashed on the blade-sharp, sapphire waves like an echo in the ocean of the pine-needles on the mountains. I always seemed to view this as if I were disembodied, somewhere out to sea, with the coast a little to my left. Then I might draw closer and hover over the stark and splendid road, which the sunlight had made dark blue, like the sea, at its centre, and which was dusty at its edges. Also hovering was an image or impression of a woman. She was Oriental in her features, and dressed in clothes that suggested some traditional status that only hundreds of years of history would allow one to understand. As enigmatic as the identity her wondrous clothes bestowed, was her relationship to the man, who may or may not have been myself. If her clothes marked her as a 'princess' – and I believe the truth was nothing so simple – then perhaps the man and woman could have been said to be on their 'honeymoon'. But I am afraid that such prosaic words can only mislead. In any case, there was something magnificent about this scene. It was the pine-freshness of the future, but it was a future in which hundreds and thousands of years of history once more came into their own, and were lived through the life of the man, and were also understood to complete satisfaction by his intellect. Perhaps the two of them, man and woman, were in that car, following the road that curved into possibility, and perhaps they passed beneath a fantastical shining pagoda of red and gold, transparent as a hologram, perched atop some precarious and verdant crag.

Such are the dreams of lost things that form my soul. Some have recurred since childhood. Others have come to me as something new in adult life. Some, like that described above, at some point seem to 'go out', their inner light extinguished. (Perhaps – so I hope – the light will return.) Others, though the strength of their visitation varies, have yet to be affected by this fatal dullness. All of them have some quality in common that I try vainly to name, but whose appeal to the heart is that undying appeal of nostalgia. Remembering them is the sweetest sensation I know, like once more coming alive. It also inspires in me the cruellest of all longings. And often – could this be simply because I grew up close to the sea, or is there some other reason? – these dreams have in them an image of branches in the air above the quiet beauty and majesty of waves.

I have said that my life and these dreams do not touch each other at any point. This is true. And yet there are certain places, certain experiences and certain memories that seem to bear some indefinable relation to or correspondence with these dreams. In childhood, for instance, some magical thing that never actually happened seemed forever about to. And that magic, in order to seem so imminent, became in some haunting, phantom way, also *immanent*. Without touching, it had to cling so closely to the outline, the movement and the appearance of things as to be identical. And yet it was not quite identical, and if one tried to grasp the memory and find the magic of a dream there, one would be left with an empty, mask-like shell, either because the magic had flown the memory and left it a husk, or because the magic apart from the memory was itself just a husk. I think about a certain face in candlelight, for instance, and remembering that face I believe that love is only possible in childhood. Is this a wax mask of magic? Is it the real face, devoid of magic? It's a heartbreaking and also a sinister line of questioning. All lovers, I think, at some point know this taste, when the loss of love becomes something macabre. And all magical places and dream-like memories are susceptible, without changing in appearance one jot, to the same kind of macabre transformations.

When I was young there was a beach known to us by the name of 'Broadsands'. I do not remember the first time we went there; it was as if there were no first time. Our visits there seemed part of a series that knew neither beginning nor end. There must have been a first time, though, that I climbed down those two hundred and twenty uneven and narrow stone steps – which seemed to me like five hundred or a thousand – set in the shadow-cool cliff-face. The way led between dark rising shelves of crumbling slate, and equally dark thorn trees that grew in dwarfed, wind-hunched clumps atop them. That first time, and on many occasions afterwards, I must have found the steps so difficult that I had to take one at a time, not putting one foot in front of the other, but only one foot, with some effort, forward and down, and the next on the same step. The descent was arduous, but it led to another world. Slowly the grim cliffs of that world would come into view, with their rocky, vertiginous ledges on which gulls nested, tufted with the stringy grey-and-green grass, and spattered with droppings. These rocks were eerie with a prehistoric loneliness, as if we had just been conveyed to an undiscovered island in the Pacific, known previously only to its wild inhabitants, to the hidden marine traffic of the solemn region, and to the soaring albatross. To me it was precisely Conan-Doyle's *Lost World*, and the seagulls were not different to ancient saurians. The very air of the place was sonorous, as with the grey and scaly skin of reptiles, and the measureless silence boomed with some memory of battling pterodactyls, like Second World War bombers. And so eerie-solemn was the place that its very silence was excitement, suggesting to the mind of a boy inexhaustible imaginations of mysterious things, and riches of invisible adventure ever-brimming in the precious, petrified treasure-chest of the landscape, whose surface was carved so intricately with the writhing of root and vine and the immemorial grey writhing done by wind, wave and rock together across millennia. The wearisome descent, and afterwards, the almost unendurably wearisome ascent, therefore, seemed a proper price to pay.

Despite its name, 'Broadsands', the beach was of no great extent. Its largeness was that of its seclusion, and of the impressiveness of the cliffs, and of the endlessness of the sea and air. The beach seemed to me something like a giant's knuckle. Between the great, hawthorn-haired fingers were narrow little coves – four of them, including that down which there trickled the broken, fossilised waterfall of steps – each with a slightly different character and geography. And after the last of these fingers a tiny isthmus of sand joined the knuckled cliffs to another rock, which was a kind of tidal island, since, when the tide came in, the murky waves would submerge the connecting bar of sand with terrifying swiftness. This island, its sides of steep and slippery slate, was crowned, like the cliffs, with ragged, thorny trees, whose insanely twisted branches, dotted with grey-green lichen, seemed to preserve in the air between them a mysterious sense of dry, still emptiness, like that of a studio set.

Broadsands was a little distance along the coast from home, so that to visit it was always something of an expedition. Therefore, I never did so alone. When we visited, 'we' were usually myself, my father, my brother, the dog, and, depending on the occasion, others. Most of the time the beach would be ours alone, few others, it seemed, either knowing the secret of Broadsands' existence, or willing to pay the price of entry to that world. As to what we did there, it seems to me that it was not possible to be bored on Broadsands. Even if there had been nothing to do, it would have been enough to sit there in the midst of the saurian mystery of the place, and watch some obscure, repetitive play of air stirring in a tuft of stringy grass on some inaccessible ledge. There was, however, plenty to do, and happily, nothing that had to be done. The only exception here was that, if we stayed on the beach overnight – as we sometimes did – then it was necessary to prepare and eat a meal.

Apart from the invisible adventures of the imagination, which I cannot hope to describe, I might spend time crawling in the perpetually damp and salty little cave at the base of the fourth knuckle of rock. In this blue whorl, smooth as the skin of a porpoise, I would try to insinuate myself in the manner of a winkle in its portable abode. I wanted to become one with the cave in just such a way, as if it were my shell. But since the cave was not portable, I was also afraid of succeeding, and being stuck there forever. Somehow, I always thought, too, that I might *discover* something in this cave, though there was nowhere to hide anything. The salt-dank spirit of that cavity had to be somewhere, though, and that spirit must have had its secrets. And yet it always eluded me, perhaps disappearing into the last vanishing point of some ever-shrinking spiral of the rock, where I could not squeeze myself, or taking the primitive, rock-flake form of a sea-louse, and escaping.

Another favourite pastime was to dig in the sand, discovering as if anew each time the damp sand that lay beneath the pleasant, dry sand of the surface. The topmost layer of sand was a crystallisation of the sun's rays as dust and grit. Therefore, to walk upon it, or lie in it, was like walking upon or lying in some essence of the sun itself. But dig and you would find the sea, and strangely it would seem that the sea was more ancient than the sun. The smell of it there in the sand was full of primitive secrets, and the cold and darkness of a time when life crept first into being as a savage, unbeautiful chaos. It was the smell of cold-blooded fecundity, hinting that the primordial soup was more a primordial stain of dampness through which there ran a thin, oily streak or seam of salt-musk that had lubricated the darkest and most horribly hag-ancient of rocks, dripping and dribbling in subterrene shadow, till the mineral fissures had turned slimy with the spawning of life. That smell, as I worked my fingers into the shaggy-wet patches of cloven sand, was enough to convince anyone, whatever the evidence to the contrary, that life had not needed the sun to begin, but had sprung forth first in all the most hidden and buried places, the cave-systems and deep ocean floors where sunlight never penetrated. And, indeed, there was a resemblance in spirit between creatures of the deep sea, creatures of the cave, and creatures of the buried sand, which had, as well as darkness, the brine of the one place and the rock of the other. Thus the sand-hopper, a crustacean not unlike a shrimp. Ugly as the angler-fish and sickly as the blind cave salamander, this creature would spring up from my childish excavations like the dehiscence of seeds flying from a suddenly burst pod. Needless to say, I would chase these slimy fleas of the beach, for no other purpose than to hold one, or many, in my closed, dark fist and feel them wriggling and trying to work their powerful spring-leaps, but having no room to.

Tiring of this, I might try some rock-climbing, being, at that age, agile with the curiosity and the natural, breathing life of the self that time and education destroys. The thrill of rock-climbing was in finding hand and foot-holds, and in discovering just how far these would take you into previously unexplored heights. There was also the thrill of seeing things from a different viewpoint, as if one had entered the world of the nesting seagulls, or the microworld of sea-lice and sand-hoppers. To be close to that inaccessible ledge with its tuft of stringy grass, at which you were looking earlier as if it were the moon, or a cloud in the sky – that was a thrill. It seemed to prove what is, after all, only the truth, though our senses tell us otherwise – that nothing is fixed.

While the tide was out I might climb the steep and slippery silver slate of the island, where finger and toe-holds were very slight indeed. Those last inches of the rock before the dusty soil, and the dry, clinging herbage where the island's crown began, were always the most treacherous. After a giddy, scrabbling struggle, I would make it, relieved not to have fallen, and explore the empty mystery of that thorny maze, which was perhaps of an acre's extent. It was a pirate's island, of course, though I had never encountered pirates or found treasure there. What I found was simply atmosphere – the stillness distilled from isolation and elevation. Something in the dry, gibbering branches of the stunted trees made me think of things Oriental and of the delicate antiquity of certain Chinese tales, seemingly wreathed in mists of wondrous pinks and yellows, like smokes emitted from the phials of potion in some sorcerer's cavern. This dry, ticking atmosphere of sorcery, which made me search and search, satisfied and yet utterly thwarted, enraptured and yet cheated, thinking it an astounding thing to cross this island in a minute or less, and see the dust between the starveling roots break in the round mouth of a tunnel at the edge of the silver-slate cliffs there, as if the whole tunnel of thorns and dust were telescoping my vision dizzily out to sea, and yet finding it sickening also that the island ended so abruptly that I teetered on that Darien brink with the weird insignificance of the island's existence – I found nothing else but this.

And there was panic added to the weird emptiness of this sorcery, since it seemed the tide, when out, was always threatening to come in, and leave me stranded on that thorny enigma of rock, where only thorns might thrive, and sometimes, more than merely threatening, did begin, sloshingly, to bury the isthmus of sand beneath the unresting dull terror of its green, so that I was forced to make a reckless escape. Therefore, all explorations of the island had a nervous quality, time, like a shrinking shadow, being short. It was the tide, perhaps, that was the guardian of the island's sorcery. If only you stayed long enough on the island, perhaps you might discover its secret, after all. But, more horrible than a swarm of octopi, the savage ocean, its speed and power as alarming as murder, ensured that no one ever would.

And still there were things to do. Even parched with the salt-terror of near death, the appetite remained. And though the pirate island could not be explored, the rest of the beach could; and every time was as strange and great as the first.

I might throw stones at the inexhaustible surge and drag of the sea, or walk back and forth along the shore where the bubbles of wavelets appeared and disappeared like temporary pebbles. And in walking from one end of the beach to the other while the rippling tide telescoped its foaming veils across the sand and shells, and retracted them, never concluding its sketchy plans, but only erasing and rearranging, I felt always as if I were a pendulum whose oscillations took me deeper into the understanding of something foreign.

Sand, it seemed, was as inexhaustible as sea. Just to scoop up a palmful and feel its weight was good. It was as if these grains each represented separate vibrations in the soothing resonance that is called pleasure. More than that, to let the sand trickle through your fingers was an exercise in letting go of all things, since nothing better symbolises time than sand, each grain having been released by the attrition of millennia from the significance it once had as a mountain, to be then hidden in the pleasant insignificance of other grains, none of which may be traced to beginnings. An hourglass does not measure an hour, but untold ages, with each speck in its trickle. On the beach, the sands of the hourglass, whisked by the wind, returned those ages to nothing. And yet, these grains seemed to accumulate the pleasure of the day. If you buried your legs with scoops of sand, dry and warm, or damp with a cool that slowly absorbs warmth, you would find it surprisingly heavy with the weight of this pleasure. This was especially true of sand dug from beneath the surface layer. Serious with shadow, the wet undersand had stored the solemn joy of time's slow passing, which began now to crawl over your legs like a displaced snail gradually growing easy in its new location and putting down once more the foot it had pulled up into its shell.

Eventually the sandy accumulation of time would begin to shift the day from afternoon towards evening. We would gather driftwood together for a fire. There were dry, smooth twigs, eaten away strangely, resembling unknown musical instruments, or sometimes great waterlogged beams of wood, as if from a shipwreck. When sufficient material was gathered from all the far-flung quarters of the beach, this was piled together on the sand, and handfuls of dry grass were used to kindle the first flames. The gathering of firewood was an activity somehow calculated to induce a satisfying tiredness in the bones, and there was nothing more appropriate then than to sit close by the newly ignited fire and watch your labour slowly reduced to ashes. Potatoes, apples and so on, wrapped in silver foil, were placed like offerings on the pyre, not in the heart of the flames, but upon the surrounding splints of wood, where the heat must have been as intense as an oven; the offerings cooked well, though sometimes slightly charred or smoky.

With the cool of evening, winds would spring up, and the smoke of the fire seemed to chase you. If you sat in one place it would pour towards you, making your eyes water, until you sat elsewhere, when, following your movements, the wind would change direction, bringing the smoke with it, and that acrid smell like shaggy, blackening hay, pleasant for a second, and then unbearable. All the while the extent of the beach would be growing or shrinking at an astonishing rate, according to the tide, ebb or flood.

At last the sun would sink, and the blue of the sky, no longer contained by the vault of heaven, would begin to dye the air itself. And as this blue permeated the air, the far sky from which it seeped down would grow darker, its opacity melting away to reveal the night that is always there.

In one of the ancient coves between the knuckles of beetling rock, like a roofless cave, we would arrange our sleeping bags upon the sand, close to the dying fire, whose heat-glow was a different kind of silence in the air, unhurriedly thickening and curling to pops and cracks when sparks would leap, or some piece of charred and ash-furred wood dropped softly into the embers below. There was no need to try to sleep. It was not tiring to lie there and look directly up at the pale night blue as the stars came out one by one. Dun-coloured bats, too, filled the air with the thrum of their half-invisible wings, issuing at last from the dark hollows that had kept them secret all through the sleeping day, and threading the nocturnal air with the needle-sharp inaudible cries by which they navigated their Baroque, fluttering flights, seeming to proclaim the night as different to day as land is to sea.

What was that difference, to human beings all but forgotten, of which the bats, like fragile curiosities always on the edge of disappearing, served to remind me? A different mode of life inhabits the sea than inhabits the land. But what mode of life is a human being? To sleep out under the stars – the phrase is fixed, and it is almost unnatural to search for another to express the same idea. It is relatively rare for a human not to shelter from the open sky at night, even if the roof that shelters is nothing more than a sheet of canvas. To sleep without a roof seems almost like sleeping upon waves – it is to enter a different habitat, not entirely human. This is the habitat of the stars, and here the stars seem not so remote. To sleep out in the open air is to share the night with the stars and the bats as the swimmer shares the sea with the fish, jellyfish, coral, krill, sea-urchins and turtles.

Lying upon the beach, the nylon-velvet of the sleeping bag so thin that I seemed to feel each grain of sand beneath me as I tried to work the sloping sand into a natural cradle with my movements, I would be at perfect leisure to gaze at the stars, without any need to crane my neck. There was the ancient jagged line of the slate cliff, like an old, inky, Chinese picture, leading steeply up to the clumps of stringy grass, and to the equally jagged trees, and then, with sudden clarity, just above them, a mere breath away, was the sky, a wondrous, soft blue in which there hung pearls. And watching one of these pearls shining on the cheek of the night, the whole sky misty and pellucid at the same time, like a detailed opium vision, I began to feel that somehow or other I might reach that pearl. The gentle caresses of air upon my face were like waves. The sand seemed to melt from beneath me. The waves of air would cradle me and rockingly float me up past the tips of the thorn trees and into a sky that was full of these gentle, invisible waves. The way was long and the night air had its own topography, which human eyes could not discern, but it was not unthinkable that I might float with that pearly star, and take the lower horn of the moon in my grasp.

So thinking, drifting ever higher, without being aware I had ever closed my eyes, I would pass some subtle gateway into sleep. Or if it were not the stars and the night breezes that ushered me into sleep, it was the endlessness of the sounding waves. There would be times that I wondered, with distinct anxiety, whether we were far enough up the sands to be beyond the reach of the waves. I knew how rapidly, and with what surprising energy, as if all composed of leaping green tigers, the tide was apt to move. I was afraid that I would awake to find myself in the unsupporting embrace of the invading waters, wrapped about with weed, the terrible salt taste in my mouth that in its harshness bespoke the true violence and strangeness of death by drowning, the violence and strangeness of that other world where human beings could not live, though life was there to witness, coldly, what would become of human trespassers. It was useless, though, to be afraid. The sound of waves was a wild thing, as untameable and cold-blooded as the prehistoric shark. But that sound was also the pillow on which I must rest my head if I wished to sleep and dream. The sound was constant, through sleeping and waking, weaving the two together. The crash and collapsing retreat of the waters achieved a sense of slow motion, as if that repeated action were the hypnotism at the very heart of existence, and though therefore the thing most real, also that from which proceeded all that was unreal. To rest one's head on this reality then was, after all, soporific. With reality beneath your head, there was nothing left to occupy you except dream. The churning of the waves was the blurry mechanism behind it all.

Then the morning would come, with a gentle, milky, all-embracing light. It was as if, in fact, the light had been there already, empty, and the world of sand, stone and sky had quietly emerged from it, only becoming complete at the moment of my waking. And there, still, was the same sound of waves, but the night was gone and everything had changed.

Whilst I slept, my body, the sleeping bag and the sand had achieved a perfect symbiosis. Somehow, though, sand had got into the sleeping bag, a smooth, heavy grit against the nylon-velvet of the lining, half cold in its separation from the massed sand of the beach, half warm with the sleep of my body. Lingering in the sleeping bag, then eventually drawing up my knees, and sitting with my arms resting on them, I would notice the subtle scents whose invisible traces remained in my simple bedding. The mixed scents of the beach, of the sand and the chill of the air, and of the breath of my slumber, seemed to make that sleeping bag more dear and familiar to me than any bed. Rising, barefoot, I would naturally go down to greet the sea, now farther out than it was before I slept. The white emptiness of dawn was in the foam of the waves as they lapped upon the sand. I felt, each time, almost puzzled at the blankness of it all. It seemed as if the world had been made anew as mystery, and that nothing before this day, on which the waves broke, had ever existed. This milky emptiness was a quiet delight. I walked along where it took form as the lacing of sea-foam. There, at the margin of sea and shore, I would find things stranger than any I had known before. There were white cuttlefish bones in abundance, though never any cuttlefish. I would pick them up and wonder, if today was the first day, where these bones could have come from.

The sea brought other offerings. Sometimes the shoreline was dabbled with the shimmering silver of tiny fish. I did not stop to think that they were dead; they only seemed beautiful, as fallen leaves are beautiful. That the sea had shed silver leaves was a matter of some wonder to me. And then I realised. These sad, beautiful slivers of silver, the shape of arrow-heads, were, in fact, the stars. In order that the new day might take form, the sea had risen up to the very sky, and then, retreating, had taken the darkness and the stars down with it. The darkness it had swallowed, but here were the stars, precious dead things, as if to show that, even though all things are made afresh, some memory of the non-existent past remains.

Perhaps, then, it was the enclosing tides that made Broadsands seem timeless, forever new and forever ancient. The days on that beach, and the memories of those days, are taken down and swallowed by the waves, where they lose all sense of order, and then are thrown up fresh again on the sands of waking. It is all the same day, vast as the sky that makes it, repeated with the variation that clouds take in that sky. And so I cannot trace any line of progress in those memories from younger to older, except that I believe it became easier to descend and ascend those steps, and at some time, for some reason, or no reason at all, we stopped going.

A single memory stands out for me as distinct, as something that happened once only on that beach and was not repeated. I had been gathering shells from different parts of the beach, and small, rounded pebbles, like boiled sweets, and twigs and feathers, and I began to arrange them in a pattern on the sand. At first, perhaps, I had no object in mind except to create something of beauty, but very quickly the emptiness awaiting inspiration was filled and a design began to form under my hands almost by itself, as if my hands were trying to catch up with it. Something delicate, something rare, something beautiful – in other words, what I invoked in this ritual of stones and shells upon the sand was magic. When I had tried to think of a design it had been no good. The inspiration needed my emptiness first, and then what came, in the manner of all inspiration, was both unexpected and obvious, that thing I had been too scared to contemplate. The stones and shells took the shape of a love heart, and inside this there appeared the letters of a sacred name. That name was 'Tracy'.

When the work was finished, I stood back from it a little dazed. The magic had, in some way, succeeded. My heart was there on the sand, tender and quivering, that had before been hidden from all eyes. And I seemed also to see there, like some essence or genie I had captured in a bottle, the face of the one to whom the name belonged. The sand was her freckles, and beneath them there was that skin not pale, not dark, but dusky with all the pure and delicate glow of dusk, and of such a rare shade of cream or hickory brown that it seemed to me almost lilac. Through all my impressions of Tracy there was woven the same tremulous thread that had made a complexion so rare, and the stitches of this burning thread had been sewn in my heart for some time with the sharpest of needles, and now I had worked that whole fine embroidery upon the sand.

I did not know what should be done. I did not want to destroy something so precious, but if I left it the sea would claim it, anyway. And then I wondered what would happen if any saw what never had been seen. My father was lying nearby, in swimming trunks, his head on his hands and his eyes closed. I looked in his direction, and then at the magical thing, and back again, and felt trapped. Perhaps sensing a change in the mood of his surroundings, he opened his eyes. Walking over, he looked at what I had done. Never in my life have I felt, before or since, as I felt at that moment. Calmly he asked me who Tracy was. I gave some brief, dying reply.

"Have you spoken to her," he asked, "to tell her how you feel?"

"No," I said.

There was silence, and my father walked away again.

A terrible sense of shame and sickness then came over me like the rippling of heavy rain on a glaucous ocean, and I wished that I had never dared to form that heart upon the sand. Sick, then, hopelessly and to my guts, and wan with shame, so that my weak fingers trembled, I dismantled that heart. A few marks remained on the sand where it had been, but time would erase them.

Recently I made an unplanned visit to the place where I grew up. I took a walk and came to a particular spot that has drawn me before. How many things there are in this world, and in my life, and this nameless spot is one of them. From a certain beach, some miles along the coast from Broadsands, there are steps leading up a wooded hill. The steps become a path, the path climbs to a corner where, to the left, there are more steps, and at this corner is a scrap of a section of wooden fence. As I picture it now, this fence is hardly wider than a stile. I suppose it exists merely to cordon off that dangerous corner, because here the trees have, it seems, naturally formed the arch of a leafy frame through which to view the sea below, and here, also, the creeper-veined ground falls away in rolling stages, and with deceptive suddenness, to some invisible and fatal edge. The fence differs from a stile mainly in that there is no plank forming a step to help you climb over. Like a signpost without writing, what it conveys to me is a mixture of the picturesque and the perilous. With the curving and crooked branches it helps to frame the view, and invites you to stop, perhaps to lean; but it also warns you against that view's allure. Stop here, yes, but stop and proceed no farther in this direction. And surely the danger implied by such a warning is also part of the allure?

When, irresistibly, I stopped on this occasion, I was reminded of Broadsands, and even decided to make a visit – the first of my adult life. However, the weather conditions during my stay were not afterwards favourable, and, inevitably, time was consumed in other ways, and I didn't go. For these reasons – time and weather – I was unable to check my memories against Broadsands as it exists today.

What I saw when I drew near to that nameless spot, framed like a picture, was the halcyon blue of the sea, now light and semi-transparent in the sun, containing the shadows of its own waves, and seeming to reveal, even in this gentle, regular mood, the vastness of its savage power. As well as being the soothing, constant ripple behind the eyes of a sunbather, the sea was monstrous. I found myself imagining a single entity filling the entire ocean, like a great, lapping jellyfish of shadow.

Superimposed upon the hushed beauty of flashing waves were the twigs of the trees, the distance of empty air between sea and twig somehow emphasising the wild inaccessibility of the latter. The sea below seemed to share this inaccessible nature, angling in sharply to a small, secluded inlet, formed on one side by a tall, shelving and slanting slice of silver-white rock. To the left, as it converged in a V with that part of the hill on which I stood, this slate cliff leaned forward so that it formed a slightly overhanging, acute angle with the sea. The hardy green of rough shrubs and thorn trees that clung to the head of this chunk of rock like scrubby hair, actually seemed to be leaning away from the lip of the overhang, as if afraid of tipping over that edge. I supposed that no human being had ever touched that edge, and this thought filled my heart with a kind of ravishing thrill. Or perhaps it would be more accurate to say that, feeling such a ravishing thrill in my heart, I guessed that no human being had ever touched that edge.

Farther to the right was a smooth slope of slate, like an open, anonymous palm that none had ever read, lined here and there only with the grey pencil lines where layers of slate came to an end, and with seams of green where vegetation had managed to take root. This slope did not rise to an overhang, but formed an obtuse angle with the sea. I had climbed similar pieces of rock as a child, and I remembered now the particular wild thrill of scaling such a bald surface. It was possible that you could find yourself clinging like a lizard, with nowhere to go. You could be stranded, the footholds and toeholds by which you came somehow having melted away, and all around you the bare, slippery hostility of rock, where no human has been and no plant can take root. What a horrible, attractive fate, to have to cling and cling, grabbing and crying like the child that you are, knowing that you cannot cling forever.

The trees that made a picture of this view were largely of the kind I remembered from the cliffs over Broadsands, and the crown of the pirate island. They were pirate trees, thorny and twisted, their branches infested with a greyish-green lichen. These branches, I felt, like those of the trees of Broadsands, were eyries. Their clutching twigs formed nests. But here there were no eagles. Instead there was air – emptiness and air. Why did this emptiness fascinate me so unutterably? It was the same emptiness as that of the pirate island, a mystery that will never be known, just as you will never know me.

Here is another tree. Not a thorn tree, this one, its branches extend some distance out into the air, and with their tips reach to a place beyond which is only air, and dizzy air. See how slender the branch is. Those last, delicate twigs cannot be so far away, but who could ever climb along to touch them? But there, in that nameless eyrie of twigs and air, is my heart. Just along, farther, inaccessible, there.

THE GWYLLGI OF THE LOST LANES

Too recently for me to write about in detail, a friend of mine died in a very horrible way. This has some bearing on what follows, so I shall say that his death appeared to be suicide (a problematical statement). He was found hanged in an area known to those who lived near as "the Lost Lanes". There are other things I could say in connection with his death that would be relevant, but as I think of those things now, they are almost too relevant. What I judge fit to write will have to suffice, and perhaps is already more than enough.

I was touched to find my friend had thought of me when making out his will. Amongst other things, I was bequeathed whatever of his books I chose to keep. I had to visit the cottage where he had spent his last days in order to collect them. I decided to take all the books and sort them once I had got home, as I was uncomfortable lingering there. As it turned out, this required three trips, because of the sheer number of books.

The library in the cottage, divided between many shelves, upstairs and down, was undoubtedly the strangest and most fascinating I have ever seen, and perhaps the strangest document I have so far examined amongst those I took is the one below.

The books in that library were of such a kind — those who only know books from high street shops will not even imagine that such books exist — that I was unable to pack them into boxes without now and then opening a volume and reading a little. I was just about to look inside an edition of Edmund Jones's, A Relation of Apparitions of Spirits in the Principality of Wales, *when some folded sheets of paper fell from between the pages. They were xerographic copies of a handwritten manuscript. The handwriting was that of my friend. I find that I don't wish to say more on the subject.*

I have changed or 'scored out' the names of places and people as I saw appropriate. I suppose a little detective work on the part of any ambitious reader would soon uncover the location of the events described. Personally, I hope never to go back. I present the following as a matter of significant mystery.

I doubt the information is of a kind that is called useful, and may even seem, in some sense, injurious, but there are some things that are of such strong interest — in every meaning of the word — to the human soul, that, even without knowing the outcome it seems necessary to make them known, if only to a few. This manuscript I judge to be such a thing.

Now that I come to write it down, it seems to me that everything begins and ends with the lanes, and the roads that lead to the lanes. This is a puzzle — a puzzle of a deadly kind. From one direction you will see one thing, from another something else entirely. In any case, you will always be tricked. The way will be switched on you, somehow, and you will find you have slipped onto the wrong track.

You might think that an aerial photograph of the hills would lay everything bare, and so answer any questions, but the world is never quite the way it is shown on a map, or even in a photograph. I am drawing a map now, of the roads and lanes as I walked them, and my experiences in them. It's a map I must draw in my mind. And perhaps, by doing so, I can find where the switch takes place.

First there is the cottage. Why first? Because this is where my father died. This is the knot through which the complex net of pathways is drawn tighter. Then, in front of the cottage, runs a road. This is not the main road, on which cars pass, and it is not yet the lanes. I turn right outside my cottage and there is the road. It runs along the walled bottoms of the gardens of a number of cottages like this one. If I turn left and follow the quiet road, the cottages are on my new left. On my right, at first, is a small paddock in which sometimes a white horse is grazing. There are crumbling, ivy-grown barns, and overgrown wasteland, and for a while, a brook is visible between trees, its silty banks prehistoric with horsetails. Opposite all this, on my left, the cottages are interrupted at one point by the grey edifice of Bethlehem Chapel, with its cemented exterior and its dull windows that speak of desertion. There is nothing here as colourful as stained glass. Some of the panes are frosted, obscuring the interior. One or two are ordinary glass, but through them can be seen, as if resting on the inside sill, only blanched, neglected books with Welsh titles and children's toys and games, similarly stale with age.

Then the cottages resume. Where they end, a narrow, cemented path runs up between the trees of the enclosing hills. Walk on a little farther, with tree-shrouded brook on one side and the slope of the hill on the other, and you will come to another such path, this a little broader, but somehow more drear in aspect, and sloping in the opposite direction, as if one might ascend this path and soon descend the other.

Now what strikes me as I draw this map in my head, is how one thing runs into another. I have made a distinction between the road and the lanes, but, of course, they are connected, and there is no difficult barrier to separate them – no barrier at all, except in feeling.

The road in front of the cottages, anyway, would generally be considered safe, despite the quietly interruptive presence of the Chapel, like an unanswered question. There are the dogs, of course, but these would probably even be thought part of the safety of this road, on which they seem to spend their entire lives, when they are not in the gardens of the cottages. They seem half-stray in the manner in which they haunt the place, but they are domestic animals and quite tame, all of them of the border collie type or thereabouts. If you come along the road from the direction of the ascending path and the overgrown brook, you'll be greeted by a doggy hollering, but this is as much welcome as warning, and perhaps none without a distinct phobia of dogs would take it too seriously. When the dogs are not shouting their nervous bravado, this is a quiet road indeed, but its quiet is not quite the unnerving quiet of the lanes, which forbids. Perhaps a human does not even think about these things consciously, but the old instincts are still there to be heard if one listens; they will tell us what the dogs know, that this is a place of relative safety.

But yes, for me, it was my father's death, there in the cottage, that started it all, and from which I must draw this map. These roads and lanes I have called a net; with his death they became a tethering noose that chafed and tightened round my throat.

After his death, I took to walking the outlying roads and footpaths of this area aimlessly. If it had not been for those wretched walks – walks whose character was formed of my grief and emptiness – I might still know nothing of the Lost Lanes, and might not now be writing this. I had already lived here for two years, after all, without taking that turning in the road. There had never been reason for me to take it, and somehow it had never been inviting. People, anyway, may live in one place their entire life and still be ignorant of where this or that lane runs, even though it starts within a minute or two of their front door. If only the turning I took had remained one of these! The air that hung above its mouth should have told me that ignorance was best.

It happened on an evening when I was returning from the lonely ramble that had become my habit. I was walking back along the road that runs in front of the cottages and anticipating the sunset of canine voice that would be the only thing to greet my homecoming.

After all the eyelessness of my stumbling, suddenly I stood in the middle of the homeward road, and I *saw*, and what I saw, in some dim, fatal way, I questioned. Here was a path I had never taken. Over it there hung, like an unmoving smudge of black cloud, the question, "Why?" For some reason, this upward turning, sly in its tilt and its silence and shadow, made me think of the dogs. The animals had often come down from the path at the end of the cottages at the sound of my tread, and the symmetry of that other path to this might have evoked in me such associations, but now I stood and wondered, I was not sure that I had ever seen or heard the dogs come down from this ascending way.

It was not, perhaps, the most exotic of mysteries, but to my barren mind it held a sense of relief – there were still things that might engage me, if only briefly and sadly. I thought, also, of the way that the tame dogs had tended to follow my father and responded to his voice, it seemed, more naturally than to the voices of their owners. Perhaps the dogs, understanding my father, also knew something of where he had gone. Although such thoughts were not conscious in my mind – thoughts that, anyway, hardly make sense – the curiosity that finally caused me to take that path was peculiar, and I am not sure how else to evoke it.

I think I stepped forward, at first, with a vaguely warm and sentimental feeling in my heart, but this feeling, though momentarily highlighted, was diffused into a colder background and quickly lost. As I moved between the tense, grey masts of the trees that lined the path, I noticed a silence, a lack of barking, as distinct as the finger-bone twigs. Soon enough, the trees shrank away from the edges of the path and the slope levelled out. The cement began to give way, also, to dirt. On my right was a hedge, bordering uncultivated fields. On my left, before the beginning of a similar hedge, was a house, or the remains of one. The stone walls, I could just discern, had once been whitewashed. The doorway and windows gaped empty, and the roof had collapsed saggingly in the centre. Around the stony orifices were the permanent black shadows that told of fire, even now conveying to me the bursting, spiky-tongued energy of licking flame. The edifice had undoubtedly been rained upon many times since the fire had occurred, but standing, as I was, at a distance of ten or twenty paces, I believed I could smell the sickening despoliation of smoke.

It must have crossed my mind to tread closer and peer inside this charred shell, but I did not. My curiosity had become chill.

And yet, there was a sense that I had not found what I was looking for. The doggy way down again? Was it really that? Perhaps I also felt, for the first time in some while, that I was not tethered, and could roam. I have heard that, when a barred door to an animal's enclosure is left open by mistake, or thrown open by a liberator, the animal does not immediately rush to escape its cage, even if it sees the new opening. Habits are already in place, and there is no need to flee them – toward what? The dirt track that meandered into the cloudy wilderness of the sky was to me like the open door of a cage. I took it hesitantly, sniffingly, as if the very air was different, and too large. Once I was outside the cage door, however, I became less hesitant. I walked with no end or direction in mind, without slowing my pace or thinking of when I might stop walking.

It must have been already close to twilight, and the air was turning subtly, mingling its tints. At some point the upward climb turned downward, though far from the road where the cottage is. Here and there the fields were dotted with small copses, each gathered mournfully about its own local secrets. I seemed to be approaching the bottom of a valley. At last I began to wonder where I was, and where I was going.

I came to a crossroads. There was a post, tall in the gloom, at one corner, and, taking it for a signpost, I drew nearer. What I had thought a sign, though, was nothing other than a projecting beam of wood, and I drew back again. In all but one direction, the ways seemed to ascend. I wondered what time it was. I had no watch. To the blue of the air soon would come a tint of silver, I thought. I looked about and saw that I was alone. There was no sound or sight of human creature. And then I heard a mewling from the bottom of the hedge, along one of the turnings. Unable to identify the sound, questioningly, I trod a little way in that direction. The road was uneven in its winding and its rise and fall, so that, at first, the child must have been hidden from my eyes. She – I felt it must be a she – was crouching at the side of the road, whimpering as if in pain. She had longish, matted hair that hung down to conceal her face, which was, anyway, half turned away from me. The peculiar thought struck me that she was urinating. She was only a tiny thing, perhaps three or four years old. The situation was so strange that I almost did not wonder what such a poor mite could be doing out here, alone, at such an hour. I did not want to approach her, either, though a part of me said that she must need help. Somehow it felt as though I were forbidden to take another step towards her. I could not tell precisely whether such a taboo came from inside me, or from outside, that is, whether it were for my own sake I held back, or for something other – something in these circumstances I did not understand and should not lightly interfere with. And yet, simply to walk away seemed impossible. Although my relation to this scene was a mystery, I could not help but be part of it now. I could only wait, to see what transpired.

My gaze must have been fixed so intently on that shivering elf that it took me a little while to realise there was some third entity here. I had not seen anything in the road a few moments ago – and I did not look now – so I supposed that the thing had come while I had been standing and watching. I knew it because, in the shivering and whimpering of the child, that seemed to gather all the swiftly falling night into itself, like a flame gathers in oxygen, there was now also a different shivering, from a different, but somehow related, source. This other shivering, I became more and more able to distinguish from the child. It was a kind of breathing, as with monstrous, phlegmy lungs. Without turning my head away from the child, I formed a very distinct and detailed outline of the other presence. It was not a visual picture, exactly, but an intimate, almost diagrammatic understanding without words.

I did not know how anything in that situation then could be resolved without me losing my soul.

I was caught up with that breathing as if it were my own and could not move away from it without, it seemed, also losing my life breath. I had, however, a growing sense of a large, physical presence, sobering in its otherness, and quite distinct from myself and the girl.

I waited for change, and dreaded it.

Something dark, heavy and inhuman weighed upon my heart. As if stumbling, I took a step forward, my shoe scraping the ground. I do not know if there had been any thought behind this move. My mind had become incoherent, full of savage phantoms. Perhaps I had meant to save the girl, or perhaps to beg her for help. Whether or not she had been aware of my presence before – and I quite believed she was watching me, through her screen of dishevelled hair, and with her face turned away – she moved as if startled at this sudden noise, and there was something in that movement that I did not like. Her face now was turned towards me, thrust out on her twisted neck, staring. There was a scream. I knew there could be no other human in the night to hear a sound like this. It told me I was alone more surely than anything else. And yet, at first, I did not know where the scream had come from. Could it be myself? It seemed it must be the girl, but even she did not appear capable of quite a shriek as this.

It was then I thought the wait was over, and my soul would be forfeit.

In my panic, my head turned, and I saw the beast that must have padded down from farther up the road while my eyes had been fixed upon the girl. It was a fresh shock to see in solid form the thing whose spirit-outline I had known in certainty. This dog, I knew, had never had a human master. And yet it seemed to stand in some dire, unchanging relation to human fate. A wolf in the wilderness is beautiful. No one could say the same of this creature skulking ownerless in lonely roads. The beast was ugly and knowing, though it would never be tamed as a wolf might. It was black, and seemed to me the size of a horse, with hair like that of a Highland ox. Its eyes, when they caught the disappearing light, were the colour of moonstone.

I did not believe at that moment that I could, but with a spasm like that which makes a dead heart beat again, I turned and ran.

It was a long time before I dared to hope that I might escape, and then this hope brought a new agony, as the numbness of instinct ebbed away again and I had to make my way in conscious terror and deliberation over the hills. It was fully dark by now. I was lost, and the fields and trees through which I passed were unearthly. At moments, I was unable to suppress the memory of that face, though I knew that, at all costs, I must forget. It seemed to me that the child must have met with some kind of accident, but this did not seem explanation enough. It was more than an accident. It was what ordinary people call a tragedy. I felt that I more than understood what they meant by that word now. When I could not fight against the memory of that face, I saw it as if externally present, peering from the side of a tree, or from thorny brakes. At other times, I was certain I heard again the stentorian breathing of the beast, but was quite unable to determine the direction of the noise, or how close it was.

The way back to the road I knew was strangely difficult. I remember a pitted field of ant-mounds and reeds, in which I was lucky not to have broken a leg, the soft ground giving way beneath me again and again, so that I despaired. Finally, I made my way back by climbing down the course of a hillside brook, soaked and torn by brambles, and having to escape, at the end, by scaling the wall of some silent building, and dropping from the other side.

It was only minutes then before I was back at the cottage and locking the door behind me. I sat up, staring into the fire. When a child has done something so wrong that he dare not tell a single soul on Earth, the memory of that thing comes back to him again and again, with about it a kind of evil certainty, as if he cannot hope to escape being found out, and he knows the consequences will be some ghoulish thing that wracks him to his fear-sick bones. That is how I felt when the face refused to dim tamely away into dark forgetfulness, and the presence of that beast seemed again to grow separate and distinct among the shadows that haunted the cottage and the surrounding lanes. When I slept, I was in lanes again, nearer to or farther from that drear crossroads, but which would always lead back there eventually.

Daylight woke me. I drew the curtains and saw to the ashes in the fire. It was possible, then, to get through a night, and maybe I would get through another, or more. But for now, anyway, grey, silent and sly, there was only daylight. Once it had been the guarantee that all was normal and sane. Now it seemed a temporary and receding safety. That daylight marked the ultimate truth had become doubtful to me. But still, for now…

I knew what I had seen, or, at least, partly. There had been the hideous cross-section of the spirit that had formed so intricately in my mind's eye while my head was turned from the beast; that was a kind of knowledge never to be gained from books, and which seemed to revive memories older than my mortal identity. However, there was another kind of knowledge, too, superficial and far more external, which I had gained, in odd scraps, from books and other written matter. This external knowledge was of such a nature that I had always believed it to be trivial and unconnected with myself. I had certainly never imagined it would come, at the end, to assume such importance that all else would be eclipsed.

The beast I had seen, others had seen before me. I remembered it had been called by different names, but those that came back to me were 'Black Shuck', 'Padfoot' and 'Shriker'. If I wished to understand what I had seen, then I needed to start with the accounts that other witnesses had left behind. To this end, I visited the library in the nearby village. I did not wish to research the subject alone in the gloomy cottage. My walks had lacked purpose for some time, but now I was able to tread the day-lit roads with conscious aim and destination.

I learnt very little that I did not already know. Indeed, there seemed little to learn. Death is the shadowy end of all earthly knowledge, and it is to death that the Black Shuck is familiar. Whatever back road the ominous hound appeared on, it was a way that disappeared out of human view, its end and origin lost in the final, overwhelming mystery that thickens from twilight to impenetrable pitch black at the edge of all life. Even the question of whether the beast was ghostly or of solid matter was hardly touched upon, let alone answered.

What I did learn, or in most cases, simply refreshed in my memory, was as follows:

There exists a peculiar pattern of folklore in this country, varying from region to region, that deals with a kind of black dog encountered in lonely lanes, in dark woods, on desolate moors, and in other deserted places. The black dog is reputed to be a harbinger of death. To see it is to know that death is near – either that of the witness or of someone close to him or her. Accounts vary as to the outward appearance of the beast. It is often described as being a mastiff in type, larger than any normal dog, and sometimes is reported to have only one eye, fiery and baleful, or, more curiously, to be without a head. To some, it appears as an ordinary animal, not distinguished by demonic features – a black Labrador or mongrel – but with something unmistakably sinister about its bearing.

The Black Shuck has been particularly associated with East Anglia, and it is the East Anglian county of Suffolk to which the most famous tale of the creature pertains. Records tell that on the 4th of August, 1577, a black devil dog appeared in the two Suffolk churches of Bungay and Blythburgh. The events, witnessed by full congregations in both cases, involved the sudden intrusion of the beast into the church buildings, where, amidst great affright, it set about killing and strewing mayhem. At Blythburgh, the dog left behind scorch marks, still visible today and known locally as "the devil's fingerprints". The Reverend Abraham Fleming described the incident as it was known to those in the other church, in his text, "A Straunge and Terrible Wunder, Wrought Very Late in the Parish Church of Bongay":

Sunday, being the fourth of this August, in ye yeer of our Lord, 1577, to the amasing and singular astonishment of the present beholders, and absent hearers, at a certein towne called Bongay, not past tenne miles distant from the citie of Norwiche, there fell from heaven an exceeding great and terrible tempest, sodein and violent, between nine of the clock in the morning and tenne of the day aforsaid.

This tempest took beginning with a rain, which fel with a wonderful force and with no lesse violence then abundance, which made the storme so much the more extream and terrible.

This tempest was not simply of rain, but also of lightning and thunder, the flashing of the one wherof was so rare and vehement, and the roaring noise of the other so forceable and violent, that it made not only people perplexed in minde and at their wits end, but ministred such straunge and unaccustomed cause of feare to be cōceived, that dumb creatures with ye horrour of that which fortuned, were exceedingly disquieted, and senselesse things void of all life and feeling, shook and trembled.

There were assembled at the same season, to hear divine service and common prayer, according to order, in the parish church of the said towne of Bongay, the people therabouts inhabiting, who were witnesses of the straungenes, the rarenesse and sodenesse of the storm, consisting of raine violently falling, fearful flashes of lightining, and terrible cracks of thūder, which came with such unwonted force and power, that to the perceiving of the people, at the time and in the place aboue named, assembled, the church did as it were quake and stagger, which struck into the harts of those that were present, such a sore and sodain feare, that they were in a manner robbed of their right wits.

Immediately hereupō, there appeared in a most horrible similitude and likenesse to the congregation then and there present, a dog as they might discerne it, of a black colour; at the sight wherof, togither with the fearful flashes of fire which then were seene, moved such admiration in the mindes of the assemblie, that they thought doomes day was already come.

This black dog, or the divel in such a likenesse (God hee knoweth al who worketh all) runing all along down the body of the church with great swiftnesse, and incredible haste, among the people, in a visible fourm and shape, passed between two persons, as they were kneeling uppon their knees, and occupied in prayer as it seemed, wrung the necks of them bothe at one instant clene backward, in somuch that even at a momēt where they kneeled, they strāgely dyed.

290

No other accounts that I uncovered at that time were as dramatic or as well-documented. I did learn, however, that the black dog had been sighted many times in this part of the country, too, where it was known by another name – "*gwyllgi*". "*Ci*", which becomes "*gi*", simply means 'dog' in Welsh. The etymology of "*gwyll*", apparently, is either 'wild' or 'twilight', although I cannot help thinking, when I see it, of 'ghoul' – ghoul-dog.

The significant information for me, was what I had, anyway, remembered – that the appearance of the beast augured death. My father's? But that had already happened. My own? Who was I close to now that it could mean someone else? However, there were still uncertainties here, even down to the question, what is death, exactly, if it is heralded by such as this?

What I read only seemed to reinforce my childish but keen sense that my experience at the crossroads prefigured something far more terrible, that it had in some way marked me out, and that to be so marked meant whatever curse had befallen me, it was hideously inescapable. There is little a human being can do in such circumstances except to repeat mentally – against the haunted and sorrowful knowing of the heart – that such things cannot be, that it is imagination, some form of mental anomaly brought on by loss and loneliness. This was what I did, too, trying not to dwell on what I would have found incredible only days before, but which now nagged at me with maddening persistence.

I went about my daily life outwardly with more purpose than I had shown in some while. I found all manner of tasks to distract me and to put some backbone in my days again, though I remained curiously absent-minded in the midst of such tasks, and often went into a trance and forgot what I was doing.

For relief, as usual, I would wander, though never now past that turning I had taken for the first and last time on the day I came upon the shivering child and the ownerless beast. It was perhaps three days after that, when I stepped from the cottage door, that I saw the white mare in the nearby paddock had just foaled. I did not have any especial thought in my head as I walked over to take a look. The foal was black, wet and trembling, the afterbirth still attached by a fleshy ribbon to is belly. At intervals it would attempt to stand, but that slimy pink ribbon was twisted around its back left leg, and each time this prevented it. I derived no comfort from the sight of new life. This birth was a kind of mystery, true, but it had taken on the hue of another mystery that ended all. What could it think of its sudden surroundings, so different, so greater in variety and extent, than those that had previously been all it knew? And yet immediately, in the spreading green of earth and in the endlessness of uncaring air, that did not resemble the containing flesh and blood, it made its repeated, shaky attempts to stand. It must learn to run, for fear of danger, and it must stay by its mother's side, until she disappeared into earth and air.

As I stood by the hedge, a man, whom I recognised as a neighbour, approached from within the paddock. The mare, I supposed, was his. Stopping where the hedge stood between us, he addressed me, and we spoke a little of the foal. I asked when it would be free of the placenta. It would wither, he said, or the mother would bite through the cord. For some reason it suddenly occurred to me to try an unrelated question – it seemed I had no one else to ask, and the question was almost involuntary.

"Do you know of a dog," I asked, "a very large dog, in this area, that might be a stray? I don't know what breed it could be, but perhaps a wolfhound."

The man turned away before my question was finished, as if something about the mare and foal had claimed his attention, and I could not be sure he had heard. When he turned back he seemed to be considering my face.

"I saw it just the other night. I'd gone up the track just after the end of the cottages—"

The man turned away again so that I was uncertain of his words when he spoke, but he seemed to say, "I know the track."

Now he was facing me again, his eyes squinting and searching.

"They call it the Lost Lanes round here," he said. "You don't go up there without a good reason, unless you want to get lost."

I could not place his tone. Was it a reproach?

"Have you heard of a stray dog there? Or a lost child?"

He turned away abruptly and began striding towards the mare as if he could no longer keep from the business of the newborn foal and was impatient at me for claiming his attention when he was occupied with more important things. I felt I had offended him in some terrible way. Perhaps I had gone too far. Somehow I had understood that I might, but there were things I needed to know. My neighbour must have thought so, too, after all. He turned once more, before he reached the mare and her offspring, and called out, "I'm not the one you want to talk to for stories of stray animals. Try number 3. Ask about the burnt cottage."

I was not reassured by his change of heart, however. Looking at his face, I understood it was no change of heart at all. It was not sympathy but a kind of necessity that had moved him. I felt a distance grow up between us. He had spoken his last words to me, and now I was nothing in his eyes but a phantom.

Who has business with the darkness to come? By the very nature of that darkness, it seems, any connection to it decays the reassuring authority, procedure and rewards that would hold in matters of worldly business. I had not been sent to consult with a doctor, a policeman or a priest who often have business with all that happens up to the threshold of darkness, and with the very threshold, but I knocked upon the door of the third cottage in the row opposite the paddock with a greater sense of apprehension than I would have known in visiting surgery, station or confessional. There had been good reason why I had spoken to no one of what I had seen – not even the police – and I wondered quite what I had expected when I broached the subject with my neighbour.

Mrs Evans is old in a way that people are no longer supposed to grow old, in a way that I do not remember people being old since my childhood – old in a way that seems to remove her more than half already from human existence. Her position is unofficial, and has no title, but she was suited to the business for which I was calling. I realised, as long as I had been resident in the area, I had never seen her before. She was a chalky, calcified presence as she half-emerged from the gloom of the hallway to open the door to me. It seemed to me that soon enough she would become entirely mineral. She looked at me with what appeared habitual suspicion, as might a half-feral cat, her surprise at seeing me evident in her silence and the sharpness of her giblet-wet eyes. But when I attempted to explain why I had come, she understood more quickly than I anticipated and told me to enter. It was afternoon, but the interior of the house was still dingy. Mrs Evans sat in a chair in the corner and I sat upon a settee against the wall. A few rays of daylight glinted on the glass of a cabinet containing a bone china tea set, but no tea was served, and all except the wall clock and the stir of its dangling pendulum was still. The silence seemed long before she started to speak, and when, at length, she did, she did not look at me, so that I almost wondered if she were blind, except that the initial look in her eye when she had answered the door had proclaimed so strongly otherwise.

Blindness of a kind, however, had taken her, and as I listened, I too seemed to suffer a similar loss, in that one kind of vision was replaced by another kind that made the hair stiffen on my neck. The room and its stilted complement of furniture remained present, but I no longer saw them. I do not think I can recall the words that were spoken, but I remember perfectly the story that was told, as if the moon had risen higher over a valley and slowly there had been revealed those features of the landscape that previously were hidden.

No one now owns the burnt out cottage, and none will claim it, or the land on which it stands. Only about twenty years ago, an old man had lived there. He had never married, and there were no children. His temperament was such that he had not made friends in the eight or more decades of his existence, and no one visited him. He did, however, own a dog, a border collie crossed with something else, very similar to the dogs that belong to the cottages lining the road today. This dog was his only companion. People did not like to go near the man, and, if they had to pass his cottage, they would take care not to turn their head and look. For one thing, the appearance of the man was very unpleasant. His skull was a grey and pink eggshell, which looked like it might crumble if you poked it. And in this skull, his eyes were sickening with the infirm anger of old age. Whatever the reason for this anger, which seemed twinned with an increasing feebleness of mind, it was not an emotion that he liked to let out in impulsive fits of rage. As if he had come to view his anger as the only harvest of old age, he saved it up with care and patience, distilling it into slow malice, which he would use discerningly, a little at a time. Since no human came near him, the only living thing upon which he could reliably spend this malice was his dog. On occasion, pitiful sounds were heard from the cottage by those who passed near. The dog would sometimes be chained outside, and with the passing of time, ugly marks and welts became increasingly visible upon its body.

Because no one cared to approach too near this miserable beast in order to examine it, the exact nature of the marks was unclear, although the most prominent of them seemed most probably to be burns. Once, when a curious child had peered in through a window, he had been frightened off by the sudden appearance of the drooling old rascal at the door, waving a poker in a grotesquely arthritic claw. After that, although no one actually saw it happening, the story was that the old man was in the habit of torturing the dog with a red-hot poker.

One day, the old man did a strange thing. He paid a visit to the minister of the Bethlehem Chapel, which, at that time, still held services, though most of the cottages preferred to attend the Church of St. C--- a little farther away, since the services in the chapel were peculiar and had appeal only for a very limited congregation. People referred to the Bethlehem Chapel now as a Spiritualist Church, though the minister, when asked, would say that this was a misunderstanding. The old man's visit to him, for this reason, and for others, was noticed. Someone within the minister's small congregation spoke to someone else outside of it, and the story began to percolate through the community that the old man had wished to consult the minister on a very grave matter concerning the welfare of his immortal soul. He had seen a great black dog, he said, waiting in the lanes that curved into the hills from his home, and he knew that this apparition meant the worst for him. He was not interested in anyone's preaching about repentance, he said. All he wanted to ask the minister was if there were anything in Hell or Earth that could save him. He seemed to expect of the minister some practical defence or special knowledge not available to the world at large. The minister said that, alas, he knew nothing – the old man was crediting him with too much power. The meeting became unpleasant rapidly, but eventually the minister was able to persuade the old man to leave.

Just over a week after this visit from the old man, the night air on the hillside above the road flickered orange and red. The fire did not spread beyond the old man's cottage, but all within was destroyed. A charred human body was found among the ashes.

At the time, no one enquired what had become of the old man's dog. Moreover, there was no one close to the old man to make trouble about investigating the fire or to fuss about details concerning the disposal of the remains, or the estate, such as it was. Presumably such things were dealt with, but of these my informer had no knowledge. The old man's reputation, his visit to the minister, and the very location of the cottage, at the beginning of the Lost Lanes, made people put caution before curiosity and keep their distance. At least no one now would feel their blood sicken within them at the sounds that had sometimes emanated from the cottage. That the old man had been taken from this Earth without causing trouble was a blessing.

A month or two passed, and people ceased to talk about the business. It was then that something else happened, and those who were part of it, or touched by it, knew that, after all, a sickness would haunt their blood for as long as they remembered. Mr and Mrs Brooks, at number 5, had been looking after their granddaughter, Nicola, and had let her play in the front garden. They did not leave her long, but when they looked again she had disappeared. Suddenly panicked, since she was nowhere in view, they began to search up and down the road, calling her name. Some of the neighbours joined them. Apparently no one had seen anything. The only sign that Nicola had been in the garden at all was that the gate was left open. Except for the calling voices, the day was silent – a lazy day in early summer, a day in which flies begin to buzz. Those searching for the child were numerous enough to split into two parties, and they went in opposite directions. It was the group who went in the direction of the Lost Lanes that finally found her. A shape was huddled at the side of the track, just a little way up the slope, inside the mouth of the turning.

What had happened could have been no accident. In fact, it was hard to say precisely what had taken place here on this quiet track where no cars passed, on a sunny afternoon, so close to the cottages, but some evil finger had poked out from nowhere and gouged a scar in the heart of Nicola's family. The girl was dead, and all knew from the start it was useless to call an ambulance – though they did – useless, in fact, to do anything. According to the pathologist's report, she had been savaged by a dog, though there were those who saw her at the end who did not believe this.

Mr Brooks, the grandfather, had some ideas of his own on the matter. There was one thing he could do, he said, and he would do it, whatever the price. He rolled a stump of wood to the side of the road, opposite his front door, buried an axe in it, and started off up the hill with a strange stick in one hand. He passed by the burnt out cottage and no one knows exactly where he went or what happened. At twilight he returned to the clamorous barking of the neighbourhood dogs. The noose on the end of his stick was fastened around the neck of a hideous, mangy, one-eyed beast, half its body covered in suppurating burns. Doors opened and people emerged to see. He called for someone to hold the stick so that the creature's jaw was firm upon the stump of wood, and then, while the other dogs set up a racket such as humans are not meant to hear, and milled about the road so that those present feared they might *turn* in some unimaginable way, he drew out the axe whose blade he had sunk into the grain, raised it high, and split the skull of the squirming, tortured beast that had escaped the fire that killed its master.

Mr Brooks and his son – Nicola's father – also paid a visit to the minister of Bethlehem Chapel. Although, it seems, they were more welcome than the old man had been, and even joined the Chapel's regular congregation, it is doubtful that the minister could help them any more than he could help the one who had died writhing and alone in the fury of flames. The older Mr Brooks came to his end, too, before the year was out, when he lost control of the car he was driving on a local road one night. There was no sign that anyone else had been involved in the accident, but the car was wrecked, and the body inside its shell impossible to identify positively until it was examined by the pathologist.

Here the story ended.

"Did Mr Brooks see what the old man saw?" I asked.

"That's all there is to tell," said Mrs Evans, as if in dreadful commiseration.

"But the minister?"

"There are no services at the Chapel any more. The minister disappeared. So did most of those in the congregation at the end. There weren't many of them. You'll not find any left who'll admit they were there."

"What should I do?"

"What do any of us do?"

"But… Why is this happening? You must have thought about these things."

"Do demons have nightmares?"

The susurration of her voice, somewhere among the shadows, hardly seemed to belong to her body at all.

I stood.

"Thank you," I said.

"Nothing can be done," came the whisper from the corner as I left.

The daylight outside was strange after the oppressive greyness of the house, but almost immediately a sense of menace, like a silent but constant rumble of thunder, returned to the air about me. I knew I could not leave the matter behind in that room; I knew, again, that the curse was not imagination.

Of course, I considered suicide, but if it now seemed possible that there was more than one kind of death, it also seemed certain to me that any kind of death was unspeakable. I decided I would find the minister. Perhaps, after all, there was a whole side to this story that I was not hearing, though I was still overwhelmed, sometimes even during the day, by memories that could not be conquered, and before which any ideas of an explanation seemed to fall apart as an irrelevance. Even so, I had to find the minister.

I had never before seriously played the detective in my life, but the darkness that now stood so close on the horizon of all things seemed to give my investigations a peculiar, leaden urgency. In any case, my brain was working, as if this hideous puzzle were precisely that upon which the maze of its cortex was designed to be exercised until it wound down in biological entropy. I knew of no one connected with Bethlehem Chapel whom I might question, and so I decided to ask the rector of the main local church – the Church of St. C--- – located at a distance of a mile or two along the main road, just beyond the high street of the neighbouring village. I found the telephone number of the rector, with his name, on a sign by the gate to the churchyard and resolved to make a telephone call to the rectory later. It seemed preferable to do that than immediately attempt a visit. Thrown out of my usual habits and patterns of thought, I returned home by a different route, this time passing the old miners' welfare and community hall, which stood in a car park a little way down from the side of the ascending street I trod. This dour, and strikingly ugly building, a hulk of rain-stained grey rising from a lower ring of pebble-dashed walls in which were set tiny windows filmed with grey frosting, or larger ones obscured by vertical-slatted blinds, was now the venue for a variety of events, though it was surprising to me that anything but slow decay took place within those walls, looking as torn by the weather as would be a giant cardboard box. Popular films were screened here, and, I noticed, for a number of days, at the cost of eight pounds, visitors could benefit from the talents of Valerie Sayers, clairvoyant and medium extraordinaire, in an evening of "entertainment and enlightenment" billed as *Somewhere Out There*. I made a note of the advertised time, and continued home.

I finally managed to speak to someone at the rectory. Since I wished, at all costs, to hide the personal nature of my motives in making my enquiries, I pretended that I was a freelance journalist writing a dull article on rural church buildings and their history. I was told by the lady who answered the telephone that if I paid a call upon the rectory at 3.00 pm the next day, the rector would do what he could to answer my questions. For the moment satisfied, I did not wish to let my thoughts range any further than the next day's appointment. Bereft of anything to occupy me now, I found it hard to make the glassy passage from one hour to the next. Any stretch of empty time was a vigil, an unending and purposeless interrogation of the soul suffered without hope of balm. There was little chance, then, that I would forget that evening's entertainment, dismal as it was. In fact, I went out early, planning to walk to the venue by a circuitous route, so that I would not have to wait too long to be admitted upon arrival.

It began raining some time before I got there, the low clouds stretching from horizon to horizon seeming to emit a sickly glowing gloom different in quality to the darkening bruise normal to that hour – it was almost fluorescent. The puddles in the uneven car park were stippled with raindrops. Fortunately, the doors were already open. It seemed that others had arrived before me. I did not linger, but bought my ticket at the camphor-smelling box office and went through immediately to the auditorium. The seats were of the joined, cinema variety, but old, threadbare and lacking plush cushioned covers. There were perhaps a dozen people already waiting for the curtains to rise, and I had plenty of choice in where to sit. I chose a seat away from everyone, a little right of centre, and half a dozen rows from the front. As I sat, a slow but regular stream of people continued to arrive. They were, it seemed to me, an audience appropriate to such a venue and such a bill. Most of them were old, but even the few younger parties who did appear were void of the glamour of life. They could only have come here because, in some profound sense, they had been barred from some more desirable venue in the world. I smelt an old, familiar smell, a cold smell that I knew from similar buildings I had visited at other times. It was the smell of a former age, containing the menthol of cough medicines, the mildew of decaying hymn books, and the various odours of soap carbolic, dust, forgotten coats left hanging forlorn in damp cloakrooms, and other ingredients less easy to identify. Such a smell was enough to put me into a kind of empty trance of fatalism. I sat in that chair, silently, without thought, waiting for anything that might happen to me, and utterly forgetful of the fact that I had ever demanded anything of life.

I suppose the auditorium became about half full. Anyway, it was not so full that anyone was forced to sit near me. It was odd, somehow, to be sitting among the sniffles and murmurs of complete strangers. There was little in the way of dramatic build-up to the night's entertainment. The entire hall, instead, had fallen under the same spell of defeat as I, to which drama was irrelevant. It hardly seemed we waited for anything. We were simply fleas who infested the seats. We were lost property, each item having nothing in common with the others except that we were not needed elsewhere, and for that reason alone shared this limbo.

Eventually, however the mangy scalloped curtains rose and drew aside. The stage was revealed, empty but for a tall chair with thin, black legs, and a microphone stand. A man came on in a dinner jacket, and began to tell jokes that were palpably agèd, their inferior quality as distinct as that of cheap clothes or stale food. With his spiked and highlighted blond hair and his orangey tan, which was not entirely successful in disguising his aging features, the man looked as if he might have been a holiday camp comedian during the era when the jokes he peddled had some currency. I suppose his role now was that of compère, a role he played as lamely as a stand-in.

Valerie emerged, after the introduction, and took the microphone from Duncan, as he seemed to be called. Then she asked him for a glass of water, perched herself on the chair, and began the preamble to her act.

"It's good to be back in the Valleys," she said. "I'm from the East End myself. Of London. But I feel a bit Welsh. I've always thought the Welsh people were very warm."

Duncan returned with a glass of water, which Valerie clearly needed, since her voice was cracking a little. She clutched her chest as she drank.

I have described that auditorium as limbo, but the evening's entertainment proved to be purgatory indeed. Duncan and another person belonging to the venue took microphones to various members of the audience, with whom Valerie then conversed, attempting to act as medium between them and vanished loved ones. I had never been to such an event before, though the basic set-up was familiar to me from television. What struck me particularly was that the dead ones who clustered in grey invisibility around Valerie in competition for her inner ear, were unable to communicate in a direct or lucid way. They had been mouldering somewhere, and now groped for words and images with decayed, dreamlike organs of speech and understanding.

"Would it mean anything to you if I were to say that your Uncle Nathan is showing me a box? Is there a box that he had, or gave to you?"

"No."

"I don't know how to describe it. Like a box, but it has glass in it. Maybe it's an heirloom."

"Well, there's the barometer."

"Barometer?"

"Yes. It's my cousin's really. My uncle invented his own kind of barometer."

"Yes. That's it. I can see it now, with the glass face, like a clock."

"Yes. It's a little like a clock."

"Your Uncle Nathan is just asking you now to remember the barometer, and why your cousin was given that. He says you'll understand. Would that mean anything to you, my darling?"

"I think so. Yes, maybe."

Exchanges of this sort were perhaps the most successful communication between dead and living that took place in the auditorium that night. More often, the audience member to whom the microphone was pointing would plainly and unapologetically state that no, they had never heard of anyone called Sheila, or that their father had been the picture of health right to the very end and had never suffered any kind of ailment, or that their departed wife had not set foot in a dancehall in her entire life. It was Valerie, in fact, who became apologetic – in tone, and sometimes explicitly. Certain of her repeated phrases became painful in this regard, with a cringing, hesitant feel to them: "Would it mean anything to you if I said…?" Again and again, the answer was a plain "no".

The other side, which the dead inhabited, began to seem to me an exceedingly depressing, worm-eaten sort of place. The dead lived through objects, such as barometers, handbags, old kitchen tables and letter-openers. This untidy rag-bag of the inanimate gave off the greasy glow of memory, around which the dead fluttered like senile moths of the spirit. And, in the end, this was all there really was. And then, perhaps, even this sickly light faded and the moths lost themselves, mercifully or otherwise, in darkness.

Just as I was thinking this, not really concentrating on the stage, or what the foundering medium was saying, it struck me: *we* are the dead, here in this auditorium. *This* is the other side. It's us that she's appealing to, us she's trying to contact, to cajole and beg into communication, and we who are staring at her blankly, uncomprehendingly. No wonder she is suffering such confusion up there on the stage.

At times her apologetic tone seemed to double back on itself and become accusatory.

"It's not a good night, tonight. I need something to work with, you know. You've got to give me something to help me to help you. It's not easy tuning in to the spirits on my own."

I had no desire from the start for the microphone to be passed my way, but with Valerie's performance proving such an embarrassment, I was now distinctly averse to becoming involved. I began to make sure that I was looking down whenever Valerie was searching for someone else to act as a conduit for her psychic abilities. I soon suspected, however, that my avoidance of eye contact was unnecessary. There were times – I think three times – during her performance that Valerie's gaze met mine. The first time she looked away quickly, almost as if offended. The second time I thought I saw some mixture of curiosity and actual dislike. The last time (I believe it was the third) it was as if she had done something she had not meant to do, and, realising quickly, checked herself. I had the strange idea, after that, that it was Valerie who was avoiding eye contact with me.

To keep watching and listening to her as she died her drawn-out death there on the stage, surrounded by those who were naturally unsympathetic to the dying, was too distressing. From perhaps halfway through, I deliberately tuned out her voice and stared at the backdrop behind her, which was nothing but a sable curtain, soft and featureless as actual darkness, on which were fixed reflective points that were too large to be sequins, but were perhaps small metal discs or mirrors. They were shining stars in an artificial night. It was a hypnotic backdrop, somehow, as the auditorium's melancholy odour was hypnotic. I could believe that I was staring at the real night sky, and that the real night was as musty and artificial as this, strangely cramped in its infinity. Between the mute stars I sensed the continual mutter and flutter of the spirits who, in their blind, feeble swarming, would choke and suffocate Valerie's poor, doomed soul.

At length, the performance came to an end. Valerie left the stage visibly exhausted. The audience rose stiffly, shuffling towards the exit more resigned than dissatisfied, as if this had been quite what they expected.

A strange lethargy had come over me so that I was one of the last to stand. In fact, I had a very particular reason for lingering, though I felt now that I was recovering that reason from a toxic daze. I stood and waited for it to become clear again in my mind. The small throng of the mundane dead, resuming drab raincoats and blowing noses in their gormless evacuation, would have been infuriatingly slow, if I had had nothing else to wait for. I stood and let the steadily growing emptiness of the building become my own. When there were only a handful of the corpse-people left at the exit, I joined them at their tail, and was soon back in the area where I had bought my ticket. Outside, darkness had fallen, and it was raining as if it would rain until the end of the world. In ones, twos and threes, the last of them passed through the narrow glass doors and into the elements. As I watched, I heard a rumble of thunder, and shivered.

I went first in the direction of the toilets. I was hoping that Valerie had been given something like a dressing room here in the building. It did not look like there was anything in that direction, so I returned to the box office area. I noticed an open doorway in the wall just past the smeared box office window, with the words "authorised personnel only" across its horizontal centre. There was one member of staff still behind the glass, but she did not look up, so I walked straight on and through the door. I entered a corridor leading in the direction that corresponded to the backstage area and passed a staff kitchen with its door open. There was no one within. Turning a corner I saw what appeared to be Duncan's shoulder and back disappearing into a closing door. Treading quietly, I approached and listened outside. I checked my wallet. I had made sure to bring a substantial amount of money with me. Inside, as I had suspected, could be heard two voices – those of Duncan and Valerie.

"You know me," Valerie was saying. "You know that I'm better than that."

"Of course I do. We all have bad nights."

"That's what I'm trying to tell you. It wasn't just a bad night. I was frightened, Duncan. Maybe, after all, I've never really known what I was doing."

I rehearsed in my head what I was going to say. I just needed to get in the room. Surely if anyone would listen to me it would be Valerie Sayers, and if she could not help me, perhaps she would know someone who could.

I knocked.

"Who's that?" I head Valerie's voice. She was talking to Duncan.

"I don't know," he said, and then, in a louder voice, towards the door, "Who's there?"

"It's… er… I've come to ask about a—"

The door swung open and Duncan was in front of me. The room was some kind of office, with two desks in the centre, and box files on tables around the sides. Sitting where one of these tables was relatively free of clutter, with a cup of tea in front of her, was Valerie Sayers. She looked at me then with disbelief, as if I were not human. No one had ever looked at me like that. I froze where I stood and felt a hot, feverish shiver rise up from my feet and from my stomach simultaneously. Gazing at Valerie's face, tired with the years, slowly parched over its fragile skull, and now confused with fear, I became prey myself to a terrible mixture of emotions, as violent within me as sudden sickness. There were pity, dread and a great many other feelings, all of them tinged with some common element previously unknown to me that made them seem more horrible than their names can suggest. Perhaps most shocking amongst them, however, was something that I can only call exaltation. It seemed suddenly as if my reason for coming here was something other than I had consciously believed. And now I knew that other reason.

"That's him," she said, hoarsely, her left hand quivering and groping as if to clutch hold of something, or raise an alarm.

I think I was actually close to fainting. There was a fizzing, fluttering in my skull, and a crackling in my ears.

"I'm afraid you can't see her," said Duncan. "She's very ill. Please go."

With that, he shut the door, and I could hear a key being turned in the lock.

After a moment to gather my thoughts and recover my breath, I turned and strode quickly away. I did not look in the direction of the ticket desk when I emerged from the corridor, but headed swiftly for the glass exit doors and escaped into the pouring darkness. I had taken perhaps two dozen steps away from the building, when I decided to double back. I began to circle round, my eyes silent and hungry upon the yellow lights that burned here and there in the shabby, permeable fortress of the community hall. Within a minute or two, I was soaked into anonymity, a melancholy forgetfulness of myself. I located the window that I supposed must belong to the office occupied by Duncan and Valerie, and approached its boiler-room blaze as if this were some last outpost of humans at the edge of the universe, and I a feral man who only half-remembered what electric light signified. I drew close to the wall and inched towards the window with my back against the wet scrape of the pebbledash.

Through the cold rattling of the rain on the glass and the sonic distortion of the wind, I could make out some of the words of the conversation taking place within.

"…like static. I just couldn't tune in." This was Valerie's voice.

"Static?"

"Yes … the radio. I don't know what I've … after all, but I began to hear this kind of … blasting, horrible. …thing was that it was so much bigger than… And that man who … through him."

"…sure you don't want to see a doctor? I've told them you need some time to recover here, but… can I do? I don't want to leave you like this tonight."

"…don't know. I just don't know. I'm frightened, Duncan. Please, just let's stay… something. God, help me. If there is a God. Only he can help me, now…"

"…hysterical. I really think you should…"

I did not hear the end of this last sentence, but before it was finished, Valerie had burst into pitiful sobs, and Duncan began to repeat her name helplessly.

Not wishing to listen further, I walked unsteadily away into the night.

I could not go straight home. There was something appalling about the idea. I simply wandered in the rain, through the empty, dripping streets of the village and the muddy lanes of the outlying areas, soaked to the skin, in utter animal solitude, noticing, now and then, that there were incandescent flashes of lightning followed by thunder that seemed to grow closer and more snarlingly violent. I am sure that at some point I had ceased to think. I knew that it was good to be away from the community hall, where I had left the wretched woman and her companion, and at one point, when I remembered this, I laughed in a way that would have sounded obscene to any who heard, even if they had not known what I laughed at. The thunder itself joined in my laughter. I laughed again, in the same manner, to realise I was walking alone in dark and unfrequented places as if it were quite safe.

I must have lost track of events entirely at some point. I do remember, as if it were a dream, though it seemed too crisp and poignant to be a dream, that I found myself on the muddy banks of an overgrown brook surrounded by brambles and horsetails, not far from the cottage. Stunted trees formed a low canopy, not high enough to allow a man to stand. In fact, I was on all fours, and around me, in the blue gloom of a twilight that I supposed only afterwards was that of approaching dawn, were three of the tame creatures belonging to the road that passed in front of the cottage, brought together here in an almost tender, though bestial communion. They lapped at the shallow water, and licked and leapt at each other playfully. There was a creeping feeling in the awareness of my situation, since it seemed to bring with it a particular kind of loneliness that was not to be desired. Then also, from somewhere behind me, I seemed to hear a deep, continuous growl that did not belong to any of the dogs I saw, or to any very much like them. I remember alarm at the thought my human wakefulness would make me visible, naked and vulnerable in some especially ghastly way. But fate must have intervened mercifully, as I have no recollection of what happened after that, or no clear recollection. There was only a dark, unseeing sense that the bestial convocation continued in some form.

Just after midday, I awoke in my bed in the cottage. I was fully dressed, and my clothes were filthy with caked mud. I showered, changed and stripped the bed. My memories of the previous night floated before me the while, but though they were heavy with melancholy, they seemed distant to me now. I felt a relief and ease of which I was almost immediately suspicious, but which remained relief and ease nonetheless. Just as the curious scene with the dogs seemed half-dream, so did the waking daylight now. I knew precisely where that soft canine revel had taken place, and it occurred to me that I might check the mud there for marks, though the thought was not an entirely attractive one. I was still contemplating this when, after a combined breakfast and lunch, I suddenly remembered my appointment that afternoon. I set out almost immediately, as if I might be late, though I was in good time. When I arrived, events took such a turn that I forgot about investigating the mud.

The rectory was set in its own grounds not far from the church. It was an airy-looking building, its exterior painted light green, but as close to being a castle, with its dormer windows and the clustered angles of its roof-ridges, as an edifice of the country cottage type can be. Even if there had not been a sign on the stone gatepost, the garden and exterior were well-tended and the place stood out from nearby residences sufficiently that I had no difficulty in finding it. Nervous, because of the irregular nature of my visit and the subterfuge I believed necessary to it, I hesitated before the white-painted front door. It has always made me nervous actually to knock on the door of someone I do not know, and it was especially bad in this case because the building was a mixture of private home and business residence, and I felt in danger of two different kinds of trespass. I did knock, however, with that feeling of fear-laden homelessness, purring vividly in all that can be seen, which has been the background to all my adult emotional life.

The door was answered soon enough by a woman in her fifties, with a brisk manner, whom I suppose was the person I had spoken to on the phone.

"Hello. I'm the journalist," I managed to say in answer to her enquiry.

"The journalist? Hadn't you better talk to the police? I don't think they've even lifted the cordon yet."

I paused for a moment. "I phoned yesterday about some questions."

"Oh, yes, I remember now. I'm afraid the Reverend can't keep his appointment. There's been a bit of an incident."

"I'm sorry. But perhaps you can help me. I won't take long."

"All right then. You might as well come in and sit down."

I followed her into a room that matched the grounds in its aspect of being perfectly kept. By a window, its short edge against the wall, was a large desk, so that the area was business-like in its domesticity.

I sat down on one side of the desk, and she sat on the other.

"What is it you want to know?"

"There are a few things, but I suppose my questions can be best answered by the minister of the Bethlehem Chapel. Do you happen to know his contact details?"

The lady looked at me oddly now, as if trying to piece something together.

"Any particular reason?"

The question seemed intrusive, but I tried to ignore the implication that I must justify myself.

"Historical research," I said. "Local history. The article mentioned."

"Well, I can't put you in touch with the minister," she said, "but I can give you the address of the steward. He might be able to help you."

"Yes. That would be good."

She tapped at the keyboard of the computer in front of her, took a post-it note, and carefully wrote down a name and street address. There was no telephone number.

"Could I take your details, too?" she asked. "Just in case anything else comes up."

That seemed a strange way of putting it, but I gave my real name and address, and even telephone number.

"What was the incident?" I asked as I put the steward's details in my pocket.

"I suppose you'll hear about it sooner or later, but don't say I've said anything. It's all a bit peculiar. There was some medium or other at the Welfare Hall last night. She's been found dead in the churchyard."

"Dead?"

"Yes. Probably lightning. You know, there was a storm last night."

"Yes. I see."

I thought of asking more, but could not bring myself to do so.

"Thank you," I said, when at last I rose to leave.

As I walked back home, I noticed now the police cordon around the churchyard gates, which were padlocked. I did not think I would at first, but as I examined the gate and its surroundings, I had a sudden urge, and, climbing up by means of an adjacent flowerbed, sat astride the stonewall and then dropped down on the other side. I walked searchingly along the gravel paths between the tranquil tombs, hoping to see anyone who might be here before they saw me. Coming to the end of an avenue of stones, I saw the small white pavilion of a forensics tent farther down the graveyard. Everything was silent, and I sensed no human presence. On a sudden conviction, I strode forward. As I drew nearer, I saw that there were scorch marks on the ground. They were strange, scattered. It was as if something had burnt into the very soil, leaving deep, lasting scars. The marks were roughly oval in shape, with sometimes what seemed a cluster of dots at the narrower end, like claws. Was this what the woman had meant by "lightning"? I was suddenly gripped by a melancholy unease at my distance from the roads that passed this churchyard, which now seemed intolerably far. If there were no other humans here, I understood why.

I left in haste, climbing over a wall into a small neighbouring park, where standing stones formed a circle around a recumbent slab. It seemed I was unobserved, or at least unchallenged. As I put some distance between myself and the church, I wondered if Valerie had remembered that churches lock their doors these days, and if it would have made a difference if they didn't.

The steward's name was Vince Mitchell. I went to his house directly from the churchyard. I showed him the post-it note, telling him I had been given his address by the Reverend Martin's secretary. I said I needed to know more about Bethlehem Chapel. He invited me in, and made some tea. I found the house to be comfortable and unpretentious. There was no clutter, but the place showed signs of activities in mid-process. The carpet was of a dour swampy green, and the décor generally consisted in various tones of green, brown and yellow, but the effect was sober rather than oppressive, as if everything was designed simply to let the daylight in and give it a natural home that yet was not stark or bare. There were large jars on the shelves containing pulses, coltsfoot, rice. Next to a patchwork tapestry on the wall was the Aum symbol as written in Devanagari. We sat at a wooden table near some sliding glass doors onto a small backyard. I felt at home, strangely.

"What do you need to know?" he asked.

"I need to know… about the black dog."

He seemed to draw a deep breath as he took this in. Looking about, it occurred to me that the room was full of symbols of protection, and that something of the consciousness of eternal vigilance was in that deep-drawn breath.

"First," he said, "tell me what you know."

I told him almost everything, only neglecting to mention that I had attended the final performance of Valerie Sayers, and that afterwards I thought I remembered a peculiar scene of which I had been part on the banks of the little brook. I suppose my story impressed him, because, when I had finished, after a silence of seeming contemplation, he said, "It will probably be easier to show you than to tell you."

He took a set of keys from a box on the bookshelf behind him.

"It'll actually be less conspicuous if we go in daylight," he said.

As we left the house and made our way to our destination, by what seemed to me a circuitous route, Vince started on an explanation that was just as circuitous, and which seemed begun somewhere in the middle.

"After Nicola died," he said, "her father began attending services at the chapel. Officially, it's not a Spiritualist church. It's not part of that tradition. But there are things that are unique to the Chapel because of its history. It's a place where people come who want to hear voices from the other side. Or it was. At the moment, it's just a kind of storehouse."

"What does it store?"

"Records. That's the other unique thing about it – the records stored there. They date back to the thirteenth century. There's been a church on the site since that time, but not always the same building, and not always the same denomination. Some of the earliest records suggest it was an ill-favoured place from the start. It seems that it was built here more to act as sentinel against some kind of evil thought to inhabit the hill than as a place for people to gather. It's a reputation that still survives, as you know. It's hard to say how old the lanes are, but they've always been the Lost Lanes as far as anyone knows. The hill itself used to be called Rhiw Gwyll – the dark hill, or the wild hill – but even the name is thought to be unlucky now.

"Anyway, there was a fire in 1564 and the church building was nearly burnt to the ground. Some of the records were saved and transferred to another church, nearby. But some time after the church here was rebuilt, the records were passed back. The same thing has happened at least twice since. Maybe the worst fire was in the early 1800s. The records have always been considered very valuable, and were always the first things to be rescued from a fire, but that time very little remained of the church building. The site was abandoned for decades, but eventually, someone decided to rebuild. The new building was the one that still stands. It was erected in 1860, and became an independent chapel. I say that, but it's always had discreet links with at least one other, larger church in the area."

Now we came from a side lane into the road that passes in front of the cottage, and Vince stopped talking. His silence was like a prohibition, and I caught it, too. He seemed watchful as we walked, and a firmness about his mouth suggested an inner marshalling of resources in preparation for something.

At last we stood before the iron gate that opened on the drab cement walkway to the doors of the two joined buildings. Vince opened the gate and I followed him through.

We did not, as I had expected, go to the larger of the two buildings, but the lesser. Set in its wall was a single door of linked planks, the grey-green paint cracked and peeling. It had a Yale lock, and looked somewhat like the door to an old storeroom. I felt something like an intake of breath as Vince fitted the key into the hole. It turned readily enough. He stepped inside with the air of one entering the unknown. After looking this way and that, he half-turned and invited me to enter.

I noticed, as I crossed the threshold, a peculiar sensation. It was a sensation with a quality of accuracy about it. This space had not been disturbed by human feet for some time. It was not a feeling of ancient desertion, however. Some atmosphere had been cooped up here almost undecayed for twenty or so years. Physically, too, this interior was odd. There were gothic features like arched stone doorways and bare stone walls, but the furniture and contents had a flavour of the 1970s or possibly early 1980s. On the floor was a grimy carpet whose swirling pattern, much dimmed, was in rather dreary shades of grey and blue. I also noticed scorch marks here. There were bookshelves, and books in disarray, and old padded chairs. It had once been something like an informal meeting room. I was a little comforted at the daylight outside the frosted window, but Vince closed the door behind us, revealing more scorch marks on its inner surface, these in places resembling scratches.

Vince strode silently through the archway into the next room, and I followed.

"You'll notice that the window here is clear glass," he said. "There's a reason for that. We weren't sure if it were a good idea, but the window is high enough that people can't see in casually from the road. Daylight is not an ultimate defence, it seems, but it helps. Sometimes. There's so much we still don't know."

He paused, as if bewildered as to where to go now he was on the brink of that unknown. While he was silent, seemingly engaged in internal struggle, I looked about the space. There was something very wrong here. My eyes were inevitably and repeatedly drawn to a perfect circle burnt into the carpet, and other marks of burning in and around it. I noticed, also, children's toys and games in boxes, as well as some scattered on the floor. There was a grotesquely melted plastic doll. I could not look at its face. There were also children's clothes strewn here and there.

"Nicola was not the first child to die unnaturally in this area. The parents came to this chapel. In the end, it was never enough just to pray. Some people knew that there was a history, and secrets. They needed to know what had happened to their children. The Minister – he's gone now – always warned them there was danger involved, but they agreed to the methods.

"There were voices. We all heard them. The Minister called them 'echoes'. He said you could never go past the echoes, that the soul of the departed, as far as the living are concerned, must be presumed beyond reach, lost, but the echoes might tell us something. For those who gathered at the chapel, I'm afraid, the echoes were never enough. One night, I opened the chapel for a meeting without the Minister. We got past the echoes. Something came, but it wasn't the soul of Nicola. Three people died, including the father. But the Minister came. The thing was scratching at the door, and he opened it. He said, 'I'm the one who called you. Take me!' Then he ran. He was never found."

Vince was silent again. After some minutes he walked through the next arch into an enclosed area of shadow and stone. I heard the keys again.

"Come through," he said.

I went.

He had opened a heavy old wooden door, backed with lead, so it seemed, and beyond I could just discern worn stone shelves stacked with books and papers.

"All we know about is the threshold," said Vince, "but these are the records, hundreds of years of them, of what we do know, at least in connection with this church and these hills."

He picked up a leather-bound volume, seemingly at random, and opened its time-browned pages.

"Here's a curious thing I think about sometimes," he said. "Just before the church fire of 1564, a man was hanged at a place referred to only as 'the Crossroads'. His death had to be recorded, and the Minister of the time was called upon to give the Last Rites. However, it says – it's in Latin, so I'll translate: 'Let all but his death be forgotten. We cannot judge such as this, but only rid the world of him. May God judge him, who only has the wisdom to do so.' It's hard to tell, but that last sentiment might be a kind of formality. I say that because the Last Rites, as recorded, were not of any orthodox kind. I think that these were them: 'He who lives as a beast, must die as one.' He wasn't hanged alone, though. A dog was hanged beside him. Whether the dog belonged to him or not is not written."

He looked at me then, as if, despite all that he did not understand, nonetheless, he understood everything about me.

"Perhaps you'd like to add to these records," he said. "It's not much, but it's all we have."

"I shall," I said.

He nodded.

"Leave nothing out."

And so I have written all I know, and the puzzle remains.

Words such as 'parochial' and 'local' can have a dismissive connotation. "That is of only local concern," we might say, or of a politician or an artist, "His vision was strictly parochial." However, now that I am forced to confront the problem of this trick knot of the Lost Lanes, I cannot help but see these local details – the mental map I have attempted to draw – are of such daunting importance that everything else in my life will be swallowed up and – yes – lost within them. The range of human life, its wondering and wandering, is, after all, deceptively limited, and the true significance of the local is deceptively vast. The deception consists especially in the fact that at first the former seems to contain the latter. As we draw close to our end we see that the latter contains the former.

It seems I have been allowed a little more time – a little more rope. I know already that it cannot help me free myself, though I cannot help but make the attempt. There is a haunting, and it has its own schemes and its own reasons, unknown to us. It does not hesitate, but it is patient, because, in a sense, all is one in this haunting.

And yet I must try.

Maps of the area, as if by secret agreement, fail to mark out the footpaths and lanes on the hills behind the cottages. I have resorted to examining aerial and satellite photographs. I suppose they are not close and detailed enough, but I find it impossible to resist the impression that they are not photographs of the area I walked at all. In particular, I have been looking for a crossroads from which all roads but one are ascending, and at which stands a lone wooden post with a projecting beam. I have found nothing like it, and the unpleasant thought occurs to me that I may only do so again on foot.

At night I seldom have any dream now but the one of the lanes that wind up and down the hill. I am nearer to the crossroads, or farther from it, but I am always, though running from it, on my way towards it. If only I could find out what the trick is, where the switch takes place.

I have written all I can. Perhaps some of my questions will be answered, but I greatly fear I will never have the chance to write of what I learn.

It occurs to me to append to this manuscript something that may have been bothering any who read this. The crossroads – apparently – was real enough, whether it had showed in the photographs examined or not. It was near the very edge of the Lost Lanes on the other side of the hills to the cottage. That's where he was found. Someone was alerted to his presence by the barking and strange behaviour of their dog. There were marks and wounds on his body that I am told could not have been self-inflicted.

Acknowledgements

I would like to express my gratitude to the following:

David Rix, Miranda Keyes, Brendan Connell.

Quentin S. Crisp was born in 1972, in North Devon, U.K. Leaving A-level college without grades, he spent five years working with Wolf and Water Arts Company before going on to study Japanese at Durham University. He graduated in the year 2000. His first collection of fiction, *The Nightmare Exhibition*, was published in 2001, by BJM Press, while he was teaching English in Taiwan. He returned to Japan later that year to research Japanese literature on a scholarship at Kyoto University, studying in particular the works of Higuchi Ichiyo. He returned to Britain in 2003, since when he has had fiction published by Tartarus Press, PS Publishing and others. He currently resides in a garret flat in South East London, and is editor for Chômu Press.

Publishing History

- The Fairy Killer, first published in *Strange Tales, Volume II* (Tartarus Press, 2007).

- Dreamspace, first published in *Postscripts 22/23: The Company He Keeps* (PS Publishing, 2010).

- Tzimtzum, first published in *Cinnabar's Gnosis: A Homage to Gustav Meyrink* (Ex Occidente Press, 2009).

- Sado-ga-shima, first published as a standalone chapbook by Rainfall Books, 2008.

- The Gay Wolf, previously unpublished.

- The Temple, first published on the now defunct Gothic Fairy Tales website, 2004.

- Lilo, previously unpublished.

- Non-Attachment, first published in *Postscipts 26/27: Unfit for Eden* (PS Publishing, 2011).

- The Broadsands Eyrie, previously unpublished.

- The Gwyllgi of the Lost Lanes, previously unpublished.